Lucia's Addiction

A novel of desire, power, and forbidden secrets
by Y O Yera

Lucia's Addiction

A novel of desire, power, and forbidden secrets
by Y O Yera

Y O Yera is a passionate author who has made sensuality and human emotions the heart of her novels. With an immersive and provocative style, she takes readers into worlds where passion breaks boundaries, and love collides with the forbidden.

Her work is defined by the fusion of intense eroticism, unexpected twists, and unforgettable characters, creating stories that not only ignite the senses but also invite reflection on the limits of desire, power, and love.

In Lucia's Addiction, Y O Yera invites readers on a journey of lust, secrets, and overflowing emotions—where nothing is what it seems, and the fire of the past can burn hotter than ever.

Lucia's Addiction

A novel of desire, power, and forbidden secrets
by
Y O Yera

Published by Amazon KDP.

To those who once let themselves be consumed by an impossible love… and discovered that the forbidden burns with greater fire.

Acknowledgments

This book is so much more than words on a page: it is the result of passion, sleepless nights, and the fire of an inspiration that refused to be extinguished.

To my husband, Jorge, who always believed in my dreams and reminded me that courage and love are the true foundations of every story. Thank you for being my light.

To my parents, Mayda and Angel, who patiently listened to my ideas and encouraged me whenever doubt tried to take hold. In every chapter of this novel beats a piece of their support.

To my readers: you are the true reason I write. Without your curiosity, without your desire to dive into stories that ignite both the heart and the senses, these pages would remain silent. Every time you lose yourselves in these words, you give life to my world.

And finally, to that part of me that once doubted my ability to create something powerful and unforgettable: thank you for never giving up. Lucia's Addiction is proof that every forbidden spark can turn into a blazing fire.

With all my heart,
Y O Yera

Lucia's Addiction

A novel of desire, power, and forbidden secrets

Chapter 1

✦ ✦ ✦ ✦ ✦ ✦

I see him coming, laughing, surrounded by friends, as if the entire neighborhood were his stage and he the inevitable leading man. Here, where women are scarce and men think themselves indispensable, he walks differently: confident, insolent, with the arrogant calm of someone who knows every gaze is on him. And yes, every gaze is on him. Mine too. But mine is different: the look of challenge, of restrained hunger.

I'm twenty-one years old and still live under the suffocating roof of parents who believe duty is the only thing that belongs to me: study, graduate, become the exemplary daughter they designed. But him... he is the opposite. Two years older, the owner of a chaos that pulls me in like an abyss. He likes to drink, laugh too loud, get tangled up in trouble that isn't his. The perfect nightmare. And the one who steals my sleep.

His laughter bursts out like a gunshot in the afternoon. His eyes—green, insolent—pierce me as if they could see straight through my skin. He's spoken barely a handful of words to me, yet I already feel stripped bare. When he passes close, the air shifts, thickens, and my body answers with an untamable pulse. I don't know if I want to escape... or surrender.

At night, when I lock myself in my room and the heat clings to my skin, it's his lips I imagine on mine. His weight. His scent. That danger that surrounds him—the danger I long to taste in silence.

But tonight, I won't settle for imagining. Tonight, I'll go looking for him. I've rehearsed lines, excuses, smiles... all useless, I know. Because when he's standing before me, no words will be enough. My body will speak for me.

I check myself in the mirror one last time: the blouse with one less button, a stolen perfume, the flush I cannot hide. I am a woman on the verge of committing a crime. My heart beats as if it wants to tear free from my chest.

Through the window I see him—already there, beneath the same tree where he always waits. Destiny calls me. I walk toward him on trembling legs, yet with a resolve I have never felt before. I don't know if he's watching me. I don't know if my voice will obey when I stand before him. But I do know this: I don't want to be a spectator. I want to be fire. And tonight... tonight I will ignite him.

"Lucia?" His voice strikes me like thunder. I don't know if he spoke my name or claimed it with that unshakable confidence that defines him. The world stops for an instant; my palms sweat, my chest pounds so hard I fear everyone can hear it. I barely manage to respond— a clumsy word that dies on my lips.

He smiles—and in that dangerous curve lies an invitation disguised as a challenge.

"What are you doing here?" he asks, his mouth tilting into a smirk, the gesture disarming. His friends let out brief laughs, but he doesn't take his eyes off me. As if no one else exists.

"I'm going to a friend's house," I lie, my voice lower than I expected.

He leans forward, resting his elbows on his knees, his gaze stripping me bare without shame.

"Then today I got lucky," he says, cruelly calm.

Something in me shifts. Fear recedes, replaced by a warm, dangerous current pushing me toward him. For the first time, I feel his interest—his eyes claiming me. The certainty intoxicates me.

Then he does it. A minimal gesture, almost invisible: he offers me a cigarette I never asked for, brushing my fingers with his. That brief touch is an inferno—his skin against mine, confident, brazen... and in his eyes, the spark of someone who already knows the answer to a question he hasn't dared to ask.

I feign indifference, holding the cigarette as if I knew what to do with it. But the lie cracks across my burning cheeks. I try to meet his gaze with defiance, even as my lips tremble.

And I discover that this vulnerability excites me— because it's part of the secret game only the two of us understand.

He doesn't hide. He doesn't pretend. His seduction is direct, brutal in its certainty. He rises slowly, and I step back until the bark of the tree presses into my spine. His body cages me without touching: his hands braced on either side of my head, his breath hot against my skin, the invisible weight of his presence forcing me to yield.

He hasn't touched me yet, and already I feel owned.

The air thickens, charged with something neither of us names, devouring me alive. His gaze pins me with brutal strength—a silent domination, as if he'd waited centuries for this moment. I should step away, pretend indifference, but I can't. I'm trapped... and in that trap is a dark pleasure I don't want to escape.

"You know you shouldn't be here," he whispers, so close his lips nearly graze my ear. A shiver rakes down my spine.

"I know," I answer—and my voice surprises me. It doesn't sound weak or trembling. It sounds eager, hungry, as if I've found a courage I never knew I had.

He smiles—just the faintest curve of his mouth, enough to set me on fire. He tilts his head slowly, testing me, as if measuring how far I'm willing to surrender. I don't step back. My fingers clutch the trunk behind me, searching for support in the midst of vertigo.

And then it happens: his lips brush mine. A fleeting touch, almost cruel in its brevity. The world goes dark in that instant. Everything disappears. Only the two of us remain, fused in that touch that shatters me.

He is steady, insolent, master of every second. I, instead, tremble—lost in the intensity of a kiss that never fully arrives. Because he doesn't kiss me... he threatens to. And that sweet torture drives me mad.

"Lucía..." His voice is a murmur against my mouth, a blade slicing through what little resistance I have left.

I want more. I need more. And when at last his lips press fully onto mine, my surrender is instant. The kiss is rough, hot, an invasion that steals my breath. I answer without thought, as if my body had been waiting for him all along.

The cigarette slips from my hand and falls to the ground. His fingers clamp around my jaw, firm, possessive, forcing me to take him in completely. My body burns. I think of nothing. Only him. Only this first spark threatening to erupt into an inferno.

When he pulls back, barely a centimeter, my breath is ragged, my mouth aching with unbearable emptiness.

"This is only the beginning," he warns, with that damned confidence that ensnares me.

And I know he's right.

When I came back to myself, I was already home. My hands trembled, my lips still burned, and my heart found no rest. That night I didn't sleep. I lay awake, eyes fixed on the ceiling, replaying every second of the kiss. Each time I remembered, my skin ignited all over again. I brought my fingers to my lips, as if his mouth had branded them, and smiled against my will.

I imagined him walking with that pride that defines him—the mischievous laugh, the way he had cornered me against the tree as if he already knew I wouldn't resist. Between fear and desire, I found no border. I felt vulnerable, yes, but more alive than ever. As if he had unearthed something dormant within me... something dark, fierce, that I could no longer chain down.

The next morning, I sat at breakfast as if nothing had happened, feigning interest in trivial talk about bread prices and the market, while my mind remained trapped beneath that tree. Every sip of coffee tasted of smoke and desire. I kept my gaze lowered so no one could read it in my eyes, because I was certain something had changed in me. On the outside I was still the obedient daughter. Inside... no longer.

A question burned within me, one I couldn't extinguish: why had he kissed me like that? It wasn't a casual brush, not the whim of a boring night. There had been something in his urgency, in the way he pinned me against the tree, that made me think he had been waiting for me. As if I had been part of a plan I hadn't known about. And that thought excited me as much as it terrified me.

When I arrived at the university, I looked for Camila, my confidant. She had always been my counterpoint: sensible, grounded, incapable of understanding that some passions are worth the punishment. I told her everything, without filters.

Her reaction was the same as always—wide eyes, a sharp whisper, reproaches disguised as affection.

"You're crazy, Lucía. That guy is trouble. What if someone saw you? What if your father finds out?"

I only smiled. I couldn't explain what I felt, because I didn't even understand it myself. It wasn't just a kiss—it was a fire that had branded my skin.

"I don't care," I said, lowering my voice as if confessing a sin. "It's like nothing existed before him."

Camila looked at me with that mix of fear and curiosity she tried to hide. I knew it too: there was no turning back. Adrián had marked me, and neither her warnings nor my own fear could save me from what had begun.

That afternoon, when I got home, I changed clothes and sat on the terrace, surrounded by books. I pretended to study, but my mind was too restless to focus. Then I felt it: a jolt in my chest, as if my own heart had sensed something before I did.

A whistle cut through the air. My skin prickled instantly. I lifted my gaze ... and there he was, on the other side of the fence. That dangerous smile—half mockery, half desire—stole the breath from me.

"So, this is where you're hiding, Lucía ..." His voice slid through the wood like a forbidden secret. He didn't shout. He didn't whisper. It was insolent—so sure of itself it froze me in my chair.

I sat motionless, the pencil in my hand my only shield. I wanted to answer, but my voice caught in my throat. All I could do was stare at him—that dark gaze digging into my most intimate thoughts.

He leaned casually against the fence, tilting his head as he studied me like prey.
"You don't seem as innocent as everyone thinks."

Blood rushed to my face, but this time I didn't look away. I tightened my grip on the pencil, as if it could steady me, and forced myself to speak.
"And you don't seem as dangerous as they say."

My voice trembled, just slightly. A mistake, I thought. But he didn't mock me. On the contrary, in his eyes I caught a flicker of surprise—something between amusement and interest.

A low laugh escaped him, closer to a restrained growl. "So you do have more courage than you let on." He leaned closer to the fence, every word falling against my skin like an invisible touch. As if there were no distance between us. As if he were already inside.

"Do you want to test it?" he asked, the spark in his gaze igniting me and freezing me all at once.

The air caught in my lungs. Part of me wanted to scream no, to beg him not to dare. But the other... the other begged in silence. My heart pounded so hard I swore he could hear it from the other side. I lowered my gaze, trying to hide the chaos consuming me.

He smiled as if he already knew my answer. A hunter's smile—cold, certain—that made me feel prey and accomplice at the same time.

"You wouldn't dare...?" I heard myself say, masking with firmness a courage I didn't possess.

His eyes gleamed, dangerous, as if I had just given him the challenge he'd been waiting for.
"Never tell me I won't dare, Lucía," he whispered. His voice ran over my skin like an invisible caress.

He didn't wait. With one swift movement, he set his foot on the wood and in a heartbeat, he was on my side.

My heart leapt to my throat. The whole world narrowed to that instant: him, me, and the certainty that we had just crossed a line with no return.

He moved closer without hurry, like a predator certain the prey won't flee. I stepped back until the terrace wall dug into my spine.

His face hovered inches from mine. I felt his hot breath, the tang of tobacco, the mix of sweat and cheap cologne—an assault on all my senses.

"And now what, Lucía?" he murmured, that crooked smile disarming me. "Do you still think I wouldn't dare?"

Fear cut through me like a blade. But something stronger—darker, more addictive—kept me from retreating. I lifted my chin, forcing myself to meet his gaze, and shaped a smile that burned more than it trembled.

And in that gesture, I knew I was lost.

"And what if I'm the one who doesn't dare let you in?" I said. My voice barely trembled, but it felt like defiance.

For an instant, his eyes widened in surprise. Then amusement sparked within them, and his smile stretched into something dangerously delicious.

It was the smile of someone who had just found the exact crack through which to slip inside.

He leaned closer, his breath brushing my lips.

"Then prove it," he whispered, with the cruel calm of someone who already knows he's won.

My heart hammered, but I didn't back away. I held his gaze as if it were my last defense.

And I understood, with brutal clarity, that I had lit this fire myself—and now it was too late to put it out.

His hand rose slowly to my face. The back of his fingers brushed my cheek—a light gesture, almost tender, yet charged with fierce intent. That contrast—his dark, challenging gaze against the softness of his touch—split me in two.

"You know you can't play with me, Lucía..." His voice sank into a murmur that barely grazed my skin. "Because if you start... there's no turning back."

And then I knew: it had already begun.

My heart pounded so hard I was certain he could hear it. I could step away, I could escape... but I didn't. I held his gaze, forcing the words out even though my voice trembled.
"And who said I want to go back?" I whispered, boldness and fear spilling out together.

He didn't wait another second. His lips crashed onto mine with a sweet violence that ripped the breath from me. There was no warning, no space to think—only the inevitable collision of two worlds that until then had only brushed against each other without touching. The kiss was wild, urgent, as if he meant to claim me entirely in a single instant.

My traitorous body offered no resistance. My hands searched for something to hold, only to find his back, sliding over the rough fabric beneath my fingers, pulling him against me with a desperation that terrified and thrilled me at once.

Then I felt it—a cold touch against my tongue. I shivered at the discovery: a piercing. Of course. Bad boy, even in the secrets hidden inside his mouth.

That tiny detail disarmed me completely. The icy metal grazing the most intimate edge of my desire turned the kiss into something else. Deeper. More electric. More addictive. An unexpected touch that shook me like lightning, and with every new brush, it dragged me further into him.

Suddenly he caught my wrists above my head and pinned me to the wall. His lips gave no respite, his hands roaming my body with the certainty of someone who knows exactly what he wants. Every caress was fire, every touch a reminder that I no longer had a will of my own.

It was intoxicating. It was forbidden. It was divine.

And the worst—or the best—was that I didn't want it to end.

A sharp sound pulled me back to reality: my mother's voice calling from inside the house. My heart lurched. He smiled against my lips, refusing to let go, savoring the danger.

"Looks like someone doesn't want us to play," he murmured. In his eyes burned a spark that wasn't just desire, but warning. No one could ever know.

"Go!" I begged, my whisper desperate.

He finally pulled away, the insolence of his smile still intact.

"Relax, Lucía," he said softly, almost as if sharing a secret. "This stays between us. Always."

With one agile leap he was back over the fence, as effortless as when he'd stolen my calm—taking with him that dangerous smile of a man who knows he holds the power. I walked into the house with my pulse racing, breath uneven, the taste of his mouth still imprinted on mine. I didn't run or hide; I simply carried with me the burning secret of what had just happened. I passed the kitchen to the sound of my mother talking about her day, but her words barely registered. I nodded, murmured something, and kept walking as if nothing had happened—though inside I was still burning.

I collapsed onto the bed, my lips still damp, my body vibrating with every memory. I closed my eyes and felt him again: the weight of his body against mine, the insolence of his smile, the cold of that piercing brushing my tongue like a jolt, leaving me trembling.

I didn't think about the risk or what people might say. I thought of nothing but him—the brutal way he kissed me, the way he held me as if I already belonged to him, how easy it was to lose myself in his hands. I caught myself smiling alone, biting my lip. I was afraid, of course—but it was a fear tangled with pleasure, with the delicious certainty that the forbidden was already becoming my addiction.

Chapter 2

✦ ✦ ✦ ✦ ✦ ✦

*T*he *morning found me wide-eyed long before the alarm rang. I hadn't slept; every time I closed my eyes, I felt him over me again—his mouth devouring mine, the cold piercing flicking against my tongue like a lash of pleasure.*

I went downstairs pretending normality, but inside I knew I was no longer the same. I was a woman carrying a burning secret beneath her skin.

Each time I remembered his kisses, a wave of heat surged through my body. It wasn't butterflies—it was fire. And the smile that slipped out on its own could betray me at any moment.

In class, the professor spoke of Philosophy, but I thought only of him. Of tasting that insolent mouth again. Of the way he held me as if I already belonged to him. Of the wild rhythm still burning inside me. It was intoxicating, being desired like that—with an intensity that consumed everything.

From her corner, Camila watched me with that piercing expression. She tore a scrap of paper, scribbled quickly, and slid it onto my desk. I opened it slowly, hiding it under my notebook. In her tight handwriting, I read:

"What did you do last night? You've got the look of someone hiding something."

Heat rushed to my cheeks. I tucked the note away without answering. This wasn't just any secret—it was too powerful to be given away in a single word.

In the cafeteria, Camila didn't wait. She dragged me to the back, away from everyone, that perfect mix of reproach and curiosity that defined her.

"Lucía, talk already," she demanded, not giving me a moment's peace. "I know you too well. That face belongs to someone who's tasted the forbidden."

I drew a deep breath, trying to hold back the smile that betrayed me—but I couldn't.

"You have no idea, Camila."

She squeezed my hand hard. "Then tell me. What happened?"

I looked her straight in the eye, as if saying it aloud would mean reliving it. I lowered my voice, but I didn't soften the words.

"He kissed me. Not like a game, not on impulse... like he'd been waiting for me forever."

Camila's eyes widened. "God, Lucía! Are you insane? I've heard he's dangerous."

I laughed under my breath, savoring the memory on my lips. "I know. And I love it."

"What if someone finds out?" she whispered, glancing around as if anyone could hear us.

"Then let them," I cut her off, leaning toward her with a new spark in my eyes. "You don't understand, Cami... when he kissed me, it felt like nothing else existed. As if he branded me."

She shook her head, though the fascination in her eyes was impossible to hide.

"That man is going to destroy you."

"Maybe," I admitted, playing with the coffee cup between my fingers. "But if he does, I want it to be with those lips."

Camila sighed, defeated, and slumped back in her chair.

"You're lost."

I smiled, biting my lip, letting the confession set me on fire all over again.

"Yes. And I love being lost."

The rest of the day at the university blurred past. Nothing could distract me: not classes, not conversations, not familiar faces. All I could think of was getting home—back to that terrace that had already become the stage for a secret too big for my age, too addictive to let go.

When I finally stepped off the bus, I sensed him before I saw him: that tingling at the back of my neck, that absurd certainty he was near. And there he was—leaning against the bench at the stop, as if he'd been waiting for me all along. He wasn't doing anything, just smoking with that insolent calm that clung to him. But the moment he lifted his gaze, he caught me.

His eyes found me instantly steady, as if my fate were already written in them.

My stomach clenched; my legs trembled so badly I feared I wouldn't be able to move. I had never seen him so brazen, so exposed—waiting for me in broad daylight, in a place where anyone could see. And still... he was there. For me.

"Were you expecting someone else?" he asked as soon as my feet hit the pavement. His voice was low, but every word scorched my skin like a brand.

I wanted to keep walking, to feign indifference, but my steps stalled on their own. There was something in his gaze that pinned me to the ground: the world narrowed to that instant—him sitting, me standing before him, trapped with no way out.

He rose calmly. Each step toward me landed like an invisible blow to my chest, a reminder that he was dangerously close and utterly sure of himself. The street went on around us—people passing—yet we were locked in a secret, dangerous game, impossible to hide.

"You know you can't escape me, don't you?" he murmured, leaning just enough for his shoulder to brush against mine.

My heart pounded like a drum. Fear and desire tore me apart, yet I still met his eyes and answered: "And what if I don't want to escape?"

The spark of triumph in his gaze stole my breath. Adrián arched a brow and let out a low, dark laugh that rippled through me like a shiver.

"That's how I like it..." he whispered. "For you to speak your mind—even if your voice trembles."

Heat flushed my skin, but I didn't back away. There was something in that moment, in the shameless way he challenged me, that made me feel more alive than ever.

And I understood with brutal clarity: I was lost. And I didn't want to be saved.

His hand slid over my waist with a cruel calm that made my skin prickle. Lower still, tracing the edge of my skirt, brushing lightly against my inner thigh—as if measuring with precision how far to go to leave me breathless. A minimal touch, yet it pierced me completely: my breathing spiked, and I bit down on my lip to stifle a moan.

I was trapped in the delicious vertigo of crossing a line from which there was no return.

And just like that, he withdrew his hand with the same calm with which he had branded me. He brushed my cheek with a light, almost mocking kiss—and smiled.

"Shall I walk you home?" he asked, as if the question carried something else—he already knew my silence would be a yes.

I couldn't answer. I only nodded, and I saw his smile widen at the sight of my surrender.

We walked side by side along the sidewalk, not touching. No one would have suspected a thing, yet I carried his imprint in every corner of my body. The silence between us was heavier than any words; the heat of his presence burned me, and the thought that anyone might see us made the danger taste even sweeter.

When we reached the corner of my house, I stopped.

"Don't come any farther," I whispered. "They could see us here."

He didn't argue. He looked at me for one more second with that unbearable calm that kept secrets I didn't yet know, then turned the corner and vanished as if he'd never been there at all.

I went inside with my heart pounding in my throat. I didn't understand what he wanted from me or what hid behind that insolence. I only knew that every touch dragged me deeper—like a dangerous dream I didn't want to wake from.

Then I heard it: that whistle. The same one that had branded itself into me the afternoon before. It wasn't just a sound—it was a command, a call that pierced me like an electric current.

My heart jumped. I could have ignored it, could have stayed put—but it was useless. The whistle was a magnet.

I rose slowly, holding my breath, and crossed the living room as if moving in secret. The terrace door creaked as I opened it. There he was—leaning against the fence, waiting. The dangerous smile on his lips said everything he didn't need to speak.

In that instant I knew: it was already too late to resist.

"I knew you'd come," he said without greeting me. His calm, mocking voice sounded like an invisible thread tugging me at will.

I stood in the doorway, my hands gripping the frame, torn between fleeing and surrendering. He didn't move; he only held my gaze, and that stillness cut sharper than any gesture.

Then he stretched his hand over the fence—slow, steady, as if he already knew I would give in. He didn't need words: the gesture was both invitation and command.

My eyes fixed on those long fingers, waiting for mine. My heart hammered in my throat. One brush, one tiny contact, and a pact would be sealed with no return.

And I gave in. My fingers found his, trembling, and the moment I touched him a jolt ran through me.

He squeezed my hand firmly, possessive, as if that contact would mark me forever.

He pulled me toward the fence, drawing us close until our breaths mixed. I knew it was madness, that anyone could see us… but the only thing that mattered was the strength of his hand gripping mine and the dark promise in his eyes.

"Come in…" I whispered, and in that instant I understood that I had surrendered.

A spark of triumph lit his gaze. He didn't hesitate. With the same agility as always, he climbed over the fence and, in a second, he was inside. My heart galloped at seeing him invade my space, my world, as if something irreversible had just been sealed.

"Don't play with me," he said then, his voice deeper, denser, almost a blade brushing my skin.

His eyes bored into me with an intensity that chilled my blood. It wasn't just a warning. It was a threat. It was a promise. And I knew with brutal clarity: that sentence would haunt me long after that afternoon… because I no longer belonged even to myself.

I wanted to challenge him, yes. I wanted to play with him. I wanted to know what it felt like to have the power, even though my hands trembled and my heart seemed ready to burst from my chest.

I looked him straight in the eyes, holding his challenge, and this time I didn't look away.

"And what if I'm the one playing with you?" I said, with a smile I could barely contain, enough to ignite a different gleam in his eyes.

He was so tall he enveloped me completely; his strong hands held me as if he could break me or protect me at will. His gaze was deep, dangerous, as if he wanted to disarm me from the inside. Yes, I was inexperienced, but the last thing I wanted was for him to notice.

So, I leaned toward him, brushing my lips against his ear, and whispered,

"Not everything you see is as innocent as you think."

I pulled away just enough to look at him, and I saw surprise on his face turn into that dangerous spark that defined him. Then he trapped me with hunger, devouring my mouth as if he couldn't wait another second.

His hands lifted me at the waist and pressed me against his body; instinctively I wrapped my legs around him. He carried me against the door and the impact of my back against the wood mixed with wet, urgent kisses that left me breathless.

He broke the kiss for just a moment, his lips grazing mine, his breathing dense, heavy with desire.

"How far do you want to go, Lucía?" he murmured, that deep voice cutting through me like a blade.

Heat rose to my skin, leaving me unable to form words. My body answered before my voice: I gripped him tighter, as if I wanted to melt into him. His crooked smile confirmed that he already understood.

And in that instant I knew: it had stopped being a game. It was a dark pact—and I was already inside.

Inside, I was afraid. I didn't want him to know; I didn't want him to discover how vulnerable I felt in his arms. But it was useless: that was the truth. I had never crossed that boundary... and yet I wanted him—exactly him—to be the one to take me over it.

His eyes trapped me, as if deciphering every secret I tried to hide. His hands were firm against the door, and there was no tenderness in his smile—only a ferocious promise, a hunger ready to devour me.

"Don't tell me..." he murmured, brushing his lips against mine, his voice threaded with malice. "Is this your first time, Lucía?"

Heat flared across my skin like an impossible blaze. I said nothing, but my eyes betrayed me. He understood before I could form a word. His low laugh sent a shiver through me, and his grip tightened as if he had just won a game only he knew the rules of.

He leaned toward my ear, his hot breath grazing my skin.
"Then let me..." he whispered, deep and dark. "I'll show you what you've never felt."

A chill ran down my spine—fear and anticipation braided together. I didn't stop him. On the contrary—I clung with my legs, surrendering to that vertigo pulling me into the unknown.

But time betrayed us. A sharp sound—the creak of a door—snapped me back to reality.

"My mother!" I breathed, my heart in my throat.

He didn't move at once. He stayed pressed to me, breathing against my neck, savoring the thrill of almost being caught. Then he smiled—that crooked smile that left me defenseless—and kissed me quickly, furtively, like an indelible mark.

"Until next time, Lucía..." he murmured, before vaulting the fence with the same agility with which he'd stolen my calm.

I stood there, trembling, caught between unfinished desire and panic. I knew the worst was still to come.

I went to my room with my body still vibrating, my skin burning as if his hands were still on me. I collapsed onto the bed without turning on the light, breath ragged, lips sore from wanting him too much.

I closed my eyes and saw him again: that crooked smile, the strength with which he'd held me, the deep voice that promised things I didn't yet know. A shiver ran down my spine—fear and hunger braided into one.

I didn't want to sleep. I wanted to stay like that— awake, replaying every second, etching the memory so it could never fade. I knew it in my bones: he was danger, the brink, my ruin. Yet it was already too late. The forbidden had become my craving.

Chapter 3

✦ ✦ ✦ ✦ ✦ ✦

*T*he next morning felt like torment disguised as routine. Coffee, familiar voices, the radio on... everything seemed the same. Everything except me. I moved among them like a ghost, answering just enough, smiling when required, while inside I still burned with the memory of his hands and the promise in his voice.

It was the weekend, and I'd made plans with Camila to go to the beach. The plan sounded innocent: sun, sea, and a book. But I knew sooner or later she'd pry the truth out of me. And the truth was that, since the night before, my body no longer belonged to me.

The road was full of street vendors and laughter—the kind of chaos so typical of Cuba that had always felt endearing to me. But that day everything fell into the background. The only sound still beating inside me was his low whisper: "I'll show you what you've never felt before..."

Camila talked nonstop, laughing at anything, greeting half the town as we passed. I watched her lips move, but the only thing I heard was the echo of him in my memory. And although a vast blue sea opened before us, my horizon had shrunk to one obsession: having him again.

"Lucía, are you even listening to me?" Camila snapped, her fingers waving in front of my face.

"Yes, of course… what were you saying?" I muttered, trying to sound attentive.

"Adrián?" she raised an eyebrow that said it all. *"That man is nothing but trouble. You have no idea what you're getting into. The stories I've heard about him give me chills."*

I looked at her in silence. Camila—always so proper, so afraid of anything that strayed from the rules. And me… I had already crossed the line. While she talked, I smiled to myself. Maybe what Camila really needed was to taste a little of the danger she was trying to steer me away from.

"Oh, Camila… stories are always exaggerated," I said with a tilted smile, feigning indifference. *"If you believed everything people say, you'd never step out the front door."*

Deep down I knew she wasn't entirely wrong, but nothing drew me in more than the thing everyone warned me to avoid. Adrián was that danger that called to me like a magnet; they could paint him as a demon, and I saw him as the most irresistible temptation of my life.

"He's playing with you, Lucía—don't you see?" Camila insisted, her brow furrowed.

"And what if I'm the one who wants to play with him?" I shot back with a defiant smile.

"And what experience do you have?" she blurted, eyebrows arched.

I leaned closer, so only she could hear.

"Enough," I whispered, wickedly.

Camila's silence lasted barely a second before she swatted my arm.

"Lucía, I can't believe what you're saying..."

But curiosity glittered in her eyes, betraying the reproach.

"He likes women with experience—or at least that's what they say," she added in a low voice, as if sharing a forbidden secret. "And when he finds out you're a virgin, he'll run."

I held her gaze without blinking, my half-smile saying more than words.

"Don't worry, Camila... he already knows."

Her expression tightened.

"And?" she asked, bracing for the worst.

I leaned in closer, a chill running down my skin as I said it.

"And that's what he liked most. As if I were his trophy."

Camila swallowed.

"When? How did it happen?" she pressed, suffocated by the need to know more, as if the secret consumed her even more than me.

I laughed softly, savoring her desperation.

"It was… intense," I said, stretching the word to torment her a little. "I'll only tell you this: when he kissed me, I knew there was no turning back."

I offered nothing more. Slipping on my headphones, I leaned back on the sand and closed my eyes, as if music could silence Camila's warnings. The sun burned, the breeze wrapped around me, and for a moment I let myself be carried by the illusion of calm… until I felt it.

A touch. Firm. Deliberate. Traveling up my legs like an electric current.

I shivered head to toe. I didn't open my eyes at once; I wanted to stretch the moment, to pretend that caress was a secret only mine. My heart pounded, and though I couldn't see him, I already knew.

When I finally opened my eyes, I confirmed it: Adrián, leaning over me with that half-dangerous smile that could say everything without a word.

Camila sat rigid beside me, lips pressed tight. Her eyes darted between us as if watching an accident unfold in slow motion, torn between intervening or staying frozen.

"I looked for you... and here you were," Adrián said softly, ignoring Camila completely, as if the world itself had vanished. His eyes locked on me, piercing straight through.

Heat rose across my skin. The sea breeze, the people around us—everything disappeared under the weight of that gaze. Camila remained silent, caught in the same vertigo that held me, but I couldn't think of anything except him.

"How do you always know where I am?" I asked, barely a whisper, caught between curiosity and the tremor of having him so close.

Adrián smiled slowly, a calm that chilled me more than the ocean itself.

"When I want to find something, Lucía... I always find it," he murmured.

In that certainty I understood it wasn't coincidence. He wasn't following me—he was hunting me.

What was it about Adrián? His deep voice, that fierce certainty in every word, the way he seemed to command everything without effort. I didn't understand it, but his mystery wrapped around me like an invisible net I couldn't escape.

He leaned in just slightly and, with disconcerting calm, brushed aside a strand of hair the wind had tangled across my face. His fingers grazed my sun-warmed skin, and his eyes sank into mine. That minimal touch sent shivers through me, charged with a dangerous promise.

"Don't ask me how, Lucía," he whispered, not breaking eye contact. "I just... always know where to find you."

A chill ran down my spine.

"You're different..." he continued, his tone less praise than verdict. "And that can't be faked."

The air left me. What did he see in me that I didn't even recognize? His voice pierced me like a secret, and in his words, there was a certainty that made me tremble more than any touch.

Slowly, deliberately, he removed the earbud I still had in one ear and set it on the towel. Then he took my hand.

"Come."

He led me toward the sea. The water rose around our legs like a warm embrace, but it wasn't calm I felt: each wave pushed me closer to him, erasing distance with silent violence.

Between the murmur of the ocean and the blinding sun, the only real thing was his fingers entwined with mine—firm, possessive, beneath the water.

"There are no witnesses here, Lucía," he whispered, that dangerous smile in place. "Just you and me."

I was trapped in his gaze. That malicious gleam told me nothing about this was innocent. And yet, instead of frightening me, it pulled me deeper—straight into a place I didn't want to leave.

I felt his hand slide beneath the water, brushing my waist with calculated slowness. The contrast between the cool sea and the scorching heat of his touch made me shudder from head to toe. I drew in a sharp breath, fighting to contain the sigh burning in my throat.

Adrián leaned closer, so near that his hardness pressed against me beneath the water.

"Tell me, Lucía…" he whispered, his deep voice wrapping around me like a spell, "how far are you willing to let me go?"

A moan escaped me, slipping from my lips like a secret impossible to hide. Heat flushed my face, and in his eyes, I saw something ignite—triumph, as if that sound confirmed I was already his.

He didn't rush. On the contrary—he stayed still, watching me, a crooked smile disarming me more than any touch.

"That's it, Lucía…" he murmured, soft and challenging, a delicious threat. "Let me hear you more."

His hand slid lower, pressing against the top of my thigh, guiding me toward him with a dominance that left me nowhere to escape. Each wave covered and concealed us, but it was his control that truly drowned me, erasing my boundaries until I no longer knew where I ended and he began.

He moved only a few inches closer—slow, sure— exploring the exact edge between what's allowed and what's forbidden. The water no longer refreshed; it burned where his fingers marked me. My whole body tensed, trapped in a vertigo that was equal parts fear and desire.

A deeper moan rolled from me, swallowed by the ocean. My hands gripped his shoulders for balance, though in truth I was surrendering even more. Adrián smiled against my skin, pleased, as if every sound he drew from me were his personal victory.

"That's it..." he murmured, his voice a warm blade at my ear. "And I'm only just beginning."

I bit my lip until a tiny drop of blood welled and stung in the salty breeze. I couldn't hold back—I began to beg in broken whispers, not to stop; I wanted more.

Adrián watched me with that crooked smile of triumph and desire. His fingers yielded a little further—just enough to make me shiver, but not enough to satisfy.

"That's what you want, isn't it?" he whispered close to my ear, that soft, dangerous voice. "And yet... I still won't give you everything."

Indifference was no longer an option. My lips trembled, my body arched toward him, and words slipped out unfiltered, broken by urgency: "Please... Adrián..."

Adrián held my gaze, and instead of giving me what I wanted he paused. His fingers withdrew slowly—cruel in their calm—while his smile widened like a predator savoring a beg.

"Not yet, Lucía," he murmured in that soft, defiant voice—a threat wrapped in a caress. "I want you to learn to crave it until it hurts."

I stared at him, lips parted and still panting, fire sparking in my eyes.

"What if I don't want to wait?" I said, daring him with a smile despite my body screaming the opposite.

Adrián arched an eyebrow, amused, as if my defiance were exactly what he'd hoped for.

"Then you'll have to take it from me, Lucía..." he whispered, moving even closer, sure that sooner or later I would give in.

He was playing a game... and I wanted to play too. I kissed him with a depth that stole my breath, letting my tongue explore his with a hunger I had no intention of hiding. I felt his body tense beneath me, and every moan that escaped my throat seemed to bend the rules of the world in my favor.

His taste was salty and sweet at once—the sea and sin mingled in my mouth. My hands clutched his shoulders, and for an instant I knew I was setting the rhythm, dominating him through desire. The water wrapped around us, warm and complicit, as I turned every touch into provocation and every sigh into surrender.

Then, with the same boldness with which I'd begun, I pulled away. I gave him one last defiant look—my lips still wet—and stepped toward the white sand. Each drop sliding down my burning skin was another way to tempt him.

"Lucía!" he called, voice laced with fury and desire. But I didn't stop. I kept walking, water dripping from me, until I slipped from his sight.

That night, back home, I locked myself in the bathroom and let the hot shower rain over me, a burning veil. I closed my eyes and saw him again: that defiant gaze, those lips devouring mine, his fingers claiming my skin beneath the waves.

My hands began to explore me—first trembling and restrained, then with the same urgent insistence with which he had branded me. Steam fogged the mirror, water slid down my body, and every caress echoed him, as if he were there guiding me, showing me what it meant to desire until I was lost.

I moaned into my bitten lips, trying to quiet the sound. Then I understood: that was the first time I had truly touched myself—because I was doing it for him. Even in my solitude, I no longer belonged to myself.

Chapter 4

✦ ✦ ✦ ✦ ✦ ✦

I was at the university, sitting by the window with a copy of Twenty Love Poems and a Song of Despair *open across my lap. I tried to underline verses, jot down notes for class, but every word pulled me back to him.* "Love is so short, forgetting is so long." *The line cut through me as if it had been written for my own damnation.*

Camila appeared suddenly, arms crossed, brow furrowed.

"Lucía... that man isn't the kind who stays."

I looked up and arched a brow, holding my composure.

"And who said anything about staying, Camila?" I replied with an ironic smile.

She scoffed—the way she always did when she wanted to keep her distance. Camila was still saving herself for the perfect man, clinging to her good-girl mantra: that her first would also be her only. The right one.

"Forget about that, Cami." I closed the book and left it resting on my lap. "Fairy tales don't exist. I don't want to be anyone's princess. I want to live. I want to feel."

"You're playing with fire, Lucía." Her voice sounded harsher than ever. But behind her hard eyes I saw something else: fear. Fear of what Adrián meant.

Fear of me. Fear of what might drag her down if she followed too close.

I closed my eyes for a moment, letting Neruda's verses blur into the memory of his mouth on mine, the touch of his hands still burning on my skin. Maybe Camila was right... but if this was fire, I'd rather burn than live extinguished.

She sighed, as if worn out from talking to me.

"You paint everything like life is a game. I don't want scraps of passion, Lucía. I want real love. A man who looks at me like I'm the only one, who protects me, who respects me."

I looked at her in silence, with tenderness and pity all at once. Her innocence was beautiful, yes, but also a weight that would drown her sooner or later.

"And what if that perfect love never comes, Camila?" I asked, a defiant gleam in my eyes. "What if the only real thing is desire? Would you really rather wait forever than risk feeling something—even if it hurts?"

She held my gaze, serious, with that unshakable firmness that defined her.

"Yes, Lucía. Because what I want isn't negotiable. I want love—not halfhearted affairs."

Camila leaned closer, her eyes burning with conviction.

"Listen to me carefully: passion burns out... and the emptiness it leaves can be worse than never having loved at all."

I didn't answer. I pretended to reopen the book on my lap, but her words dissolved the moment I closed my eyes. In their place Adrián appeared—still dripping seawater from his skin, wearing that dangerous smile that pierced right through me. I felt his fingers again along the inside of my thighs, the pressure of his hand beneath the waves, and a shiver ran through me as if, right there in the middle of the university, he had truly touched me. A moan stuck in my throat, and I understood the inevitable: warnings and promises of perfect love no longer mattered.

I shook my head, trying to banish his image, and snapped the book shut. Reality returned like a cold reminder: I had to get ready for my night shift.

I'd been working as a waitress in a city restaurant for almost two years—the black-and-white uniform, my hair tied back, my hands always busy with glasses and trays: my nightly routine, the other life few knew about. There, among tables and murmurs, I felt free, as if the night itself gave me permission to be someone else.

That night, while wiping a table on the terrace, I saw him: Adrián. His silhouette cut against the dim light, insolent gleam in his eyes, the aura of danger that never left him. He sat with the calm of someone who knows he's being awaited, as if the entire city belonged to him. He didn't order anything.

He pulled out a cigarette, lit it slowly—savoring the ritual—then offered it to me.

"Want one?" he asked, his voice always a challenge.

I hesitated. He didn't let me answer. He took my hand, brought the cigarette to my lips, and, leaning in far too close, showed me how to inhale. The smoke burned my throat and intoxicated me all at once. It wasn't tobacco I tasted—it was him.

Each drag felt like his command; every exhale my surrender. The addiction wasn't in the cigarette—it was in him. I knew it, though I couldn't—wouldn't—stop.

Adrián took the cigarette from my lips with two fingers, slow and deliberate, savoring the instant as if it were part of a ritual. Before I could react, he gripped my chin and his mouth crashed onto mine—deep, claiming me right there on the restaurant terrace.

Smoke danced between us, mingling with his tongue, burning me from the inside out. The kiss wasn't a caress— it was a challenge, a public mark, a delicious threat.

The murmur of customers, the clink of cutlery, the city lights... everything remained, but it faded to distant noise. The only real thing was him—his strength, the addictive vertigo of knowing anyone could see us.

And it was precisely that possibility—that brazen exposure—that made my body burn even more.

"Lucía," he whispered against my lips, smoke still drifting between us. "What do you have that poisons me like this... that won't let me stay away from you?"

His voice was a confession disguised as reproach— soft and dangerous, like everything about him. And in that instant I understood: the addiction was no longer mine alone. It was consuming him too.

I looked at him with a crooked smile, my mouth still burning from his kiss.

"It's not me, Adrián," I murmured, a sharp edge in my voice. "It's you—you who can't let go."

His eyes narrowed, first with surprise, then with a fierce gleam that made my skin prickle. My defiance only fed him more.

"Then hold me tight — never let me go., Lucía," he said in a low murmur, an order wrapped in a challenge.

I stepped back just enough to lift the tray I still held, pretending everything was normal. The restaurant stayed full, customers coming and going, but the only presence that felt real was his—watching me as if he had already stripped me bare right there.

"Get back to work, waitress," he ordered with a crooked smile, lowering his tone until it became an intimate command, as if he were speaking directly to my

skin. "Act like I'm not here... though you know you won't be able to."

My hands trembled as I set the glasses down; the cutlery clinked louder than usual, and I bit my lip so I wouldn't betray myself. He was right: even if I walked away, he stayed on my skin, in every runaway heartbeat, in every ragged breath.

"I'll be out in ten minutes," I whispered, barely audible—a secret and a promise at once.

Adrián held my gaze, leaning back in the chair with the insolent calm of someone who had already won. Smoke curled from his lips in slow spirals, each puff a countdown. A sentence carrying me toward the forbidden.

The clock on the wall crawled with unbearable slowness, each second pounding like a hard blow against my chest. I forced a smile for customers, carried trays, feigned routine... but inside I burned with the certainty that he was there, waiting.

When I finally stripped off the apron and handed over the tray, the air caught in my throat. I smiled at my coworkers as if nothing were wrong, but my steps down the hallway were no longer mine: I walked, pulled by an inevitable force.

Pushing open the door and stepping outside, I saw him. Adrián.
Leaning against his gray car, cigarette smoke curling

from his lips, one hand in his pocket, his profile haloed by the streetlamp. He didn't look like he was waiting. He looked like he'd been hunting.

"You took your time," he said without moving, his voice low chilling me, igniting me all at once.

There was no time for more. He crushed the cigarette under his boot and in two strides had me pinned against the cold metal of the car. His hand gripped my wrist with fierce certainty, dragging me into his gravity.

His crooked smile brushed my lips, his breath hot against my ear.

"Look at you..." he murmured, eyes devouring me as though stripping me bare. "Beautiful. And you smell... exquisite."

He held me with that half-smile—a promise, a threat.

"Tell me you don't want it," he whispered, his voice a low blade. "Dare to lie to me."

I didn't answer with words. My hands locked around his neck, pulling him toward me as if surrender itself had become my only choice. His mouth devoured mine in a kiss that burned, desperate, claiming me as if there were no turning back.

I kissed him hungrily, intoxicated by the smoke and danger that clung to his tongue. Every moan that broke from my throat only made him press me harder into the car, his urgency branding me as his.

Adrián lifted me with brutal assurance, my back scraping the cold metal while his hands roamed me with merciless precision. My legs wrapped around his waist, the kiss deepening—wet, frantic—until I could no longer breathe, until the night itself seemed to belong only to us.

The world vanished. There was only the crash of his breath against mine, my muffled moans swallowed by his mouth, the delicious friction of his body grinding into me. Each caress was fire, and I wanted nothing but to burn.

A sharp noise jolted me: a group of voices, laughter too close. My pulse spiked, but Adrián didn't flinch. His eyes locked on mine, hard, defiant. Without a word, he seized my hand with that dangerous authority that unraveled me.

He opened the car door and pulled me inside—not rushed, but with the calm inevitability of someone who had written this scene long before I surrendered. The engine roared, the city lights dissolved behind us, and the dark road carried us to the coast.

The sea waited beneath the moon, vast and complicit. Adrián parked in the shadows, the rhythm of the waves pounding like a secret drum. He killed the engine and turned to me again, his gaze so intense it stole my breath.

He leaned over me without mercy, his hand locking at the nape of my neck as his mouth crashed into mine— savage, wet, desperate, as if the wait had been unbearable. His fingers slid up my thighs, parting the fabric with the certainty of a man who never asked, only took.

He shoved me back into the seat; his body covered me completely, claiming me with every savage kiss and every demanding touch of his hands. The cold leather beneath my back clashed with the burning heat that wrapped around me. The car creaked beneath us, as if even the metal bore witness to the violence of that desire. His breath seared my neck, and my nails dug into his back, clinging as though letting go would make him vanish.

His lips paused over mine for a moment. His eyes drilled into me with an intensity that pierced straight through.

"I want to be your first man," he whispered, deep, enveloping—like a sentence passed down. "I want you to be mine."

That damned tone of his shattered every defense. In that instant my upbringing, my fears, even Camila's cautionary voice disappeared. Only he remained... and the certainty that I was about to cross a border from which I could never return.

But I wanted him. With every fiber of my body, with every feverish thought that had devoured me in silence. Adrián wasn't just a dangerous man—he was temptation made flesh. And even if it cost me my soul, I wanted him entirely.

"Do it…" I moaned against his mouth, trembling, my lips brushing his. "I'm yours."

I didn't need to say more. My body spoke when I pulled him closer in desperation, my legs locking around his waist, my nails clawing down his back.

Adrián smiled against my lips, satisfied, and I understood then: I wasn't only giving him my first time… I was giving him everything I was.

He reclined the seat with a sharp motion, the leather squealing in the silence of the night. With one tug, he tore my blouse open, exposing my bra, and shoved my skirt up to my hips. With his mouth, he slid my panties down slowly, a divine torment, undressing me with a cruel patience that sent shivers ripping through me.

"God…" I gasped, losing control as his hand plunged into me with a sudden twist. His fingers moved in slow circles, marking me from the inside, tearing moans I tried to stifle, while his breath grew heavier and his eyes burned in the shadows.

Each twist of his fingers carried me higher, dragging me to the edge of an unknown abyss, until I thought I would break from sheer pleasure.

But suddenly, in the middle of my rising climax, Adrián stopped. He withdrew his hand with cruel calm, holding my gaze as if savoring my desperation.

Then I felt him settle between my thighs. He opened me slowly, with a fierce delicacy that clashed with the raw intensity of his desire. My breath caught as he began to enter me—slow but relentless—tearing the veil of my innocence with every thrust... and claiming what was already his.

Adrián held me firmly, his hands making each movement claim me rather than teach me. His voice— low and hoarse—slipped between my moans:

"Relax... surrender. Tonight, you will learn what it means to be mine."

I felt trapped, possessed, consumed all at once. Each of his gestures drew a new shiver from me, and though it was my first time, fear melted beneath the certainty that my body had been waiting for him all along.

The initial pain dissolved into a burning wave that coursed through me, turning into something unknown and brutally addictive. My nails sank into his back, marking him as he marked me, and I understood there was no turning back: I belonged to him, and I accepted it with every moan.

His rhythm was relentless; each thrust drew a muffled cry that echoed against the car windows. The leather beneath my back creaked, blending with the wet sounds of our bodies and the distant pounding of the waves that accompanied our frenzy.

Adrián paused for barely a second, eyes fixed on mine—wild and dominant.

"You okay?" he murmured, his voice broken.

I answered without words, kissing him desperately, my tongue begging for what my voice could not form: more. His crooked smile was my sentence. He moved again with a deeper, more intense force, as if he wanted to carve himself into me forever.

Every time my name slipped from his lips in a hoarse moan, a new wave of pleasure tore through me, making me tremble uncontrollably.

The climax struck me like lightning—violent and devastating. I screamed his name, convulsing beneath his weight, feeling pleasure set me ablaze from the inside until I had no breath left. It was extraordinary, brutal—a fire I no longer wanted to survive.

His kisses were pure poison, each touch igniting a different corner of my skin. His hands gripped my breasts with a cruel expertise, as if he'd known my body forever even though it was the first time he possessed it.

"Again..." I begged between moans, my voice broken, consumed by a need without end.

Adrián looked at me with a wild gleam—surprised and aroused by my desperate surrender. His crooked smile sealed it. He leaned over me and now there were no pauses, no mercy: each thrust grew deeper, more brutal, marking my body as his.

Everything inside me tightened, a burning whirlwind about to explode. The world vanished; only he remained—his strength dominating me, driving me toward an abyss I did not want to leave. Then I shattered again, fiercer than the first time—a ripping scream that dissolved against his mouth as my body convulsed beneath him.

Hot tears blurred my vision—whether from pleasure, vertigo, or the brutal certainty that Adrián had crossed every one of my limits. I broke in his arms; I surrendered—irreparably his.

He didn't pull away. He held me inside him, panting against my neck, his lips brushing my ear like a blade.

"Now you're mine, Lucía," he murmured, deep and triumphant.

I thought my body couldn't take any more, but Adrián smiled against my skin—dangerous, insatiable.

"Did you think this was enough?" he whispered, his voice both promise and threat. "The night is just beginning."

His gaze burned on me, devouring me, and my trembling body ignited again at that single sentence. It was a delicious sentence of doom: I knew he could claim me over and over until he broke me...and I wanted it.

His mouth descended to my breasts, taking my nipples with gentle bites that wrung louder moans from me. The cold scrape of his tongue and the shock of his piercing jolted me like lightning: a metallic, wildfire that pushed me toward delirium. Between sweet pain and absolute *bliss, I understood that all I wanted was more of him, even if it consumed me.*

He continued slowly down my torso, tracing a path of fire with his mouth, until his burning tongue found my center with a precision that erased all reason. The cold, wet brush of the piercing against my sensitive skin pulled from me a stifled cry; it was an unfamiliar, exotic pleasure that made me arch my back and lose all control.

"What is he doing...?" I tried to think, but it was useless. Only the vertigo of pleasure remained—a savage wave that swept me whole.

"Come for me!" he ordered in a deep, domineering voice, and I obeyed without resistance. The climax broke me completely, shaking me in tremors as his playful, cruel tongue stretched my orgasm until I lay spent, my legs trembling around his head.

I was left gasping, my chest rising and falling out of control, unable to believe what I had just experienced. I had never imagined pleasure could be so devastating, so absolute—as if my own body had been torn from me only to be handed over to him.

Adrián straightened slightly, his lips wet, his eyes blazing—he looked at me as if he had tasted forbidden fruit and knew he would never abandon it. A dangerous smile curved his face.

"That was only an appetizer, Lucía," he said, his voice deep. "I'm only just beginning with you."

He kissed me suddenly, deep, and I tasted the wet echo of myself in his mouth. My heart lurched—never had something so forbidden felt so unbearably exciting.

Adrián held my gaze, smiling against my lips.

"The best thing I've ever tasted..." he murmured, voice low as he licked faintly, as if wanting to keep it to himself. "And I want it again and again."

I reached for him again, trying to lose myself in his mouth, but Adrián gripped my chin and pulled back just a few centimeters. His eyes flared, controlled and cruel.

"No, Lucía..." he whispered with that crooked smile. "You won't always get what you want—not so quickly. Learn to crave it, to suffer for it. That way, when I give it to you, you'll feel it multiplied."

"What do you mean?" I asked, voice trembling, as if I couldn't understand how he could want more when my body was at the limit—exhausted and sated. But with him... it never seemed enough.

Adrián cupped my face with both hands, his gaze hot and steady. "You don't get it, Lucía," he said, hoarse with desire. "You will never be enough for me. I could have you a thousand times and I'd still need you."

A shiver ran through me. These weren't just words from a man in the heat of passion; it was a dangerous confession; an abyss shared between us. And though I should have been frightened, I sank deeper into him—

because being his addiction made me feel powerful and damned at the same time.

Then I glanced at the dash clock and felt a jolt. "The time!" I cried, pulling away, my heart in my throat. "My parents will kill me if I don't get home now."

Adrián studied me for a long, heated second, that intense look refusing to let anything else matter. Then he smiled, dangerously calm. "Then let's go, princesa... but remember: this is only the beginning."

He pulled the car to a stop a few streets from my house, cut the engine without looking at me, and said, firmly: "Here."

It wasn't a question. He took my face and devoured me in a searing kiss—so deep it stole my breath and reignited the ache inside me. It lasted only a moment, but it left me trembling, knowing no other kiss could compare. I lay down on the bed still tasting his mouth on mine.

Every heartbeat reminded me I was already his, that I had crossed a border with no return. While my mother's voice echoed like a verdict, I understood the inevitable: I lived under a roof of rules and watchful eyes... but my skin, my desire, my hunger already belonged to Adrián.

Chapter 5

✦ ✦ ✦ ✦ ✦ ✦

I *dreamed of him. Or maybe it wasn't a dream.*

His hands gripped me; his voice whispered in my ear with that deep cadence that shattered me inside: "There's no escape, Lucía. You're already mine."

I woke gasping, skin slick with sweat, heart pounding as if I were still pinned beneath his body. His name burned on my lips, and when I pressed a hand to my chest it trembled, as if my body couldn't tell the difference between dream and reality.

The room was silent, yet the sense of him lingered— stuck to my skin like an invisible mark. Adrián wasn't just forbidden desire; he was danger itself, one that had chosen me, that followed me even into sleep, stealing my calm and filling every corner of me with his presence.

I rose slowly, my body still vibrating, and opened the window. The morning breeze stroked my skin, cool but powerless to quench the fire devouring me inside. I closed my eyes, and for a heartbeat I swore I heard his whistle— the insolent sound that called me like a magnet. I snapped my eyes open, holding my breath... but the street lay empty.

I smiled, though there was nothing amusing about it. Because I knew: even if he wasn't there, even if my mother watched me with her inquisitive eyes and my father demanded the perfect daughter... Adrián already lived inside me. And nothing in this world could pry him out.

As I dressed for university, I paused before the mirror. Something in me had changed. My honey-colored eyes gleamed with an intensity I didn't recognize, as if they guarded a secret too big to hide.

I ran my fingers through my still-damp hair and traced the flush on my cheeks. It wasn't shyness—it was the invisible mark of the night before, the imprint of the man who had set my body and soul ablaze.

I straightened my blouse and stood still, wondering if Camila would notice. She'd always had that cruel radar for spotting me—reading my eyes like an open book. Would she be able to see what had happened in the darkness of that car, what had turned me into someone new?

The thought alone made my skin prickle. That secret wasn't something to share lightly: it was fire under the tongue, a poison that could consume everything if I let it slip. And yet the temptation to spill it, to watch Camila's reaction, was almost as addictive as the memory of Adrián on my skin.

"Lucía!" Camila greeted me as she entered the classroom, her wide, clean smile reminding me how opposite we were. Her voice carried the freshness of someone who believes the world is simple—without shadows or abysses.

I paused for a second, returning her smile though inside I felt her eyes undress me more thoroughly than her expression let on. What if she noticed? What if she could read the ember still burning behind my gaze?

I bit my lip, hesitated the barest moment, then let myself drop into the desk beside her. I leaned close, my voice folding down into a whisper as if the words themselves might catch fire.

"I'm going to tell you something... but promise me you'll keep it as if it were your own," I said.

Camila lifted her brows, curiosity sharpening into something nervy. Her smile fluttered, less certain now.

"What did you do now?" she breathed, drawing nearer as if she both feared and desired the answer.

I swallowed, feeling heat bloom across my cheeks. I didn't force the confession. I let the name come slow, like a prayer or a curse.

"Adrián."

The air between us tightened. Camila's smile vanished; surprise and alarm carved her features. She froze, lips parted, as if I had named a ghost.

"Adrián...?" she whispered, incredulous, the word trembling toward panic. "Tell me you're not serious, Lucía."

I leaned in, unable to hide the tremor of a smile. The sound of my voice felt foreign and true at once.

"Camila... I'd never felt anything like it. Being with him is like stepping off the edge of the world and finding a new gravity—time unravels, everything else quiets. The way he looks at me, the way he touches me..." I stopped, biting my lip; the flush on my face spoke louder than any confession.

She drank my words with wide eyes, that shadow of alarm in her gaze curiously intoxicating. It was as if listening to me thrilled and terrified her in equal measure.

"It's like he's opened an entire other world for me," I whispered, leaning nearer still. "And the worst part is... I can't stop thinking about him. Not for a single second."

Camila buried her hands in her hair and exhaled, long and defeated.

"I don't even know what to say... but now I'm sure of it, Lucía. You've completely lost your mind."

I laughed, soft and dark, as if her reproach were the sweetest compliment.

"Maybe I have," I said with a half shrug.

"Lucía, I don't mean to ruin your thrill," Camila said more softly now, the seriousness undercutting her usual brightness, "but I've heard he has other women."

I held her eyes, the smile tilting like a knife-edge.

"I already told you, Camila. I'm not looking for marriage or promises. I don't want to be anyone's *future—right now I want to be all edge and no safety. If that's madness, then let me be mad."*

"This isn't love. It's the pleasure of the forbidden. It's feeling danger so close you can taste it. It's the rush of power... it's sex, nothing more."

She looked at me as if she didn't believe a single word—and maybe she was right. Because even as I spoke, my mind had already left the classroom. I closed my eyes for a moment and saw him over me again: his mouth devouring mine, his hands mastering my body as if he knew me better than I knew myself. I felt his breath at my neck once more, the edge of his voice burning me from the inside out.

A shiver ran through me; I bit my lip to keep from betraying myself in front of Camila. "Just sex," I had said. But the truth was different: Adrián was a sweet, lethal poison already coursing through my veins... and my body was begging desperately for another dose.

The professor's voice dragged me back to the present. Somewhere in the distance he spoke of exams and deadlines, but his words blurred into a meaningless murmur, impossible to hold.

My phone buzzed. I glanced at the screen and my breath caught: an unknown number. I hesitated before opening the message...and nearly dropped the phone when I read it.

"Don't let that boring class fill your head. Tonight, you're mine."

A chill tore through me. I had never given him my number. There was no way. And yet... there it was. The certainty seared through my skin: there was no barrier Adrián couldn't cross.

I pictured him in some nearby shadow, smiling with that dangerous calm, watching me even from a distance.

With trembling fingers, I typed before I could change my mind: "I can't. I must study. My parents won't let me go out—especially now with finals." I sent it knowing it was useless—that excuse wouldn't stop him. Deep down, the one I was trying to convince was myself.

Nothing. The silence felt worse than any reply. I imagined Adrián punishing me with absence, letting me burn alone, knowing I would think of him every second of the day.

I bit my lip until it hurt. Had he grown angry? Or was he simply playing with me—confident that even without answering he already had me exactly where he wanted?

The professor droned at the front, but his voice was a distant hum. I could copy what he said, feign attention...but inside me Adrián pulsed on, a burning memory that devoured everything.

The day dragged like an endless torment. When night finally fell, the house sank into silence. My parents slept, the lights were out... and I remained awake, unable to shut my mind.

My phone buzzed on the nightstand. My heart jumped so hard I nearly screamed.

"Come out to the terrace. Now."

No emojis, no softness—just a command. I swallowed, hands trembling as I pushed the sheets aside. Every step toward the terrace felt like a small crime, another secret pulling me down without escape.

I eased the door open, holding my breath so it wouldn't creak. The night air hit my face—cool, laced with salt. And there he was.

Adrián leaned against the railing, half-hidden in shadow, a lit cigarette throwing a thin glow across that crooked smile. The moment I crossed the threshold his eyes found mine, and I knew it didn't matter how much I resisted—this night was his too.

He stood beyond the fence, the moon carving his silhouette, the cigarette's ember sketching his mouth with each drag. I slipped the door wider; the hinges sighed like a traitor. He stepped across the threshold without hesitation, and the hush of night became an accomplice to our secret.

In the patio's corner, beneath the tree's heavy shadow, he trapped me. His body blocked every exit; the air condensed, danger and desire beating inside me.

"My parents are inside…" I whispered, pressing my palms to his chest, trying to push him away. "Are you crazy? They could hear us."

He smiled that dangerous calm that always undid me.

"Exactly for that reason, princesa…" he murmured, leaning close until his hot breath brushed my skin. "Danger makes everything more intense."

Instead of kissing me he slid a hand from my shoulder and captured my wrist—slow, deliberate. His touch was soft and cruel at once, each second of delay an exquisite torment. I shuddered but couldn't pull free; control had never been mine.

He brushed my lips without kissing them, breathing over them with obsessive patience.

"Are you afraid they'll hear you, Lucía?" he whispered, his low voice vibrating against my mouth. "Maybe they should know what their perfect daughter provokes."

I wanted to answer, but he pulled back just a fraction, that crooked smile driving me wild. His finger traced my jaw and stopped at my lips.

"Look at you… shaking, yet your body begs for me. Tell me, princesa… do you want me to own you right here, right now?"

My heart hammered in my throat, but this time I didn't retreat. Very slowly I placed my hands on my thighs and lifted my dress, letting the night breeze caress the bare skin. The movement wasn't accidental—it was a challenge.

Adrián watched me in silence. Something new flared across his face: a wild, dangerous spark that made me feel as if I'd ignited a blaze impossible to extinguish.

With trembling fingers, I slid my panties down, each motion deliberate, as if the very air were tracing my skin. When they were in my hand, I met his eyes and, with a daring gesture that burned me from the inside out, offered them to him. He didn't hesitate; I slipped them myself into the pocket of his pants, as if I had hidden my most intimate secret in his possession.

The dangerous smile that curved his mouth was enough to disarm me. He leaned to my ear; his deep voice pierced me like a dagger wrapped in silk.

"Now, princesa... you're provoking me like a real woman."

His fingers brushed the pocket, stroking the fabric with a calm that was torture, then his eyes locked on mine again—blazing with more than desire.

"You have no idea the fire you've lit," he murmured with cruel serenity. "Do you really think you can play my game?"

His breath scorched my skin. My hands shook, but I refused to step back. I took one step closer and, with a bravery I hadn't known I possessed, slid my fingers *slowly down his chest until they rested at his belt. "What do you want from me?" I whispered, my voice splitting between fear and defiance as I toyed with the edge of his pants.*

I felt him inhale faster; for a second, I fancied I'd surprised him. His lips twisted into that half-smile— danger, promise, threat.

"That's good…" he murmured, his deep voice thick with lust and warning. "But remember this, Lucía: when I unleash what you've stirred in me, you'll never escape."

Suddenly Adrián seized my wrist with impossible force and slammed me against the tree trunk. The sharp impact drew a gasp from me; my boldness dissolved in the night air like smoke.

His gaze burned—wild, triumphant—as if this exact moment had been waiting to be unleashed.

"Never forget who's in charge here," he growled, his hoarse, dangerous voice brushing my skin as he held me pinned. His mouth crashed onto mine in a fierce, merciless kiss—punishment and reward at once.

With a harsh motion he spun me around, leaving my back to him. The cold night air slid across my thighs as he yanked my dress up, exposing me under his absolute control.

Then, without warning, his palm came down hard— two sharp slaps that ripped a muffled cry from me and set my whole body alight. The mix of sting and pleasure hit me like lightning, erasing every scrap of resistance. My skin sparked, my legs trembled, and even as my body begged for more,

I felt a small, fierce part of me surrender.

"That's it..." he whispered in my ear, that low, ruinous voice cutting right through me. "Obedient... trembling... and a little more mine each time."

I wanted to scream with pleasure, to let my flesh speak for me, but I bit my lip until it tasted of iron. It wasn't fear; it was the delicious vertigo of being exposed to the night, knowing the forbidden burned hotter when discovery was possible. Every strike flared with risk, every caress a secret that set me on fire.

Two more slaps, each harder than the last, made my knees wobble as if I might collapse. There was no time to think. Pressed to the rough trunk, Adrián fucked me with fierce urgency—driving into me with a carnal hunger that overflowed him.

His breath seared the back of my neck as he held me tight, claiming me as if to brand me forever. There was no tenderness—only heat, hunger, and domination—and I, far from resisting, gave myself wholly to the instinct consuming us both.

His hands crushed my hips, steering the rhythm with brutal precision, dragging me further from myself with every brutal thrust. Each strike of pleasure tore through me like lightning, erasing boundaries I had once known.

I clung to the bark in desperation, nails scraping the trunk, my body trembling on the brink of total surrender. If I let go, I knew I would lose myself—yet part of me wanted to fall, to dissolve in his hands and his ravenous need.

The pace became frantic, savage, as if the night itself burned with us. My body tightened to the breaking point and then shattered: a brutal climax ripped me open, a raw cry lost against the wood. I shook uncontrollably, undone by pleasure, while his hands kept me upright so I wouldn't collapse.

Adrián roared in my ear, losing himself with me in the same devastating wave. His body convulsed against mine; he came deep inside me in a feral explosion that split the world in two.

We stayed pressed together, gasping beneath that tree, our sweat mixing with the humid night air. In the heavy silence—still pulsing with danger—I understood the truth: it hadn't been only a moment of pleasure. It was a pact—an invisible mark binding me to him.

I hated him and wanted him at once, realizing the forbidden was no longer a passing game but a delicious damnation I had no desire to escape.

We collapsed onto the damp grass; the world reduced to the tremor of my body and the hot weight of Adrián atop me. When the climax finally subsided, I let myself fall against his chest, exhausted, searching his ragged breaths for a rhythm to steady mine. My legs trembled, my heart pounded mercilessly... and yet desire still smoldered, demanding more.

Night folded around us, silence broken only by our gasps. Adrián tipped his head toward my ear; his deep voice cut through me like a sentence:

"This isn't over, princesa. I'm only beginning to teach you what it means to belong to me."

A new heat ignited my chest, fiercer even than the orgasm. It wasn't a promise — it felt like fate written in stone. And there, pressed to him, I understood there was no escape... though I didn't want one.

Adrián rose slowly, all insolent calm. He straightened his clothes without hurry, cast me one last burning look, and vaulted the fence without a word. He didn't say goodbye; he knew his absence would bind me just as tightly.

I was left alone, dress rumpled, and skin branded by his fire. The echo of his footsteps faded, but inside me his imprint still burned like an invisible tattoo. I closed my eyes, hugged myself, and knew with brutal certainty: the forbidden was no longer a game. Adrián was my mark, my sentence... and my addiction.

Chapter 6

❋ ❋ ❋ ❋ ❋ ❋

I woke with my body still burning from marks no one else could see. Days had passed since that night under the tree, yet I could still feel his imprint on my skin—as if Adrián were still inside me, breathing through every memory.

I searched for him without meaning to: in every corner of the university, in the places where he used to lean with his friends, in the noisy hallways. But there was no trace of him. And his absence burned me even more than his presence ever had.

Camila noticed, though she pretended not to. Every day she repeated the same question, as if trying to snap me out of a fever dream:

"Did you see him today?"

I only smiled, shrugged, and changed the subject, as if it were all a fleeting game. But inside, the only truth was that I longed to see him again—even for a single second.

"Remember, it's Marta's birthday today. What time should I pick you up?" Camila asked on the bus, pulling me out of my thoughts.

I nodded, answering something vague, but my mind wasn't there.

The ride felt endless. The small talk, the laughter—everything sounded distant, like it belonged to someone else.

Because with every mile, with every stretch of silence, the only thing that pulsed inside me was his name.

Adrián.

The bus stopped halfway, and most of the passengers got off, half laughing, half complaining. I moved on autopilot, my feet dragging, my mind drifting, as if the whole journey were just a meaningless parenthesis.

When we finally arrived, the party was already a whirlwind of smoke, colored lights, and thundering music. The air was heavy with cheap rum and tobacco, laced with perfumes soured by sweat. The girls looked like dolls ripped from a shop window—heels too high, lips too red, makeup flawless and brittle.

The men strutted around with their glasses brimming, their laughter too loud, desperate to prove something no one cared about. At the center reigned Marta: tall, blonde, with those green eyes that always seemed to look down on everyone, surrounded by admirers like a queen already bored of her own court.

Camila and I danced a couple of songs, toasted with watered-down rum, and for a fleeting moment I managed it—I convinced myself I could be just another student celebrating the end of the semester, that Adrián was nothing but a ghost.

Then it happened.

A murmur swept the room, a ripple starting at the shore and swallowing everything in its path. I turned without thinking, and there he was. Adrián.

The door still open behind him, cigarette smoke curling around his crooked smile, and that insolent calm that made him stand out even in a room full of noise. He didn't dance, didn't speak, didn't need to do anything… and yet the entire party froze around him.

My breath caught in my throat. Amid the crowd his figure gleamed like a declared danger: a dark shirt clinging to him, green eyes blazing under the lights, and that confident stride that seemed to split the world in two. The party roared on—music and laughter everywhere— but for me there was only him.

From across the room Adrián found me with his gaze. He needed nothing more than to lift his glass a fraction— a slow, calculated motion, a private toast meant only for me—then turned back to his friends as if I didn't matter.

But I knew. I felt myself burn because of that tiny gesture: a precise blow, a reminder that I belonged to him even when he didn't touch me.

Camila laughed beside me, talking about anything, and I forced a smile, pretending to listen, pretending to belong to a normality that no longer fit. "I'll get a drink," I murmured; my own voice sounded far away.

I pushed through the crowd like someone in a trance, pulse racing, skin prickling with hungry anticipation. The cool night air hit me as I crossed the patio, but it did nothing to tame the fire in my chest. Then I felt him— before I saw him—the prickling at the back of my neck that only he could provoke.

As I slipped into the dim hallway toward the bathroom, strong hands seized my waist and slammed me into the wall in the half-light.

"Beautiful... pretending you don't want me," Adrián murmured against my ear, his deep voice spilling over my skin like sweet poison.

His mouth traveled down my neck—slow, dangerous. It was not a kiss so much as domination; his tongue grazed tender skin and the cold, wet edge of his piercing teased me, sending a violent shiver through my spine. My body knew him before my mind could protest, and I understood I was lost.

Then, with the same composed cruelty with which he'd arrived, he pulled back.

"I'll see you in a while," he murmured, leaving that promise burning in my chest.

And he was gone. Just like that—he left me pressed to the wall, trembling, breath unsteady, desire leaking like an open wound. Adrián toyed with me with surgical precision: igniting me, denying relief, chaining me to my own hunger.

I smoothed my clothes, fixed my mask of calm, and returned to the party as if nothing had happened. The truth was every step scorched me.

"Where were you?" Camila asked the moment she saw me, her curious gaze cutting into me the way it always did.

I just smiled, unable to give her an answer that wouldn't sound like what it truly was: a sin.

"Bathroom," I said, forcing a casual tone as I sipped from my glass. I tried to look composed, but my cheeks still burned, my breath wasn't steady... and I was certain that if Camila looked at me too long, she'd know something had happened.

When the party wound down, we gathered to leave. Between tired laughter and comments about how good the night had been, we walked to the bus stop. We waited beneath the yellow glow of a streetlamp, counting the minutes until the next bus.

Camila chatted animatedly with the others, but her voice barely reached me. My eyes scanned the empty street, restless, as if expecting Adrián to emerge from the dark the way he always did—stealing my breath.

And then he appeared. Adrián, with three of his friends, laughing as if the whole night belonged to him. No car this time. He walked, blending his darkness into the neighborhood shadows, and my heart went wild.

He came closer without hurry, wrapped in that insolent calm that made everyone stare without knowing why. Then, wordlessly, he offered me a cigarette. Our fingers brushed—barely a touch—but the spark raced through me like lightning. To everyone else it was nothing. To me, it was a silent pact.

He pulled out his lighter. The flame lit his face for an instant; his clear eyes fixed on mine as he brought fire to the cigarette between my lips. But he didn't let go.

His face leaned closer, slowly, until the heat of the flame mingled with the heat of his breath.

"Not here..." I whispered through clenched teeth, my pulse hammering. "Too many eyes."

Adrián's smile curved faintly, malice flashing in its edge. He exhaled smoke aside, unconcerned, and murmured just for me:

"Precisely because of that, princesa."

He leaned in closer, smoke curling through his words.

"They're not neighbors, Lucía," he whispered, his voice a silk-wrapped blade. "They're witnesses. And that makes it even more exciting."

The group burst into laughter at some unrelated joke, unsuspecting. But I felt the burn of another gaze— Camila. Her eyes were fixed on me, sharp, furrowed, cutting into me like a scalpel. She wasn't smiling *anymore. She wasn't playing. Her suspicion scorched hotter than anything Adrián could whisper.*

Before she could speak, Adrián let out a dry laugh and raised his voice with practiced ease.

"Well, so when the hell is this bus coming?" he quipped, careless and brazen.

Laughter rippled through the group, dissolving the moment into trivial jokes. But my skin still burned, knowing the truth hadn't dissolved with it.

I glanced at him from the corner of my eye, my pulse still racing. He was a master of it—dragging me to the edge of disaster, and with a single gesture, turning fear into fire.

I hated him for that insolent calm... and I craved him precisely because of it.

When the bus finally arrived—empty at that late hour—we climbed aboard as a group. But Adrián didn't give me a choice: his hand seized mine with a firmness that was both command and sentence. He led me to the very back, unhurried, as if the entire vehicle belonged to him, and pushed me gently into the seat by the window.

The others filled the front, their laughter and chatter spilling into the silence of the night. But in the back seat there was only shadow, the low hum of the engine, and the heavy air thick with everything he and I had yet to do.

Streetlights flashed across his face in fragments of gold and darkness. His fingers tangled with mine, and his heat invaded me inch by inch. The whole world had shrunk to that seat, that closeness, and the dizzying certainty that no one could stop what was already burning between us.

Adrián turned his head slightly. Without releasing my hand, he whispered so close his lips brushed my skin:

"Ready to tempt fate, princesa?"

The gleam in his eyes under the flickering light made my pulse explode. A few seats ahead, people kept talking, oblivious, but I knew the back of that bus had already become ours.

His mouth crashed onto mine—deep, urgent, devouring me as if the risk itself made him hungrier. His other hand slid up my thigh with maddening patience, lifting my skirt inch by inch until the night air kissed my bare skin. Pleasure and danger coiled together, suffocating me.

I couldn't think. I couldn't resist. With a feverish impulse, I turned and straddled him. The sudden press of his erection against me ripped a moan from my throat, muffled against his mouth. I kissed him savagely, biting his lip, tangling my tongue with his, the cold brush of his piercing electrifying me until my whole body trembled.

Adrián growled into the kiss, surprised by my audacity, but instead of stopping me he crushed me closer. His hands gripped my hips with bruising force, grinding me against him as if he wanted to fuse me to his body. The bus rocked gently, but it was his rhythm that truly unbalanced me.

He pulled back just enough, his lips grazing my ear, his voice rough, dangerous, and thick with lust:

"Careful, princesa... you're playing with fire. And I don't know how to stop once I'm burning."

A nervous laugh, sharp and reckless, escaped me. I leaned in, my breath hot against his neck, and whispered with all the defiance I could muster:

"Then don't stop."

I bit him lightly on the neck, just the brush of my teeth against his hot skin, while my hips moved slowly over him, daring the danger with every stroke.

The growl that escaped his throat was pure menace. With a sudden movement he grabbed the back of my neck and forced me to meet his eyes. His gaze burned, intense, as if he wanted to devour me whole.

"You don't run the show here, Lucía..." he snapped in that deep voice that made me shiver. "Never forget it."

His hand slid down my back and pressed me against him with a force that left no doubt: the game was over, and I was his.

All the rebellious strength I had tried to hold onto melted away in an instant. My body surrendered to him as if it had been waiting for that command forever. I let my forehead fall against his shoulder, breathing hard, while my hips obeyed the pressure of his hands.

Adrián didn't wait any longer. His firm grip lifted me slightly and, with a confident motion, he settled me onto him. He pushed my panties aside, unbuttoned his pants, and right there—in the dimness of the moving bus—a moan tore from my throat as I felt him fill me completely. Breath left my lungs, leaving only the vertigo and the tremor of having him inside me. His thrusts were deep, relentless, each one carrying the force of someone claiming what he considered his.

He kissed me without pause. His lips moved across my skin like a sweet sentence: my mouth, devoured in deep, bruising kisses; my neck, bitten lightly, pulling ragged sighs from me. Every touch, every wet stroke of his mouth wrapped me tighter in his control.

"Lucia!" he groaned against my lips, and the sound of my name on his voice only inflamed me further. I moved harder, finding the rhythm he had carved into me, riding his desire with mine.

"Adrián!" I cried, and when my voice broke in his ear, something changed in his eyes.

"Come with me…" he ordered, his tone fractured by the agony of fire consuming him. And that was the key.

Our orgasms detonated in unison, shaking our bodies with violent tremors of madness and forbidden passion. In that instant, I knew Adrián wasn't just a man: he was danger, he was addiction, and I was already completely lost in him.

A shout from the front of the bus snapped us back to reality.

"Adrián!" one of his friends called out.

My heart froze. What if they saw us? What if they realized what we had done back here? My blood was still boiling, and at the same time fear surged up, closing around my throat.

"Lisa says the new club downtown is amazing—should we head over there?"

Adrián looked at me then, and in his eyes still burned the same wild desire that had just undone me. His hand didn't release mine, as if the entire world had narrowed down to that single choice.

With my voice unsteady, trembling with both desire and defiance, I dared to ask:

"Do you want to go with them… or would you rather get off at our stop?"

Adrián held my gaze for a few endless seconds. Then he smiled. It wasn't sweet or calm—it was the smile of a predator, pleased, proud of my boldness, as if he had been waiting for me to take that step.

"That's how I like it…" he murmured, squeezing my hand tight.

His eyes flared with dangerous fire.

"We're getting off," Adrián said, his voice cutting through the air like a sentence. He rose in one swift motion, still gripping my hand, and the whole world shrank to that single gesture. Friends, music, the laughter drifting from the front of the bus—none of it mattered. Only him, deciding for both of us, pulling me into the unknown.

As we walked toward the door, I felt eyes stabbing into me. Camila. A few rows ahead, she was staring as I passed, her look of reproach sharp enough to slice through me. Her expression said it all: I saw, Lucía. I know what happened back there. I dropped my gaze, unable to meet hers, guilt knotting with the euphoria still racing in my veins.

We stepped off the bus in silence, my blood roaring in my ears. Adrián's grip on my hand was firm—more command than gesture—and he spoke only once, low and grave, without even looking at me:

"We're going to my place."

I followed him as if there were no other choice. Just a few streets away, a back door swallowed us into his world.

The moment we entered his room, the air shifted: tobacco, clean sweat, and that harsh cologne I already recognized as sin.

The bed, wide and unmade, ruled the center of the space. To the side, a computer spilled its cold glow over scattered papers. Closets overflowing with shoes and shirts, arranged in meticulous order, stood in sharp contrast to the feral intensity of the hands that still burned on my skin. Everything in that room breathed Adrián—dark, virile, controlled even in its chaos.

I stood frozen for a few seconds, my eyes tracing every detail, fully aware that I was stepping into a space that wasn't just intimate… it was dangerous. And yet, in that very danger lived the desire consuming me.

I felt his gaze fixed on me, so intense it raised goosebumps without him even touching me. Adrián didn't speak. He simply leaned against the doorframe, arms crossed, watching me as if savoring the sight of me standing there invading his world and, at the same time, already trapped in it. His lips curved into the faintest smile of satisfaction: the smile of a hunter who knows the prey is inside his territory, with no escape left.

"Do you know what it means to be here, Lucía?" he finally said, his deep voice filling the room. "In my space, on my bed… there's no room for doubts or games. Only for what I decide to do with you."

I crossed my arms, trying to hide the tremor in my hands, and met his eyes head-on.

"There's nothing left that could surprise me, Adrián," I shot back, voice sharpening with a defiance I hadn't known I possessed.

The dangerous smile that spread across his face made me doubt my own words in an instant. That spark in his eyes said the opposite—that I hadn't seen anything yet, and that I was about to find out.

He watched me in silence, all unsettling calm—the kind worse than any sudden move. He took slow, deliberate steps toward me, each one both chill and ignition.

"Do you really think there's nothing left that could surprise you?" he whispered, leaning so close his breath ghosted my ear. *"All you've done so far is open the first door... and I have an entire world waiting behind the next."*

"Or are you bored already?" he added suddenly that half-smile razor-sharp, unraveling me. His tone wasn't a question; it was a dare—to see how far I'd go.

My heart hammered. I didn't know whether to match his provocation or let the current pull me under. Every word he spoke sank me deeper into the addiction I could no longer deny.

I kept his gaze, tipped my head with a smile that I knew would light him on fire.

"Bored with you?" I said, thick with irony. "I doubt it, Adrián. Though perhaps you talk too much and do too little."

His smile widened—darker, harder. In a flash his hand closed on my waist and slammed me against the wall; his body pinned mine so tight there was no room to breathe.

"Do too little?" he breathed in my ear, low and dangerous. "You'll beg me to stop."

"Beg you to stop?" I breathed against his lips, teasing but not kissing. "No... what terrifies me, Adrián, is begging you never to stop."

He didn't let my provocation pull him in. He stayed perfectly still, his mouth a breath from mine, his chest contained like a predator who already knows he has won. His eyes bored into me with a cold intensity that froze me in place.

"You have no idea what you're saying, Lucía," he murmured, dangerously calm. "When I decide not to stop, there won't be a living thing that can resist me."

I didn't answer with words. Instead, I tipped my face just enough to catch his lower lip between my teeth, biting down hard enough to draw a guttural growl from his chest. I released him slowly, savoring the taste, and smiled with shameless defiance.

Adrián didn't pounce the way I'd expected. His fingers clamped around my chin with unyielding force, holding me there and forcing me to meet his gaze.

"You're going to pay for that, princesa," he murmured, dangerously calm. "I don't think you'll be able to walk home."

With a slow, deliberate motion unlike any he'd shown me before, Adrián turned me and swept my long hair aside, leaving my back completely exposed to his stare. His fingers found the zipper of my dress and began to slide it down with excruciating patience. Every inch it descended sent a shiver tearing through me.

"A little short, isn't it?" he murmured, soft and laced with irony—disorienting me in an instant. I didn't know whether to laugh or tremble. The air burned in my lungs; my voice was trapped. All I could feel was how each of his movements stole my control, how the sound of the zipper mingled with the frantic beating of my heart. I closed my eyes and surrendered to the exquisite torment of his touch.

The zipper stopped halfway, as if leaving me half-dressed were part of the punishment. His fingers traced a slow line down the bare skin of my back—a calculated caress that raised goosebumps to my very bones. He didn't hurry; he kept me teetering on that border where desire burns hottest because it never quite arrives.

My ragged breath betrayed me. He knew he was driving me insane; his game had me completely under his control. Adrián lowered his face until his lips brushed my ear, his hot breath melting any last attempt at resistance. His scent hypnotized me. His voice—low, husky—cut through me like a sentence:

"Your silence tells me more than your words, princesa... and tonight I'm going to tear out every moan you try to hold back."

I couldn't contain it. A moan slipped from me—deep, uncontrollable, as if ripped from my very core. The sound filled the room and shattered the fragile silence that had held me safe.

His body barely touched mine, and yet I felt wetness betray me between my thighs. It was maddening he wasn't even fully touching me, but the command of his voice and the heat of his breath were enough to set me ablaze. My skin burned, my legs trembled, and I understood I no longer needed his hands to surrender; his presence alone was enough to addict me.

Adrián returned to the zipper, dragging it down so slowly that every second became delicious torture. The dress slid off my shoulders like a slow caress, leaving me exposed to his gaze—a gaze that stripped me long before his hands ever did. His fingers traced my skin with the lightest touch, savoring every inch as if he wanted to take my sanity away drop by drop. I held my breath, torn between the desperation to hurry the moment and the desperate wish for it never to end.

"Let me see you," he murmured, tone as firm as it was hungry. "Don't hide anything from me, Lucía. Everything about you is mine."

My heart raced. Despite the consuming desire, I hesitated to turn. I'd never felt comfortable with my body: my breasts weren't as full as I would have liked, and those one hundred and fifteen pounds had always felt more like a sentence than a gift. The fear that he would discover my insecurities froze me for a moment.

I turned to him slowly. My hands trembled as I tried to cover myself, but he gently moved my fingers aside, forcing me to reveal myself exactly as I was.

Adrián took his time, devouring me with his eyes from head to toe, as if every inch of my skin had belonged to him forever. I felt him undress me more with those green eyes than with his hands, and I wanted to pull away, to hide again. But then he spoke in that deep voice that dismantled my defenses:

"Stop hiding, Lucía. Your breasts? Perfect for my mouth. Your body? Exactly how I want it. Everything in you was made for me… and I'll prove it to you until you have no doubt."

"I want to see you touch yourself," he ordered, his voice steady. I stood stunned, wide-eyed, unable to respond at once. I'd never imagined he would ask that. Silence wrapped around us, my ragged breathing betraying the clash inside me: shame against desire, fear against the dangerous addiction pulling me toward him.

"The truth… I wouldn't know how," I confessed, cheeks burning. I felt my face light up—a maddening mix of shame and inexperience. I dropped my gaze, unable to

meet his. Deep down I knew that confession was exactly what he wanted: my naked surrender, my innocence handed straight into his hands.

"Never?" he asked, voice low, loaded with surprise and hunger.

I looked down. "Once…" I murmured so quietly I wasn't even sure the words had left my mouth.

Adrián wasn't satisfied. He stepped closer, invading my space. "Once? Where, Lucía? How was it?" he whispered, soft and dangerous.

Shame consumed me; my cheeks flamed. "It was… a stupid thing," I stammered, trying to dodge his eyes.

"I don't care if it was stupid," he cut in, gripping my face to force me to look at him. "I want details, princesa. I'm dying for details."

"It was… once, alone," I admitted, barely a whisper, my heart thudding so hard it felt like I couldn't breathe. "It didn't last… I didn't even know what I was doing," I babbled, biting my lip. "I was in the shower… I thought of you and—" My voice broke, and I couldn't finish the sentence.

The silence that followed was unbearable. My ragged breathing filled the room, the flush burning my skin. I didn't know whether he would punish me for confessing or devour me on the spot.

A dark gleam lit his eyes, sharper than any caress. His smile tilted with dangerous satisfaction as he leaned in, trapping me between his voice and his desire.

"In the shower, thinking of me..." he murmured, savoring each word. His thumb brushed my lips, lingering at the bite that still trembled.

"That, princesa, is the most exciting thing you've said—and I intend to prove it."

I wanted to hide, but he didn't allow it. His firm fingers forced me to hold his gaze, and then I understood: he wasn't after my shame—he wanted my surrender.

"This time you won't do it alone," he declared, his voice low enough to chill my bones. "I'm going to teach you how to touch yourself for real... until you scream my name."

His dangerous smile pressed into my skin like an invisible brand. It wasn't a promise; it was an order. Trembling with desire and fear, I knew there was no escape.

"Now I want to see you do it... here, in front of me. Show me how you did it, but this time knowing it's me watching."

"No... I can't," I stammered, lowering my eyes, the flush climbing to my ears. The very idea made me shake: what if I did it wrong? What if my awkwardness ruined the desire I'd sparked in him?

Adrián didn't accept doubts. He took my hand firmly and guided it toward my body, his deep voice a cruel caress in my ear:

"Calm down, princesa... let yourself go. I'll show you how."

A choked breath escaped me as his strong hands guided mine. I wanted to close my eyes and hide in the shadow of my shame, but he wouldn't let me. He grabbed my chin roughly, forcing me to meet his stare.

"Don't you dare look away," he ordered, low and uncompromising. "I want to see you break. I want you to understand that now you belong to my eyes... and to whatever I decide to do with you."

His control crushed and aroused me at once. There, trembling under his dominance, I realized the true pleasure wasn't in my hands but in being forced to discover myself—and I wanted it more than anything.

At first my fingers shook, my body rigid between shame and desire. But his eyes held me—consumed me— until I understood there was no escape. The flush on my cheeks became part of the fire coursing through me. Guided by his hands, mine began to move clumsily at first... then with a desperate, obedient rhythm.

"You're mine, Lucía... only mine," he whispered.

A moan burst from my lips—deep, freeing—and I couldn't hold it back. I looked him straight in the eyes, moaning under his burning gaze, knowing this was exactly what he wanted: my complete surrender, my pleasure placed in his hands.

Adrián didn't break eye contact for a second. His smile widened—dark, proud of what he'd provoked in me. He held my chin, forcing our eyes to stay locked even as my body continued to shake.

"That's it, princesa…" he murmured, dangerously calm. "I want you to remember who made you cry out like that. No one else will take you this far. You're mine, and you just proved it."

Still gasping, legs weak, Adrián squeezed me to his chest and lowered his voice—hoarser now, more commanding.

"We're not finished, Lucía…" he whispered in my ear, nibbling my earlobe. "Now I want more. I want to hear you scream my name until you have no voice left."

His gaze burned like a brand, and I understood the climax that had shattered me seconds before was only the prelude to the delicious torment he planned. I clung to his shoulders as he guided me with fierce resolve, and in that instant I accepted the inevitable: Adrián was my owner, and I—unwilling but unable to resist—surrendered again.

Suddenly his calm vanished. Adrián seized me with a force that ripped a muffled gasp from my throat and hurled me onto the bed. His hands roamed my body as if claiming it with fury. He leaned over me and, giving me no respite, drove into me with a brutal rhythm—each thrust stealing the air from my lungs and returning only raw, scorching pleasure.

"Now you'll understand why no one gets away from me," he growled, his lips crashing into mine in a wild, punishing kiss. His hands pinned me in place—branded, owned, completely under his control.

In the midst of his relentless rhythm, Adrián lowered his face until his mouth brushed my ear. His voice—rough with desire—cut through me like a command no one could ever disobey.

"There will never be another man, Lucía... promise me."

The world narrowed to that demand. His words burned as much as his body inside me; it wasn't a question—it was a command. Breathless and pounding, I could only nod, giving him that promise without a second thought.

Adrián caught my wrists with one hand and pinned them above my head against the sheets. The weight of his control intensified everything—being unable to move made every thrust sharper. His unrelenting rhythm stole my breath and filled me with such overpowering pleasure that I lost the line between where I ended and he began.

Adrián pressed my wrists harder and sped up, his pace becoming brutal and relentless. Each thrust was a blade of fire that ripped a muffled cry from me, a sound I couldn't stifle no matter how I tried. The world fell away: there was only him—claiming me with savage force, breaking down the last of my resistance until I became pure pleasure under his control.

A tearing scream escaped my throat as my body arched beneath him, trembling uncontrollably. Each thrust hurled me closer to an abyss, until I was finally thrown headfirst with no net. Pleasure crashed through me in brutal waves—one after another, more intense than anything I had felt before; my body could hardly bear it. I clung to him, shouting his name as I dissolved into a devastating climax that left me empty and full at once.

I lay undone beneath him, shattered into a thousand pieces of pleasure, but Adrián did not let my release dictate him. He held firm, gripping my wrists even tighter, prolonging each movement with cruel precision, proving that not even my surrender could loosen his control.

His breathing was heavy, his muscles taut; still I felt him restrain himself—teetering on the edge, absolute master of himself...and of me.

He sat up with a quick, predatory movement, as if the next step had already been planned. He opened the nightstand drawer, pulled out a dark handkerchief, his eyes burning as he did. In an instant he took my ankles and rolled me easily until I lay face down, my cheek pressed into the sheets.

"Don't move," he ordered, low and absolute.

A tremor ran through me—fear, shame, or the fierce curiosity to see how far he'd go. He slid the handkerchief over my face and tied it across my eyes, plunging me into velvet darkness. My breath hitched; the world vanished and only his voice remained—deep, possessive—filling me with unbearable vertigo.

"You don't need to see, princesa... just obey."

Every sound, every brush of his breath became exquisite torture. I tried to guess where he'd touch first— my neck, my hips—but not knowing suspended me on the razor edge: my skin prickled, my heart wanted to leap from my chest. Each silent second was an agony, a countdown toward a pleasure that already consumed me in anticipation.

His lips began to travel over me in slow kisses and nips, from the base of my neck down over my curves. Each mouthful of attention drew deeper sighs from me, stealing my control bit by bit. I felt his erection press against me from behind—hard, unforgiving—reminding me with every push that I belonged to him.

His touch moved lower, slow and deliberate, until he reached the pulse of me. The first circle of his fingers drew a shuddered breath I tried to smother in the sheets—a futile attempt to contain the storm he'd set loose.

"Stay still," he warned in a low, dangerous voice — a threat that made me shiver more than his touch.

I bit the sheets hard, trying to hold back the moans that threatened to escape. Each circular stroke set me alight, and yet the only thing in my head was his command: stay still.

My body trembled under the sweet torment, arching against my will as I fought to remain motionless. Pleasure struck me, and still, between stifled gasps, I obeyed—moaning with the contained force of someone about to break.

Adrián paused his fingers just enough to make my body cry out for more. He noticed the tension in my muscles and smiled darkly, like someone who delights in another's desperation. He leaned over me, his breath burning the back of my neck, and whispered in a low, rough voice—dangerous and erotic all at once:

"Not yet... wait a little longer. It will be more intense, you'll see."

His words hit like a blow, forcing me to hold back the unholdable, to prolong the delicious agony that was destroying me. His command left no room for choice, only the ache to obey.

Each second felt like an eternity, a torment that kept me on the verge of collapse. I knew only he had the key to free me, and I surrendered to that waiting, trembling beneath his power.

Just when I thought he would grant mercy, when I expected to shatter, Adrián withdrew his fingers with cruel calm. The empty space left me with a frustrated, desperate moan. My hips searched instinctively for the lost friction, but he pinned me down, pressing my body into the sheets.

"Not so fast, princesa…" he whispered in that dangerous calm that unmade me from the inside. "I want to see you beg for it."

The blindfold's darkness grew unbearable by the second. I couldn't see—only feel his breath near me, his erection brushing me like an unfulfilled promise—and that exquisite torture made me lose my mind.

I refused to beg, even though my body betrayed me, trembling and crying out for him. Adrián knew it. He grabbed my hips and hauled me up with fierce ease, forcing me onto my knees. With one hand he seized my long hair and swept it into an improvised ponytail, yanking until my bare back pressed against his torso.

"More… please," I begged.

His teeth bit into my skin, pulling a broken gasp, while his other hand descended mercilessly to find my most vulnerable spot once again. The same circular, rhythmic caress reignited the sweet agony, slowly undoing me. I was insane, lost—and yet I remained silent, enduring the unbearable, claimed by his will.

"How much more, Lucía?" he growled against my skin, and for the first time I heard a trace of desperation in his voice. The need to claim me completely burned him

as fiercely as it burned me, and that mix of power and hunger made him even more dangerous.

I couldn't take it any longer. The tremor in my legs betrayed me, my breathing fractured, and the heat inside consumed everything it touched.

"Adrián... please..." my voice came out trembling, choked between moans and tears of sheer need.

"You drive me insane, princesa," Adrián roared, and in a fierce movement he lifted me as if I weighed nothing.

Instinctively, I wrapped my legs around his waist, clinging tight while he held me with absolute dominance. He caught me against the door; one breath later he was inside me, the shock tearing a broken gasp that tangled with his uneven breathing.

The wood creaked with every thrust, my nails digging into his shoulders, and I lost myself between sweet pain and savage pleasure. In that moment there was no world, nothing else... just Adrián making me his again and again, against the door that could barely contain us.

Each drive was harder than the last; the door trembled to our rhythm, and between gasps I felt his mouth brush my ear.

"You're mine, princesa..." he murmured in a hoarse voice, each word punctuated by a beat of pleasure. "No one else can touch you, no one else can make you feel like this. Only me. Always me."

His hot breath on my neck, the weight of his body pressing me against the door, and those possessive phrases etched into my skin made me lose control. Every movement reminded me there was no escape: I was his, and he made sure to repeat it with every word.

The fire exploded inside me—an uncontrollable, fierce orgasm that shook me through and ripped a tearing cry from my throat. My body convulsed against the door, my nails sank into his back to anchor myself, while my voice rang out his name. I melted simply hearing him, knowing my total surrender was what aroused him most.

"That's it... I want to hear you, princesa," Adrián panted against my ear.

He didn't stop. He kept taking me, steady and brutal, while my body shook and came apart in his hands.

When my legs finally gave out, I thought he would let me go—but he didn't. Adrián held me tight, as if I were made of paper, and in one swift movement hauled me up and pressed me against his chest. My breath was still broken, my body still shaking from the climax, and yet he strode purposefully to the bed, giving me no respite.

He threw me onto the sheets with a mix of brutality and fierce care, like someone placing a treasure that belonged only to him. He bent over immediately, capturing my mouth in a hungry kiss, and I felt him harder, more demanding.

I understood the storm wasn't over.

He gave me no chance to breathe. No sooner had my back hit the sheets than Adrián claimed me again, every motion rough with need. A sweet sting ran through me, braided with the pleasure of the previous orgasm—an insatiable ache.

His hoarse voice wrapped around me, rough and dominant:

"You're not finished, Lucía... and neither am I."

His relentless rhythm dragged me to a place I wasn't sure I wanted to return from. I was barely recovering from one shattering climax when another struck, ripping his name from my throat as if it tore straight from my soul. There was no pause, no mercy—each thrust was a new wave, an explosion of sensation that consumed me.

I clung to him, trembling beneath his power, realizing I'd lost count of how many times I'd come.

My body no longer obeyed me—it was his now, answering only to him, trapped in an endless chain of orgasms that left me spent... and still desperate for more.

His pace grew more chaotic, more savage, as if he could no longer contain himself. I felt his muscles knot above me, his breath turning into a feral growl that ran down my spine—seconds before he finally shattered.

"Lucía!" he roared my name like a beast unchained, driving into me with one last punishing thrust that yanked another orgasm from me in perfect unison. His body

convulsed against mine, every spasm releasing what he'd held back with such fury and control.

I held on to him, breathless beneath his body and the heat between us, while the last wave broke through him— and dragged me down with it.

It was the roar of a man claiming me—sealing me as his with every drop of release. Even at the moment of letting go he never lost dominance. His grip on my hips stayed firm, unrelenting, making it clear that pleasure didn't weaken him—it made him more masterful.

His breath was heavy, but in his eyes, there was no exhaustion... only that dangerous calm.

He leaned down, voice rough and thick with appetite:

"Lucía. I'll want more... more of you, of that mystery that pulls me in," he murmured against my skin, desire and danger threaded through each word. "Even knowing you're forbidden."

That last word made my thoughts spiral.

Forbidden? *What did he mean by that?*

My heart pounded wildly—not just from the weight of his body over mine, but from the echo of that confession.

Was there something I didn't know?

A secret binding me to this addiction without me even realizing it?

"What do you mean... forbidden?" I whispered, barely audible between his lips and my skin. My body still burned beneath him, but my mind clung to that word like a blade.

Adrián watched me in silence, those green eyes blazing with a fire I couldn't read. The dark smile that curved his mouth wasn't an answer—it was a provocation. That silence maddened me more than any touch ever could.

His smile widened just a fraction, and when I opened my mouth to press him, his voice cut me off like ice.

"Do you take the pill?" he asked, matter of fact and brutal, as if he were discussing logistics rather than something intimate and urgent.

What kind of man moved so easily from dark mystery to that intimate control over my body?

"Yes, I take it," I answered, lifting my chin defiantly so he wouldn't see the knot in my throat. Without waiting for his reaction I climbed off the bed, grabbed my clothes, and dressed in quick, sharp movements.

His question stabbed like a dagger — not for what it implied, but for what it suggested. Didn't he mind the possibility of leaving me pregnant? Or was he simply reminding me he had no intention of staying?

The sting of offense burned in my chest. Of course, I wasn't ready to be a mother either, but the way he skirted the issue, the way he toyed with me at my most vulnerable — I refused to fall into his game. Not this time.

I didn't get the fury I expected. Instead, Adrián's low, dark laugh filled the room and chilled me to the bone.

"I like it when you rebel, Lucía," he said in that calm voice that always undid me. "Because sooner or later you always come back to me... and you know it."

His gaze roamed over me like an invisible caress— slow, devouring. There was no anger in his eyes, only a disturbing satisfaction, as if my fury were just another of his conquests.

"Don't be so sure, Adrián," I whispered against his mouth, defiance trembling in my voice. "I'm not as easy to tame as you think."

He rose slowly and stepped in close, his fingers brushing my chin to force my eyes to meet his. In a low, certain voice he said the sentence that shattered me from the inside:

"I don't need to tame you, Lucía... because deep down you already know you're mine."

I turned without another word and walked out the door, the dawn air hitting my face like a slap.

I walked fast, wanting to leave behind his house, his scent, his shadow... but it was useless.

The words kept drilling into my mind, repeating like a sweet poison coursing through my veins: You already know you're mine.

I hated him for the calm in his voice, for the certainty behind those words—and even more for the heat that came with admitting he was right.

Every step I took away from him only sank me deeper into the truth I didn't want to face.

Adrián wasn't a passing chapter.

He was a sentence.

Chapter 7

✦ ✦ ✦ ✦ ✦ ✦

*C*amila met me at the door with her usual energy—
barefoot, hair tied in a messy ponytail and that smile
that seemed to shine brighter than the summer itself.
"Finally!" she exclaimed, wrapping me in a tight hug. "I
thought you'd forgotten me." The smell of freshly baked
flan drifted from the kitchen, and for a second, I let myself
imagine staying here, in her house—her simple, sunlit
refuge where nothing dangerous seemed able to reach
me.

Her mother greeted us warmly from the living room;
she had always been our accomplice, so different from
mine, who saw threats lurking in every corner.

Camila's room seemed suspended in a time that no
longer belonged to me: stuffed animals neatly arranged,
soft-colored walls pinned with inspirational quotes,
bottles of perfume lined up on the vanity. Everything there
was innocence and order. And me—I stood in the middle
of that light carrying a secret too raw, too forbidden to
belong.

We were two faces of the same coin: she still believed
in princes and happy endings, while I had already let
myself be consumed by a man who tasted like danger
itself. Yet Camila was still my refuge—the only one who
could face my shadows without running.

She flopped down beside me, hugging a cushion, but her eyes pierced into me with an insistence that made my skin prickle. The silence lasted only a breath before she asked, sharp as a blade:

"Lucía... what happened after you got off the bus with Adrián?"

There was no reproach in her tone, but curiosity tangled with fear—and it cut through me, because she had seen. Her eyes were an accusing mirror, telling me I could no longer hide.

I dropped my gaze, fidgeting with the floral bedspread as if I could knot my sins into its threads.

"It was... intense," I confessed, my sigh betraying me more than I wanted. "Adrián has a way of trapping you, Cami. It's like he knows exactly which string to pull so the whole world disappears."

"Lucía!" she cried, tossing a stuffed animal to the floor, clutching her head in disbelief.

"That isn't magic—that's manipulation. Don't you see? He wants to confuse you, to make you feel like you're nothing without him. That's not normal... and you know it."

Her voice dropped suddenly, soft but urgent, as if even the walls might conspire to keep my secret. "That man will devour you. And the worst part is—you'll let him. You'll believe you need him."

I looked at her in silence. She trembled from fear for me.

And I—I trembled from desire for him, the memory of his hands still burning on my skin, proof that she was right and that I didn't care.

Camila called him poison... and I felt him like the drug that kept me alive.

She breathed deeply, as if trying to pass calm into me, then took my hands with that firmness that always undid me.

"You need fresh air, Lucía." Her voice was soft, but a plea hid beneath it. "My mom rented a house on the beach this weekend. Come with us. It'll do you good. You need to remember yourself without him."

For a second the image of the sea felt like a balm: salt on the skin, the sound of waves, the sun wiping away thought. I wanted to believe it would be enough. I wanted to think I could shake him off like sand after a swim.

"All right... I'll go," I whispered, forcing a tired smile. Camila hugged me, convinced she'd pulled me back from the edge. I hugged her back, too, but inside I knew: no sea could wash out a poison already running through my blood. Adrián wasn't a memory I could flee— he was a sentence I would keep returning to.

The rest of the afternoon passed in easy laughter and the warm comfort of Camila's house, as if for a few hours I lived inside a parallel life. The food tasted delicious, neighbors drifted in and out, the flan's sweetness filled the air... everything was simple enough that, for a moment, I believed I could breathe unchained. Yet with every laugh, every sip, his name pulsed— invisible, forbidden, impossible to scrub from my skin.

The following days were a mirage of calm. No messages, no whistles in the street, no late-night calls. No trace of Adrián. But his silence didn't free me—it devoured me even more than his presence. It was as if he'd moved into my head, crouched in every corner, reminding me that even emptiness belonged to him; he owned the void as much as the fire.

So, when Camila insisted we go to the beach, I agreed without hesitation. I needed to run or at least pretend I could. Maybe the ocean would offer a truce—though deep down I knew even the waves couldn't wash away the poison already in my veins.

"A weekend at the beach with Camila?" my mother repeated, peering over her glasses with that look that could strip a lie bare. I nodded, calm on the surface though she sensed something was wrong.

"Yes, mamá. That's all—just a break," I said, keeping my voice steady as if I could convince her too.

She said nothing more; that silence was worse than a sermon. I recognized the look: suspicion glimmered in her eyes, the certainty that I was no longer the obedient daughter she'd hoped to raise.

I didn't wait for her to speak. I kissed her on the cheek and crossed the doorway as if the street itself could cleanse the guilt burning on my skin. The fresh air hit me, and I inhaled deeply, knowing the only thing ahead was a trip to the beach... and the illusion that I might find freedom there.

Tight jeans, a backless blouse, and my worn-out sneakers were my choice. I didn't need anything else. I caught my reflection in the window before leaving and saw someone different: strong, sensual, dangerous. For the first time in a long while, I felt my body was my armor.

The beach house was a perfect mirage: the pool glittered under the moon, music throbbed like a wild pulse, and the neighbors' laughter filled every corner as if tomorrow didn't exist. I danced, I drank, I laughed—and for a fleeting moment, I believed I was free. That I could simply be Lucía without chains, without secrets, without Adrián's shadow chasing me.

Carlos came closer, that clean smile of his always setting him apart.

"Dance?" he asked, extending his hand. I had known him forever; I knew about the feelings he kept quiet... and yet, I also knew he wasn't the one who burned my skin at night. Still, I accepted. We danced two songs, and I found myself smiling, lighter, as if the rhythm itself returned a power I had forgotten.

The party went on until dawn. Glasses raised, bodies dripping from the pool, laughter dissolving into music.

But as fatigue crept in, the frenzy faded, and one by one we drifted to the bedrooms. In the room I shared with Camila and two other girls, we turned off the light amid whispers and jokes, and soon the only sound left was the sea cradling the house.

I was slipping into sleep when the vibration of my phone jolted me awake. The screen lit the darkness and, when I saw the name, the air caught in my lungs. Adrián.

I didn't need to read the message to know the mirage was over.

With my heart racing, I got up quietly, careful not to disturb the steady breathing around me. On tiptoe, I made my way to the door and slipped into the hallway. The message was clear, short—more command than invitation:

I'm outside.

Through the glass doors to the patio, I saw him— outlined against the murky light of the pool. He sat at the edge, a cigarette glowing like an ember in the shadows, his jaw clenched, his gaze locked on me. It wasn't calm; it was contained danger, a fire waiting to erupt. The smoke curled upward slowly, as if even the air itself knew to fear him.

I mistook that tension for desire. I thought it was hunger for me, as always, and I refused to see the shadow burning behind his eyes. I walked toward him in cautious steps, each one pulling me deeper into the abyss.

When I got close enough, he looked up. His voice dropped to a low whisper, poisoned with control.

"Did you enjoy dancing with him, princesa?"

I froze. The question landed like a sharp blow, brutal in its simplicity. Then I understood: he'd seen me. Every smile, every turn in Carlos's arms was tattooed in his memory. He didn't need to shout—his dangerous calm was the most terrifying punishment.

"And what about you—what's your problem? Are you stalking me now?" I shot back; my voice edged with defiance though my heart hammered like a drum. I held his gaze, determined not to give in, even knowing my rebellion was a thin thread against the blaze in his eyes.

Adrián let out a low, dark laugh that both chilled and ignited me. He rose slowly, letting the cigarette smoke dissolve between us as he advanced, each step more calculated than the last.

He stopped so close his heat wrapped around me like an electric field. His voice dropped to a grave whisper— intimate and dangerous, slicing right through me:

"Careful, Lucía... careful. Remember who's in charge here."

He didn't need to shout or touch me; the words split the air and bent my will. My chest burned with defiance, but the vertigo of surrender unraveled me at the same time.

"I don't want to see you anywhere near another man," *he said, his voice so sharp it hurt. "I'm not sharing you* *with anyone. Ever. Do you hear me?"*

He leaned in further, his mouth barely grazing mine, *and the sickly-sweet poison of his whisper stole my* *reason:*

"Only I can take you to heaven... and drag you back *again."*

My lips parted; no words came. I hated the arrogance *of his line... and yet my body recognized its truth.*

"Prove it," I finally breathed—low, steady, a dare that *scorched my skin. It wasn't a plea; it was a challenge. I* *wanted to push him, to see how far his control reached...* *or how hungry he was to break it.*

The spark in his eyes flared into a blaze. A dark, *almost cruel smile twisted his mouth, and in that instant* *I knew I'd crossed a line of no return.*

Adrián took one last drag and stubbed the cigarette *out on the pool's edge with a sharp motion—as if* *pronouncing the end of calm. He gripped my face, hard,* *and kissed me with calculated violence, pressing smoke* *into my mouth like a poison I had to swallow. The harsh* *taste made me dizzy—the mix of tobacco and desire* *blurring my senses—and still my body opened to receive* *him.*

His eyes never left mine; they burned with that dangerous spark that stole my breath. He was a hunter savoring his prey, branding me with the taste of fire.

"Prove it?" he echoed, his deep voice a dark caress against my ear. "Princesa... you just called on the devil himself. Let me show you what happens when you push me."

With one confident motion, Adrián stripped the nightgown from me, peeling it away like a ceremony. I stood exposed under the stars, trembling in my panties, and he knelt before me with a dark devotion that made me feel both queen and captive.

His lips descended to my center with hungry precision, and a moan tore from me at once—lost somewhere between vertigo and desire.

His firm hands held me from behind, imprinting their strength on my skin, forcing surrender without a choice. He toyed with me, savoring the torment. His tongue moved slowly, deliberately, the way an executioner draws out the wait. The faint metallic brush of his piercing against my sensitive skin sparked like electricity, pulling muffled sounds from my throat. Cold and heat. Torture and delirium. Each contrast sent a shudder through me I couldn't control.

"Adrián... please... more..." The words came out broken, turned into a plea. Shame no longer existed—only pure addiction, the certainty that he held the power to break me and raise me in the same breath.

He lifted his gaze for a heartbeat, eyes glittering with triumph, then plunged back in.

My body opened to him—slick, receptive, already his. I knew, in the marrow of me, there was no returning: I was branded, ruined, and already needing more of what only he gave.

When my plea broke into a strangled moan, he tightened his grip on my hips and unleashed a brutal storm—tongue and mouth working with ruthless ferocity. He drove me higher and higher; the contact of his mouth and the pressure of his hands ripped ragged screams from me. My back arched, my nails sank into his shoulders, and my body shattered in an overwhelming, burning cum that left me gasping and raw.

There was no mercy in his giving—only the certainty that he tore me down and rebuilt me in the same motion, claiming every fiber of me.

While I lay spent and trembling, Adrián rose with the same disconcerting calm, as if nothing could unsettle him.

"That's what happens when you provoke the wrong man," he murmured.

Then he tilted his head, eyes burning into mine. "Never forget, Lucía: only I can take you that high... and only I can strip you of everything."

Without taking his eyes off me, Adrián began to unbutton the black shirt I loved, revealing his hard torso under the moon's trembling light. He slipped off his shoes in one agile motion, yanked down his pants and shrugged off his boxers; the raw intensity of his desire stole my breath. Before I could react, he scooped me up in his arms and the ground disappeared beneath my feet.

The heat of his skin against mine collided with the humid night air. He walked to the pool's edge and, without hesitation, plunged us together into the water. The cold hit like electricity, but his lips finding mine beneath the surface reminded me there was no escape. Everything burned—even in that blue that swallowed us.

The cold water braided with the heat of his body, and that duality drove me into a frenzy I couldn't control. Every touch beneath the surface felt amplified, more dangerous—as if the water multiplied the press of his skin against mine. I felt him everywhere: hungry kisses claiming me, hands mastering every curve and hollow until desire blurred into the vertigo of drowning in him. There was no air, no thought—only surrender to that mix of water and flesh that dragged me deeper than any wave.

His hands locked on my waist and pushed me down, submerging me while his mouth still demanded mine. The world became liquid silence—bubbles, pressure, the burn of his body against mine. I couldn't breathe, and the dizzy lack of air braided with the pleasure coursing through me. It was a test—I knew he wanted me to endure, to let him conquer me even against the urgency of my lungs.

Until the water gave way and air existed between us again.
On the surface, the game became unbearable; the need to feel him inside me grew like an uncontrollable fire. My breathing quickened with every second, drowned by the urgency that ruled me.

"You're mine, Lucía. Only mine... until your last breath."

He lifted me by the hips with a firm motion, pressing me to him beneath the water. I felt him fill me—deep, brutal—and a strangled cry left me, dissolving into bubbles that raced to the surface. Cold collided with the fire of his thrusts, a savage contrast that tore my control to pieces.

The water became prison and release at once. He moved inside me with ruthless precision; reason bled out, leaving only the pulse of his control. When his gaze locked on mine, he rasped through wet, hoarse moans,

"Come with me, Lucía — I want to hear you come."

The climax detonated inside me, obeying him like a command; my body shattered into a thousand hot fragments of pleasure. Waves slapped around us, furious, as my back arched and my nails dug into his skin searching for an anchor in the midst of ecstasy.

A guttural roar ripped from his chest so deep the water seemed to shudder. He held me tighter, driving into me as his orgasm hit with brutal force. His moans braided with my name—

"Lucía... Lucía"—a possessive litany drowning the night.

My name tasted intoxicating in his mouth; every syllable made me tremble again, as if each one were another thrust claiming me. Afterward there was a thick silence, broken only by our ragged breathing and the soft lap of water against the pool's edge. I clung to his shoulders, still feeling tremors run through me, while he kept me pressed to his body as if he never wanted to let go.

The water was no longer refuge but echo—of what we'd unleashed. The night's cold brushed my wet skin and pulled me back to the world, little by little. Adrián lifted me with the same force he'd used to possess me and hauled me out of the water.

I fumbled for a towel and handed it to him, my hands shaking. He took it without breaking eye contact and dried himself with lethal calm—each slow stroke a declaration that I remained under his control.

I stepped out of his arms and grabbed another towel, clumsily wrapping it around my body. The rough fabric against my wet skin didn't warm me; it was only the illusion of cover after having been bared, vulnerable, surrendered. I clutched the cloth to my chest, breathing deep, trying to convince myself I still controlled something.

Adrián didn't rush to touch me. He took one step closer, his gaze dark. His eyes traveled over the towel I held as if he could see through it, and a crooked smile curved his lips.

"Listen to me, Lucía," he growled, voice rough as a lash.
"Let them look. Let them burn for you. But only I touch you. Only I take you. Only I own you."

The towel trembled in my hands as if it might fall.

The worst part was that my body burned—aroused by his possessiveness, by a domination that should have frightened me and instead made me beg for more.

For a moment I thought I had him at my feet. Behind that dangerous calm and his voice that chained me, I imagined he might be mine too. In my mind every possessive look, every order that stole my will felt like a confession: that of a man who could not escape me even when he pretended otherwise.

I watched him get dressed, each movement charged with eroticism. A strange impulse rose in me, as if I could match the game—and in a low voice I dared to ask,

"Do you want to do something next weekend?"

His gaze fixed on mine, and the answer landed like a sharp blow, freezing the night around us.

"I can't, princesa... I shouldn't even be here tonight," he said in that deep voice that seemed to hurt him.

He looked at me for a second, then brushed my lips with a small, fleeting kiss that tasted like farewell and punishment.

Without another word he turned and disappear into the darkness, leaving me stunned—confused, my skin still burning from what had happened... and from what had been left unfinished.

I returned to the room on tiptoe and collapsed onto the mattress. The others slept peacefully, oblivious to everything, as if they lived in a clean world that no longer belonged to me.

I closed my eyes, but all I saw was his silhouette fading into the night, his deep voice burrowing into me like poison: "You're forbidden. I shouldn't even be here tonight." I clenched the blanket until my knuckles ached.

What was Adrián hiding? What secrets lurked in that darkness that drew me more fiercely than any promise of light?

They weren't just words. They were keys to a mystery that consumed me—chains I clasped onto myself. Sleep never came. His voice echoed endlessly in my head, and my body still burned with the need for him.

It wasn't simple desire. It was obsession, curling through my veins like liquid fire. And the worst part was knowing it: the more I tried to run, the deeper I would sink into him.

Chapter 8

✦ ✦ ✦ ✦ ✦ ✦

*T*he weekend at the beach was over, but the poison
remained inside me. Back home everything seemed
normal: my parents lost in their routines, calm settled
into every corner... too calm, as if the stillness itself
conspired to make me remember what I'd lived.

I lay back on my bed, the window open and the night
breeze slipping in. I closed my eyes, trying to convince
myself I could sleep—that I could be an ordinary girl,
oblivious to the fire Adrián had lit in me. Then I smelled
it. That unmistakable scent: tobacco braided with danger,
desire and night.

I opened my eyes abruptly. It wasn't memory or dream.
Adrián was there—standing in the shadows of my room,
framed against the open window like a forbidden
silhouette that had crossed every border. His eyes shone
with an intensity that stole my breath.

"Are you crazy?" I managed to whisper, my voice
breaking between fear and vertigo.

He didn't answer. His lips curved into that half-
smile—the dangerous one a man wears when he knows
he no longer needs permission to invade every corner of
your life.

"I can't control it, Lucía..." His voice was lower than ever, a rough whisper, almost broken. *"I don't know what you do to me. I try to tear you out of my head... and all I do is want you more."*

For a second something different appeared in him: not only the predator devouring me with his gaze, but a man chained to his own obsession—just as much a slave to me as I was to him. That vulnerability made him no less dangerous; it made him lethal.

He advanced with the calm of someone who knows there is no escape. The air in my room thickened—charged, electric. Each step sent a jolt of adrenaline over my skin. His madness hummed in the space, an overflowing addiction that pulled me toward losing myself in it, even knowing it could destroy me.

His hand took my face—not tenderly, but possessively, firm, as if claiming what he already considered his. Then he kissed me: a clash of fire that tore an involuntary moan from me.

"I want you to dance for me," he ordered, his voice low and leaving no room for refusal.

He pulled a pair of headphones from his pocket and settled them over our ears as if sealing a pact. Earned It began to play, the bass thudding in my chest like a second heartbeat.

There was no stage and no audience—just him, his gaze fixed, and me reduced to his private show.

At first my hips moved shyly, the music nudging me to loosen up little by little. But his stare devoured everything, stripping me more thoroughly than any clothing. Heat rose beneath my skin and shyness soon became impossible. My movements grew sultry, daring— swaying to the slow, poisonous rhythm of the song.

I ran my hands down my thighs, up over my curves as if they were his, teasing myself until I lost sense. The light blouse and the too-short shorts left little to the imagination, yet my fingers toyed with the fabric anyway, barely tugging at the edges like an offering. His breathing deepened; I understood that every move of mine aroused him...and enraged him, because control seemed to slip toward me.

"Slower," Adrián whispered, barely audible over the music. I obeyed, letting myself be carried by a game where my body was the weapon and his gaze the chain that held me captive.

I slid my hands up my waist, lifting the blouse just enough to let my breasts peek before covering them again. It was a cruel dance—skin and fabric, reveal and conceal—that lit his eyes more than any words. With a slow roll of my hips, I let the shorts fall a little, then a little more, until they pooled at his feet.

I stood before him vulnerable, nearly naked, breathless. In that instant I understood the truth: every inch I showed no longer belonged to me—it belonged to him.

"Take it all off, Lucía," he ordered, voice low and dangerous.

The air thickened. My hands shook as I clung to the fabric that still covered me, as if it were the last barrier between my will and his control. But his look stripped me bare before my fingers could. Resistance felt useless.

Heart hammering, I slid the straps of my blouse down my shoulders and let it fall slowly to the floor. The silence became unbearable—until I heard him.

"You drive me crazy, princesa..." he said, low, as if the word burned on his tongue. *It wasn't praise or confession; it was a threat—a warning of the obsession devouring him.*

That word cut through me like lightning. My hands stopped belonging to me and obeyed only him, moved by that searing gaze that consumed everything.

The crooked smile on his lips vanished in an instant. Adrián rose with a sharp movement and before I could step back he was already in front of me. His hands clamped onto my hips and, with a brutality that ripped a gasp from my throat, forced me to feel the full weight of his desire.

With one violent tug he fisted my hair and tilted my face up until our eyes locked.. Pain stung, braided with pleasure, and I bit down on my lip.

My hands slid up his torso, fingers finding the fabric of that black shirt that carried so many memories. I pushed it upward, slowly, devouring every inch of his heated skin while the fire of his body fused with mine. The shirt fell onto my pajamas with a soft rustle—silent witnesses to the inevitable.

I continued the ritual, sliding his pants and briefs down. Fabric whispered against skin; the cloth fell and a low, animal sound left him as his erection sprang free, urgent and heavy.

The air thickened, charged; the room held its breath, waiting for the collision of our bodies.

With that cruel calm of his, he let his fingers toy with my clit—brush, withdraw; brush, withdraw—each tease drawing deeper, lower moans from my throat. He bent to my ear and his voice, low and dangerous, cut through me:

"Shhh, princesa... I don't want anyone else hearing what belongs only to me."

My chest seized. His warning lashed through me like an invisible whip, mixing risk and a heat that set me burning inside. I wanted to scream, to let my body speak, but the delicious threat of discovery forced me to clamp my teeth together.

His mouth descended to my hardened breasts. The wet sound of his tongue on skin made the room shrink to that single, slick noise—slurp, drag, inhale. When he grazed my nipple the cold kiss of the piercing sent a sharp cry up my throat. He circled it—soft tongue, then metal—each *rotation a tiny electric shock that tore another sound from me.*

I arched into his mouth, a wet, ragged cry escaping as pain and pleasure tangled and unraveled me. Each nip, each soft bite, was delicious torment that erased everything else. The wet smack of his lips, the suck, the tiny hiss of breath at the back of his throat became the rhythm that ruled me.

"Is that your way of staying quiet, princesa?" Adrián murmured against my skin, voice thick with venomous mockery. The metal provoked another treacherous moan from me. His crooked smile said what I already knew: every sound I made was his victory.

"You're mine in every sound you make, Lucía... even your body betrays you," he whispered with lethal calm, his teeth grazing my skin until I shuddered.

I bit my lip, desperate not to scream, but the certainty devoured me: he was right. There was no silence, no defense—only him.

"Then scream, princesa..." he said into my mouth in low voice. "I want to hear you tear yourself apart just for me."

His lips descended without mercy, and his tongue— wet, playful—tormented me in ever-faster circles. He sucked, nibbled, devoured me with feral skill, as if he intended to wrench my voice out of me with pure ecstasy.

Heat rose to my head, my nails dug into the sheets, and a cry tore from my throat. Adrián intensified his assault, pleased, driving every caress, every wet stroke of tongue and metal to an unbearable pitch.

The world fractured around me; pleasure hit like detonation, and escape stopped existing. Everything shattered—heat, breath, thought—until there was nothing left but him. My body broke open under the force of it, every nerve burning with the knowledge that I was lost to him.

Every nerve arched into a devastating orgasm, and still Adrián didn't pull away. He drank in every shudder, every moan, until nothing remained of me but absolute surrender. Then he lifted his head, eyes blazing and fixed on mine, and in a hoarse voice—still warm from my skin—he marked me with words that sounded like a verdict:

"That's how I want to see you, Lucía. Let your pleasure bear my name. When you close your eyes, let it be proof you are mine—and that I alone can take you and strip you."

Those words sank deeper than his touches, tattooing me from the inside. They were not mere phrases but invisible chains binding me to him with a force I no longer wanted to escape.

"You don't own me..." I managed to whisper, breathless, my voice weak but carrying that thin thread of defiance that let me cling to the illusion of control. My

body still trembled from the orgasm he'd torn from me, and yet I dared to meet his gaze. "I'm not yours, Adrián."

The dark smile that spread across his lips chilled my blood. It was the smile of someone hearing a lie he did not intend to tolerate—the smile of a predator who knows his prey has not yet understood there is no escape.

He grabbed me by the waist and, with overwhelming force, turned me face down on the bed. One hand pressed into the center of my back, pinning me, while the other hauled my hips up in a single, ruthless pull. The sound that escaped was a choked breath, trembling between resistance and want.

"I'm going to remind you in the only way you understand," he growled, voice rough, his touch as brutal as his intent.

He shoved my face into the pillow with one hand, pinning me effortlessly. His breath burned at my ear as, in a low, cruel whisper, he issued the order:

"Don't move...and stay quiet. I don't want anyone interrupting us."

The threat pulsed in every word—dark and dangerous—and yet desire surged through me with a violence that stole my breath. The softness of the fabric against my face and the brutality of his control split me in two: the Lucía who wanted to resist and the Lucía who burned to obey.

The strike came without warning—fast, merciless— ripping a sound from my throat that I buried in the pillow. Another hit followed, just as fierce, the rhythm measured and deliberate, his breath breaking over me like heat, each movement stamped with the fury that claimed me.

Then came the final punishment: his thrust—deep, savage—driving into me without mercy.

The world vanished beneath the echo of his slaps and the delicious violence of his merciless pace. Every movement was a sentence, a reminder of who was in charge, and I—caught between ruin and worship—let the fire take me, knowing there was no redemption in it.

Just when the fire was about to consume me, when my body trembled on the brink of explosion, Adrián stopped. The thrust cut off abruptly, leaving me panting into the pillow, trembling, muscles tight with unbearable frustration.

"Do you feel it, princesa?" he murmured with dangerous calm, squeezing my hips to pin me harder. "You're one second away from losing yourself...and I decide when."

A sob of pent-up pleasure escaped me; my nails dug into the sheets as if I could tear free what he denied me. The void of his absence was worse than any blow—the waiting, his favorite cruelty.

"Adrián... please..." I begged, voice broken, a thin thread between gasps. "Don't stop... don't torment me anymore."

Tears burned my eyes—not from pain, but from the unbearable tension pulling me to the edge. Each second without him inside me was torment; each withheld touch was a delicious knife. My hips trembled, seeking the contact I was denied; my whole body pleaded for what my lips could no longer hide: I needed him, I wanted him, I begged for him.

"That's what I wanted to hear," he murmured with a dark smile, and without notice he plunged into me with a sudden, brutal thrust that ripped a raw scream from my throat.

The dangerous calm was gone; in its place came raw power and possession. Each movement was both punishment and reward—a merciless rhythm that stripped away my pleas until only the delirium of him remained.

My back bowed against the mattress, muscles taut as he drove into me with unspent rage. A cry formed and broke, stifled behind my bitten lip, while dread and pleasure tangled in my chest.

Adrián's own pleasure broke free in a low sound that vibrated against my skin like thunder. It excited him to watch me struggle—to see me bite the pillow, to smother every sound I wasn't supposed to make. That restraint drove him mad; I felt it in the rough urgency of his rhythm, in the way his fingers bit deeper into my hips, as if trying to claim the cries I refused to give.

With a sudden, agile movement he lifted me and sat up in the middle of the bed, his back straight, his eyes glowing like embers. He guided me without giving me a choice, positioning me on top of him—still trembling, vulnerable, my heart racing.

His erection filled me at once, stretching me until I gasped. And though it looked as if I had control from above, it was him setting the rhythm—his hands clamped hard on my hips, forcing me to ride him the way he wanted. Each rise and fall was a lash of pleasure, his strength directing every motion, reminding me that even here, even when I thought I was leading, I was still entirely his.

Our bodies collided in a frenzy without end, as if the world had shrunk to that savage back-and-forth consuming us.

His grip on my hips grew tighter, commanding me to obey his merciless rhythm.

Our moans tangled into broken whispers, and I couldn't hold it back any longer. The fierce pace, the crushing pressure of his hands, the burning look that never released mine... my body seized suddenly, and a cry ripped from my throat—stifled by fear of being overheard, but so raw it felt like it split me open from the inside.

Pleasure crashed through me in unstoppable waves, leaving me shattered and trembling, collapsing against him with no strength left to resist. And Adrián, that dark smile etched on his lips, held me tight to his chest, satisfied as if my orgasm was nothing more than proof of his dominion.

My hips bucked under the brutal rhythm he forced, and then his body trembled violently beneath me. His hands dug into my flesh as he held me fast, refusing to let go, until he exploded inside me—wild, ruthless—his ragged groans vibrating against my skin as if marking me from the inside out.

"Lucía..." he panted my name, each syllable drenched in possession, as if branding me with his voice were as necessary as the fury of his release. In that instant I understood it wasn't just sex; it was a battle of dominance he always won, claiming every fiber of me even while surrendering himself.

We both collapsed onto the bed, a smile slipping from our lips at the same time, as if we had lost and won a war in a single instant. Our breaths remained ragged, clashing in the heated air of the room, while the sweat from our tangled bodies wrapped us in a feverish, humid embrace. For the first time in a long while, I felt something close to calm... though deep down I knew that with Adrián, nothing ever was. Only the dangerous pause before the fire returned.

As the warmth of his body still surrounded me, my mind began to drift, unable to stop the questions striking silently inside me. What was this between us? Just sex, addiction, a dangerous game? My lips still tasted his kisses, my skin still burned with his marks— and yet, there was something in his gaze, in those cryptic words he whispered between moans, that reminded me I didn't really know him. Adrián was desire, he was madness, he was fire... but he was also a mystery beginning to consume me from within.

The silence grew unbearable. I turned toward him, breathless, and forced the question that had been clawing at me.

"Adrián," I said, voice low but steady, "what did you mean when you called me forbidden? And the other night—when you said you shouldn't even have been there?"

His eyes locked on mine—intense, unreadable—as if I'd opened a door that had to stay shut. My heart hammered; one part of me wanted the answer, another dreaded it might be worse than his hunger.

Adrián's mouth curved into that half-smile that hid more than it revealed.

"By day I deal with numbers—accounts, balances... the boring side of accounting," he murmured, eyes burning into me. "But at night... at night I'm something else."

He stopped there. The dark spark in his gaze made my skin prickle. I tried to press him, but his finger on my lips silenced me.

"Don't ask, Lucía. Trust me... you don't want to know."

His lips brushed against mine with a tenderness that contrasted everything we had just done— as if, for an instant, he could pretend to be gentle.

Then he straightened, unhurried, dressing with calm precision while I watched in silence, trying to etch every detail into my memory.

Before leaving, he stepped toward the window he had come through, and with one foot already outside, he turned his face back to me. His gaze burned with a fire that could never be extinguished.

"Remember this, princesa," he whispered, voice low and lethal. "You belong to no one but me. If anyone ever tries—I'll end them."

And before I could react, he was gone—swallowed by the darkness of the night, leaving me trembling beneath the sheets. My body quaked between fear and fascination, chained by the fire only he knew how to ignite.

Chapter 9

✦ ✦ ✦ ✦ ✦ ✦

We're leaving!" I announced, slinging my backpack over my shoulder with a mix of impatience and eagerness to get away from everything.

"Take care and call me when you arrive... and before you go to bed," my mother replied in that controlling tone that reminded me that, even at twenty-one, I was still her daughter who had to answer for herself.

Camila and I set off for Varadero with our excitement on edge. We had worked for months at the restaurant to afford this treat, and the plan was simple: a few days by the sea, hoping the sun and salt could—if only for a moment—wash away the poison Adrián had left running through my veins.

The hotel looked like it had been lifted from an impossible postcard: crystal chandeliers gleaming like jewels, floors reflecting every step, and a sweet scent drifting through the air unlike anything I had ever known. The room exceeded all expectations: a wide balcony opened onto an infinite sea, a turquoise so perfect it seemed unreal. I leaned on the railing and let the breeze tousle my hair. For a moment, I thought maybe here I could finally breathe without chains.

Camila, meanwhile, was like a kid on Christmas morning—running from one side of the room to the other, opening closets, throwing herself onto the bed with laughter that filled the space.

Her carefree joy was contagious, and yet it cut me with a sharp edge of envy: she could be free, without ghosts, without secrets. I couldn't.

Digging through her backpack for something to wear, her choice was immediate: a red bikini with ruffles, playful and dazzling, as if it had been made for her. I chose a black bikini, simple but powerful, one that made me feel strong, almost dangerous.

In front of the mirror, we fixed ourselves up between jokes, trying on sunglasses and painting our lips as if the night were already waiting for us. Everything felt perfect... too perfect, as though fate itself were preparing the stage to remind me that not even the sea could make me escape Adrián.

I lay back on a lounge chair under the umbrella, letting the breeze play with my hair while I opened The Alchemist by Paulo Coelho. Between the pages, a line hit me like a gunshot straight to the heart:

"When you want something with all your heart, the entire universe conspires to help you achieve it."

I closed my eyes for a moment, feeling those words carve themselves into my skin. What if the universe wasn't saving me, but instead pushing me straight toward Adrián? What if the abyss I was falling into wasn't madness... but destiny in disguise?

Camila suddenly appeared, radiant, with a different kind of smile—lit by a glow that surprised me.

"I just met someone," she whispered, as if she were guarding a treasure between her lips.

I raised an eyebrow.

"Who?"

She pointed discreetly toward a boy waiting a few meters away, restless, as though he were seeking her permission to approach.

"He invited me to lunch. Want to come?"

I shook my head slowly, offering her a conspiratorial smile.

"No, Camila. Go. Enjoy."

She said goodbye with a quick, light hug, running toward him with that innocence that still protected her. I watched her walk away and sank back into the lounge chair, aware that now I was left alone with the silence, with the sea... and with my own addiction.

The book rested closed on my chest, but its words kept echoing like an incantation I couldn't silence. The sea was calm, the breeze fresh, the sun caressed my skin; and yet inside me there was only fire. That fire had a name. Adrián. And even if I didn't say it aloud, it burned in me with the force of something I no longer knew—nor wanted—to extinguish.

I want him. I need him. The phrase pounded in my mind with the same insistence as the waves licking the shore.

If he were here… if he appeared suddenly, there would be no possible resistance: I would surrender, again, without thinking. It was the only thing my body demanded. Neither the endless sea, nor the apparent calm, nor Camila's distant laughter could fill the void Adrián left each time he disappeared. He was a drug, and I was nothing more than his addict, trembling as I waited for the next dose.

My teeth sank into my lower lip until it bled, the metallic taste reminding me how alive I felt in that moment. My thighs rubbed together instinctively, searching for friction that never came, an impossible relief. I closed my eyes tightly, but it was useless: simply recalling his deep voice, the brush of his tongue marked by the piercing, made my body burn as if he were there, claiming me in secret beneath the paradise sun.

I sat up abruptly, as if movement could chase away the whirlwind consuming me. I stowed the book in my bag, grabbed the towel, and walked toward the bar, letting the cool sand run between my bare feet. The music and laughter wrapped around me as I approached, a necessary noise to mask the chaos in my mind.

I ordered a mojito almost without thinking, as if the ice could put out what was boiling inside me. The chilled glass numbed my hands; the fresh mint hit me with a reality check... but neither the drink, nor the noise, nor the beauty of the place could hide the truth: without him, all that paradise was an empty stage.

The ice melted slowly in the glass, like me consuming myself in his absence. I ran my tongue across my lips and tasted the bitterness of mint... as bitter as the waiting.

And then I saw him.
His silhouette emerged from the crowd like a memory I could never erase.
The white shirt clung to his sun-kissed skin, every step radiating certainty—
the kind that made distance feel irrelevant.

The air grew thick; my lungs burned.
It didn't matter how far I ran—Adrián was everywhere, even in the places where I had tried to forget him.
The first time he touched me, I understood that fire doesn't kill; it feeds.
And now, insatiable, I had learned to crave the burn as if it were the only way to feel alive.

He leaned toward me, his shadow swallowing the bar's light, and his deep voice caressed my ear

"Didn't hear you mention you were going on a trip, princesa."

My heart hammered so loud I thought he might hear it. His scent—rum and sea—wrapped around me like a sweet poison I could never escape. I swallowed and forced a smile that never reached my eyes.

"I didn't think I owed you any explanations," I murmured, trying to sound firm, though the tremor in my voice revealed the truth: it wasn't fear—it was hunger for him.

His fingers brushed my wrist—barely a touch, but enough to set me alight. He held my gaze with that lethal intensity that left me trapped between fleeing and total surrender.

"There's no escape from me," he whispered, low. *"Not here, not anywhere in the world."*

The music, the laughter, the bustle—all faded. There was only him, devouring me with his eyes.

"How do you always know where I am?" I asked, attempting defiance though my breath trembled.

Adrián smiled sideways—the arrogant smirk that both killed me and bound me.

"Because wherever you are, Lucía... that ground becomes mine."

He tilted his head, eyes fixed on mine—dark, intense—like a predator that stalks its prey with endless patience.

"Let's just say I know the right people," he added finally, unsettlingly calm, each word designed to pierce my resistance. *"That's enough to find you. Always."*

I stood frozen, chest tight. The ease with which he appeared, again and again—no matter the distance or the secrecy—was no longer coincidence: it was a real *danger. A danger that smelled of obsession... and of a mutual addiction.*

Suddenly he took my hand. He said nothing; his gaze charted our course. He led me through the crowd as if an invisible chain pulled us, each step a silent command.

Laughter and curious glances washed away until all that remained was his fingers tightening around mine, the frantic pulse at my wrist, the vertigo of knowing that with every step I drifted further from my own will...and inexorably closer to his.

We crossed the hotel lobby and each footfall felt like a step toward fate. The gleaming marble, the crystal chandeliers, the hollow stares of strangers—everything dissolved beneath the fierce magnetism radiating from Adrián. It was as if the luxury surrounding us existed only to hide the raw hunger smoldering between us.

By the elevator the silence thickened, an almost audible hum. The doors opened and he guided me inside, that insolent certainty folding us into a private world. He pressed the button for a suite. The thought pierced me— desire and vertigo twined into one.

The air inside the elevator turned electric. Before I could say a word, his hands pinned me against the wall, and his mouth devoured mine with brutal hunger.
The confined space magnified every touch, every gasp, every friction of his body against mine.

"You're driving me insane, Lucía…" he murmured between kisses, his voice so deep it cut straight through my bones. *"I've never felt anything like this."*

His desperation burned through me. Control had slipped from his hands, and yet he was still the one setting the rhythm—the one guiding me to the edge of the abyss.

The elevator stopped with a faint jolt. The soft chime announced the top floor, but he barely pulled back for air.

When the doors opened, he didn't let go. His grip stayed firm as he dragged me down the carpeted hallway, every step heavy with a dark promise: upstairs, in that suite, there would be no limits.

The world blurred around us—golden lights, framed paintings fading into haze, the echo of our hurried steps swallowed by the silence of the corridor.

All that existed was the heat of his hand pulling me forward and the intensity in his eyes, locked on me as if every second apart had been a punishment.

The keycard slid into the lock with a metallic click that both froze and ignited me at once.

The door opened, revealing the suite—a dark stage of forbidden promises: heavy curtains sealing off the world, the salty scent of the sea drifting through the cracked window, golden lamps casting dense shadows on the walls. Everything conspired to trap me there, alone with him.

He pressed me against the wall with deceptive gentleness that turned into delicious violence. His mouth crashed against mine with restrained fury, devouring me as if trying to erase the days he had been gone.
His hands gripped my waist, possessive, a reminder that there was no escape.

"Is this a game to you, disappearing like that, princesa?" he growled against my lips, his voice vibrating with the same dark rage that fueled his desire.

I tried to answer, to explain myself, but he didn't give me the chance. His tongue invaded my mouth with a wildness that broke and ignited me all at once, and I understood that his anger wasn't the enemy of pleasure—it was the fuel.

"You disobeyed me, Lucía..." he whispered, his hot breath searing against my ear. "Now I'm going to remind you who's in control."

His gaze was pure shadow—dangerous, like a secret he refused to confess but that burned through his skin, through the way he claimed me. Adrián wasn't an ordinary man; he was a forbidden mystery pulling me into him with no escape. And still, trapped between his strength and the weight of his desire, the only thing I could think was that I didn't want to get away.

He pinned me against the wall with the precise strength of a man who enjoys power. His body pressed against mine, his breath mingling with my own, and I realized there was no space to flee—not even to think about how I'd ended up there.

His hands caught my wrists above my head—firm, commanding—like invisible shackles that sent shivers through me. The most disturbing part was the certainty that even if I could break free, I wouldn't.

The world shrank to his presence. Every movement, every breath, belonged to him. I could only follow the rhythm he imposed, caught between fear and the need to please him.

"That's how I like it..." he murmured, hoarse and dark, breath grazing my lips. "When you remember exactly who holds the power."

He freed one hand only to slide it up around my throat, applying just enough pressure to remind me he was in charge. My pulse hammered beneath his fingers; that blend of fear and need unraveled me. I met his eyes and found something wild there, something dark I could not fully fathom—yet it pulled me like an abyss I couldn't resist.

His grip tightened on my wrists, each motion vibrating with restrained force, as if punishing me for daring to stray. His mouth continued to devour mine, the scrape of metal against my tongue a delicious lash that tore guttural gasps from me.

With ruthless ease his other hand moved to my bikini. I heard the soft sound of fabric yielding to his fingers, mingled with my ragged breath. In one swift, precise motion the top slipped free and fell to the floor. Exposed, my breasts trembled under the light and under his ravenous gaze. I felt vulnerable and owned—yet a searing heat spread through me as he looked at me like something that belonged to him by right.

His fingers slid immediately over my bare skin—possessive, firm—exploring like a master claiming what was his.

"That's how you learn, Princesa," he whispered, voice hoarse, laced with control and threat. "You can't run from me... ever."

He gripped my hips hard and, with effortless strength that stole my breath, lifted me into the air. Instinctively I wrapped my legs around his waist, clinging to him, feeling the press of his body tight against mine.

My breasts hovered at his mouth, and Adrián didn't hesitate—he leaned in, warming my nipples with the heat of his breath. His eyes locked onto mine with a dangerous intensity, and then, in that deep molten tone that unmade me, he murmured:

"The perfect size... for my mouth."

A shiver ran through me from head to toe. His mouth took me with purpose— I searched for balance against his body, as pleasure swallowed what little control I had left.

My breathing grew ragged and wild as he claimed me, but the most unsettling discovery was that his words inflamed me more than his touch. Every time that rough voice called me princesa, every time he reminded me, I was his, my body answered with a hunger that terrified me.

His lips devoured me, yet it was the phrases he breathed against my skin that struck deepest; they kindled a heat no touch alone could reach. In his mouth I found a fierce pleasure—the metal at the tip of his tongue an electric sting that tore moans from me—but in his voice I found the true damnation: his possessive words outweighed any caress.

Still tangled in his arms, Adrián carried me toward the balcony. Sunlight filtered through the curtains and licked our skin, turning every touch incandescent. He held me as if I weighed nothing—absolute master of my body and will.

The salty air slapped my face. From the twelfth floor the sea spread beneath us, an endless, glittering blue; the world stretched away below, but up here the only reality was him and the way he owned me completely.

He pressed me against the railing with dangerous confidence. The cold iron bit into my hips while the heat of his body crushed me from behind. I felt control slipping away; his tongue moved over my breasts like a brand, leaving trails of fire in its wake.

"Feel that princesa?" he whispered, his low voice making me tremble. "Right here, where anyone could see... and yet you belong only to me."

My legs tightened around his waist; adrenaline and desire braided into one. The risk of being seen inflamed me, and every possessive word, every deliberate movement, dragged me deeper into the addiction I no longer wanted to fight.

One of his hands slid my bikini aside with practiced ease, the fabric parting like an invitation. Without warning his finger slipped inside me, drawing precise circles that pulled me toward the cliff's edge of pleasure.

My body arched against him, surrender spilling through shallow sighs *he caught against my lips.*

"That's it..." he murmured into my ear, his voice a low, dominant promise. "There's no escape, Lucía. Up here, with the whole world below us... you exist only for me."

His movements grew fiercer, relentless, as if he intended to wring every sound from my throat. His hand dominated me, torturing me with a brutal tenderness until the knot inside me tightened unbearably. Then, with a violent pull, I broke—shattering into him, collapsing into the hand that held me, into the mouth that claimed me.

I heard his dark laugh brush my ear. His fingers kept playing with my wetness—slow, cruel—delighting in my captured surrender.

"Mmmm… you're soaked," he whispered, that low voice sending shivers across my skin. "Admit it, princesa… you love the way I break you."

Only a raw moan escaped me; words would have betrayed too much. He smiled, satisfied, knowing my body had already told him everything.

Then, without breaking eye contact, Adrián dropped to his knees. The sight of him there—below me yet absolute in command—stole my breath. With deliberate calm he tugged the last scrap of fabric free and let it fall; I stood naked before him, exposed to the night and to him.

His mouth descended to my inner thighs, hot and possessive, tracing a path of kisses that made me quiver against the railing. When his tongue—pierced metal flashing cold—found me, circling with feral precision, a cry tore from my chest that I could not hold back.

"You taste like innocence corrupted," he murmured against my skin, voice rough with hunger. "And now you're mine."

He moved with predator patience, teasing, keeping me balanced on the razor's edge. Each minimal brush was a calculated sting, and I arched into his mouth, pleading without words as he drew me out of myself, inch by intoxicating inch.

His tongue grew firmer, wetter, alternating delicate strokes with sudden thrusts that tore broken moans from me. He gripped my thighs hard, holding me open for him, forcing me to remain exposed to his cruel, delicious game.

"That's it, princesa... surrender," he murmured against me, the vibration of his voice fusing with the wet strokes, dragging a ragged cry from my throat.

"More... more," I begged. Every flick of his tongue pulled me closer to the abyss, my body trembling beyond control. The pressure inside me built to an unbearable peak, a strangled moan slipping from my lips. I was ready to break, to explode in his mouth...

But suddenly, Adrián stopped.

His lips withdrew with cruel slowness, leaving me gasping, desperate, trembling with the climax he had stolen. I clutched at his shoulders, confused, tears of frustration burning in my eyes.

He looked up from below, his hands still gripping my thighs, holding me in place so I couldn't escape. His smile was dark, dangerous, satisfied.

"Not yet, princesa," he growled, his voice rough and still wet with me. "Not after you disobeyed me."

I tried to protest, but his gaze silenced me. He was savoring my desperation—the way my body cried out for him with a will stronger than my own. His fingers traced

*slowly along my thighs, barely touching, provoking me
further, chaining me to that edge.*

*"With me, you'll never be in control," he whispered,
his voice igniting me more than any caress ever could. "I
decide when, how... and if you've earned it."*

*The punishment was exquisite—painful and addictive
all at once. My breath came in ragged sobs, and I hated
him for doing this to me... yet at the same time, I craved
him more than ever.*

*His tongue moved with diabolical precision, the cold
spark of his piercing setting every nerve ending ablaze.
Just when I felt myself about to break, to surrender... he
stopped again.*

*A cry of frustration tore from my throat, and he smiled
against my skin, savoring my despair.*

*"Not yet, princesa," he rasped, his voice shaking me
to the core.*

*He dove back into me, slow at first, then ferocious,
playing with my limits, forcing me to tremble between
pleas and moans that unraveled into the night air.*

*The pressure built again, and when I was on the verge
of shattering, he stole it away once more.*

*"Look at you..." he growled as he pulled back, his
dark, dominant gaze locking on mine. "You're dying for
me. And I'm the one who decides how much you can
take."*

My hips writhed, desperate to chase his mouth, but his grip tightened, punishing me with that merciless wait.

He took me to the edge again, then denied me once more. My body cried out for him, my mind swam. I was broken, surrendered, addicted to his absolute control — and yet the only thing I wanted was for it never to stop.

I couldn't take it any longer. My legs trembled, my breath a choked sob of pleasure and frustration. He kept me imprisoned in that cruel cycle.

"Adrián... please," I begged in a broken voice, tears threatening.

His smile was dark and dangerous, cutting me like a whip. His fingers pressed hard against my thighs, holding me open for his mouth as he looked down at me with that devastating intensity.

"Do you hear what you're saying, princesa?" his hoarse voice vibrated against my skin, driving me mad. "You're begging me... and I'm only just getting started."

I closed my eyes, humiliated and aroused, feeling myself unravel in his hands. Nothing else mattered now — not the balcony, not the danger, not the imagined eyes below. I only wanted to surrender to him, to give him my body, my will, my addiction.

"Please... I beg you," I moaned, hot tears running down my cheeks, my body arching in pleading.

He lifted me roughly and carried me to the bed without giving me a choice. He threw me onto the sheets with a dominating motion that ripped a stifled gasp from me.

I watched him come closer, his shadow devouring me in the golden light pouring through the window. The dark, dangerous look in his eyes reminded me I was playing with fire — with a man who didn't belong to the light or to the world I knew. But his control over me was absolute.

He leaned over me, pinned my wrists to the mattress, and his deep voice struck me like a blow. "You thought you could escape... you belong to me, Lucía."

"Did you learn, princesa?" he murmurs, his voice vibrating against my skin more than his hands do. "Or do you want me to carve it into your body, so you won't forget?"

His fingers stroked between my legs, barely grazing me, making me arch in desperation. My breath cut off; my body begged him, but he denied

"Your body begs me... but it's not enough," he whispered slowly nibbling my nipple. "I want to hear your soul begging too, Lucía."

The denied pleasure became exquisite torment.

I was trapped between unbearable desire and the delicious humiliation of knowing he controlled everything. My tears mixed with moans as I unraveled — Adrián shattered my defenses and rewrote me from the inside out.

I lay sprawled on the bed, gasping, unable to move. My whole body ached, but it wasn't the ache of injury — it was the exquisite torment of being kept on the edge, denied release. My skin burned, my muscles trembled, and my mind drowned in a desperate haze.

Through eyes blurred with tears of held-back pleasure, I watched him. Adrián began to undress, every movement laced with that dangerous confidence. He removed his shirt slowly, revealing a torso mapped with scars I don't know — silent proof of the dark life he keeps from me.

His gaze never left mine as he unbuttoned his pants, savoring my state — broken, humiliated, unable to free myself. I knew it excited him even more.

Naked, he was as imposing as his presence. He approached radiating raw eroticism, each step a sin in motion. There was no salvation in him, only delicious damnation.

His hands slid up my legs from below, slow and firm. When he reached my knees, he parted them with that practiced mastery — a fierce hunger that stole my breath.

Then I felt it: his erection grazing me, pressing into my most sensitive place with a searing force that made me shudder. He captured my mouth, devouring it, and without warning he thrust into me hard, a brutal motion that ripped a scream from my throat — agony and rapture braided together.

"I warned you, Lucía—you were never meant for me," he growls, every thrust sealing his words into me. "And yet here you are... cursed to be mine alone."

Pain and pleasure fused until they were indistinguishable.

With every thrust he broke me down and rebuilt me, until only Adrián remained — completely dominating me.

My body trembled beneath him, unable to resist, begging in ways my mouth would not. I hated myself for surrendering and yet wanted nothing else.

Suddenly he stopped. He stayed buried in me, motionless. He looked down at me with that dark intensity that trapped me; his hot breath brushed my lips.

"Do you feel it, princess?" he whispers, voice laced with cruel control. "Only I decide if you fall—or if I hold you right at the edge."

Then he moved again, slow and delicious, torturing me with gentleness. Every drive of his hips turned into an exquisite punishment, dragging a sob from me with every restrained wave of pleasure.

Another brutal thrust ripped a torn scream from me. Then another pause. Another slow caress. The back-and-forth was perversely methodical, humbling me, setting me alight until I lost my mind.

"I will make you beg again and again," he growled into my neck, his teeth grazing the skin. "Until you understand that pleasure isn't yours... it's mine."

My body could no longer bear it.

He seized my hair, forcing me to meet his eyes as he took me without mercy.

"Now, princesa," he snarled, low and ragged, "you're going to come for me now."

The command cut deeper. As if some part of me recognized that only he could decide, pleasure detonated inside me — a brutal, uncontrollable orgasm. I screamed his name, torn and surrendering, everything inside me erupting from head to toe.

My body convulsed beneath him, every nerve aflame. Adrián held me tight, buried in me, making it impossible to believe this climax meant freedom. Deep inside I knew: what he had given me was no gift — it was punishment, cleverly disguised as reward.

But he didn't stop. Adrián kept moving inside me, filling me again and again. Every motion carried the same cruel truth—his desire would always outlast mine.

I screamed, the sweet ache of overstimulation made me quake; my body still convulsed from the recent orgasm, and he reveled in it, feeding on every reaction.

"Did you think it was over, princesa?" he growled, his voice hoarse and sharp as a lash. "I decide when this ends. And I want more."

His lips searched for my neck, biting with fury while his pace never slowed—wilder, more inhuman. Tears ran freely; my legs shook, but I remained bound to him, unable to escape his dominion. Every time I thought I couldn't take any more, that I was about to break, Adrián pushed me further, proving that my body belonged to him and that my limits didn't exist as long as he was inside me.

I was lost. And I knew it: he didn't come to be satisfied — he came to consume me whole.

His rhythm intensified, relentless, as if he wanted to breach every barrier of my body and mind. I was exhausted, shattered, and yet something inside me ignited again under his control. I didn't want to; I couldn't take any more... but my body betrayed me, answering only to him. Adrián stared down at me with dangerous darkness in his eyes, pressing my hips to his as he thrust with fury.

"I can't get enough of you..." he whispers against my lips, his voice rough with desire. "It feels so good to have you like this... you're my downfall."

Then it happened — a wave stronger, more devastating ripped through me.

His breath burned at my neck, and I heard him growl — wild, restrained — a sound that made my soul shiver.

He let go inside me with the controlled fury of a man who, even at climax, must claim his territory. His roar fused with my moan, and for one suspended instant the world vanished: no balcony, no hotel, no secrets — only this abyss we fell into together, chained and damned.

Chapter 10

✦ ✦ ✦ ✦ ✦ ✦

Still tangled in bed and consumed by a pleasure that feels infinite, our sweat-soaked bodies entwine like colliding worlds. My breath shatters, lost in the heat of his skin against mine, and for a single instant time ceases to exist.

Two opposing souls: me — the one who should flee, always under the world's scrutiny — and him, the dark, dangerous man who isn't mine, yet brands me as his. His arm presses heavy across my waist.

The echo of his words resounds in my mind like a sentence:

You are my downfall—and my possession. Even though reason screams for me to run, my body, my desire, and something deeper keep me chained to him.

I watch him in the shadows: his scars barely visible beneath the faint light slipping in from the balcony. They are traces of a life he hides — a dangerous life I sense but don't fully understand. Still, with every heartbeat I sink deeper into his damnation.

Silence settles over the suite, broken only by the distant murmur of the sea. I lie beside him; his heavy arm rests across my waist like an invisible shackle. I glance at him from the corner of my eye; his chest rises and falls calmly, but his gaze remains lit — dark, unreadable.

The suite is too luxurious, too perfect: heavy curtains, sheets that smell expensive, a window that seems to open onto the whole ocean. A shiver of curiosity runs through me because I know nothing of his life — nothing of what he does when he isn't devouring me.

"Adrián..." I dare, my voice low as I trace nervous circles across his skin. "How is it that you have this room?"

He holds my gaze for a long moment, and I feel his hand tighten around my waist, reminding me that even my questions fall under his control. His lips curl into that dangerous smile that hides more than it reveals.

"Let's just say I know the right people," he answers finally, his calm more unsettling than a shout. His hoarse voice vibrates through my chest.

He grips my face roughly, but in his eyes, there is something beyond desire — fire tempered by storm.

"You don't understand what you do to me, Lucía..." he murmurs in a broken voice, as if speaking to himself as much as to me. "I am darkness. I am danger. But you... you are the only pure thing that's ever touched my life. And for that reason alone, I won't let you go."

"What are you hiding?" I whisper, daring to challenge him. "Adrián... can you tell me?"

His gaze hardens instantly. The hand that had been caressing my thigh tenses, and for a second, I think he's going to pull away. But he doesn't. Instead, he leans over me, trapping me between his body and the mattress, and in his deep voice there's a blade of fury mixed with something that sounds like pain.

"Lucía..." he breathes, brushing his lips against mine. "What I hide is not for you. Believe me, princesa... if you knew, you'd never look at me the same way again."

His words cut through me like a knife. There's truth in them, a truth that chills my blood even as it fuels my desperate need to know him. And though I should stay silent, though I should surrender, I feel I can't stop pressing.

The air between us thickens, charged with something I can't fully name. I'm about to push again when suddenly the sharp ring of the phone shatters the calm of the suite.

Adrián freezes, his eyes fixed on mine — dark, aflame — as if the bell had awakened the beast he keeps inside. He clenches his jaw and sits up, leaving my skin prickling and my heart racing.

I watch him stride, naked, to the table where the phone keeps ringing. He answers without looking back; his voice is low, dry — short, clipped sentences I can't make out.

When he hangs up, he returns to me. Though his gaze burns as always, now there's something else: tension, urgency, restrained anger.

"I have to go, princesa," he murmurs, hoarse. "I need to be somewhere else tonight."

"How do you mean, you're leaving?" I ask, my voice breaking between disbelief and held-back fury. "You came from Havana for this trip... for only a few hours?"

He pauses, halfway through gathering his things. His broad back, marked with scars I still don't dare ask about, tightens under the soft lamp light. He doesn't look at me at once.

Finally, he turns, and his light-colored eyes pierce me like a blade.

"You don't understand, Lucía," he says in that low, grave voice laden with danger. "I didn't come just for a few hours. I came because I couldn't bear not having you."

He walks toward me, cups my face in his hands, and his mouth grazes mine — a threat disguised as a caress.

"But my life doesn't belong to me the way you think. And if I stay longer than I should... I'll drag you down with me."

His words tear me apart more than his gaze. I want to stop him, to scream for him to stay, not to leave me here with this silence that burns fiercer than his hands ever did on my skin. But my voice dies in my throat.

Adrián gives me one last kiss—hard, brief—more a seal of possession than a farewell. His breath still scorches my lips even as he pulls away. He dresses with quick, almost violent movements, as though his body must leave before desire forces him to stay.

I watch him take his keys, his phone, his jacket. At the door he turns, and for an instant I think I see his eyes break.

Then he's gone.

The door closes with a dry click that pierces my soul. The suite falls silent, too large, too cold. My body still trembles for him, my skin still burns everywhere he touched me, but his absence weighs heavier than any orgasm ever could.

I sink into the sheets, the taste of his mouth lingering on my lips, and only one question hammers through my head: Who are you, really, Adrián?

I walk the hotel hallway on legs that still tremble, each step recalling the force with which he claimed me. My chest aches with unanswered questions; the weight of his farewell presses down even harder than his body had. I take a deep breath before opening the door to my room, trying to pull myself together.

Camila is sitting on the bed, her hair still damp from the shower and a mischievous smile lighting her face.

Her eyes sparkle the moment she sees me, as if she's been anxiously waiting for my return.

"At last!" she exclaims, patting the bedspread. "I was dying to tell you."

She leans forward with the youthful excitement that always follows her, and before I can get a word out, she's talking in a rush.

"Lucía, you can't imagine... He's gorgeous—tall, that killer smile. And the best part... I think he really likes me."

I listen with a faint smile, but inside I'm torn apart. Her excitement feels light, pure, normal—and it makes my own story feel unbearably different.

While she gushes about a summer romance, I still wear the marks of a dark man I shouldn't want, yet one I cannot let go of.

"We're meeting for dinner tonight—hope you don't mind," Camila asks, trying on a light summer dress in front of the mirror, her face alight with innocence.

I watch her smile, her eyes bright with the promise of something clean and simple. A pang of envy stabs me. She lives love the way it's supposed to be. I—on the other hand—am trapped in a dark whirlwind I can't even name.

"Of course not," I reply, forcing a smile as I let myself fall onto the bed. The softness of the sheets contrasts with the burning I still feel on my skin—Adrián's invisible marks scorching me from the inside out.

Camila doesn't notice. She keeps talking about her beach boy, about how attentive his eyes were when he saw her, how he made her laugh.

By nightfall, the lights of the bar seem colder, the conversations more distant. No matter how many glasses of wine I drink, I can't silence the murmur of his voice in my memory. Adrián is absent... and yet I feel him here, on my skin, in my breath, in every racing heartbeat that refuses to calm.

I catch myself glancing at the door repeatedly, waiting for the impossible. For him to appear. For his dark shadow to cross the room and drag me away. But the door stays closed, and the world keeps spinning as if no one else notices my damnation.

When Camila sighs, blissful, resting her chin in her hand as she dreams of her beach boy, I sink into a thick silence. And I realize that Adrián's absence weighs more than anyone else's presence. His void burns me more than his body ever did. That is the true addiction.

Back in the room, Camila falls asleep quickly, cradled by the lightness of a romance just beginning. I, instead, slip out silently onto the balcony.

The night in Varadero is a black sea scattered with stars. The salty wind caresses my face, and I toy with the glass of wine still in my hand, gazing down at the dimly lit beach below.

I close my eyes, and I can almost feel him: his hands on my skin, his hoarse voice at my ear, the weight of his body claiming me as his own. It's absurd, I know. He isn't here. He's gone. But his absence has a weight—so crushing it steals the breath from my lungs.

I wrap my arms around myself, trying to quiet the tremor running through me. And in that silence, I repeat over and over the question that has consumed me since the moment I met him:

Who are you really, Adrián?

The breeze picks up, lifting the hem of my dress. The wine sways in the glass, and with it my mind—lost between desire, fear, and addiction. I stay there, trapped in the night, waiting for a return I don't know will ever come.

The sun barely filters through the curtains when I feel someone shake my shoulder. I open my eyes with difficulty and find Camila's face leaning over me, her eyes sparkling with excitement.

"Lucía, wake up!" she laughs, tugging at the sheet. "You have to see this."

I sit up slowly, still carrying the weight of the previous night pressing against my chest. On the table sits a perfectly served breakfast tray: fresh juice, fruit, steaming coffee, and a basket of bread that smells like heaven. Among the dishes, a small, folded note.

My heart stumbles in my chest.

Camila claps her hands, amused.

"Looks like someone's got a secret admirer!" she teases, mischief bubbling in her voice.

I take the note with trembling fingers, the world narrowing to those firm strokes, written with certainty:

"Have breakfast, princesa. I need you to remember I'm still here, even when you don't see me. —A."

Air lodges in my throat. Adrián. Even from a distance, even in shadows... he finds me.

I lift my gaze. Camila is watching with a curious smile. I pretend calm, but inside the storm rages again. His hold isn't just over my body—it surrounds me, tracks me, and even with doors locked I am never free of him.

"Well?" Camila presses. "Who sends you breakfasts this... elegant?"

I swallow hard, the note burning like a brand between my fingers. I don't want to lie, but I don't know how to explain what I barely grasp myself.

"It's... Adrián," I finally whisper, my voice a fragile thread.

Her expression shifts instantly. The eager smile vanishes, replaced by disbelief.

"Adrián?" she echoes, eyes widening with alarm. "Lucía, for God's sake! That man was here last night?"

I raise a hand, trying to soothe her, but she's already pacing, a storm contained in four walls.

"Don't you see how unsettling this is?" Her voice cracks, torn between worry and anger. "He always knows where you are, he always appears—as if he's following you. Lucía, that isn't normal. That's obsession."

I stay silent, the note clenched in my palm. Camila's fear is real, but the fire Adrián left on my skin won't let me let him go. I know the truth: he is dangerous. I know he hides shadows from me. And yet that danger is the very thing I crave.

"Camila, I'm not blind," I say at last. "I've told you already—I know Adrián keeps secrets... but I can't stop."

She stares at me, confusion and anger twisting in her eyes, as though she can't reconcile me—the one who always kept her feet on the ground—with the woman surrendering to this.

"Don't you see?" she pleads, folding her arms. "This isn't love, Lucía. That man isn't for you."

Her words cut because I know they're true. But while she speaks, my mind drowns in the memory of his dark eyes locking on mine, his deep voice calling me princesa, his body consuming me as if he needed me to breathe.

I look at her, unable to explain the inexplicable.

"It's addiction, Cami," I whisper, more to myself than to her. "And I don't know if I want to… or if I even can… be cured of it."

Silence settles between us, thick and suffocating. Camila exhales sharply, her sigh heavy with resignation, as though she no longer knows how to save me from myself.

"I can't believe this, Lucía…" she mutters, her voice tight with restrained anger as she snatches her purse from the chair. "I'm telling you that man is wrong, that something about him feels dangerous—and you… you're letting yourself be dragged under."

Her tone lashes through me like a whip. I know she loves me, that every word is born of worry. But I also know nothing she says can undo what I feel.

Camila rubs her forehead, as if I were an impossible puzzle.

"Do whatever you want," she says at last, her voice clipped and cutting. "But don't say I didn't warn you."

The door slams behind her, leaving me alone with the echo of her anger. My gaze drifts to the note on the table, those firm letters still burning my fingers. I know she's right—that all of this is dangerous, that Adrián is a mystery built of shadows.

And yet the only thing I crave... is to see him again.

The day crawls by without Camila. She's truly angry, and I can't blame her.

Dusk descends in muted colors, a palette of oranges and violets streaking the horizon. I walk without aim, the sand slipping between my sandals, following a path that doesn't promise an end. Time dissolves into thought, each step dragging me deeper into the labyrinth of my unanswered questions.

Who is he, really? What secrets hide in that silence that cuts into me like a blade? His shadow haunts me— even in calm, even in his absence.

A rustle behind me makes me stop. I turn slowly, heart pounding in my chest—

And there he is.

Standing in the middle of the path, as if he had been waiting all along. His shirt hangs unbuttoned, his hair tousled by the sea breeze, his dark gaze piercing me from head to toe. I don't need to ask how he found me. I already know, he always does.

"Adrián?" I whisper, my voice weaker than I wish.

He walks toward me with calm certainty, the steady grace of a predator closing in on its prey. The sun bleeds across the horizon, painting his silhouette in gold and crimson, as if the entire sunset were bowing to him.

When he reaches me, his hand clamps onto my face with a force that leaves me no choice but to meet his eyes.

"You shouldn't be walking alone, and this far," he growls, his voice hoarse, laced with danger. "You have no idea what you do to me when you disappear."

Before I can form a reply, his mouth crashes onto mine with brutal urgency. It isn't a kiss—it's a violent claim, a clash of rage and hunger that steals my breath and forces me to cling to him just to remain standing. Adrián tastes of fury and desire woven together.

His hands imprison me against his chest, as though he wants to fuse me into him, as if the kiss itself were both a warning and a caress

"Mine or no one's, understand?" he bites my lip, rage and desire fused into a single gesture that hurts as much as it burns.

The path is deserted, but the thought that anyone could appear makes my breath falter, quicken, break. My mind screams of danger, of madness. But my body betrays me, seeking him, needing him, surrendering as it always does.

When he finally pulls back, it's only to drag air into his lungs. He doesn't release me; instead, he seizes my wrist in an unyielding grip and leads me off the path. No time to think. No time to protest.

"Where are we going?" I ask, though my voice emerges more like a ragged whisper than a demand.

He gives no answer. He strides forward with the certainty of someone who knows every secret corner of this place, and I can only follow, bound by the magnetism that coils around him. The sand beneath my feet grows coarser, wetter, until the rush of the waves grows louder, swallowing everything else.

And then I see it: a secluded beach, hemmed in by towering rocks that rise like sentinels, shielding us from the world. A hidden sanctuary, raw and wild, as though it exists only for him... and now, for me.

He stops abruptly, pinning me against one of the rocks, his body pressing into mine, cutting off any thought of escape. His eyes blaze—dark, consuming—as if this ground is his territory and I, his captured prize.

"Here, nothing can disturb us, princesa," he whispers, his lips brushing mine, each syllable molten. "Here, unseen by every eye but mine, you exist only to please me."

The sea roars behind us, its wild thunder the perfect echo of what he awakens inside me. His mouth claims mine again, but this time there's more than rage—there's something else, something that feels like a secret slipping through his lips.

"You don't know what I risk coming to you, Lucía..." he whispers, biting at my neck. *"You don't know the shadows I try to keep you away from."*

I stare at him, stunned, my breath ragged. His words strike as hard as his touch, and the contradiction burns me from within. I want to demand answers, but his hands are already sliding up my thighs, forcing them apart, and my body surrenders before my reason can resist.

"You're light..." he murmurs, his voice lower, darker, as if speaking only to himself. *"And I... I am the darkness that should never touch you. But look at me, princesa... I can't stop."*

I feel myself splintering. Each word confuses me, wounds me, traps me. His kiss tastes of sin and confession, of danger and redemption all at once. And still, the only thought blazing through me is that I want more.

"I've done things..." he whispers, his deep voice sending a shiver through me. *"Things you can't imagine. Things you should never know."*

His tongue trails slow, torturous lines along my collarbone, and I arch against the rock, powerless.

I want to scream at him to tell me the truth, to finally explain what this all means—but the weight of his body crushes my will.

"There are people who would give anything to keep us apart..." he goes on, his fingers branding my skin with

invisible fire. "And if you ever knew the truth, princesa, you'd hate me."

My mind screams the question—Who are you, Adrián? —but my lips know only how to surrender to his.

"Undress for me, princesa," he commands, his voice hoarse, thick with desire and dominance.

I obey. Slowly, I unbutton my floral blouse, revealing the nakedness beneath. The humid air of the beach caresses my breasts, yet the only heat I truly feel is the scorch of his gaze devouring me.

Without breaking eye contact, I slide down the shorts clinging to me, exposing the thin scrap of fabric that's left. Adrián steps forward like a predator no longer capable of restraint. His fingers graze the edge of my underwear, tracing it slowly, savoring every inch of my skin.

His touch steals a broken sound from my throat, feeding his hunger. With cruel precision, he peels the fabric away, his palms claiming my hips as the cool air stings where his fire lingers.

Adrián lifts me and lays me onto the damp sand, right where the tide reaches. The chill of seawater clashes with the fever of our bodies, drawing another moan he silences with a fierce kiss.

His mouth is sin, his piercing chaos, and his touch a wild prayer against my skin. The ocean rages around us, waves crashing like the echo of his anger and my surrender.

He parts my legs with a force that allows no resistance, his hips locking against mine, and in a single, violent motion he drives into me. The cry he tears from me blends with the crash of the waves breaking on the shore.
He moves like the sea when it claims the sand—insistent, inevitable, beautiful in its destruction.Each thrust drags me deeper into the sand; each touch is a reminder that here, in this secret place, there is no one but the two of us.

"Don't you dare run from me, Lucía..." he growls, voice breaking with something raw. "Not even the ocean could wash you out of me."

Saltwater slicks our burning skin, cooling the surface even as his movements ignite me from within. My nails dig into his shoulders, my breath frays, and I let myself be swept away by the storm that is him.

The rocks stand as silent witnesses, and I feel marked, lost, trapped in Adrián's secret... and in my addiction to his darkness.

The taste of his lips reveals something deeper, something fractured. Adrián clings to me like a man drowning, finding in me the only refuge from his shadows.

"You don't know what you do to me, Lucía..." he whispered, voice ragged, almost desperate. "I don't know how or why... but with you, the void disappears."

I froze, caught between the weight of his words and the press of his body. I had never heard him like this: unarmored, undone, as if I were the only refuge for a man made of shadows.

He wanted to sound strong, to remain the dominator who always overpowered me—but his gaze betrayed him. Behind those dark eyes, I saw storm and pain. And for the first time, I felt that Adrián needed me as much as I needed him.

For one fleeting instant, he had let me in, had shown me the wound beneath his mask.

But the moment shattered as quickly as it came. His eyes hardened, punishing himself for revealing too much. His mouth crashed back onto mine, fierce and possessive, erasing the fragility with violent urgency.

His hands seized my waist, grinding me deeper into the wet sand as his body resumed its brutal rhythm.

"Don't get it wrong, princesa," he growled into my ear.. "I'm not a man who loves... I'm a man who takes. And you are what I need right now."

The cruelty of it should have broken me. Instead, it ignited me. My body yielded even as my soul trembled at the shadows I sensed behind his fury.

His thrusts grew more brutal, as though he needed to bury the memory of his own weakness inside me, to prove he was still the predator I could never escape. The sand clung to my damp skin, and the waves crashed cold and merciless against our entwined bodies.

Adrián took me with savage desperation, every movement claiming not just my body but my soul. And when he crushed me to him, growling my name like a dark vow, I shattered. Pleasure detonated inside me, a devastating orgasm ripping through me like lightning.

The wave of pleasure crashes over me, drowning, devouring. I scream his name into the wind, lost, as I feel him release inside me too—his voice a guttural roar, his body trembling against mine. The sea swallows our burning bodies, cooling our skin, yet inside me everything still burns.

There's no room for fear.
No room for reason.
Only Adrián.
Only this tide that drags me under without promising shore.

Adrián lets his fingers wander over my skin as if they own every inch of it. His hand glides slowly down my stomach, over my hips, and stops between my thighs, pressing hard—marking me, as if he wants to leave his touch carved into me.

His breath burns against my ear, and his hoarse voice slices through me with a shiver:

"You're mine, Lucía. Your body, your pleasure, even your voice... everything belongs to me."

There is no escape. I am trapped, dominated, and although my mind screams that this is dangerous, my body surrenders completely, breaking me and thrilling me at once.

He smiles against my neck as he feels me tremble, his tongue—cold with the piercing—brushing my sweaty skin. Then, lower, almost like a dark vow, he adds:

"It doesn't matter where you run, or who tries to take you from me. You will always come back here... beneath me."

Suddenly, his hand snatches the chain at my neck. He pulls hard, forcing me upright. My breath cracks, my eyes lock onto his, and I understand the game is not over yet.

"Kneel, princesa," he growls, his voice rough, charged with power. "I want your mouth on me... now."

The tug of the chain leaves me no choice. He drags me down, and my body submits before my mind can even react.

The damp sand bites into my knees as I settle in front of him, his shadow covering me like an unbreakable wall. Adrián locks his gaze on mine, a dangerous glint sparking in his eyes that makes my skin prickle. With one hand tangled in my hair, he forces my face upward.

"Eyes on me, princesa," he commands, his deep voice cracking like a whip. "I want to see in your eyes how you surrender to me."

I swallow hard, trembling, and slowly bring my lips closer to his hardness. The first touch rips a guttural growl from his chest, a feral sound that quickens my pulse. My hands instinctively move to rest on his hips, but he shoves them away with brutal ease.

"No... only your mouth," he murmurs with delicious cruelty, his thumb pressing against my lower lip. "Nothing else."

I shift, taking him in slowly, tasting him, letting my tongue trace him in a steady rhythm. His deep groans tell me I'm doing it right—but he never gives up control.

His hand tightens in my hair, guiding me, setting the pace—deeper, faster—until I choke and tears sting my eyes. But even that only seems to arouse him more.

"That's it, princesa... let me feel your throat clench around me."

He pulls me back just enough to let me breathe, his fingers firm against my jaw, forcing my mouth open for him. Then he guides me down again, slower this time, savoring the contrast between my desperation and his dominance.

Every movement, every choked gasp, every tear sliding down my cheek belongs to him. Lost in the rhythm,

I discover I relish being used—possessed in the rawest, most addictive way.

His groans grow deeper, harsher each time my mouth takes him further. He tightens his grip on my hair, controlling me without choice, and the chain at my throat tugs like a gleaming shackle condemning me to obedience.

"Don't stop, princesa..." he growls, his broken, commanding voice locking with mine. "You're going to swallow it all; do you hear me? Every drop."

The yank of the chain forces me to look at him just as his body shudders— His moan came out rough, like something primal clawing to be free. Heat floods my mouth in an instant, and though every instinct screams to pull away, his hand in my hair and the metal at my throat keep me bound to obedience.

I swallow slowly, tears streaming down my face, the salt of the sea mingling with his bitter taste. Adrián watches me; in his gaze there is no mercy—only dark possession that ignites me as much as it terrifies me.

When he finally releases me, I gasp for air, exhausted, my chest heaving violently. He brushes his fingers across my cheek with startling tenderness, a softness that clashes with the brutality of the moment.

"That's how I want you, Lucía... surrendered, mine until your last breath."

As the metal still burns against my skin, I know there is no escape. I don't want one.

He picks me up effortlessly, as if I'm weightless in his arms. His mouth crashes against mine in a fierce, consuming kiss—like he wants to brand his fire into me before he's gone. When he pulls away, his eyes lock on mine, dark and dangerous.

"You are my greatest temptation, Lucía... and also my damnation."

He hands me my clothes, helping me cover my nakedness with a strange, controlled calm—as if he suddenly wants to erase the violence of the moment. Still holding my hand, he walks me back along the path; silence presses between us, broken only by the crunch of sand underfoot.

At the hotel door he stops. His hand tightens around mine—strong, steady—yet his gaze is distant.

"Rest, princesa," he says in a low voice that brooks no argument.

I grab his arm, desperate; words slip out before I can stop them.

"Stay with me... even if just for tonight. Tell me something else—anything—about that life that punishes you, about what you hide from me."

His expression darkens, and for a moment I think he might relent. But then he strokes my cheek with the back of his hand—a tender gesture—and whispers:

"If you knew more, you'd stop looking at me the way you do now."

He kisses me once more, quick and poisonous against my lips, then steps away. Before I can stop him, he's already vanished down the corridor, leaving me with a burning heart and a throat knotted tight.

I collapse onto the bed, still smelling of the sea, my clothes clinging damp to my skin, as if every scrap of him insists on marking me. The silence of the room strikes hard and raw after his voice, his strength, his body claiming me as if I'd never had another choice.

I closed my eyes, and it all came rushing back—the chain around my neck, the fury of his kisses, the unexpected tenderness as he dressed me, the coldness in his voice when he left.

A storm that binds me, wounds me, and feeds.

I should hate him.

I should run.

But all I feel is that I need him more than the air I breathe.

I don't know what shadows follow him, what secrets haunt him, or what abyss lives inside him. All I know is this: sooner or later I will tear that truth from him.

Chapter 11

✦ ✦ ✦ ✦ ✦ ✦

The routine at home was a disguise: the same walls, the same inquisitive glances, the same suffocating silence... yet I felt everything was about to shatter. My father paced back and forth with sharp, restless steps, his voice a storm each time he barked an order. I tried to vanish within those walls, weighed down by the certainty that my secrets were already carved into my skin.

"Lucía!" Camila's voice burst from the doorway, so urgent it jolted me upright.

She rushed toward me, hair disheveled, eyes blazing as though a fire burned inside her chest. She seized my arm tightly, tugging me from the hallway as if she needed to drag me out of the world itself.

"You have to listen to me..." she gasped, breathless. "You're not going to believe what just happened."

My heart leapt instantly. Part of me feared to hear Adrián's name on her lips; another—far more dangerous—longed for it.

But what spilled from her mouth was different. A shot straight through my chest.

"I'm getting married!" Camila exclaimed, her radiant smile so bright it blinded me for an instant.

"What...?" was all I managed, breathless, feeling the ground tilt beneath my feet.

She laughed nervously, pressing her hands to her face as if she still couldn't believe her own confession.

"I met him recently, but he's perfect, Lucía. He asked me to marry him, and I couldn't say no."

I watched her in silence, a strange pang tightening my chest. She spoke of a future, of certainty, of peace. And I... I was chained to a dark man, to a desire as dangerous as it was addictive, to a destiny that offered neither clarity nor promise.

That word cut through me like a knife. Peace. Something I hadn't known since Adrián had stepped into my life.

"I don't know, Camila..." I said slowly, trying not to sound cruel but unable to mask my shock. "We haven't even finished university—don't you think this is all a bit rushed?"

She stared at me, wide-eyed, as though she couldn't comprehend my resistance.

"Rushed?" she repeated with a nervous laugh, biting her lip. "Maybe... but when you feel it, Lucía, you just know. And I know. I don't need more time."

"I mean... it's different, Cami. It's a huge commitment." I tried to sound calm, as if reason could shield her from a mistake.

She sighed, sat beside me on the bed, and took my hand.

"I know. But for the first time, I feel like someone truly sees me. Like he chooses me. And you, more than anyone, should understand what it means to be unable to say no to what seizes you."

Her words froze me. Because she was right: I understood too well. Only in my case, what bound me wasn't pure love... it was Adrián.

"If you're sure, then I'm happy for you," I finally said, forcing a smile. "But I want to meet him, okay?"

Camila laughed nervously and hugged me hard, almost knocking the air out of me.

"Of course! You'll see, Lucía—you'll love him. He's so different from everything we've lived... so steady, so safe..." Her eyes gleamed with unshakable hope. "I think I've never felt so at peace."

The word struck me again like a cruel echo. Peace.

I nodded, concealing my contradiction behind another forced smile.

"Then I'll wait for the introduction."

Still glowing, Camila pulled her phone from her bag.

"You'll get along with him, you'll see," she insisted, dialing with trembling fingers.

I remained silent, watching her. Her joy was contagious, and yet in my chest a bitter unease throbbed—the cruel contrast between the light she lived and the darkness devouring me.

"Víctor!" she exclaimed as soon as the voice answered. "Yes, my love... I'm with Lucía. How about dinner tonight, the three of us, so you can meet her?"

She paused, biting her lip, listening intently. I could only read the seriousness in her face, the glow in her eyes that brightened with each word he spoke.

"A restaurant?" she repeated, almost breathless. "Perfect. That sounds amazing."

Hanging up, she squeezed my hand.

"It's decided. Tonight, dinner—the three of us. I want you to meet him, Lucía. I want you to see how special he is."

A smile curving my lips but never reaching my eyes. Because while she prepared to introduce me to a man who seemed straight out of a fairy tale... all I could think of was Adrián: where he was now, what darkness he was hiding in, and why I could never seem to escape him.

The afternoon slipped away in preparations. Camila fluttered in front of the mirror, trying on dresses, applying makeup with a lighthearted excitement that made her seem transformed since meeting him. I, on the other hand, dressed on autopilot: a simple black dress, hair loose, just a touch of lipstick.

The black car pulled up in front of Camila's house, and I saw him immediately: Víctor. Tall, immaculate, with a polished smile designed to inspire trust. Nothing about him was improvised; every gesture, every word radiated calm, security.

"A pleasure to meet you, Lucía," he said, shaking my hand firmly. His voice was deep but steady, without a trace of menace—the kind of voice anyone would want to hear every day.

The contrast hit me like a blow to the chest. His serenity should have been attractive, should have invited me to lower my guard. But it didn't. All it did was remind me how much I missed the vertigo, the dangerous edge of Adrián. Víctor's perfect smile unsettled me, because I realized calm had no taste. I was already lost to a different flavor: smoke, fire, poison.

Camila looked at him as if he were the sun. I, on the other hand, saw him as a cruel mirror of what I would never have with Adrián.

I smiled back, out of courtesy more than feeling.

"The pleasure is mine."

During the ride, Camila never stopped talking—sharing anecdotes, laughing, intertwining her hand with his. I stayed quiet, staring out the window, my reflection betraying me: I couldn't stop imagining what Adrián might be doing at that very moment.

The restaurant was as chic as promised: dim lights, minimalist décor, waiters in white gloves. A movie-perfect scene for my friend's romance. We were led to a table by a wide window overlooking the glowing city.

"I hope you like this place, Lucía," Víctor said with that unshakable calm. "It's important to me to know the people Camila loves."

I nodded, toying with the stem of my wineglass.

"It's lovely, yes. Very elegant."

Dinner unfolded with Camila's laughter, Víctor's stories of work, travel, and projects. He was a proper man, well-mannered, everything in order.

And with every word, I felt the sharp contrast. While Víctor spoke of future plans, I heard again the dark whispers Adrián had breathed against my skin. While Víctor smiled with serene warmth, I remembered the burn of hands that gripped me as if I were both sin and salvation.

Camila watches me expectantly, as if seeking my approval.

"See? I told you you'd like him," she says, her smile radiant, her eyes shining with hope.

I return a polite grimace, gripping the wineglass between my fingers. "Yes... he's charming," I answer, the word hollow, borrowed.

Víctor is charming, yes. Too charming. Every gesture measured, neat, correct—the kind of man any sane woman would want by her side. The kind of love that offers peace.
But I am no longer that sane woman.

While Camila clings to his hand as if holding the future, I remember Adrián's fingers digging into my skin like punishment. While Víctor speaks of projects and travels, I hear Adrián's deep voice in my head, claiming me as his.

I smile again—courtesy, not feeling—and I hate myself for it, because the truth burns inside me: Víctor is perfect, but I'm already damned.

Then I feel it before I see him: that invisible current that makes my skin crawl, that flame no other man can ignite. My breath catches: my hands clench tighter around the wineglass.

I lift my gaze... and there he is.

A dark suit tailored perfectly to his frame, an immaculate tie, his hair slicked back as if born to dominate any scene. He doesn't belong in this elegant restaurant, and yet the moment he crosses the threshold, the room itself feels too small for him.

Víctor is calm.
Adrián is a contained hurricane with every step.

His eyes found me in the crowd—green, burning, lit with that flame that had already scorched me from the inside. *And then I understood: no matter how polite his smile, no matter how refined his manners, that man was danger. My body recognized it instantly.*

He stopped in front of our table, his deep voice cutting through the air—polite and sharp, like a knife wrapped in velvet.

"Good evening."

He doesn't look at Camila. He doesn't look at Víctor. Only at me.

Camila smiles, startled by his sudden presence. Adrián gives her a brief gesture, almost like a poisoned compliment.

"Congratulations on the engagement. I wish you both the best."

Then his hand closes over mine. The contact is an electric shock that shakes me to the core, and I cannot hide the tremor in my fingers as I return his grip.

"May I steal Lucía for a second?" he asks, his gaze fixed on me, leaving no room to refuse.

Víctor arches a brow, polite but confused. Camila's eyes dart to me, searching for an explanation. I, meanwhile, feel the world split in two: the false peace before me and the dark hurricane that has just stormed in.

And even knowing I should refuse… my body has already surrendered to following him.

He pulls me from the table without waiting for an answer, his grip firm, his burning gaze leaving no room for hesitation. I barely hear Camila calling after me; every part of me already trembles with Adrián's nearness.

He leads me down a side corridor, each step purposeful, a predator dragging his prey. I can't take my eyes off the breadth of his shoulders beneath the immaculate jacket, the perfect cut of his suit—never has elegance looked so erotic, knowing the brutality that lurks beneath it.

"What are you doing here, Adrián?" I whisper, though it sounds more like a moan than a protest.

He doesn't answer.

At the end of the hall, he wrenches open a narrow door: a storage room, dimly lit, shelves and boxes steeped in the scent of wood and dust. A place no one is meant to enter.

He shoves me inside, locks the door, and pins me with his body until I can barely breathe.

"Here…" —his voice drops to a low, steady murmur— "Here, only you matter."

Under the dim light of a single lamp above us, his gaze trails over my body, slow and possessive, stopping at the black dress I'm wearing.

"This black dress looks beautiful on you," he whispers, his fingers brushing the fabric as if he wants to tear it away. "But I'd rather see it on the floor."

The lash of his tone burns through me. His hands clamp hard on my hips, devouring me with his eyes before his mouth seizes mine with the urgency of a man who can't wait.

The scrape of his suit against my bare skin beneath the dress makes me shudder. It's a dangerous contrast: the pristine elegance of his appearance and the ruthless brutality of his touch—an alchemy only Adrián can conjure.

My breath quickens. Without realizing it, my fingers clutch at the lapel of his jacket, desperate to reassure myself that he's real, that he's here, that he isn't just the ghost haunting me day and night.

His hands move with dangerous calm. His fingers trail down my back, barely grazing, until they find the zipper of my dress. With slow precision, he slides it down.

The faint rasp of metal mingles with my ragged breaths.

"I want to savor every layer, princesa," he murmurs, voice low and fierce. "I'll strip you down like a secret only I get to keep."

The dress slips from my shoulders, falling in languid folds until it gathers at my waist. He doesn't rush—his palms guide the descent, caressing every inch of revealed skin as though each touch is a claim he refuses to leave unmarked.

When the fabric clings at my hips, his fingers toy with the edge—lifting, lowering, grazing—until a moan breaks free, and his mouth curves into a dark, triumphant smile.

"Look at you, trembling at my touch," he whispers at my ear. "This isn't a dress... it's just an excuse to remind you that everything it hides belongs to me."

At last, the dress pools at my feet like a surrendered trophy. I feel naked long before I am, because his gaze—those burning green eyes—strips me more completely than his hands.

The fabric lies discarded, but his stare continues to peel me apart, layer by invisible layer. His hand slides to my waist, fingers brushing the fragile barrier of my underwear, teasing the thin fabric that fails to conceal the heat radiating from my skin.

"Too beautiful to be hiding under this," he whispers, his voice husky, warm breath ghosting over my ear.

He tugs the cloth gently—just a centimeter down—then slides it back up, savoring the desperation he provokes. His mouth trails along my neck, slow and deliberate, each burning kiss paired with that cruel rhythm of fingers shifting the fabric down, then up, until I writhe in unbearable anticipation.

When he finally chooses to strip it away, he does it slowly—agonizingly slow. The fabric whispers against me, falling inch by inch, while his stare devours every second of my unveiling. I gasp, trembling, as it slips past my thighs, my knees, until it joins the dress at my feet.

His hand returns to my hip, tracing the path the cloth left behind, and a broken moan escapes me. He gathers it with a dark smile.

"This is how I like you, princesa*," he growls, the words a dark blend of order and truth. "Shaking. Exposed. Only for me."*

His mouth leaves mine, starting a slow descent that robs me of breath. He finds my neck first, leaving soft bites mixed with searing kisses—each one a brand, a silent claim. His lips trail down to my collarbones, slow, wet, deliberate, painting a path of heat across my skin.

His tongue follows, unhurried, and a moan slips out before I can stop it. He smiles against me, tasting control. His hands grip my waist, tilting me back against the wall as his mouth lowers to my breasts, alternating between gentle worship and sharp bites that make me arch into him.

"Perfect," he growls, voice dark and unsteady with need. "Built to be mine."

His mouth keeps descending along my stomach— kissing, biting, claiming every inch of my skin. My hands tangle in his hair, my legs trembling as he slowly presses me against the wall, his tongue still exploring me.

When he reaches the edge of my body, he leaves a burning trail along the inside of my thighs—the heat of his lips, the scrape of his teeth—a cruel game that tears moans from my throat.
He has me on the brink, and he knows it.
I shudder, breathless, waiting for him to finally devour me— but he stops there, smiling.

"I want you desperate, Lucía. I want you to beg."

His mouth reaches the spot I crave, and a helpless sound slips past my lips. His tongue moves slow, exploring, tasting me with a dark, perfect precision that unravels me completely. Every motion deep and knowing—like he's learned my body the way one learns a prayer.

"Adrián..." The sound of his name falls from my lips—shaky, desperate, more plea than word.

He answers by pressing harder, his rhythm punishing and precise, desire sharpened to cruelty. His fingers grip my thighs, spreading me wider, holding me up when I'm ready to collapse. His mouth takes everything—my breath, my sound, my control. Pleasure rises like a relentless tide, crashing again and again until my body trembles, wrecked, helpless against the storm he's become.

I'm right at the edge.

Adrián lifts his head just enough to meet my eyes. His mouth, wet and tasting of me, curves into a dark, knowing smile.

"You don't have to say it, Lucía..." he growls. "I'll prove there's not a single part of you that doesn't carry my mark."

Adrián straightens, his mouth still wet from me. His green eyes blaze, alive and dangerous, as he lifts me with effortless strength.
He slams me gently against the wall, my back meeting the cold surface while his hands grip my hips hard enough to bruise.
His suit is still perfect—flawless, composed. He only unbuttons his pants with one quick motion, like a man who never needs to strip to own what's his.
That power—his control—unravels me, makes me feel small, breakable... his.
One thrust, and my breath shatters against his lips, desire consuming everything else.
The contrast is maddening: I'm naked, trembling, exposed; he's immaculate, untouchable, utterly in control.
His rhythm is a violent wave, driving me into the wall until there's nothing left of who I was.
Only this remains—two lost souls breathing the same air, trembling in the silence between us.

"That's it..." he growls in my ear, voice low, broken with desire. "I want you to remember who makes you tremble. There is no place, no man, no life outside of me."

My nails claw into the fabric of his jacket, my legs cling tight to his waist, my body arches seeking more.

His strength holds me in the air, his body locked with mine, and for a moment I think he'll break me in a savage frenzy. But then—suddenly—he slows. His thrusts become deliberate, deeper, each one calculated to dismantle me piece by piece.

The shift destroys me. I expected fury, frenzy... but what I find is exquisite torture: him sliding in and out with cruel calm, pausing just enough to make me burn, to let release approach only to recede again, a wave that never crests.

"Look at me, princesa,*" he murmurs, his voice low and rough, his green eyes locking on me with lethal focus. "Every sound you make belongs to me. Every heartbeat I steal from you... is mine."*

He smiles against my neck, fully aware of the torment he inflicts—pleasure given drop by drop until I unravel.

The slow rhythm turns into torment.
Every deep, measured thrust pulls me to the brink—
only for him to drag me back, denying the fall.
My body trembles, my sounds tangled in the thick air around us, and the not-yet of it all makes me lose my mind.

Adrián's eyes never leave me, green and burning with that cruel blend of power and want.

His mouth brushes my ear, his voice a dark, shivering growl that tears through me.

"You won't come until I say so, princesa... and only if you beg."

A desperate moan escapes. I try to move against him, to quicken the pace myself, but his hands clamp me against the wall, dictating every motion. The helplessness scorches me. The desire breaks me.

"Adrián..." I whisper, panting, my voice broken.

The heat inside me is unbearable, my body trembling, pleading for mercy I no longer want. I dissolve in his arms, lost to him completely— and the words escape before I even realize I've spoken them.

"Please... let me... let me come. I beg you."

The look in his eyes says it all—he's won again. He doesn't just possess me; he owns every inch of me. His smile ghosts against my skin before he breaks the calm with a single, savage motion.

His hips slam into mine, hard and unyielding, each thrust deeper, wilder—like he's trying to pull the soul out of me. The sudden change wrecks me. My body, already trembling from the waiting, detonates under the violence of his rhythm.

"That's it, princesa..." crushing me violently against the wall. "That's how I wanted you—begging, obedient, lost in me."

Pleasure overtakes me. I scream his name into his mouth, unable to hold back, as my body detonates in an orgasm that shakes me to the core. My legs go weak, my back arches against the wall, my chest trembles under his control.

Adrián holds me tight, not letting me escape a single second of that climax that rips tears from me, his body claiming mine until the end. I feel him release with me— his ragged breath in my ear, his low roar merging with my torn moan.

I collapse against him, exhausted, my heart racing, knowing he has broken me again... and that I would beg him again if he asked.

His breath still fans my ear—rough, overflowing. I expect him to pull away at once, to leave me as he always does, with that cutting coldness that hurts me so much.

But he doesn't.

Adrián remains still, holding me against the wall as if afraid that letting me go would shatter me into a thousand pieces. His lips brush my forehead in a gesture so soft, so unexpected, it steals a sigh from me. I close my eyes, feeling for the first time a caress that doesn't seek to mark or possess... but to stay.

When I look at him again, I notice a crack in his mask: his green eyes, still burning, now hold a different shadow—something that isn't fury or desire, but something closer to fear.

"Lucía," he breathes, savoring the name like a claim. "You have no idea the hold you've got on me."

That moment lasts only a couple of seconds, but it brands me. Because for the first time, I feel that behind his brutality there is a broken man... and that I am the light he cannot help but seek, even if it consumes him.

Then he blinks, and his gaze hardens again. He lowers me slowly until my bare feet touch the cold floor once more. I reach blindly for the dress lying crumpled on the ground, mute witness to what just happened. I slip it on clumsily, trying to compose myself, though the weight of his eyes on me makes calm impossible.

As I adjust the straps, my gaze collides with his. The burning green is still there, but colder now—more calculating. The question sears on my tongue until I can no longer hold it back.

"How did you know Camila got engaged?" I whisper at last, my voice a fragile thread, wavering between fear and reproach. "It's impossible... no one knows yet. It's too soon."

The silence thickens between us. Adrián doesn't answer right away. He only watches me with that unsettling mix of power and danger, as if weighing just how much truth to reveal.

My heart hammers, because deep down I know it isn't coincidence. He always knows. He always appears where he shouldn't. He always discovers what no one else does.

And for the first time, the vertigo of desire mingles with a chill of real fear.

Adrián doesn't smile. He doesn't deflect. He only holds my gaze, and when he finally speaks, his voice is so deep it freezes me from the inside out.

"I know the fiancé."

The air vanishes from my lungs. My hands clutch at the fabric of my dress as if it could shield me from the shadow his words have cast.

"What... what do you mean you know him?" I stammer, disbelief tearing through my voice.

He takes a step toward me, slow, deliberate—like a predator choosing to show just a glimpse of his world.

"Let's just say our paths have crossed before," he murmurs, his green-eyed stare unyielding. "And believe me, princesa... not everything that glitters is gold."

My breath quickens. A shiver crawls down my spine. Because if Adrián knows Víctor—the man Camila loves—then nothing is what it seems. And worst of all... I don't know if I want to uncover what truly binds those two men together.

Adrián closes the distance with another step, and the air between us thickens. I feel the heat radiating from his body, the taut line of his shoulders beneath the immaculate suit, and that gaze that grants me no reprieve. His hand brushes my chin, tilting my face up until I have no choice but to drown in his green eyes, burning like dark fire.

"Take care of your friend," he whispers, a threat disguised as advice. "Víctor... is not what he seems."

My stomach knots.

"What do you know about him?" I ask, barely a thread of sound, though deep down I already fear the answer.

Adrián smiles—but it's a bitter, dangerous smile.

"Enough to tell you that his fairy tale is thick with shadows. And believe me, princesa... I know how to recognize them."

His breath brushes my neck, and a shiver courses through me. The contradiction devours me: I should be afraid, I should push him away, but the intensity of his warning only pulls me closer. As if the deeper I fall into his secrets, the less possible it becomes to escape.

When he pulls back, leaving my body burning and my mind in chaos, his gaze flickers with one last spark of danger.

"Come, I'll take you," Adrián says, his deep voice reverberating inside me.

We leave the small room side by side, feigning composure, as if our bodies weren't still aflame from the pleasure that had consumed us minutes before. My breathing remains uneven, and every accidental brush of his hand against mine hurls me back into images I long to erase... and relive.

As we approach the table, I feel the weight of every gaze. Camila smiles, though her curious eyes search mine with that old complicity only she and I share. Víctor, in contrast, watches me intently, as if trying to decipher something just beyond his reach.

"Adrián is taking me home, Cami," I say, forcing a smile, as if it were the most natural thing in the world.

Camila arches her brows in surprise but stays silent. Víctor only nods with that flawless calm that defines him.

Adrián leans toward them with perfect courtesy, his presence more imposing than when he first entered.

"It's been a pleasure," he says, shaking Víctor's hand firmly before congratulating Camila again with a brief gesture. Then his eyes shift to me—those green flames only I can read: burning, possessive, impossible to mask.

In that moment, I knew it didn't matter how much we tried to hide. Adrián would always leave a trace— something that lingered, even in a room full of elegance and masks.

The cool night air meets us as soon as we leave the restaurant.
I walk next to him, the fabric of his suit grazing my bare skin, his hand at the small of my back—gentle, commanding—a silent reminder of who leads.

"What were you thinking?" I whisper, unable to hold back. "Showing up like that, in front of everyone... in front of Camila, in front of Víctor."

Adrián smiles to one side—that dangerous smile that never promises calm.

"I was thinking I can't stand seeing you in a world where I don't exist."

My steps falter. My heart pounds violently.

"You don't understand, Adrián... Camila is happy," I begin, my voice unsteady. But before I can say more, he closes the distance, invading my space, his shadow engulfing me under the dim streetlights.

"I know him," he says in a low voice, as if confessing a secret that drags me deeper into his darkness. "And I won't stand by while you surround yourself with lies."

His intensity disarms me. Part of me wants to shout, to push him away—but the other part, the most dangerous part, burns with the fire only he ignites.

"Why do you always have to know everything?" I breathe, my voice breaking between reproach and desire.

Adrián cups my face in his hands, his gaze locked on mine, and I feel him undress me all over again without even touching me.

"Because you're mine, Lucía. And no one—do you hear me? No one will come near you without me knowing."

His words cut like a blade: cruel, possessive... yet so addictive that my body trembles just to hear them.

I freeze, my heart hammering, my anger struggling against the pull of him.

"Are you saying you don't want me surrounded by lies?" My voice shakes with reproach and pain. "And you, Adrián... you're the first one who lies to me—you hide your life."

His jaw clenches. For a moment, I think he'll answer with fury. But he doesn't. He stands there, silent, his green eyes burning with something I can't quite name: anger, guilt... and desire.

He takes a step closer, and the air thickens unbearably.

"You don't understand..." he growls, his voice low, almost broken. "It's not the same, Lucía. Mine isn't a lie—it's a secret. And I keep it to protect you."

"Protect me from what?" I demand, tears stinging my eyes.

His silence wounds deeper than any reply. Then he seizes my wrist and pulls me back against his chest, his breath grazing my lips.

"The day you learn everything..." he whispers, a dark fire blazing in his gaze. "You'll either hate me... or you'll never be able to leave me."

My lips tremble. My body follows. My mind screams. And there—right there, in the middle of the street— everything in me goes still.

Turning the corner, I see it: his car, looming, waiting like a silent accomplice. My heart races the instant I recognize it. This is not just a car... it is the place where it all began.

A memory strikes me like fire: the first time he took me there, with an endless passion that ripped away my innocence and branded me as his. The trace of that night still burns on my skin, in my memory, like an indelible scar.

My fingers brush the cold metal, and a shiver cuts through me at once: every desperate kiss, every stolen caress from that night floods back like a violent storm.

"Any memories?" Adrián murmurs at my ear, his deep voice wrapping around me like a tether. "This is where I made you mine for the first time. Where you stopped being innocence... and became addiction."

The weight of his words, mixed with the memory, makes me bite my lip. That car is not merely a vehicle— it is much more.

I stand frozen, my hand still on the door, while the past consumes me. Adrián leans over me:

"Don't worry, princesa..." he whispers, dark and enticing. "You'll have memories like this all over Cuba."

His promise isn't a comfort. It's a threat. I see it in his green eyes—lit with that dangerous obsession that doesn't recognize boundaries. He doesn't plan to fade into memory. He plans to become the map itself— marking every part of me until there's no space left for anyone but him.

Opens the door with a confident gesture, as if refusal doesn't exist. I step inside almost in a trance, and the moment the door shuts the air fills with him—his scent, his presence, the burning memory that still scorches me.

Adrián slips behind the wheel, starts the engine, and as the city lights streak past the windows, his hand slides without permission over my bare thigh.

At first it simply rests there—heavy, possessive. But soon his fingers begin to move, tracing invisible shapes on my skin: circles, lines, marks that raise the hairs on my arms and make my breath falter.

"You're my canvas, princesa," he growls, his voice a dangerous whisper. "I'll carve memories into you until nothing of you remains that isn't mine."

The heat in my belly flares with each invisible stroke, and I close my eyes for a moment, aware that even in silence—even while he drives—Adrián owns my body and my mind.

"Where are we going?" I ask once I realize we've passed my street, headed farther away.

My fingers grip the edge of the seat; my heart pounds so violently I'm certain he must hear it. His hand doesn't leave my thigh. Instead, it tightens, as if my question were insolence worthy of punishment.

Adrián smiles faintly, his gaze fixed on the road. That smile carries no relief, no tenderness—only a reminder that with him there are never certainties.

"Trust me, princesa," he replies at last, his voice hoarse and grave, leaving no room for argument. "Not all marks are made in bed."

His finger sketches another slow circle on my skin, closer now to where I burn, and a muffled moan trembles on my lips.

I turn to the window; the city lights fade, swallowed by a lonelier, darker road. With every passing kilometer, I feel myself pulled farther from everything I know… and deeper into him.

The tension inside the car coils tighter with every second. Music hums in the background, little more than a murmur, yet enough to set the rhythm of blood in my veins. His hand moves slowly up and down my thigh, firm and deliberate, transporting me into another universe: Adrián's universe, where nothing is safe and the only certainty is fire.

We don't speak. For more than an hour, silence reigns—delicious, oppressive—where only our bodies converse: his thumb grazing my skin, my breath hitching whenever his fingers draw too close, the way our eyes catch in fleeting reflections on the glass.

Then the car stops. My heart lurches when I look out: ahead of us rises an imposing lighthouse at the edge of the world, solitary and watchful against the vast dark of the sea.

Its beam sweeps slowly, casting brief flashes across the wild coast. The roar of the waves crashes against the rocks with ancient power. The world falls away, leaving only us, trapped in this hidden corner where no one else can see.

Adrián cuts the engine, but his hand remains firm on my skin. He turns toward me, green eyes burning with the same fierce intensity as the lighthouse's light, and his hoarse voice envelops me.

"This will be another of your memories, princesa. One you'll never forget."

He steps out first, then opens my door and takes my hand. The salty sea air rushes around us, the roar of waves against the rocks sending a shiver through me—part fear, part anticipation.

"Come," he ordered, his voice low and impossible to refuse.

He led me to the base of the lighthouse. The structure rose, solitary and imposing, its light sweeping above us like an eternal eye that watched everything. The door creaked as it opened, revealing a spiral staircase that wound upward into the dark.

We climbed in silence, my footsteps echoing against the metal, his firm hand in mine—guiding me, possessing me even in something as simple as the ascent. Each turn of the stairs stole my breath, and with every step I felt myself leaving reality behind and sinking deeper into Adrián's dangerous world.

When we reached the top, the world unfurled before my eyes: the endless, furious sea; the wind slapping against my skin; the lighthouse beam bathing our bodies in intermittent flashes. It felt as though we were the only two souls left on the planet, suspended between sky and tide.

Adrián took me by the waist, pulling me until my back met the cold railing. His gaze burned brighter than the revolving light above us.

"Look at what you have in front of you, Lucía," he whispered in my ear. "The sea, the sky... and me—ready to write my name on your body where no one will ever erase it."

The icy wind cuts against my skin, but the heat of his hands eclipses everything else. Adrián holds me against the railing, his body mastering mine without the need for force.

"Up here, the world ends with you..." he murmurs, his voice blending with the roar of the sea below. "There's

no one else—only you, the darkness, and me deciding how much pleasure you can take."

I close my eyes as his hand slowly slides down to my thigh, lifting the fabric of my dress.

"Look at me, princesa," he ordered in a dangerously soft voice.

I obeyed. His green eyes flashed beneath the lighthouse beam, and the intensity of his gaze stole my breath. He smiled at my surrender, pleased to see me caught in his perverse game.

"You like this, don't you?" he murmured, his mouth grazing my lips without kissing me yet. "You like the feeling of me pushing you to the edge... knowing I control even your breath."

His hand rises higher, touching me exactly where I need him, but instead of giving relief, he toys with me— the slow cruelty of an executioner. My body arches against him, pleading, begging with every gasp... and Adrián stops at the last second, savoring the desperation he extracts from me.

"You're going to ask me for it," he says with cruel calm, his finger tracing the edge of my desire. "Here, under the light of the lighthouse, you're going to beg me to fuck you good."

His finger keeps me poised at the brink of delirium, but I clamp my lips shut, clinging to the little control I have left. My breathing turns frantic, my body burns and trembles against him, but I don't give in. I don't give him the plea he wants.

Adrián watches in silence, his green eyes burning like fire beneath the sweep of the lighthouse beam. A dark, dangerous smile crosses his face.

"So, you want to resist..." he murmurs. "All right, princesa."

His hand grips me hard, his fingers plunging without warning.
His mouth claims my neck in a fierce kiss—almost a bite—as his fingers draw relentless circles, faster and faster, pushing me to the edge without mercy. My back arches against the railing, my voice breaking into desperate gasps, but still I hold on, refusing to say the word he wants.

Then he pulls back just enough, his hand gripping my face with rough insistence, forcing my eyes to meet his.

"I will break you until you beg," he growls, voice torn, his breath scorching my lips. "And when you do, you'll never forget who holds your will in his hands."

His fury feels like a hurricane—every touch turns into punishment, every kiss into a wild act of possession that drags me closer to the edge. I know I can't last much longer, but I still refuse to surrender. And that resistance drives him mad.

His fingers sink into me with cruel mastery. I try to fight it, to hold on to the last thread of pride I have left, but my body betrays me. Adrián knows. He feels it. His eyes, burning, lock onto mine with feral intensity.

"Say it," he growls, gripping my jaw roughly, forcing my mouth open under his control. "Surrender, princesa. Beg me."

"Adrián, please!" I sob between gasps. "I beg you."

A dark smile crosses his face—part triumph, part lust. Then he gives me what he'd been denying: he quickens his pace, pounding into me with force, driving me straight to the edge.

The climax takes me, and there's nothing left but trembling. My whole body shudders, my throat releasing a cry that mingles with the roar of the sea. It's devastating, brutal—so much pleasure it almost feels like pain. Adrián holds me firmly, keeping me bound to him as my body breaks again and again beneath his control. His lips brush my ear while my breath still comes in fragments.

"That's it... just like that. Never forget who made you beg." I know I never will.

Adrián spins me roughly against the railing, and suddenly my face is turned to the vastness of the night. The lighthouse beam sweeps across the ocean's endless black, as if the whole world were watching—but only he has me at his mercy.

His body presses into mine from behind—hot, solid, unyielding. I feel his breath at my neck before his lips devour it, burning kisses and bites that make me arch helplessly into him.

In one swift motion he drops the straps of my dress. The zipper gives with a sharp tug, and the fabric slides down my body until I stand naked to the cold wind.

My nipples harden instantly—not only from the chill, but from the way his hands seize them without hesitation, claiming them as his right.

My fingers clutch the railing as my legs weaken. His mouth keeps marking my skin from behind while his hands never stop—kneading, stroking, tormenting my breasts.

One of his hands begins to descend, unbearably slow, across my abdomen.. His hot palm slides lower, grazing the edge of my need, and my knees threaten to buckle as his fingers find me—barely touching, yet already undoing me.

"Hold on to the railing, princesa..." his hoarse voice orders, and I obey, gripping the cold metal in desperation. "Don't let go."

His hand invades me with cruel slowness, circling in perfect patterns that ignite me from within.

"Do you feel that, Lucía?" he murmurs, his breath hot against my ear. "Up here, bare, so helpless... not even the ocean could drown the moan I'm going to take from you."

My body trembles, my back arches, and I know I'm on the verge of begging him again. Because Adrián doesn't just touch me—he breaks me, he dominates me, he makes me his beneath the lighthouse's beam and before the vastness of the world.

Then his hands stop. My body shakes, incomplete, desperate.

I feel him step back, only to pull me from the railing just enough to grind me against him. My hands cling tighter to the frozen metal, my back stretched, my body trapped in his control.

And then I feel it—the unmistakable press of his erection, hard, brutal, still restrained beneath the fabric of his trousers, rubbing against my bare flesh. The contact rips a moan from me, carried off by the wind.

Adrián lowers his voice, hoarse and commanding, directly into my ear:

"Do you like this, princesa? *This is what you do to me... every time you fight me."*

His hips roll against me in slow, punishing strokes, dragging the rough fabric across my naked skin until I can barely breathe.

The friction burns, unbearable—then comes the sharp snap of his belt, the low rasp of the zipper sliding down. My body locks tight, bracing for what I already crave. The heat of his release presses against me for a heartbeat before he drives into me—hard, consuming—until I'm lost in the crash of salt and flame. My scream breaks into the night, swallowed by the sea and the wind that seem to echo our hunger.

His hands dig into my hips, holding me without mercy, marking me as he thrusts again and again with that brutal violence I can't stop craving. Each snap of his hips against mine makes the metal railing shudder, as if even the lighthouse were bowing to his fury.

"Lucía..." he growls, his voice low and ragged. "No man will ever erase my name from your skin."

"Let go, princesa," he rasps, his breath scorching my ear. "Come for me."

And I do. The orgasm rips through me—devastating, absolute. My legs collapse, my back bows painfully, and a raw scream tears free, carried off by the sea's roar. Pleasure shatters me, wracking my body until tears of pure intensity blur my vision.

But even as I come undone, he doesn't surrender. He keeps me open, trembling, his body still hard, burning against mine—as though prolonging my vulnerability is part of his punishment.

Suddenly, he seizes my shoulders and spins me roughly. My hands slip from the railing, and I meet his green eyes blazing with dark fire.

"We're not finished yet," he murmurs, a feral smile twisting his lips as he positions me, already claiming me for another round.

He spins me hard. The air cracks. The world fractures with it.

Light from the tower slices through the dark, flickering over his body—shadows and fire battling across his skin. He faces me now, shirt gaping open to reveal the hard lines of his chest, pants hanging dangerously low on his hips.

My breath turns ragged as my shaking hands find his shirt, peeling it from him inch by inch, stripping away the power he wears like armor. My fingers slow, deliberate, tasting the heat of his skin with my mouth, kissing the trail I leave as the fabric falls away.

His torso lies open to me like a map of scars and desire. I trace his abdomen with my tongue, while his chest rises and falls in heavy breaths. A dangerous smile curls his mouth as if he knows I believe, foolishly, that I have him under my control.

Reaching his waistband, I pause only a moment before he seizes my wrist and yanks me up against him. His green eyes catch mine, gleaming with a wild light.

"Now come, princesa," he orders, his tone carrying a dark undertone—as though he offers me a choice already made long ago.

I straddle him, my thighs trembling, and lower myself slowly onto his burning length. A moan slips from me as he fills me, stretching me completely. This time I set the rhythm—slow at first, deliberate, savoring the intoxication of riding him.

He watches me in silence, eyes dark and unblinking. His hands close over my breasts, matching my movements, his lips wet with restraint. He lets me think I'm in control, but I can feel it—the power still belongs to him.

My hands press against his chest, the rapid beat of his heart pounding against my palm as I start to move faster. My moans rise, my hair falls loose, wild, and for a heartbeat I think I've taken over— until his hand finds my hip and forces me to his rhythm, reminding me exactly who I belong to.

"Look at you..." he murmurs, his rough voice setting me ablaze. "You think you're dominating me, but all you're doing is losing yourself further in me."

My hips grind faster, the motion turning feral under the flickering light that shields us from the world. Each thrust pulls a louder sound from me, and I catch the tension in his jaw—the way he's fighting not to flip me, not to take back what he always owns.

It's intoxicating. That caged strength. That stare that never wavers. His body trembles beneath mine, and I move harder, chasing the illusion that I'm the one in control— that he's the one coming undone for me.

My moans break into screams, my nails tearing at his skin as I fall apart—my body trembling, giving in to the *quake, the crash of waves, the chaos inside me that refuses to be held back. I shake against him, every breath a shudder, every pulse a surrender. For a heartbeat, I believe I've taken him, broken him.*

Then I see it—his mouth curves, that dark smile that says it all. He let me think I'd won. I stay straddling him, breathless, sweat cooling on my chest, my body wrecked and open. Adrián doesn't move. His hands, once cruel, are soft now, tracing my back in slow, tender lines.

Each touch feels like a confession, like he's trying to calm the storm he started. His eyes—green, burning— meet mine. No rage. No dominance. Just something raw, unguarded... dangerous in its honesty.

"Lucía..." he whispers my name in a deep but fractured voice, as if speaking it were a burden too heavy.

I freeze. That unexpected tenderness confuses me more than all his savage thrusts. Because I know this man is not only brutality: he also carries secrets that break him from within. And for an instant, under the lighthouse's intermittent light, I feel he is letting me see a part of him no one else has ever known.

I rest my forehead against his chest, listening to his heart pounding beneath my ear, and I realize I'm lost.

Because if Adrián can also be this—soft, human, tender—then there is no way to escape him.

Adrián never gives in. But this time, he doesn't stop me—his hand clutches my hip, not to command, but to keep himself from falling apart.

Then I hear it—his voice, low and rough, breaking on a moan I've never heard from him before. It rips through me like fire.

"Keep going..." he whispers, almost a plea disguised as a command. "Don't stop, princesa."

Power floods through me. I watch him lose control. His fingers dig into my skin, his breathing deepens, and a low growl breaks from his throat as he finally lets go. His body arches, chest straining against the air, and for a fleeting moment—it's him who's exposed, undone.

I watch him tremble, feel him surrender to my rhythm, and the realization strikes me like lightning: this is the first time Adrián has ever let himself be conquered, the first time a woman has taken him to the edge without him holding the reins. I lean over him, still breathless, my hair brushing his face, and his green eyes find me with a new light—wild, dazed.

What I see in them isn't just desire. It's awe.

"Lucía..." he whispers my name, hoarse, as if he cannot believe what just happened.

I've just watched him surrender. I've just felt him vulnerable in my hands, and for a fleeting second, I believe that the Adrián who always hides in shadows has finally fallen into my grasp.

But as soon as his breath steadies, his eyes change. That soft green hardens again, and in one swift motion, he grabs my face, forcing me to look at him.

"You're the only one who's ever pushed me this far..." His voice cracks, low and rough, before hardening again. "But that doesn't mean you have power, princesa. It just means I'll have to hold you tighter."

His thumb presses against my chin, firm where a moment ago he'd been soft. And that's when it hits me— he can't stand it. The loss. The surrender. The idea that he let me take something from him. He needs to reclaim it, to remind us both who he thinks owns the game.

But the fracture is already there. I saw it. I felt it. For the first time, it wasn't only my body that broke—it was his. And while he hides behind that possessive tone, I know the truth: something cracked open inside him. Something he won't be able to bury.

I stay over him, breath ragged, eyes locked on his, unflinching.

"Stronger?" I reply, my voice trembling but steady, letting each word cut into him like a wound. "Don't fool yourself, Adrián. This time it wasn't you who decided... it was you who surrendered."

For an instant the silence is absolute. His jaw tightens, his breath catches, and in his green eyes I see a savage spark—a mixture of rage and desire.

He is not used to being challenged, least of all in his moment of vulnerability.

I press my hands against his bare chest, still damp with sweat, and bring my mouth close to his, not kissing him, just brushing his lips with the edge of my smile.

"And you saw it, you felt it. For the first time it wasn't me who got lost in you... it was you who got lost in me."

I feel his body harden beneath mine—not from pleasure, but from that dangerous tension that precedes a storm. And I know I've stepped into forbidden ground. The dark, dominant Adrián will never let this challenge go unanswered.

His silence weighs more than a roar, more than any threat. He watches me intently, green eyes blazing under the lighthouse's intermittent beam, and in them there is no tenderness, no defeat. Only a dark shadow that raises the hairs on my skin.

I feel his chest rise and fall beneath my hands, each deep breath as if he were struggling to contain himself. He doesn't push me away, doesn't touch me, doesn't speak. And yet the threat is there—latent, burning in that unbearable silence that leaves me breathless.

I bite my lip, unsure if I've just won something... or if I've just condemned myself. Because I know that look: Adrián is swallowing his words, choking back his fury... and that means that when he finally unleashes it, there will be no escape.

The lighthouse keeps turning, bathing us in flashes of light and shadow, and I remain astride him, trapped in that silence that strips me barer than any caress.

The tension is unbearable. Each second of his silence drills into my skin, and the intermittent beam lights his face like that of a dark god restraining his fury.

"When you defy me, princesa..." His voice drops to a dangerous whisper. "All you do is make me want to break you until your body remembers who it belongs to."

"You thought you could play games with me?" he breathes, his lips brushing mine, slow and deliberate. "I'll make you beg—and when I'm done, you'll understand there's no pleasure that doesn't carry my name."

He parts my legs with impossible strength, eyes blazing like molten green fire, locking on mine just before he takes me again. Each movement is deeper, harder, until the rhythm becomes chaos—my nails raking down his skin, my cries lost to the sea and the night that swallows us whole.

"Say my name," he murmurs, low and broken, pushing deeper until his voice turns into a growl. "I need to hear it—your lips, my name—while I tear you apart with pleasure."

And I do. I scream it. Because in that moment nothing else exists—not the sea, not the night, not the danger.

Only Adrián and the wild storm dragging me under without mercy.

"Say my name, princesa... scream it."

I cry it out again and again, until my throat burns. Adrián moves over me with the fury of a hurricane, every thrust of his hips marking me as his, every groan claiming my soul.

Pleasure rises—builds—roars. A massive wave swallowing me whole. My nails dig into his back, my legs tighten around him in desperate need, and then—suddenly—it all explodes.

The orgasm hits with merciless force, shattering every boundary, pulling me away from the ground, from thought, from myself. In his strength, I am nothing—and I am his.

Adrián follows, a deep growl tearing through his throat as his body claims mine until the very last second. The heat of his release merges with mine, fusing us in an ending so fierce it feels as if the lighthouse itself might collapse.

I lie trembling beneath his weight, breathless, body spent and soul chained. And when I finally lift my gaze, all I find in his green eyes is that dangerous blend of possession and darkness.

The silence that follows the climax feels almost unreal. Only the sea below, the frantic pounding of my heart, and Adrián's ragged breath pressed against me.

I close my eyes, trying to steady myself, the roughness of the lighthouse floor scraping my bare skin—reminding me that nothing we just lived was a dream.

Little by little, the trembling fades, my breathing slows, and I don't know when it happens—when sleep claims me, cradled in the warmth of his body. When I wake, the first light of dawn is spilling over the horizon.

The sea, which last night was a dark and furious beast, now lies calm—endless, blue, at peace. The lighthouse, once the stage of my storm, rises silent and watchful above a world that almost feels serene.

Adrián sits beside me, eyes fixed on the ocean. The wind stirs his hair; his shirt hangs open in the morning breeze. His jaw is set, his green eyes heavy with thoughts he doesn't share.

I sit up slowly. The calm of dawn contrasts with the fire still burning on my skin. I look at him, wondering who this man really is—the one who breaks me in the night, and at sunrise seems like a stranger.

He turns toward me and strokes my cheek with unexpected tenderness. Just a fleeting touch, like a sigh dissolving into the air. And then he speaks, his voice low, deep, as if meant more for himself than for me:

"Too much light for someone like me."

The words chill me and draw me in at once. Because I know he's right: I am light, he is shadow. And yet, I cannot stop seeking him.

The sun finally breaks across the horizon, painting the surface of the sea in gold. Everything that was dark, violent, and wild just hours before now lies wrapped in serene calm, as if the brutal night had never existed.

I keep my eyes on the endless ocean, the fresh breeze caressing skin still marked by him. The lighthouse, witness to it all, remains tall and imposing, bathing me in its intermittent glow.

Adrián says nothing. He only stays beside me, his face turned toward the sea, as if searching that horizon for an answer. I don't speak either. There are no words capable of naming what we were in the darkness... what we are now in the clarity of dawn.

And for an instant, beneath the immensity of the dawn, I stop fighting my questions and simply feel. I carve this moment into memory, knowing that even if tomorrow everything changes, even if he retreats once more into his shadows, this scene will remain tattooed on my soul: the calm after the storm.

I close my eyes. I breathe. And I understand—this is not an ending... only a pause.

Chapter 12

* * * * * *

*T*he ride back was thick with silence, broken only by the muted roar of the engine and the searing memory of what had happened at the lighthouse. My skin still bore the marks of his dominance, each touch branded like fire, while he kept his gaze fixed on the road, impassive, as if nothing had occurred.

A few meters from my house, he slowed and stopped in the shadows, away from prying eyes. He didn't want to be seen. He couldn't. His green eyes found mine in the dark, more eloquent than any words.

"I'll leave you here, princesa," he murmured at last, and his hoarse voice disarmed me once more.

His hand brushed my cheek and, instead of the brutality I always expected, he gave me a soft kiss—almost tender. That unexpected calm split me in two: I understood then that the true danger wasn't only in his violence, but in the sweetness that could confuse me, make me believe that what we had could be love.

When he pulled away, silence reclaimed everything. I watched him disappear around the corner, swallowed by the shadows, and the void he left felt more unbearable than his presence.

I turned toward my door, seeking refuge. But before I could set a foot inside, the blow of reality stole my breath.

"Lucía!" My mother's broken voice.

"Where the hell have you been?" my father roared, the razor edge of fury slicing through me like a whip.

I stepped in, and their stares pierced me like knives. There was no room for excuses: they knew. They knew there was a man in my life.

"Who is he?" my father bellowed, his face flushed, eyes bloodshot, his fist pounding the table like a hammer about to fall.

My mother watched me with tears barely held back, her hands clenched in her lap as if she feared that naming him could drain the life from us.

I stood there, motionless, throat dry and skin still marked by Adrián's prints. How could I tell them when I couldn't even fully understand what it meant to belong to him?

The air in the living room was unbearable, a courtroom where the sentence had already been passed. Their voices lashed at me: my father's fury, my mother's silent plea. And I, trapped in the middle, could only feel the vertigo of my secret about to explode.

"Who is that man?" my father repeated, roaring, the table trembling under his fist.

I swallowed hard. The trembling in my hands betrayed me, but something inside me hardened. I couldn't keep lying, I couldn't keep pretending anymore... but I also wasn't going to betray what I had with Adrián.

"Yes, I'm with someone," I finally said, my voice steady even though inside I was falling apart. "And I won't deny it."

Silence fell instantly, heavier than any scream. My mother clutched her chest, her eyes brimming with tears. My father stared at me as if my words had struck a hidden nerve, something he didn't want anyone to name.

"With someone?" he repeated, his voice tense, charged with a rage that seemed to go beyond me. "Who is it?"

I held his gaze, drawing a deep breath, determined not to give him what he wanted.

"That doesn't matter. The only thing you need to know is that I'm fine."

Fury tightened his jaw, but behind his eyes there was something else... a different shadow. It wasn't just anger: it was fear. As if my words had brushed against a buried secret, one he had been hiding for years.

The air became unbreathable. His stare pierced me, not searching for the truth about Adrián... but terrified that I might uncover the truth about him.

I didn't want to drag the conversation out any longer. I went upstairs and locked myself in my room, slamming the door shut. I leaned against the wood and released the breath I'd been holding. My hands shook, my skin still burned with the marks of the night... and in my chest thundered the certainty that the real danger wasn't just my parents finding out.

It was that my father was hiding something. And sooner or later, I was going to uncover it too.

I walked to the window and pulled back the curtain. Outside, the sunbathed the streets in a deceptive calm: everything seemed normal, quiet, routine. But inside me there was no calm. I collapsed onto the bed, burying my face in the pillow, trying to smother the memory. Useless. He was in my skin, in my mouth, in every breath. And worst of all, he was also in my mind, like a question chasing me without mercy:

How long can I keep this hidden?

The morning passed with Camila's calls, her excitement spilling through the line.

"Happy birthday! What are we doing today, Lucía? Dinner? At least go out for a bit?"

I smiled, though the smile never reached my eyes.

"Nothing, Cami. It's Thursday... I'll just stay home and watch a movie."

Her silence weighed more than any reproach. I didn't understand why I said no either. It was my birthday. I should have felt special, loved, celebrated. Instead, I was here, trapped between the knot in my chest and the echo of my own secrets.

I kept telling myself it was better this way: a day without complications, without risks. But deep inside me, doubt burned hotter than any birthday candle:

Would Adrián be able to let my day pass as if nothing had happened?

The television murmured in a corner, but I wasn't watching. I was waiting. Waiting for a signal that never came.

Until the phone buzzed on the bedside table. My heart punched in my chest even before I looked at the screen. When I did, the air left me.

I'm waiting for you at home. Don't be late.

No greeting, no explanation. Just that dry, dangerous order, written with the certainty of someone who doesn't accept no.

I froze, the phone trembling between my fingers. It was my birthday, and he didn't even mention the date. And yet that single sentence said it all: he didn't forget. He knew what today meant... and still he claimed me as his, as if my celebration only existed to the extent that I belonged to him.

I felt breathless. Part of me wanted to resist, to say no. But the truth hit me hard: I had no choice. When Adrián calls, the whole world disappears.

I dressed quickly, though every movement felt dictated by a desire that wasn't mine. I opened the closet, and my hands chose on their own: a pale pink dress, light, innocent... the perfect irony against the darkness I knew awaited. Beneath it, black lace clung to my skin like a secret made only for him.

A few drops of perfume brushed my neck. The flush on my cheeks wasn't from makeup: it was the fire his message sparked. I pulled my hair into a high ponytail, leaving my face exposed, vulnerable... ready.

The mirror returned a brutal truth: I was no longer the naive Lucía I once was. I was a woman running toward the forbidden, aware this road had no return.

I stepped out in silence, heart racing, the cool street greeting me like an accomplice. My sandals struck the pavement—quick, eager. Each step brought me closer to him, to that house that was no longer a place but an altar of danger where Adrián waited.

I raised my hand to touch the door... but I didn't make it. The latch clicked, and suddenly he appeared. His dark shirt contrasted with my light dress; his eyes devoured me before I could breathe.

He takes me by the waist and pulls me to him with a brutality that steals my air. The door slams shut behind me with a hard thud. His mouth falls on mine—fiery, voracious—a kiss that leaves no space for words.

His tongue invades mine with fury, the cold of the piercing burning against my mouth. He pins me to the hallway wall, immobilizing me at the threshold of his world. My hands reach for his shoulders, but he captures them, dominating me even on the first breath.

"I knew you'd come, princesa..." he whispers against my lips, his hot breath igniting me more than the kiss itself. "You can't escape me, not even on your own birthday."

His knee wedges between my thighs, parting them, pressing firmly right where I burn. I gasp, lost in his control, in the way he claims me from the very first second.

The danger isn't outside anymore. It's here, inside this house.

"I'm preparing something for you," he murmurs, brushing my lips with his, wearing that dangerous smile that both excites and confuses me.

He takes my hand and leads me into the kitchen. The sweet scent of sugar and batter hits me before the surprise does. My eyes widen at the scene before me.

"Are you... baking me a cake?" I ask, incredulous, my voice breaking somewhere between laughter and disbelief.

Adrián arches a brow, his green eyes glinting with that spark that mixes tenderness with devastation.

"What did you think, princesa? That I only know how to devour you?"

Before I can answer, he lifts me effortlessly—pure strength, pure virility—and sets me on the cold marble counter, face to face with him. His hands return unhurriedly to the bowl where he's beating egg whites for the meringue. The scene is as absurd as it is erotic: the man who pressed me against a railing just nights ago now plays with sugar as though nothing could be more natural.

His strong arm moves with precision, and the contrast burns inside me: that mix of restrained brutality and hidden tenderness. I watch him in silence, my heart racing, knowing that even while whipping meringue, Adrián is still the most dangerous man in my life.

And more addictive than ever.

"Sweet... but still not enough," he murmurs, tasting it from his finger with the tongue.

Adrián smirks, and this time the whisk dips back into the mixture. Slowly, he approaches me, dips his fingertips into the meringue, and traces a line across my collarbone, leaving a sticky white trail on my skin.

"Now... perfect," he whispers before leaning down and licking me with a deep, hungry groan, his piercing grazing my flesh as he sucks the sugar from my body.

My fingers clutch the edge of the counter, my legs part instinctively to draw him closer. He smiles, scoops another portion of meringue, and this time places it at the center of my chest, right between my breasts, letting it drip slowly downward.

"I want to taste you sweeter than you already are, princesa..." his husky voice drives me insane as his tongue descends, savoring every drop, every curve.

Adrián, once again, turning me into his dessert.

The cold meringue slides down my skin as his tongue follows it—licking, savoring, dragging moans from me I can no longer contain. His hands grip my waist, pulling me against him as though he's afraid I might escape that delicious torture.

With a sudden, controlled movement, he pushes me back, my body meeting the marble behind me. His hands grip the edge of my pale pink dress, lifting it slowly—painfully slow—up my legs, over my waist, until the last slip of fabric is gone.

I'm left exposed beneath him, and the way his green eyes move over me feels less like he's looking—and more like he's claiming what he's always believed was his.

"Look at you, princesa..." he murmurs, his gravelly voice rough, his sugar-stained fingers gliding across my abdomen. "Covered in sweetness, and still the most addictive thing is you."

His mouth finds my breasts, lips closing around my hardened nipples, sucking hard, the taste of meringue melting against my skin. My gasp echoes through the kitchen.

I can feel his erection pressed against me, only the thin lace of my lingerie keeping us apart. He grins against my chest, rolls his hips once—and I tremble, already undone. With a single pull, he rips the lace away, leaving me naked beneath him, vulnerable and wanting.

Adrián dips his fingers into the bowl, thick white meringue clinging to them as he lifts his hand. That wicked smile returns as he spreads it over my thighs, slow and deliberate, like he's tracing ownership into my skin.

My legs tremble, trying to resist, but he spreads them open with that ruthless control that always leaves me breathless—his, and only his. The sticky sweetness slides upward, slow and deliberate, until it reaches the place where I'm most vulnerable.

I freeze when he smears the meringue over my skin, branding me with a wicked sort of tenderness. And then his mouth follows. His tongue—hot, possessive, merciless— licks every trace of sweetness from me, until all that's left is heat and him. The touch of his piercing brushes my clit, a metallic shock that tears a cry from my lips.

My body arches, trembling, and in that instant, I'm gone—consumed, undone, a captive to the pleasure he feeds like an addiction.

"That's it…" he growls against my skin, never stopping, devouring me as if sugar alone could never be enough. "There's no dessert sweeter than you, princesa."

The world disappears. There is only his mouth, his tongue, the fire that consumes me every time he reminds me, I'm lost in him. And as he plays with me this way, I know there's no escape: Adrián is pure ecstasy.

His lips cling to my flesh with hunger, his tongue tracing every corner with a slow, torturous rhythm—then faster, sharper—until I lose my mind.

I feel his hands forcing me open, holding me down against the cold stone as he plays with me like he already knows every secret I try to hide. His tongue moves in slow, perfect circles over my clit— wet, patient, devastating.

My breathing shatters into helpless gasps, my fingers gripping the edge for balance, my legs trembling as he keeps me open, bound in his control— no escape, no mercy, only him.

"That's it, princesa… I need to hear you," he whispers against me, his voice rough, trembling through my moans— before sinking back in, slower, deeper, moving like a man who's memorized my every weakness, every secret my skin ever tried to hide.

I can't take it anymore.

My back arches as the tremor rises from deep inside and tears me apart. Everything in me fractures, surrenders, and for a moment I can't tell where my body ends and his begins. My legs try to close, but Adrián doesn't let me; he holds me firm, making sure to drink every shiver, every drop, every sound he pulls from my throat.

When my body finally gives in—spent and trembling—all I can do is sink my fingers into his hair, unable to speak, still shaking from what he's just given me. He smiles against my skin, satisfied, like a predator savoring his favorite prey.

The taste of climax still pulses through me as Adrián straightens slowly, as if he's just finished a task, calm where I am undone. He glances at me, lips wet and glistening with my essence, and smiles with that dangerous calm that breaks me all over again.

"Time to put the icing on the cake," he says in that husky, gravelly tone, the innocent phrase carrying a double edge only I can understand.

And then, without giving me another second of attention, he turns back to his bowl, whisking with precision as if nothing had happened as if he hadn't just stolen my soul with his tongue.

I remain there, sprawled on the cold marble, naked, my legs still trembling, my skin ablaze. Stunned. Obsessed. Feeling like his unfinished dessert while he continues preparing as though I'm just another ingredient in his recipe.

And in that calculated abandonment, in that erotic indifference, I discover Adrián's true power: he doesn't just claim me... he reminds me that he alone decides when I burn and when I'm left alone with the fire he's lit inside me.

I watch him with his back to me, moving with infuriating calm, as if nothing we just lived through had actually happened. His shirt hangs open, his broad back framed under the dim kitchen light, his steady hands whisking the mixture with absurd focus.

He dips a finger into it, tastes, and smiles with the quiet satisfaction of someone who controls every detail. And me, burning in my own skin, I understand that nothing is more erotic than this silent power with which he dominates me without even touching me.

He doesn't look at me, doesn't hurry. He keeps me there, naked on the counter, suspended between the pleasure he gave and the pleasure he denied. And I let him—I watch in silence that unravels me, every second stretching the tension tighter, sharper, until it's unbearable.

Finally, he opens the oven and slides the tray with the cake inside. He shuts the door with a sharp thud, wipes his hands with a towel, and then he turns toward me.

His green eyes find mine—devouring, blazing—as if dessert isn't the only thing he plans to taste tonight. He takes a few steps toward me, slow, with the certainty of a man who never loses control, and his gravelly voice slices the air like a whip.

"Now... where were we?"

Adrián approaches slowly, like a predator savoring the moment before the strike. He stops in front of me, tilts his head, and smiles—that dangerous smile that melts me. His stained fingers trace along my thigh, brushing the sticky meringue left on my skin. He gathers it with unhurried ease and brings it to his mouth, sucking it off.

"Still sweet..." he murmurs, his husky voice stroking me like a threat. "But I know I can make you even more delicious."

His hands climb—one to my hip, the other to my breast—squeezing, shaping, forcing a moan from my lips. I lean back, searching for support, as he continues his exploration unhurriedly, as though every inch of me were part of the recipe he's perfecting.

His mouth finds my neck, licking the sugar that melted there, biting down hard enough to wrench another gasp from me.

"You can't imagine how much I enjoy tasting you like this... covered in sugar, trembling, waiting for me to devour you again."

I arch against him, my breath unraveling, while his tongue follows a slow path downward, tracing the sweet trails clinging to my skin. The waiting becomes *unbearable, because I know that any second now, he'll cross that line and plunge me back into the fire.*

But he doesn't. He stops just before, his hand gripping my hips firmly, his smile stretching wider.

"Do you want more, princesa? Ask for it."

Once again, he traps me in that exquisite mix of frustration and desire that threatens to consume everything.

I lock eyes with him, my breathing uneven, his hand still anchoring my hips, his mouth so close to where I need him most.

I know what he wants: for me to beg, to yield. But instead, I smile.

"More?" I repeat, my voice trembling but laced with defiance. "No, Adrián… I don't think I'll be asking this time."

His green eyes ignite, as if I've just lit a dangerous fuse. The smile on his lips tightens—half lust, half restrained rage.

I lean into him, bring my lips to his ear, and whisper with wicked intent:

"Today it's your turn to beg."

The silence that follows is so thick it prickles my skin. I feel his breath pounding at my neck, the heat of his body vibrating with tension, the subtle tremor in his fingers now digging harder into my flesh.

And then I understand: I've just challenged a man who does not accept defeat.

He pulls back slightly, his eyes locked on mine, and smiles with that darkness that both melts me and terrifies me.

"You love playing with fire, princesa..." he murmurs, low and gravelly, thick with danger. "Very well."

"I think you need a bath,"

I don't have time to respond. He lifts me against his body with the same ruthless determination he uses to claim what's his. I cling to his neck, adrenaline flooding hot in my veins as his steps carry me from the kitchen to the bathroom.

The door swings open, and warm steam coils around us. He sets me down beside the shower, my feet barely grazing the cold tile, while his green eyes devour me whole.

He moves slowly, every motion deliberate, calculated, like a man who knows exactly how much power he holds over me. His shirt is the first to go, revealing a body sculpted by control and sin, the dim light sliding across his skin like a lover's touch. He lets the fabric fall carelessly, knowing the effect it has. I bite down on my lip, helpless beneath the weight of his gaze. The sound of the zipper lowering sends a tremor through me, my breath catching as the tension builds. His erection strains against the fabric, a promise and a threat, and when he finally strips the last piece away, he stands before me— bare, commanding, devastatingly calm—the embodiment of everything I crave and everything that could ruin me.

My lips part; my breath quickens. I am overflowing with need, caught in the spectacle of seeing him like this: naked, dangerous, devastating.

He smiles with that blend of lust and control that poisons me.

"Do you like what you see, princesa?" he asks.

The shower roars to life, water pounding down, filling the room with steam. Adrián guides me inside, his hands anchoring my hips, until the hot cascade strikes my bare skin.

He positions himself behind me, his hands exploring— stomach, waist, breasts—as though the water itself could never be enough to cover me. His fingers circle languidly over my wet skin, and his mouth finds my neck, kissing, biting, licking the streams that run between us.

"Look at me, princesa..." he whispers at my ear. "What is it you want from me?"

His hand slides lower, between my thighs. The heat of the water sharpens every sensation. He parts me firmly, his fingers exploring with cruel precision, tormenting every nerve until my knees weaken. I press against the *cold tiles, arching my back as his touch and the relentless heat drive me mad.*

I feel him—hard, powerful—rubbing against my skin from behind, but he doesn't hurry. He teases me, grinding into me, marking me with his erection without entering, as though making me wait is part of the punishment.

The steam wraps around us, my moans drowned by the shower, and each brush drags me closer to the edge. I want him inside me now, but he keeps playing, stretching out the torment, savoring my desperation.

He grabs my hair, tugging it back just enough to force me to meet his gaze from the corner of my eye.

"Say it, Lucía," he commands. "Tell me how much you need me."

I glance at him sideways, breathless, my soaked hair clinging to my cheeks.

"Say it?" I whisper with a defiant smile. "No, Adrián... I won't give you that pleasure."

His eyes gleam with restrained fury, and for an instant it feels as if the water itself begins to boil around us. I feel his hand tighten around the back of my neck, his grip firm, his lips curve into that dark, dangerous smile.

"You keep playing with fire, princesa..." he murmurs against my ear, his deep, vibrating voice making every pore on my body rise. "And you know better than to play with me"

His fingers reach me again, the rhythm quickening, deeper now, more deliberate, circling my clit until breathless moans escape against my bitten lips. The water runs between us, tracing every line of heat and want, blurring where my control ends and his begins. Then, suddenly, he turns me and lowers himself, his mouth finding the exact spot that shatters me.

"So sweet..." he growls, his husky voice vibrating against my flesh. "And still, you dare defy me."

My knees buckle, but he holds me steady—one hand on my hip, the other spreading me wide—dragging me closer and closer to the edge. Hot water pours down my back, his mouth consumes me, and I unravel into gasping moans, still refusing to give him what he craves: my plea.

My breath fractures, the climax hovers dangerously close—when suddenly he stops. He pulls away, leaving me shaking, and I can feel the curve of his dark smile even without seeing it.

"Not yet, princesa," he murmurs, biting into my thigh hard enough to make me cry out. "Not until you beg."

And in that instant, I know his game: he will play with me until I have no choice left but to break.

My legs tremble, my breath is chaos, waves of pleasure crashing through me, threatening to tear me apart. Adrián holds me with brutal strength, playing with my body as if it belongs to him... and it does. Yet I cling to *the only weapon I still possess, denying him what he wants most.*

"I'm not going to beg," I whisper between gasps. "Even if you kill me with pleasure, Adrián... I won't."

With unexpected strength, I seize his chin, forcing him to look at me. His green eyes blaze with fury and desire, but I don't falter.

"Today, you'll be the one begging for me," I say, my voice trembling but laced with defiance.

Silence falls—thick, suffocating. Water streams down his face, tracing every line of his jaw, every tense muscle in his neck. For a second, I think he'll break me in half... but he doesn't move. He gives me space. He lets me.

And I don't waste it.

Slowly, I slide down until I'm kneeling in front of him. The hot cascade runs down my back, relentless, while my hair clings to my skin. My hands trace his hips before wrapping around the rigid length of him. I take him in my grasp, gentle at first, locking eyes with him, savoring the flicker of surprise, the tremor in his breath.

"Look at me, Adrián..." I whisper, low and provocative. "Today, I'll be the one to make you lose control."

His hand braces against the wall, muscles taut, and when I slide my mouth over him—slow, wet, deliberate— a guttural growl escapes his throat. That savage sound confirms what I already know: this time it's different. This time I have him caught in my game.

My lips move with a measured rhythm; my fingers tighten; my tongue teases the steel of his desire. And then I feel it—his body trembling beneath my control. For the first time, it's Adrián who moans, who gasps, who fights against the pleasure overwhelming him.

Kneeling under the shower, water pouring over me, I savor every second of watching him lose himself.

I take him deeper, playing with the rhythm, my tongue dragging slowly, then quickening, forcing guttural groans from deep in his chest. Sounds that aren't just pleasure.

I lift my gaze. And there it is. His green eyes, usually sharp and unyielding, are locked on mine, burning with a dangerous mix of lust and something else... something that steals my breath. Fascination.

I never imagined I'd see that expression on his face. Adrián—the man who never falters, who commands every moment, who consumes me without mercy—now looks at me as if he's found something that terrifies and mesmerizes him at once. As if I were the secret he was never meant to touch. His fingers slip into my hair, not to control me, but to anchor himself, as though I've become the only solid thing left in his world.

"Lucía..." he breathes my name between gasps, his voice raw, laced with a vulnerability I barely recognize.

And in that moment, I know: I have him. I've dragged him to the edge of himself. Adrián is as lost in me as I am in him.

A strange, delicious, dangerous sensation floods me. Because as he looks at me in fascination, I realize that for the first time... the power in this storm is mine.

I pull back slowly, letting the water wash away the traces of my daring. Rising to my feet, lips still wet, my eyes never leave his. He follows me with that searing gaze, burning, stripping me bare more than the water cascading down my body.

I step closer until my mouth hovers just a breath from his. My hands press against his soaked chest, feeling his heart pound violently beneath my touch. And then, I whisper against his lips:

"You'll never find another who tastes like me—ever."

His pupils dilate, his breath falters, and a guttural growl tears from him, as if my words had shattered his last restraint. His hands clamp hard around my waist, and his mouth crashes onto mine in a searing kiss— fierce, overflowing, devouring my defiance until it bends into his.

And in that kiss, I feel it: I drive him mad. I lose him. I find him. All at once.

His kiss is wildfire—savage and desperate. Yet within that fury, his arms wrap around me, lifting me effortlessly into the air. My back slams against the slick shower wall, water cascading over us like a burning veil.

Every touch is a collision of opposites: slow tenderness, kisses that feel like worship... tangled with the pressure of his hands branding me, with the insistent rub of his hard length, aching to be inside me.

"I don't know if I'm possessing you or losing myself in you..." he murmurs, his voice rough and breaking against my skin.

His green eyes meet mine, and for the first time, I see more than control—more than dominance. I see the hunger of a man who needs me as much as he fears it.

His lips find mine again, slow, deep, each kiss a confession he'll never speak. The water burns between us as he presses me harder against the wall, and it hits me— Adrián may own me, but in this moment, he's the one unraveling. His mouth stays on mine as he shifts, holding me firmly, his erection sliding against me, teasing, testing every ounce of patience I have left.

When he finally pushes inside, it's with a slow, deliberate power, each movement a prayer, a punishment, a promise carved into my skin. The water flows between us, amplifying every gasp, every tremor he drags from me. My body meets him in frantic need, but he keeps control—stretching every second into torture, every thrust into surrender—until there's nothing left of me but the way he moves inside me.

"Feel every second, princesa..." he murmurs, his deep voice crashing hot against my lips. "I want you to remember this for the rest of your life."

My eyes flutter shut; moans escape me, lost in that intoxicating mix of tenderness and absolute possession.

His breath scorches my neck before his lips claim my collarbone, marking me with kisses and bites, all while subjecting me to the relentless sway of his desire.

The dark, dangerous, brutal man now takes me with devastating slowness, as if he wanted to savor me whole, to carve every piece of me into memory. And I melt, trapped in his poisoned tenderness, knowing this moment is not just sex—it is a silent confession he will never dare to speak aloud.

Each stroke pulls soft, lingering moans from my lips, my body trembling with every push and pull.

His gaze never leaves mine. He pins me to the wall with his usual unyielding strength, but his green eyes blaze with a different fire. His mouth returns to mine, kissing me slow, wet, in sync with the sway of our hips.

"That's it... let go," he murmurs against my lips, his husky voice stroking every nerve in me.

And I give in. The tremor starts deep, crawling up through me until my breath splinters and disappears. Pleasure claims me slowly, in steady, burning waves—a patient fire that devours every corner of me until I'm emptied, undone. The climax takes me completely, slow and consuming, each pulse dragging another sound from me, each shudder echoing through the steam until nothing exists but him.

Adrián holds me tight, guiding me through the fall, prolonging it, shaping it, owning it. I break apart under his touch, and in that ruin, I find the closest thing to peace.

When the tremors fade, I bury my face in his neck, gasping, trembling, unable to move. He smiles against my skin, the kind of smile that feels both satisfied and dangerous—like my pleasure was the masterpiece he'd been creating all along. I think I'm spent, but he doesn't stop.

His rhythm stays deep and steady, each thrust slower, heavier, as if determined to draw every last tremor from my body. His mouth moves along my throat, my shoulder, murmuring my name like a prayer and a claim. His hands tighten around my hips, keeping me where he wants me, until I feel another wave rise—fierce, unrelenting.

My breath breaks into ragged moans, my back arches against the wall, and when it hits, it's wild, uncontrollable. The second orgasm tears through me, and as the steam swirls around us, I scream his name— without knowing if it's out of pleasure, surrender… or addiction

Adrián tenses with me, his chest pounding against mine, his ragged gasps turning into a deep, guttural growl as he finally surrenders. He explodes in one final thrust, hard and absolute, releasing all of his force inside me.

The water keeps falling, mingling with the sweat and the electricity still vibrating between our bodies. His arms hold me while my legs tremble, and for an instant we are not shadow and light, not danger and addiction... we are just two broken bodies, fused in the same shiver.

I rest my forehead against his shoulder, panting, feeling his breath mixing with mine. And in that moment, in the midst of steam and water, a dangerous certainty seizes me: Adrián is my ruin.

He is very still. His hands remain firm on my waist, holding me as if he were afraid to let go. Then he lowers his head and rests his forehead against mine, closing his eyes. His voice, when it comes, is barely a whisper, trembling, unlike anything I've ever heard from him before.

"I don't know what the hell you do to me, Lucía..." he murmurs, and I feel the warm brush of his breath against my lips. "But with you... everything is different."

I shiver. That unexpected tenderness, that crack in his voice, shakes me more than all his rages combined. Because what I hear is not the man who dominates me, but someone lost, searching for shelter in me.

I lift my hand and brush his damp cheek with my fingertips. And in his green eyes, open once again, I see something that breaks me: fascination. Vulnerability. As if, for one second, he had forgotten the darkness that surrounds him.

Then he kisses me, slow, deep, unhurried. A kiss that doesn't claim or punish—only gives. And that gesture confuses me, terrifies me, because in it I discover a danger greater than his hidden world: the possibility that I might begin to love him.

"Come on, princesa…" he murmurs, brushing my lips with his before giving me one last gentle bite. "Your birthday cake should be ready."

The phrase tears a shaky laugh from me, tangled with the knot in my chest. Because in that impossible contrast—the brutality of minutes ago, the tenderness that nearly melted me, and now the man who bakes a cake as if it were the most natural thing in the world—lies the true poison.

He lowers me slowly from the wall, my bare feet slipping on the wet tile, and offers me a towel. I wrap myself in it, still trembling, while he dries his torso and slides back into his pants with that provocative calm that drives me insane. I follow him in silence toward the kitchen, my heart racing, still torn between the fire of his possession and the impossible tenderness of that gesture.

I search for my pale pink dress, pick it up from the floor, and slip it back on with clumsy hands, still feeling the burn of his skin against mine.

Adrián opens the oven, carefully pulls out the pan, and sets it on the table. The contrast is as absurd as it is beautiful: the man who devoured me with brutal hunger minutes ago now checks, calmly, to see if the cake is baked through.

He turns toward me with a crooked smile, his green eyes gleaming under the dim light.

"It won't be perfect, princesa... but it's yours."

I step closer, hesitant, my heart pounding hard. He cuts a slice and places it before me on a plain plate. No candles, no decorations, nothing that resembles a party—but I feel like no birthday has ever been this intimate, this mine.

I take a bite, the sweetness filling my mouth, and suddenly my eyes sting with tears. Adrián watches me in silence, that serious expression of his never fully softening, yet I know he's truly looking at me, as if waiting for my reaction.

"It's... perfect," I whisper.

He barely smiles, tilts his head, and wipes a trace of sugar from my lip with his thumb. That simple gesture shakes me more than any of his furious outbursts—because in it there is something that seems impossible for Adrián: tenderness.

And as I savor the last bite, I realize this cake isn't just a gift. It's his way of telling me, without words, that I am different to him. And that thought terrifies me more than any secret he still hides.

I'm about to take another bite when a sharp noise bursts at the front door. I flinch, and Adrián stiffens instantly, the warmth in his eyes vanishing in a blink. The sound of heavy, dragging footsteps echoes down the hall, followed by a slammed door that rattles the house.

"Adrián!" A hoarse, slurred voice, thick with alcohol, shatters the silence. "Adrián, damn you, get out here now!"

The plate trembles in my hands. I turn toward him, searching for answers, but Adrián is already on his feet, jaw clenched, his green eyes lit with barely contained fury. He strides over, seizes my face in both hands, and forces me to meet his gaze.

"Lucía, leave. Right now," he orders, his voice low, rough, laced with danger that leaves no room for argument.

I try to protest, to ask what's happening, but the drunken roar shakes the house again, and Adrián grips my chin tighter, his eyes cutting straight through me.

"Don't argue. Go out the back door and don't stop."

His gaze pins me, merciless, and I know there's no space for defiance. I swallow hard, my heart pounding against my ribs, and give him the slightest nod. Adrián lets go of my face, but not of my eyes—he holds me in that silence heavy with orders, as if making sure I understand that this time there is no game, no challenge.

I rise clumsily from the table, leaving the plate behind, and walk toward the back door. Each step feels heavy, as if leaving now were betrayal, but the roar of the drunken voice echoing down the hall forces me to hurry.

I push the door and step outside. The cool night air slaps my face, but it brings no relief. My hands tremble, my chest burns, and my legs move on their own until I find myself out on the dark, empty street.

I stop, breathing hard, watching the house from a distance. I want to go back, to know what's happening… but his words ring in my head: Don't argue.

When I finally get home, the glare of the lights hits me like a warning. I push the door slowly, trying not to make a sound, but it's useless: they're already waiting.

My mother sits rigid on the sofa, fixing me with a sharp, probing look as if she could strip every secret from my skin. My father, meanwhile, doesn't need words: his silence burns, fierce, a contained fire that could erupt at any moment.

"Where were you, Lucía?" my mother asks, her voice edged with something that cuts deeper than a shout.

I swallow. My throat is dry, my hands shaking, my lips still hot with the taste of Adrián. The contrast suffocates me.

"I went out... I needed to clear my head," I answer, my voice a fragile thread that sounds weaker than I mean it to.

My father leans forward, elbows on his knees, jaw clenched. There's more than anger in his gaze: a darker flash, as if the fury conceals a fear he refuses to name.

"With whom?" he spits, each syllable a blow to my chest.

The silence that follows wraps around me like a rope. His stare cuts through me like a knife, and I feel myself bleeding from the inside. I can't tell the truth. I can't name him. And yet I know my body betrays me—that guilt smolders on my skin.

I clutch my hands in my lap, avoiding those eyes that seem to know too much. And then I understand: the storm isn't only Adrián. It's here too, in my own house, pulsing in my father's secrets.

He leans in closer, so near I can feel the weight of his breath. His voice, low and hoarse, thunders like a cursed secret ready to shatter everything:

"Don't lie to me, Lucía... I know who he is."

The words rumble through the room, relentless. He pauses, and his eyes darken as if speaking the name tears at him.

"That man... Adrián."

The air cuts sharp. His name hangs between us like a sentence. I lift my head abruptly, lips parted, but no words come out.

My father clenches his jaw, muscles tight, and in his eyes there's not only fury: there's something deeper—fear, raw and unspoken.

"We've been neighbors our whole lives," he continues, voice hard as stone. "I know who Adrián is… and I know what he's involved in."

He leans closer, his stare slicing into me.

"I'm warning you, Lucía: don't ever go near him again."

Heat rises in my throat, burning hotter than his words.

"I just turned twenty-two, and you still think you can decide for me?"

He straightens in the armchair, eyes dark, braced for my rebellion.

"I can take care of myself. I don't need you forbidding me anything."

The silence that follows shatters like glass. My mother presses her lips together, unable to intervene, while my father closes his fists, fury trembling through his hands.

In a sudden move, he's on his feet. The room fills with his shadow. His eyes burn into me, but behind the rage there's something else: a darker shadow, a secret he won't name.

"You don't understand anything, Lucía," he growls, his voice more a plea disguised as a command. "That man is not for you. He never will be."

He steps closer, the air tightening around us like a noose.

"Adrián is not someone you should get involved with. I know what he carries... because I watched him grow. Because I know what he hides."

His jaw tightens; fury and fear collide in his gaze.

"And that's why—even if you hate me, even if you defy me—I won't allow it."

My heart jolts. The way he says it... it isn't simple hatred toward Adrián. It's knowledge. My father knows something—something he's keeping from me. And his anger isn't just against me. It's against a past he's desperate to keep buried.

I open my mouth to ask, but he cuts me off with a sharp, final gesture.

"Don't insist. There are truths you should never know."

His words strike me like an invisible wall, leaving me with more questions than answers. And as I look at him, a chilling realization grips me: my father doesn't just want to keep me away from Adrián... he wants to shield himself from a secret he's entangled in too.

The silence between us thickens until it suffocates. My father stands there, face carved in stone, fists clenched, as if holding back costs him more than letting go. I study him, searching for a crack, some trace of truth—but there's nothing. Only a cold, impenetrable wall.

Without a word, I rise. My steps echo hollow against the floor as I head for the stairs. I feel their eyes on my back, heavy with reproach and fear, but I don't stop. I climb with my pulse racing and lock myself in my room.

I collapse onto the bed, still in my dress, and cover my face with my hands. The echo of his words won't leave me: "I know what he carries... because I watched him grow, because I know what he hides."

I don't know what dark secret binds Adrián and my father, but I know this: the more they try to keep me away, the deeper I'll be dragged toward the truth. And when I finally uncover it... not even my own blood will be spared from what comes next.

Chapter 13

✦ ✦ ✦ ✦ ✦ ✦

The doorbell rang early, cutting through my thoughts like a sharp blow. I went downstairs and found Camila stepping in with her usual energy—radiant, carrying several bags that clinked against her body. Her aura of enthusiasm lit up the room in a way that felt almost cruel: she seemed to shine brighter than ever, while my own world felt dimmer each day.

"Lucía!" she exclaimed, dropping everything onto the couch. "You have no idea the chaos in my head right now. The wedding is in two days, and I still have half the things left to do."

I watched her in silence, struck by how differently her universe pulsed compared to mine. She rushed, laughed, spoke fast; every word of hers brimming with plans and certainty. I, on the other hand, remained chained to Adrián's shadows... and to my father's secrets that weighed on me like invisible shackles.

Camila began pulling out envelopes, fabrics, flower samples—little details that had to be ready before the big day. Her hands moved quickly, her laughter filled the room, and I forced a smile just to avoid bursting her bubble. I picked up one of the bags, peeked inside, and something sparked within me: two days. Just two days before her life changed forever. And I couldn't even be sure if mine wouldn't explode before then.

I sank into the armchair, but Adrián's words returned, sharp and relentless: Not everything that shines is gold. They pierced my mind, and before I knew it, I had turned them into a question.

"Cami... how well do you really know Víctor?" I asked, trying to sound casual, though my voice shook more than I wanted.

She lifted her gaze, raising an eyebrow, surprised.

"What kind of question is that? Well enough, Lú. We love each other, and that's what matters."

I swallowed hard, uneasy, playing with the edge of a fabric sample.

"It's not that I'm not happy for you... but don't you think this is a little rushed? You've only been together a few months, and now you're two days away from getting married."

Camila let the flowers fall with an exasperated sigh.

"Not this again..."

I lowered my voice, but I didn't back down. Adrián's warning kept drilling into my head like a thorn I couldn't ignore.

"It's just... I don't want you to blind yourself. Sometimes what looks perfect can be hiding the opposite."

She looked at me with her arms crossed, and for a second, I thought I saw a flicker of doubt in her eyes.

But immediately she straightened, lifted her chin, and gave me a look heavy with annoyance.

"Lucía, enough." Her tone was sharp, harder than usual. "I know what I'm doing. Victor is the man I want to marry, and nothing you say will change my mind."

I opened my mouth to insist, but she raised a hand—decisive, cutting my words before they could even form.

"I don't need your doubts right now. I need your support. So, if you really are my friend, help me make this day perfect."

Silence fell between us like a wall. Camila bent back over the flowers, the envelopes, the little details—feigning enthusiasm, as if with every gesture she were trying to bury the cracks I had just exposed. Her smile returned, but it was forced, a fragile veneer over the tension still hanging in the air.

I stayed frozen, a knot in my throat. I knew that if I kept pushing, I'd lose her. Pressing my lips together, I swallowed the words that burned inside me and finally forced a smile to preserve what little lightness remained.

Camila held out a bouquet, her tone suddenly light, as though the argument had never happened.

"Here, help me with this."

I nodded slowly, swallowing my anger and my fear.

"Of course, Cami. Whatever you need."

The days leading up to the wedding slipped away in a blur of ribbons, envelopes, and white flowers. Camila talked endlessly about dresses, guests, eternal promises... and I nodded, smiled, pretended to share her excitement. I buried my doubts beneath layers of routine, letting the tide of preparations carry me along without resistance.

And then, without realizing it, the morning of the wedding arrived. The house overflowed with movement: nervous laughter, sweet perfumes, shimmering fabrics flowing everywhere. Everything seemed bathed in a contagious happiness that, somehow, never reached me.

In front of the mirror, dressed for the occasion, a knot tightened in my stomach. Outside, Camila's life was about to change forever, while I remained trapped in my own shadows.

The garden smelled of fresh flowers and promises. The murmur of guests filled the air, glasses clinking under the sun. As maid of honor, I was supposed to smile, take care of details, calm Camila... and yet, I felt disguised. The soft tone of my dress wrapped me like a second skin that wasn't mine—a mask of serenity when inside me there was nothing but unrest.

Then I saw her. Camila appeared radiant in white, her happiness overflowing with a light that almost hurt to look at. And yet Adrián's words cut through me like a shadow: Not everything that shines is gold.

I looked up—and froze. Among the guests, at the back, Adrián was there. In a dark suit, flawless, magnetic even surrounded by strangers. Our eyes met for barely a second—enough to freeze the air. He didn't smile. He made no gesture. He only looked at me, as if his green eyes were a silent warning no one else could hear.

The ceremony flowed without a hitch: applause, vows, raised glasses. A perfect postcard. And yet, beneath the surface, I felt the danger pulsing, as if all that shine could shatter into a thousand pieces at any moment.

When we all moved into the main hall for the reception, lights, music, and laughter filled the air. I drifted among the guests, returning smiles and congratulations, but the tight dress clinging to my body felt like a constant reminder of his eyes fixed on me.

The din of the party seemed distant, muffled by the walls of the bathroom. In front of the mirror, I tried to compose myself: touching up my lipstick, smoothing a rebellious strand, pretending I still had control. Then the door slammed shut, and the air vanished.

I saw him reflected behind me—Adrián. His dark suit, his burning gaze, that presence that made the space too small for both of us.

"You look beautiful in that dress, princesa..." his husky voice grazed my skin, though he hadn't touched me. "The whole hall is watching you... but only I know what you're hiding underneath."

My heart pounded so hard it seemed to echo off the tiles. In the mirror, his eyes caught me, devouring me. The hall, the laughter, Camila's wedding... everything disappeared. It was only him and me, locked in that forbidden corner.

His steps were slow, sure, like a predator closing in. He stopped right behind me, so close I felt the heat of his body through my back. He didn't touch me; his hands hovered a breath from my skin, tracing my silhouette in the reflection as if he already owned me.

"Look at you..." he whispered in my ear, his breath burning like fire. "So perfect that all I want is to tear that dress off you, right here."

A traitorous gasp escaped my throat, and in the mirror, I saw the crooked smile form on his lips. He didn't kiss me. He simply let his mouth brush my neck—a cruel, fleeting touch, knowing the smallest contact was enough to drive me wild.

His hand slid slowly up my bare arm until it caught my wrist. He guided it to the mirror, forcing me to press my open palm against the cold glass.

"I want you to look at yourself, Lucía..." his breath scorched my ear. "I want you to see what you do to me."

His other hand finally settles on my hip, gripping hard, claiming me. My legs tremble, my lips search for air, and my eyes lock on my own reflection: a woman caught between danger and desire, surrendered to the dominance of a man who burns me with nothing more than words and barely-there touches.

His gaze in the mirror devours me with an intensity that shatters me. He doesn't need to do more; his green eyes alone strip me bare. But Adrián isn't in a hurry. That's his punishment.

The hand on my hip slides lower, tracing the curve of my tight dress. The fabric strains under his grip, and I bite my lip, watching in the mirror how I tremble beneath his control.

"Do you see how you shake, princesa?" he whispers in my ear, his tone dark, almost satisfied. "I don't need to tear this dress off... your body already begs, even if your mouth doesn't."

His lips graze the line of my neck, trail up to my ear, and the brush of his breath raises every hair on my skin. He forces me to keep my eyes open, to confront the reflection that betrays me: flushed cheeks, parted lips, chest rising and falling in desperation.

His hand leaves my hip, gliding over my stomach, stopping right where the fabric becomes an unbearable barrier. He caresses slowly, never quite reaching where my body craves him most. Each stroke is torment, a promise broken in slow motion.

"Look at yourself, Lucía..." he whispers, voice rough and low, the sound pulsing with the rhythm of my heartbeat. "That innocence you hide behind—no one else knows that here, with me, you melt with nothing but a touch... and you love it."

A strangled moan escapes me. His fingers keep teasing at the edge, denying me release, and the mirror becomes my cruelest judge: a woman flushed, vulnerable, completely his.

The reflection stares back at me, panting, glassy-eyed, lips swollen from biting. I'm one step from the edge—I know it, and Adrián knows it too. His hand moves with precision, drawing slow, perfect circles that set me ablaze through the thin fabric. Pleasure swells like a wave about to break... and just when I think I'll fall, he stops.

A ragged cry tears from me. My legs tremble, my body silently begs. But instead of giving in, Adrián smiles in the mirror, cruel and enthralled.

"Easy, princesa... we're not there yet," he murmurs, pressing my wrist harder against the glass as if to remind me who owns my reflection.

Then his fingers move again—faster, deeper—and the heat consumes me, dragging broken moans from my throat. My back arches, my breasts strain against the dress, and the mirror throws back the image of a woman undone by desire. I'm about to shatter again... when once more, he stops.

I close my eyes, desperate, but his grip seizes my chin, forcing them open.

"Eyes on the mirror, Lucía," he commands, his voice sharp and unyielding. "Look at what I can do to you without even taking your clothes off."

A sob, tangled with a moan, shakes me; the climax remains trapped inside me like an exquisite punishment. My reflection hurls back the truth: I'm lost, chained to him, prisoner of a desire only he can grant—or deny.

I'm on the verge of breaking when a sharp knock echoes against the door.

"Is it occupied?" a nervous female voice asks from the hallway.

Air seizes in my lungs. My eyes widen in the mirror, and the reflection betrays me—panting, caught in the storm Adrián has unleashed. I try to pull away, but his firm hand on my abdomen pins me to the glass.

He smiles—a dark, dangerous smile that prickles my skin. Leaning close, his lips brush my ear as he whispers with demonic calm:

"See, princesa? Even fate conspires to remind you your pleasure depends on me."

Another knock, louder this time. I hold my breath, terrified someone might push the door.

Adrián releases my wrist slowly, as though he has all the time in the world. With one final graze of his fingers, he steals a shudder from me yet still denies me the release my body craves. Then he steps back, smooths his jacket, runs a hand through his hair—impeccable, as if nothing had happened.

My breath is still ragged when he opens the door with ease and slips out, leaving the waiting guest behind. I remain glued to the mirror, trembling, frustrated, burning with the desire he once again refused me.

"Lú!" Camila's cheerful voice bursts through the hallway like a ray of light. "I've been looking for you everywhere."

Her reflection appears behind me, wrapped in her flawless white gown, eyes gleaming with excitement. She suspects nothing. Not the fire coursing through my skin, nor the poison gnawing at me from within.

"Are you okay?" she asks, stepping closer with an innocent smile, gently smoothing a stray lock of my hair. "I thought you got lost."

I force a soft laugh, lowering my gaze to hide the heat in my cheeks.

"Yes, yes... I just needed a moment to freshen up."

Camila hugs me tightly, oblivious to the storm raging inside me. Her sweet perfume surrounds me, and a pang stabs my chest. She is so pure, so radiant. And I, her best friend, stand trapped in a double life: the smiling bridesmaid at her wedding—and, at the same time, the secret addict to a dangerous man who just left me trembling.

The hall overflowed with laughter, music, and toasts, but I could barely breathe. The heat, the tension, the memory of what had happened in the bathroom... it all tightened around my chest. So, I excused myself with a smile and stepped outside, searching for a breath of fresh air.

The night greeted me with silence, broken only by the distant echoes of the reception. I inhaled deeply, letting the cold air steady me. But when my eyes drifted toward the parking lot, the world stopped.

Adrián was there.

Leaning against his car, a lit cigarette balanced between his fingers, smoke rising in lazy spirals that twisted into the night. His posture—relaxed, insolent—radiated danger, as if every small movement were a ritual meant to tempt me. Under the dim lamp glow, his figure seemed even more forbidden, impossible to ignore.

My steps faltered, but his gaze pinned me instantly. That green fire I knew too well burned from across the lot. He didn't smile, didn't speak, yet his presence alone was enough to make me tremble.

I walked toward him without thought, as if my feet no longer obeyed me. With each step, I remembered I was lost—that no matter what happened at Camila's wedding, no matter what my family suspected, Adrián was waiting. And I would always go to him.

When I reached him, his rough voice broke the silence, heavy with possession:

"Shall we go?"

I didn't need to think. There was no space for doubt. The moment I heard those two words; my body had already answered for me. I nodded, heart racing, and watched a dark smile curve his lips.

Adrián opened the car door with that confident gesture that always disarmed me, and I let him pull me inside—forgetting the music, the guests, the wedding itself. Everything vanished. Only his presence remained, wrapping me in danger, reminding me that once again I was throwing myself into the void with him.

I sank into the seat, and when he fired up the engine, the roar of the car fused with the pounding in my chest. I didn't know where he was taking me. I didn't know what awaited. But I knew I didn't want to be anywhere else.

The drive unfolded in charged silence, broken only by the growl of the engine and Adrián's steady hand gripping the wheel. My eyes drowned in the darkness of the road until the car finally slowed and stopped.

I looked up—and my stomach dropped. We were at a harbor, lit only by the yellowish lamps. The smell of salt and wet wood clung to the air, while the sound of water lapping gently against the docks filled the night with mystery.

Adrián killed the engine and got out without a word. He opened my door and offered his hand—strong, the same hand that always dragged me where he wanted. I took it and followed him, my heart burning.

At the end of the dock, I saw it.

A small but beautiful boat, anchored in silence as if it had been waiting only for us. Its white paint glowed beneath the moonlight, its reflection shimmering on the water like a fragile mirage.

"It's mine," Adrián said, his voice low, husky, heavy with possession. "And tonight, so are you."

The shiver that raced through me wasn't fear—it was desire. Because I understood that here, on this boat, there would be no witnesses, no rules. Only him... and me, trapped in my own addiction.

We stepped aboard in silence. The creak of the wood beneath our feet, the gentle sway of the waves—they created a secret music just for us. Adrián switched on a dim light inside the cabin and opened a small fridge, pulling out a bottle of red wine.

"Sit." The word was an order, though his tone carried an unusual softness.

I obeyed, settling onto a wooden bench. My eyes wandered over every detail: the neatly coiled ropes, the mast swaying in the wind, the silver path of the moon across the water.

Adrián poured two glasses and handed me one. His fingers brushed mine, and that fleeting contact set my skin ablaze—more intimate than a kiss. He sat across from me, his presence filling the cabin even in stillness.

"I've never brought anyone here," he said, his eyes locked on mine as he took a sip of wine.

My heart slammed against my chest. His words were simple, but the weight of everything left unsaid pressed down on me.

"Why me, Adrián?" I dared to ask, my voice barely a whisper tangled with the murmur of the sea.

He set his glass down, leaned forward, and let the silence stretch until it felt unbearable. Then, finally, he answered:

"Because with you… everything becomes dangerous in a different way."

His green eyes blazed under the moonlight, and for a moment I didn't see the brutal man who consumed me, but someone who had just allowed me a glimpse into a hidden corner of his life. The sight unsettled me more than his rage ever could.

The silence thickened, so dense I could hear every beat of my heart. The sway of the boat, the wine warming my hand, the mirror of the moon on the water— everything seemed to conspire to push me toward the truth burning in my throat.

I set my glass down. My lips trembled, but the words came out anyway.

"My father knows about us."

Adrián's gaze fixes on me, unblinking. For a second, even the sea seems to hold still, as if the waves themselves were waiting for his reaction. His lips tighten, his jaw hardens, but it's his green eyes that unravel me: burning with restrained fury, with something I can't tell if it's fear, rage... or both.

"What did he tell you?" His husky voice breaks the silence—low, dangerous, like distant thunder.

I swallow hard, holding his gaze even as my body trembles.

"That you grew up next to me. That your father is a drunk. And that you're not on the right path."

The wine burns in my throat like fire. I don't know if I expected denial, an explanation, or a touch that could erase my doubts. But all I get is Adrián's heavy silence, as if he's torn between telling me the truth... or protecting a secret that could destroy us both.

He stands abruptly, the glass rattling on the table with the force of his movement. His silhouette cuts against the moon, rigid, like a man holding back a hurricane.

"I shouldn't have brought you here," he says, his voice dry, harsh, so different from the calm of a moment ago.

The air leaves me all at once, as if his words had slammed straight into my chest. He takes a step toward the stairs leading up to the deck, and panic jolts through me.

"Wait!"

I spring to my feet, circling the table and grabbing his arm with both hands. I look into his eyes, pleading, searching for that spark of tenderness I know exists in him, no matter how hard he tries to bury it.

"Don't leave me like this, Adrián." My voice cracks. "Not after bringing me here, showing me this place. If I truly shouldn't be with you... you wouldn't have let me into your refuge."

His breathing quickens, his green eyes flickering between fury and something deeper—something fighting to break free and leaving me consumed by uncertainty.

For a moment, I think he'll pull away, break the distance, leave me standing there with empty hands. But he doesn't move. And in that stillness, the tension between us becomes unbearable.

With a sudden motion, he yanks me against him, and his mouth crashes onto mine with restrained rage—with the desperation clinging to his every breath.

His lips devour me as if he could erase my words, rip out my suspicions by the root, silence all the questions he'll never answer.

The taste of wine mixes with his scorching breath as my back slams against the wooden wall of the cabin. His hands roam my body without patience—gripping, claiming—as if touching me were the only way to make sure I'm still his despite everything standing between us.

I drown in his kiss—in the brutality and desire that consume me—realizing this is his language: the fury of a man who would rather possess me than open the door to his secrets.

And I... I let myself be swept away. Because even though I know he's silencing me, my body only wants to lose itself in the rage with which he kisses me.

He strips the dress from me with brutal speed, the straps sliding off my shoulders as if they'd never belonged there. The cold night air brushes my skin, but his heat devours it all. His mouth travels down my neck, leaving a trail of bites that burn like marks of possession.

"You're my ruin, Lucía..." he growls, his voice hoarse, trembling with lust and fury.

He steps back just enough to tear his shirt open, buttons scattering under the violence of his hands. The thud of fabric hitting the floor is almost as erotic as his fingers on my skin. Then he rips off his belt and pants with the same urgency, until he stands before me—naked, imposing, his virility claiming me without words.

The boat sways with the sea, matching his rhythm as if the waves themselves were pushing us to the edge of madness. He presses me against him, his hard, demanding erection grinding against my center, and a desperate moan rips from my throat.

Suddenly he spins me, bracing me against the cabin table. My hands clutch the edge, and before I can think, he drives into me with a brutal thrust that tears a strangled cry from my lips. The sound mingles with the creak of the wood and the roar of the sea outside.

Each of his movements is savage, devastating, as though he's carving his rage into my body because he refuses to confess it with words. I arch beneath him, lost, my skin gleaming under the moonlight, my voice shattering into moans that fill the cramped space.

The boat rocks harder, the world disappears, and only we remain: his fury, my surrender, and the fire consuming us in a wild encounter that threatens to destroy and save us all at once.

His rhythm is merciless, each stoke precise and punishing, breaking me open with unbearable pleasure. My nails rake the wood as my body gives itself without resistance, trembling, undone.

Suddenly his hand rises and comes down with a sharp smack across my buttocks. The sound cracks through the cabin, mingling with the boat's creak, and a ragged scream bursts from me. The sting burns, ignites me, and before I can catch my breath another slap lands—harder, desperate—as if each blow were his way of exorcising the frustration that consumes him.

"More!" I gasp, trembling beneath his control.

Adrián growls in my ear, plunging deeper, his hoarse voice drilling into my skin:

"I want to hear you, princesa…" another brutal thrust, another scream I can't hold back— "Give me your voice, give me your surrender."

My throat opens into an endless moan, my body vibrating with every command that strips me of will. His hand slides slowly down my back until it tangles in my hair. Suddenly he yanks, tearing out a strangled cry as my body yields without resistance. He forces me upright, my back crushed to his burning torso, slick with sweat— the feel of his skin against mine driving me mad.

His hands seize my breasts with cruel, exquisite precision, molding me as if I were only his to shape. I gasp, undone, and then I feel it—the wet, electric graze of his piercing along my ear. The shock bolts through me like lightning, leaving every nerve raw, my body begging for more.

"You're pure addiction, princesa," he murmurs against my ear, his tongue stroking each word like a sin. "And the worst part is you love being it."

My voice breaks in a sob laced with pleasure, and in the invisible reflection of the moon over the water, I understand I'm lost—every part of me answers only to him, to his strength, to his control, to the delicious damnation of surrendering to Adrián.

His breath crashes against my ear, matching the frantic rhythm of his relentless drive. One hand claims my breasts with ruthless precision, the other locks around my waist as if he'll never let go. The boat rocks. So does he. Each surge steals my breath. His tongue, his heat, his piercing—a flash of electricity that erases me. There's no escape. Only his craziness.

"Give it to me, princesa..." he growls, voice ragged, as though he's on the brink himself. "I want to feel you break against me."

And I break.

An orgasm detonates through me, ripping screams that vanish into the cramped cabin. My body convulses in his arms, my back arched, my skin slick against his as he presses me tighter, as if he wants to fuse me to him until no part of me exists apart.

His strength unmakes me. He lifts me in his arms, and sets me onto the cabin table. The shock of the cold wood bites into my fevered skin, and when I meet his gaze, he towers over me—imposing, merciless, his bare torso gleaming with sweat under the moonlight pouring through the hatch.

His hand clamps my chin with brutal control, forcing my eyes upward.

"Look at me, princesa," he orders, his hoarse voice leaving no room for doubt. "I want to see your face when you lose yourself in me again."

With every thrust, my body unravels, my voice breaking into desperate cries I can't contain. I'm raw, still shattered from the last climax, and each movement feels like fire pouring through my veins. I try to close my eyes, to escape the intensity, but his grip tightens.

"No," he growls, plunging deeper. "Look at me."

And so, I do.

His green eyes consume me—possessive, merciless— binding me tighter than his hands ever could. My body trembles, burns; my nails dig into the wood as pleasure drags me down again, fiercer, unbearable.

"That's it..." his voice rumbles against my lips, almost a roar. "Fall apart just because I command it."

The orgasm crashes into me violently, even more devastating than the first. A scream tears from my throat, echoing through the boat, my body arching toward him, vision dissolving into haze. The only thing keeping me tethered is his stare, holding me captive while I shatter.

"You drive me insane, Lucía..." he growls into my mouth, his thrusts a furious rhythm that robs me of air. "I want more—give me more."

His kiss is madness incarnate, his tongue—cold from the piercing—ravaging me, igniting me further. I devour him back with equal desperation, clutching his shoulders, clinging to his strength.

"I need you..." he whispers, voice broken, so close to my ear it splinters me. "You have no idea how much."

The boat beats beneath us, pulsing with his desire— each drive an echo of the sea and of his body. My moans drown in his mouth, and still he persists, as if there's always more of me left to claim.

In that blur of pleasure, I know nothing can stop us. The rhythm quickens, brutal and desperate, as if the boat itself trembles beneath the weight of our hunger. My body arches toward him, giving everything, unable to hold back until control shatters completely.

"Lucía..." he growls. "Come with me."

The heat in my core erupts just as I feel him shudder inside me. His strength breaks through me, my body unraveling beneath his as our voices merge into one. Everything turns to light and shadow, pleasure and delirium—a burst that dismantles me completely.

We collapse together, breathless, skin aflame, our souls splintered in the same blinding release that erases everything else. I hold on to him, and he to me, as if letting go would mean losing what's left of us—as if the addiction that binds us is also the chain that dooms us.

His breath grazes my neck, hot and erratic, while my body still trembles in fading waves of pleasure. The hands that once gripped me in fury now rest still at my waist, as though making sure I'm still there—anchored to him.

There's no haste, no rage. Only the quiet echo of two bodies finding themselves again in silence.

Adrián rests his forehead against mine, his lips trembling against my skin. His green eyes, always so intense, shine now with something softer, something I can't name.

"I've never given this to anyone..." he murmurs, his voice rough, broken, as if every word costs him. "No one's ever had me like this."

My heart tightens. I look at him, speechless, because I know he's not only speaking of sex or desire. It's more: a crack in his mask, a confession that strips him barer than any caress.

I lift my hand to brush his sweat-damp cheek. And though I know that any moment now he'll become the cold, dangerous Adrián again, this instant belongs to me—the moment he admitted what I never thought I'd hear: that I had marked him, that with me he feels vulnerable.

And that revelation makes me feel like a queen—his queen.

"Do you want to sail?" he asks suddenly, his voice rough, still heavy with everything we just lived.

I blink, surprised. It's not the answer I expected. His confession still hangs thick between us, and now he offers me the sea—as if inviting me into his hidden world.

I nod slowly, unable to refuse.

Adrián rises, adjusting the sail with sure, powerful movements, and soon the boat glides forward, cutting the water beneath the moon. The salty air wraps around me—cool, freeing—and for a moment I feel as if we're flying over the infinite skin of the ocean.

I watch him at the wheel, his silhouette etched against the night, and I realize this man doesn't only drag me into danger—he also leads me into intoxicating, unforgettable moments where the world falls away and only his shadow remains over me.

The boat advances in silence, rocked gently by the waves. The fresh wind caresses my face, tangling my hair, and I don't mind. For the first time in a long while, I feel like I can actually breathe.

I fold my arms around my knees as I watch him steer. The moon lights his profile: strong, perfect, serene. For an instant he doesn't seem like the dangerous man who pushes me to the edge, but someone made of sea and night—someone who belongs to another world.

I close my eyes and let the sound of water striking the wood lull me. The sway makes me drowsy, and a strange hollow opens in my chest: peace, because here in the middle of nowhere I feel like I am only his; fear, because I know that calm is fragile and the hurricane could return at any moment.

When I open my eyes, he is watching me. He says nothing, but his silence speaks louder than any confession. And I, trapped in that moment, think that if time could stop, I would freeze it right here: out on the sea, under the moon, two souls seeking each other even as the world tries to pull us apart.

I don't know how long we remain like that, lost in silence that says everything words cannot. Eventually sleep pulls me under, and I drift off clinging to a single certainty: even if only for a few hours, he is mine.

The murmur of the sea wakes me before the sun fully rises. I open my eyes slowly, and the sky greets me painted in pink and gold, as if dawn itself has decided to give us a private show.

A light blanket covers me. My body still aches, trembling faintly from everything we lived through the night before. I sit up, feeling the breeze on my bare skin, while the boat rocks gently like a cradle on endless water.

I look around until I find him. Adrián is sitting at the bow, his torso bare, a cigarette resting between his fingers though he doesn't smoke it. He just stares at the horizon, as if wrestling with thoughts too heavy to release.

For a moment I watch him without his knowing, memorizing the lines of his body in the soft morning light. And in that instant, he is neither the brutal man who consumes me nor the secret my father fears—he seems like a boy lost in a sea too vast.

I want to go to him, wrap my arms around him from behind, whisper that he's not alone. But something holds me back. The calm feels so fragile that even a single move might shatter it. So, I stay where I am, keeping this dawn to myself as if it will never return.

His footsteps startle me when his shadow falls over the blanket. Adrián leans down, his green eyes serious, tense, stripped of the serenity of morning.

"Get dressed, princesa," he murmurs, handing me the dress wrinkled from last night. "We're almost there."

I clutch the fabric in my hands, my heart tightening. I don't want this moment to end. I don't want to return to the world where secrets divide us, and every gaze carries judgment.

"Adrián..." I whisper, searching his eyes. "If my father already knows, what's the point of hiding anymore? There's no sense in keeping us a secret."

He stops, and in his eyes, I see something that chills me: worry. He straightens, runs a hand through his hair, and exhales heavily.

"On the contrary, Lucía..." His voice is low, laden with shadows. "Now is exactly when we have to be more careful."

My chest tightens.

"Why?" I ask, searching for answers he never gives.

He looks at me as if he's about to tell me everything— then pulls back, as always. At last, he leans closer, his breath scorching me with words that slice deeper than silence:

"Because things aren't what you think. From your world everything looks simply, all light... but it's not. I come from another place, princesa. A place where darkness rules. And that darkness does not forgive."

His confession shakes me, like he's dropped a key into a labyrinth I don't yet know how to enter. But instead of fear, what I feel is a fiercer pull to stay beside him, no matter the cost.

A thousand questions rise to my lips, but I swallow them. I know him too well: if I press, he'll retreat behind his silence, and I'll lose my only chance of reaching him. So, I nod quietly, pretending to focus on slipping the dress over my skin, while inside I burn with the need to know.

Every word carves itself into me: "I come from another place. One where darkness rules. And that darkness does not forgive."

I finish dressing without meeting his eyes, though I feel the weight of his presence—so close and yet impossibly distant. The harbor looms ahead; the air thickens until it's hard to breathe.

He thinks my silence is submission. But it isn't. My silence is a vow: sooner or later I will uncover everything he hides from me—even if it means sinking with him into that same darkness.

The boat docks in near silence. Within minutes we're back in the car. The ride feels nothing like last night: then, every mile burned with fire; now, the air between us is leaden. Adrián drives without looking at me, profile rigid, brow furrowed, hands gripping the wheel as if dawn's fragile calm had never existed.

The car stops a few blocks from my house. I recognize the corner. He doesn't kill the engine. He only glances at me—those green eyes that were soft under the moon now sharpened into weapons.

"Get out here," he says, voice flat, stripped of warmth.

My heart contracts. I open the door slowly, the cool morning air slaps against my skin. I turn to him, searching for a gesture, a word—anything to recover the man who bared his vulnerability to me under the moon. But all I find is coldness.

"Adrián..." I murmur, my voice a fragile thread.

His gaze hardens, as if even my name were a threat.

"Don't make this harder. Go home, princesa."

He presses the accelerator just enough to force me to shut the door. I watch him drive away until the taillights vanish down the empty street. Alone, I stand rooted in place, the echo of his chill lodged in my chest.

I finally turn toward my house, steps heavy, but inside I burn—because I know the man who left me with such coldness is the same one who, only hours before, revealed a fragment of his soul.

Chapter 14

✦ ✦ ✦ ✦ ✦ ✦

*T*he phone vibrates on the bedside table, and when I see his name on the screen I can't help smiling. I answer immediately, and Camila's voice explodes on the other end—radiant, bright, as if happiness spills out of every word.

"Luuu, you have to see this!" she laughs like a child; I can hear the murmur of the sea and exotic birds in the background. "This is a dream—everything is perfect. Víctor and I... oh, girl, I feel like I'm living in a movie."

I close my eyes for a second, letting her joy wash over me. She talks about heavenly beaches, dinners under the stars, how he looks at her as if she were the only woman in the world. Every word paints her as the happiest bride on earth.

"I'm so glad to hear that, Cami," I answer, my voice soft and sincere.

Camila keeps talking, laughing, radiant. I listen, congratulate her, shower her with affection. But inside, I feel like I'm living in a different movie: a dark, dangerous one where love means something else.

"I'll be back this weekend, I have so much to tell you. Love you, Luuu," Camila says, her joy overflowing even through the line.

I smile, though my lips tremble a little. "I love you too, Cami. Enjoy every second."

The call ends and the screen goes dark, leaving my room wrapped in silence. I press the phone to my chest and close my eyes. Camila is living her honeymoon— radiant, in love, convinced she's found the man of her life. And I... I'm still trapped in a forbidden whirlwind with Adrián: half-confessions, touches that burn, and a silence that kills me more than any truth.

I take a deep breath, but calm doesn't come. When Camila returns, nothing will be the same. And what I'll have to tell her won't be as bright as her story. The room is dim, lit only by the lamp on the bedside table. Silence wraps around me and sleep won't come; my body still remembers the boat's sway, the fury of his hands, the fleeting tenderness of his words.

Suddenly the phone vibrates on the sheet. My heart jumps.

A message. From him.

"Don't think that because I left you on that corner I'm far away. You can't escape me, princesa. Not by day, not by night. And when you least expect it... I'll come back for you."

I swallow, a shiver running through me. The coldness of his goodbye at the harbor collides with the fire of those words—a threat that is also a promise.

I hug the pillow, unable to erase the trembling smile that slips out. Even though I know his presence drags me toward an abyss, I can't help it: I want him. I need him. That certainty is as addictive as it is dangerous.

I type slowly, savoring every word:

"Come soon, Adrián... I want to see you lose yourself in me."

I take a deep breath before hitting send. The screen lights up with my own boldness, and a wave of heat runs through me. It's a challenge, a dangerous provocation— and I know it.

I leave the phone on the bedside table but don't take my eyes off it. The silence in the room becomes unbearable; every second stretches into an eternity. No sooner has my message left the screen than Adrián's reply appears, as if he'd been waiting for my dare.

"Be careful what you wish for, princesa. You know what happens when you challenge me. Next time you won't even have a voice to provoke me... only moans when I make you remember who's in charge."

My heart races; my breath catches. I bite my lower lip, feeling heat travel from my chest to deep inside me. He's returned my audacity a thousandfold, and the worst—or the best—is that it drives me crazy with desire.

I open the chat again, reading each word as if it were fire carved into my skin. I know I should stop—playing at this level is like dancing with the dark—but I'm already lost. With Adrián, every threat is also a promise.

My fingers shake, but this time not from fear—only pure arousal. I won't let his warning silence me. I type slowly, each letter a provocation:

"Who said I was going to resist, Adrián? What you don't know is that the idea of you punishing me drives me mad... of you taking me so far that I don't even remember my own name."

I hit send before I can regret it. The screen blinks; my pulse drums in my temples.

I drop onto the pillow, breathing fast, certain there's no turning back from what I've just done. I provoked him, and Adrián never leaves provocations unanswered. The question burns into my skin: what will he do now that I've opened the door to his darkness myself?

The silence lasts only a few seconds. Then the screen lights up with his answer.

"You asked for it, princesa. Next time it won't be a game: I'll tie you up, deny you until you cry my name, and when I decide to give you relief... it will be so brutal you'll beg me to stop."

A shiver runs through me. My hands shake as I hold the phone; my breath becomes a sharp gasp, and the wetness flowing through me betrays everything.

I close my eyes and bite my lip, but it's useless: each of his words pierces deeper than any touch. Even though I know his promise is pure danger, my whole body wants it with a desperation that scares me.

I rest the phone on my chest; the only thought I can hold is that I want him — that I want exactly what he promised. I reopen the chat; my fingers steady this time and type a single word.

"Do it."

I close my eyes; the phone pressed to my chest. With that word I'm not just daring him; I'm surrendering. I'm telling him there's no turning back — that I want to be his in the darkest, most dangerous way.

Silence stretches on. My entire body trembles, caught in the delicious anxiety of knowing Adrián never ignores an order like that. Sooner or later, he will obey. I stay awake, eyes fixed on the dormant screen, waiting for a message that never comes. The tension lulls me into a fitful half-sleep between craving and frustration until a creak wakes me.

I jerk my eyes open. The dimness of my room surrounds me; for a second, I think I'm dreaming. Then I feel it: his presence — that heavy air that is only his.

"Adrián...?" I whisper, voice trembling.

He steps out of the shadows, his green eyes burning in the dark, and my heart stops. He says nothing. He simply comes closer, the fire in his gaze fiercer than any word.

*From his jacket pocket he pulls a dark handkerchief —
the same one he once used to blindfold me — and folds it
with dangerous calm.*

*"You said 'do it,'" he murmurs, barely audible, his
voice restrained thunder. "And here I am."*

*He takes my wrists and, with precise movements, ties
them to the headboard. My breath quickens; fear and
desire mix until it hurts.*

*"I don't want your parents to hear what I'm going to
do to you, princesa," he whispers in my ear. "But I do
want to hear every moan, even if it's muffled."*

*The world collapses into that moment. Hands bound,
voice contained, my body trembles under his absolute
control. In his eyes is the gleam of a man who hasn't come
to play — but to fulfill every dark promise he made me.*

*I feel the rough warmth of his strong hands sliding
over my two-piece pajamas. There's no rush in his
movements; that deliberate slowness drives me insane.
His fingers trace the light fabric, testing the edges,
searching for a way to peel it from my skin.*

*The knot in my stomach tightens as he begins to undo
the top buttons, one by one, with cruel patience. The
fabric parts, releasing the heat of my body, and the cool
dawn breeze raises goosebumps across my skin.*

Adrián barely smiles, his dark gaze dismantling me.

"So fragile, princesa... and yet, utterly mine."

His hands push the fabric aside, capturing my breasts in a firm touch that wrenches a muffled moan from me. The sound makes him growl with pleasure; his lips descend to my neck—kissing, biting, marking me with absolute dominance.

Then his fingers find the edge of my pajama shorts. He tugs them down slowly, as if every inch were a punishment. The fabric slips down my thighs until finally I'm left bare beneath his burning gaze, breathless and surrendered.

Adrián straightens; his green eyes lock on me, gleaming with the dangerous spark that unravels me. He unbuttons his shirt with malicious calm until the fabric falls away, revealing his hard, carved torso, slick with sweat and desire.

He never takes his eyes off mine as he unfastens his belt. The metallic clink echoes through the room like thunder, and my heart pounds so hard it hurts. He lets his pants fall with the same calculated slowness, each movement another torment—trapped in the sheets, unable to move, forced to devour him with my eyes.

When at last he stands completely naked, he runs a hand through his hair, confident and damned in his savage beauty. He takes a step toward me, and I, bound and silenced, can only tremble under his control.

His hands wander over every inch of me—down my thighs, then up again, his fingertips barely grazing my skin, sending tremors through me.

Then he retreats, pulling the contact away, leaving me aching for more. A sound catches in my throat, trembling between fear and want. He senses it, and his smile grazes my neck like a silent promise.

"I love watching you fight your own need, princesa..." he rasps, before biting softly at my collarbone.

His mouth continues downward, leaving a trail of wet, slow kisses that burn me. He pauses at my breasts, biting them with savage devotion; his tongue plays with my nipples until I arch, bound and trembling.

When he thinks I can't take it anymore, he moves down my abdomen, licking, savoring every inch of skin. My breathing becomes frantic; my hips search for what he still withholds.

When he reaches my center, his hand forces my legs apart. The heat of his breath hits me before his mouth does, and that moment of waiting feels like an eternity. The wet touch of his tongue pulls a muffled cry from me that vibrates in my mouth.

His piercing traces cruel, controlled circles. My hips arch, my bound hands claw at the headboard, and my body begs for what he still refuses to give.

His hands dig into my hips—strong, possessive— holding me steady even as I tremble and buck.

His mouth is a lethal weapon. I feel him dragging me to a place where I no longer belong to myself.

My moans die in my throat as I bite my lip to keep them in, but he doesn't need to hear them. His tongue moves with reckless hunger, wild and consuming, searching for one thing—my plea.

My mind dissolves in the heat, the tremor of every touch. There's no escape. His mouth claims me completely, drinking from me as if he could swallow my very soul. I know I can't last much longer.

Adrián lifts his gaze slightly, those green eyes glinting between my thighs.

"Let go, princesa..." he whispers against my damp skin before sinking into me again, deep and sure. And I obey, because what lives in his voice isn't command—it's fate.

I can't hold it anymore. His tongue, his piercing, the strength of his grip—everything conspires against me until control shatters into a thousand glittering pieces.

The sound I try to suppress turns into a heartbeat, pulsing through every inch of me. My body yields on its own, caught between emptiness and fire, undone by pleasure that burns and soothes all at once.

The wave overtakes me, spreading like wildfire through every nerve, every breath. My tied hands pull against the headboard, my back arches, and I give him everything I have left.

Adrián doesn't stop. He holds me, claiming every last tremor, drawing my climax out until I break—silent, lost, blissfully his.

His mouth travels upward until it finds mine. He kisses me, rough and certain, making me taste myself on his lips. The flavor is sweet, electric, laced with surrender. My eyes fly open, startled, but he doesn't let me resist. I moan into his mouth, and feel his smile curve through the kiss.

"You like it like this, princesa?" he whispers between rough caresses. "You taste so damn good."

Heat rushes to my head. I'm wrecked, still trembling from release, and yet all I can think about is more. He kisses me with that same brutal intensity that always breaks me open, and when his lips barely pull away, I see that look—the one that always means trouble.

"You ready for something new tonight, princesa?"

My world stops. My heart pounds so hard it nearly drowns out the silence of the room. I'm tied, naked beneath his absolute control—and still, or maybe because of it, I nod without thinking.

Adrián smiles—dark, satisfied—the smile of a predator who knows his prey has nowhere to run.

His fingers trace my skin with maddening calm, caressing every line of my body as if already plotting the next way to break me. And in that moment, I understand with him, there are no limits. There will always be something new, always another step deeper into his addiction.

I feel him untie my wrists from the headboard, but before I can speak, his strong hand wraps around my throat, pulling me up to him. My heart races wildly. My voice dies in my throat.

His green eyes blaze with dangerous malice as his breath grazes my lips and his husky command falls between us:

"Turn around."

I obey, trembling—not to escape, but because the force of his gaze leaves me no choice. He guides me until I'm on my knees, my back pressed to his chest, my body arching, skin burning with anticipation.

His hands move over my waist, down my hips, tracing every curve as though mapping what's already his. He draws me closer, the hard pulse of him against me making it impossible to breathe.

"You're mine completely, princesa... and tonight I'll take whatever virginity you have left."

Fear. Desire. Madness. It all blurs together as his hands prepare me for the inevitable, and I know there's no turning back—he wants all of me, every inch untouched by anything but him.

His fingers move with a deliberate rhythm, exploring slowly, as if to teach me that true torment isn't in pain, but in delay. My chest rises and falls in frantic rhythm, yet he keeps that merciless control. Then his tongue finds me, and the first touch sends a shock so fierce through me I almost break in his hands.

"Relax, princesa," he murmurs, his deep voice vibrating against my skin. "I want you to enjoy every second."

His fingers join the game, slipping in just enough— stretching, preparing me with cruel precision that forces me to swallow a cry. Every movement is a blend of tension and pleasure, a reminder that he owns me.

I tremble, my hands clawing at the sheets, my mind dissolving between fear and arousal. He takes me with merciless patience, prolonging the torture on purpose.

A muffled moan escapes when the pressure sharpens. Pain comes first—a raw burn that tightens every muscle. Fear slams into me, and for an instant I want to pull away, but his hands on my hips hold me captive.

"Adrián..." My voice cracks, eyes squeezed shut.

He pauses—not to release me, but to bring his mouth to my ear.

"Shhh... trust me, princesa," he whispers, his voice leaving no room for defiance. "Don't think about the pain... feel the pleasure."

His tone is hypnotic, a command that seeps deeper than any touch. And when his fingers move again—

slower, deliberate—I realize that beneath the burn, something else rises: heat, forbidden and consuming, shaking me to the core.

My body, traitorous, begins to yield. Fear lingers, but it collides with desire, and I understand what he's teaching me: in his hands, even pain can turn into pleasure.

"That's it, princesa..." he growls against my damp skin, his voice rough, dangerous. "Let it in. Let it become what it was always meant to be."

And it happens.

My moans twist into strangled cries against the fabric biting my lips. My legs quake, my hips betray me, chasing what I swore to resist. Waves crash through me with brutal force, a climax that rips the air from my lungs. Pain melts into ecstasy so sharp I feel myself unravel completely.

Adrián doesn't stop until he's taken it all—until I'm screaming with a trembling body that no longer belongs to me, proof that even the impossible can be delicious in his hands.

When at last he lets me breathe, his fingers trail my back with dangerous gentleness, as though he's branded me with a lesson I'll never forget.

The echo of my climax still pulses through me when I feel him shift behind me, his grip tightening at my hips. A violent shiver runs through me as his hardness presses close, stealing my breath.

"Now, princesa," his voice rumbled—deep, dark, dripping with dominance. "I'm going to make you mine completely."

I had no time to breathe. He thrust into me with brutal force and a muffled scream tore from my lips. Pain ripped through me—sharp, searing—but tangled with it came a pleasure so consuming it stole what little strength I had left.

His hand fisted in my hair, yanking my head back until my spine pressed against his sweat-slick chest. His other hand clamped down on my breasts, owning me as he drove into me again and again—merciless, claiming every inch.

Tears blurred the strangled moans that escaped me. The burn was fierce, yet each thrust twisted and reshaped it until it became a forbidden pleasure that devoured me.

"Mine," he growled with every pounding stroke. "All mine... even the parts you never meant to give."

The relentless rhythm was unbearable and savage, and my traitorous body began to yield, craving his brutality as if it were the only truth keeping me alive. And I know there's no turning back—Adrián has taken me in the darkest way, and he's ruined me for any other man.

The searing burn lived inside me, and alongside it rose another fire—wild, overwhelming—dragging me somewhere I might never return from. His grip never eased: one hand crushed my hips, forcing me to take him deep; the other stayed tangled in my hair, keeping me exactly where he wanted me.

"Come for me, princesa..." he snarled, his voice ragged, almost animal. "I want to see it in your body; I want to hear it in your strangled moan."

And then I shatter.

The orgasm takes me by surprise—fierce, blinding, like thunder splitting the night. My muscles give in, my voice cracking into a broken moan, and all that remains is the trembling of a body that has surrendered completely.

I scream into the pillow, my body shaking as each thrust pulls me higher, stretching the pleasure until it blurs into oblivion.

The ecstasy tears through me, and I feel him breaking too—his body shaking against mine, every movement wild, urgent, and unstoppable.

His breath rasps into a guttural snarl at my ear, his hands clamping me tighter as if terrified I might slip away at the last second.

"Lucía..." he groans—raw, feral, torn straight from his chest.

The heat of his release floods me just as my muscles convulse in unison. A muffled cry rends from my throat when he comes with brutal force, his growl lost to the night—too powerful to contain.

We lie tangled, trembling and sweating, our breaths mingling in a whirlwind of pleasure and wreckage. Each final thrust echoes until finally his strength collapses against me. The world narrows to the two of us—broken and sated—joined in a ravenous, shared pleasure that leaves me certain that, even if it destroys me, I will never stop belonging to him.

"In which room do your parents sleep?" Adrián asks, voice hoarse, edged with malice.

"In the next one," I answer without thinking, still breathless. "But don't worry... they're not home tonight."

He pauses, arches a brow, and a dangerous smile curves his lips.

"And why didn't you tell me that before, princesa?"

I roll over, my back sinking into the sheets still mussed from what we just did. He positions himself over me, weight supported on his arms, green eyes flashing with that intensity that strips me bare more surely than his hands ever could. His gaze is possessive, hungry, as if searching for a new secret in every inch of my skin. He tips his head; his lips brush mine and his low voice shakes me to the core:

"Tell me... did you like it?"

Heat climbs from my chest to my face. My whole-body trembles beneath him. My lips want to deny it, but my eyes betray me. Yes. I liked it. He destroyed me. He made me addicted all over again.

I lock my eyes on his, still breathless, letting a mischievous smile curve my mouth.

"Like?" I repeat slowly, savoring the word. "Let's just say it wasn't bad... but you're not as irresistible as you think."

The light in his eyes shifts: a dangerous spark, a low growl rumbling in the back of his throat. His hands clinch the sheets at either side of my body, pinning me beneath him.

"Be careful, princesa..." he murmurs, his deep voice thick with threat and desire. "You know I don't tolerate being challenged."

I bite my lip, feigning calm while adrenaline floods me. Inside I'm shaking, surrendered to the burning memory of what he's just done, but outwardly I hold his gaze, provoking him on purpose.

"Then prove it," I whisper, letting the taunt vibrate in my voice. "If you can."

A low roar escapes him, and I shiver—I know in that instant I've ignited a new storm that will sweep me away. Adrián leans over me; for a moment I expect him to claim me with the fury that drives me mad. He doesn't. He stays too still, a malicious smile curving his lips.

"So, I'm not as irresistible as I think?" he murmurs, letting the words sink in. "We'll see how long that pride of yours lasts."

His hands begin a slow tour across my skin, lacking the urgency from before. He barely grazes me, toying with the idea of touch; his mouth hovers at mine without fully kissing—brushing, denying. Each caress is torture. He moves down my breasts, takes them firmly, wringing broken moans from me while withholding the pressure I silently beg for. His tongue traces my neck, the piercing leaving a trail of cold and fire; his fingers stop dangerously close to where I want him most—but don't reach.

I writhe beneath him, frustrated, and I know that's exactly what he wants: to watch me lose control, to make me beg.

"I'm not going to take you until you ask properly," he whispers in my ear, voice hoarse. "I want you to admit you need me more than you need air."

Anger and desire consume me. I try to keep my gaze defiant, but my body trembles and arches, searching for what he denies me. I understand that this time it won't be brutality that breaks me, but the slow torture of his absolute control.

His hands rise with certainty to seize my breasts, filling them in his grip. My lungs empty in a muffled cry as he leans in, his mouth devouring my nipples with a slow, cruel hunger that dismantles me. The piercing grazes my sensitive skin, sending shivers tip to toe.

It's a delicious contrast: the warmth of his tongue and the icy edge of metal—a game that drives me insane, making me arch against him even as I try to keep my pride intact.

Adrián alternates between licking, sucking, and gentle biting, testing my resistance, knowing each motion pushes me closer to breaking. His hands never stop: one grips me firmly while the other pinches with cruel precision, sparking jolts of painful pleasure.

"Do you feel what I'm doing to you?" he growls against me. "This won't fade, princesa. Not even if you try."

I close my eyes, trying to resist, but my body has already betrayed me—trembling, wet, lost, on the verge of begging for what I swore I'd never give. The pleasure he gives me is too good to be real.

"Adrián..." My voice breaks, pleading for more, begging without meaning to.

I lose control. The tension inside me snaps, and his mouth keeps moving against my skin, claiming every breath. The pleasure hits hard, violent and consuming, and I bite down on my hand to keep from crying out his name.

I tremble, sweat dripping down my body, my breath shallow and broken. Adrián pulls back just enough, his mouth still glistening, lips curled into a dangerous, knowing smile.

His gaze locks with mine—surprised, turned on, carrying that spark that always comes before the storm.

"Very receptive, princesa..." he murmurs with wicked amusement. "I didn't know this alone could make you come."

I bite my lip, ashamed and burning, realizing I've given him yet another reason to play with me... to break me further.

Adrián doesn't rush. He grants me no rest, refusing to surrender to urgency.

His fingers trace the curve of my chest, sliding down my slick abdomen, stopping just before the place where I ache for him most. I shudder, instinctively seeking his touch, but he withdraws, denying me.

"Do you want more?" His voice is low, dangerous, as he presses a kiss to my belly. "Because I do."

My hips writhe, bound to longing, a choked sob escaping me. Adrián smiles—cruel, charming—relishing my surrender.

"Look at you... trembling already. His words lash at me. "And I still haven't decided when to give you what you crave."

My body begs, every fiber straining for more, but he stretches the torment, absolute master of my pleasure. When his mouth finally finds my clitoris, the first brush of his tongue ignites me completely, forcing a ragged sigh from my lips as my legs quake violently. He doesn't rush. He teases me with deliberate slowness, savoring me as if he has all the time in the world to unravel me.

His piercing traces soft, deliberate circles, each stroke pulling me higher, holding me at the edge of a sweet abyss. He drags me there and halts, savoring my torment, letting me dangle in that exquisite cruelty.

"That's it, princesa..." he murmurs against my soaked skin, his deep voice rumbling like distant thunder. "I want you to understand—I can not only tear you apart. I can make you beg with sweetness too."

I arch, tears of pleasure clouding my vision. Every slow caress, every delicate suction sparks another fire, until my body yields completely.

The orgasm comes—endless, devastating, drawn out until it consumes me from within, dismantling me piece by piece.

I scream, raw and unrestrained, as my body convulses beneath his mouth, caught between pain, sweetness, and absolute possession.

When he finally lets me go, my skin burns, my breathing is chaos, and the only thought that remains is this: Adrián hasn't just destroyed me—he's shown me that sweetness, in his hands, is an even crueler punishment.

I sit up abruptly, trembling still, but unwilling to leave him all the power. I kiss him hungrily, tasting myself on his lips, savoring the mingling of my pleasure and his restrained desire. My gasps break into his mouth, and I feel how it ignites him further, as if my boldness dares him to lose control.

I shove him back until he falls against the bed, his green eyes flashing with surprise and hunger all at once. My body slides over his, seeking the hardness straining beneath me. I find it, wrap it in my hand, and his guttural growl vibrates deep, animal and unrestrained.

"Now you..." I whisper. "I want to hear you moan for me."

I lower myself, trailing kisses down his abdomen, leaving a wet path that unravels him. When my tongue finally brushes his erection, a raw, broken moan escapes him—a sound so intoxicating I could come from hearing it alone.

His control slips beneath my mouth, and watching him surrender to me fills me with a dark, delicious power.

I am the one unraveling him, and every rough, unrestrained moan becomes my most addictive triumph.

I straddle him, feeling his thickness stretch and fill me completely. A guttural cry tears from me, the mix of pain and pleasure flooding through in violent waves. I seize his hands, pressing them against my breasts, forcing him to touch me the way I crave—to feel every desperate beat of my body.

I move slowly at first, a rhythm soft yet merciless, each sway wringing gasps from me. Adrián growls beneath me, his fingers pinching, obeying my command—but his gaze... his gaze refuses to yield.

Those green eyes sear into me with an intensity that scorches. He studies every gesture, every cry, every tremor, as if engraving them into memory—and it only excites me more.

I fist my hair, yanking my head back, opening myself wider to his dominance as I quicken the rhythm. My hips crash down against his, and his lips part in a raw groan that reverberates through my chest like a forbidden victory.

For a fleeting moment, I feel I own him. That he's mine. That I'm driving him to the brink—and nothing is more intoxicating than watching Adrián unravel beneath me. I ride him harder, setting the rhythm with my hips, each thrust sharper, more defiant.

The sensation of his hardness filling me tears cries from my throat that twine with his, a savage duet of pleasure.

His hands clutch my breasts with desperate strength, obeying the way I command him. I stare down at him, hungry for his surrender. His green eyes glow like embers, clinging to control, but his ragged breaths betray him.

"Look at you..." I pant with a taunting smile, leaning close enough to graze his lips without granting the kiss. "You're about to lose yourself in me."

I quicken the pace, my hips striking his with furious insistence. His body tenses beneath me, his sounds growing deeper, rougher—each one a dark nectar I drink like victory.

Sweat trickles down my spine, my legs tremble, but I don't relent. I drive him to the precipice with every thrust, every grind, every broken sound that escapes him. He's about to shatter—I know it. This time, it's my turn to watch him beg.

The rhythm turns frantic, ripping gasps and cries from us both until they blend into one unrestrained chorus. Heat engulfs us, sweat slicking our bodies, the tension in him mounting unstoppable, matching mine. His fingers dig into my hips, his eyes darken, his jaw clenches, fighting a battle he can no longer win.

"Lucía..." he rasps, my name leaving him in a desperate roar.

And then I break. The climax detonates inside me— violent, consuming—my scream tearing through the air as my nails rake his chest. In that same instant he surrenders with me, his body arching, a guttural cry erupting against my ear as his release floods into me, tangling with mine, destroying us both in one merciless wave.

We move together, frantic, possessed, until the ecstasy is unbearable and I collapse onto him, gasping, trembling, still convulsing around the fierce pulse of his body inside me.

Adrián wraps his arms around me, and for the first time I offer no resistance. His chest heaves against mine, our breaths tangled, and for a few seconds there is no control, no danger, no masks—only us, stripped to the same raw truth.

Then his hands change. No longer binding, they wander softly along my back, tracing invisible patterns across my skin. His lips brush my forehead in a fleeting, tender kiss—so unexpected it steals my breath.

"Lucía..." he murmurs my name—not like before. Not with anger, not with lust, but with a dangerous tenderness, as if a secret had slipped from him. I close my eyes, letting myself be cradled by a gesture I never imagined he possessed. For a minute I am neither his forbidden addiction nor his favored punishment; for the first time I feel like something more.

Chapter 15

✦ ✦ ✦ ✦ ✦ ✦

The silence in the room is as heavy as the heat that still thrums between our bodies. I remain draped over him, his breath colliding with my neck, his hands caressing me with a sweetness I'd never known from him. I move just enough to meet his eyes. His green still smolders, but not with the usual fury; now it looks like a fire about to die down—vulnerable, fragile.

"Adrián..." my voice comes out soft, trembling.

"Why do you treat me like this?"

He frowns, as if the question surprised him more than any of my provocations. His lips part, but he doesn't answer—he only watches me, and for the first time I feel that it isn't me who trembles, but him.

I place my hand on his chest, feeling his heart race, and lean closer.

"You're so hard on me, so dark... and then suddenly you kiss me like your life depends on it," I say, staring without looking away. "Why?"

For a moment I think I'll lose him—that he'll stand, dress, and leave as he always does. But he stays, held by my question, by my skin. His silence feels like a confession, as if the answer lives in everything he refuses to say.

Adrián closes his eyes for a beat, fighting an inner battle. When he opens them again, they pierce me with that intensity that always breaks me—but this time there's something else: a flash of truth he rarely let's slip.

"Because with you... I can't be the same bastard I always am," he finally murmurs, his voice low, hoarse, almost a contained growl. "You confuse me, Lucía. You break my rules."

My heart pounds so hard it hurts. I listen and know that each word costs him, as if he tears them from himself. "You are..." he stops, jaw clenched, averting his gaze for a second before meeting mine again. "You are the only one who makes me forget who I am. And that... that fucks me up more than you can imagine."

His hand rises slowly to my face, stroking my cheek with a tenderness that contradicts the harshness of his confession. I could cry, but I don't. I lose myself in his touch and in words that don't answer everything but reveal something vital: I am his weakness.

And I know that for a man like Adrián, being weak is the most dangerous thing he can allow himself. I say nothing. His words echo in my chest like a burning refrain, and I know that if I push him—if I try to pry more out of him—I'll only make him raise his walls again.

So I kiss him.

I lean over him and seek his mouth—no hurry, no anger—only the quiet surrender of someone who realizes too late there is no escape. His lips meet mine instantly, steady yet trembling, as if that kiss were the only truth he allows himself.

His hand cups my cheek, slides to my neck, down my back, pressing me closer as though he feared I might disappear. And in that wordless kiss I accept both what he offers and what he withholds.

I don't need him to say it. His silence screams it: I am his weakness, his sentence, his addiction.

The kiss lingers, then fades. When his lips leave mine, the hollow rushes in like an open wound. Adrián holds my gaze for a few more seconds, as if trying to brand something into me before stepping away.

He rises without a word, gathers his clothes with deliberate calm, and begins to dress. Each movement is a cruel reminder that the tenderness he gave me moments ago cannot last.

"I have to go," he says at last, his voice deep and composed, as though nothing remains of the vulnerable man I had just held.

I want to stop him, to beg him to stay—but I can't. Something in his eyes forbids it: that dangerous distance rebuilding the wall between us.

He brushes my face one last time, the briefest touch of his fingers, then bends to press a fleeting kiss to my forehead—a contradictory gesture that wounds me more than any words could.

The room feels too large, too cold. I clutch the sheets still warm with his body and know, no matter how I deny it, there is no turning back. Adrián owns me, even in his absence.

I'm still gripping the sheets, his echo burning on my skin, when the sharp ring of the phone shatters the silence. My heart leaps—just for a second, I think it's him. But it isn't. The name glowing on the screen drags me back to reality.

Camila.
"Cami?"

"Lucía... we need to talk." Her tone alarms me instantly. It isn't her usual bright, playful voice—it's tight, heavy, holding back something she won't say over the phone.

"What's wrong? Are you okay?"

"Not on the phone. Come over." She hesitates, and I can almost see her biting her lip—that nervous tell she's never managed to hide. "It's important."

My heart races as I throw on my clothes. Camila's voice still echoes in my ears, taut and breaking, like someone on the verge of collapse.

When I reach her place, she's waiting in the living room—barefoot, pale, her hair half-tied as if she hasn't slept. Her anxious eyes search mine, and before I can even hug her, she blurts the words that strike like a blow:

"Lucía..." Her voice trembles, then shatters. "I think I made a mistake with Víctor."

The words hit my chest like a strike. My breath falters, my throat tightens. I stand frozen, trying to grasp whether I truly heard what she just said.

Camila collapses onto the sofa, hiding her face in her hands. Her breathing comes short and uneven, the sound of someone confessing a sin.

"What happened?" I finally ask, my voice more fragile than I'd like.

She runs her hands through her hair; fingers tangled in loose strands and looks up with eyes shining with fear.

"Last night... I heard him on the balcony." She swallows; each word is heavy. "I didn't know I was awake. He was on the phone... talking about money, about bets."

My heart hammers in my chest. A cold shiver slides down my spine.

"Bets?" I repeat, incredulous, the tremor in my voice betraying me. "What do you mean, Cami?"

"He said strange things, like… 'that fight is fixed,' 'the guys can't find out.'" She bites her lip, voice cracking. "Lu… it didn't sound clean. It wasn't him."

A shiver runs through me. Adrián's words loop in my head: Not everything that glitters is gold.

Camila squeezes her eyes shut, on the verge of tears. "I married him just a few days ago and already I feel like I don't know who I'm with."

I wrap my arms around her, but my mind is elsewhere—fights, bets, dirty money. It's impossible not to think of Adrián: his scars, his absences, the constant danger that shadows him.

My breath catches when a hard idea plants itself in my gut like a knife: what if the worlds aren't separate? What if Víctor and Adrián are connected—threads of the same dark web pulling me deeper every day?

My stomach knots. I can't tell her. Not now.

"Cami… maybe it's a misunderstanding." I stroke her arm, faking a calm I don't feel. "But if it isn't, we'll find out together. You're not alone."

She nods, but the trembling won't stop.

As I hold her, the ground beneath my feet begins to crack. I know it even if I'm not ready to admit it: Víctor's situation isn't accidental. It's another strand in the web that will, sooner or later, trap me too.

I can't take it anymore—Camila's anguish, Víctor's words looping in my head, the memory of Adrián's dangerous look all burning inside me. I need answers, even if they hurt.

My hands shake as I dial his number. He's slow to pick up, as always, and the wait suffocates me. When his deep voice finally answers, a chill runs through me.

"Lucía... what's wrong?"

"I need to see you," I say bluntly, my voice steady though I'm trembling inside.

"Now."

Silence—only his heavy breathing on the line, as if he's weighing how much risk granting my request would be.

"Where?" he asks at last.

Two hours later the boardwalk becomes our battleground. The salty breeze tangles my hair and my pulse thrums so loudly it nearly drowns me. I see him coming from afar: a powerful silhouette, a white shirt clinging to his torso, green eyes burning in the dim light. Each step reminds me I have no escape.

He stops in front of me—too close, commanding the scene.

"What's going on?" he asks, direct, with that lethal calm that strips me bare.

Fear and anger war inside me. My voice shakes, but I fire it out like a shot:

"Adrián... are you involved in illegal fights?"

The wind dies. His gaze slices into me like a blade, and for a second the silence is more dangerous than any reply. I watch him go still. His jaw tightens; his eyes scan me with a mixture of fury and surprise. For a moment I expect him to yell, to turn and walk away. He doesn't. He steps closer, the scent of his skin enveloping me, and lowers his voice to a dangerous whisper.

"Who told you that?"

My chest feels like it will burst.

"Camila heard Víctor," I say, voice cracking but steady enough to keep going. "And it all fits, Adrián— your money, your absences, your scars. Don't lie to me."

His breath quickens; his hands clench into fists as if restraining a storm. His green eyes burn in the darkness, and I know I've touched the heart of his secret. He holds my gaze so fiercely the air thins. Fire and shadow live in his stare, and when he speaks his voice is a contained growl.

"Yes, Lucía. I'm mixed up in things you wouldn't understand." He moves even closer, breath grazing my lips as if to steal away the courage from my question.

"Dirty, dangerous things that could drag you down with me."

My lips tremble. The truth cuts sharper than any lie.

"So it's true?" my voice breaks. "The fights, the bets—everything?"

He shuts his eyes briefly, guilt flickering across his face. When he opens them the hardness returns.

"You don't need to understand it," he says. "The only thing you need to know is that world isn't for you. You…" He pauses, his fingers ghosting along my jaw and sliding slowly down my neck. "You are the only light I have left."

The touch ignites and destroys me at once. I want to hate him for what he won't tell me, but his partial confession only draws me in further.

"And Víctor?" I whisper, barely audible.

His expression hardens—darker, colder.

"Don't speak his name." His voice is a blade of steel. "You don't know what you're doing if you drag him into this."

I stare at him, my heart threatening to burst from my chest.
"Tell me, Adrián…" I whisper, voice broken. "What do I have to do for you to get out of that world?"

For a moment his green eyes soften, as if my question wounds him more than any blow from those fights. Then he looks down, clenches his jaw, and steps back as if he needs air.

"You don't understand, Lucía," he says at last, his tone so low it prickles my skin. "I don't control my fate."

The words cut through me.

"What do you mean?"

He runs a hand through his hair, frustrated, his muscles coiled like a rope about to snap.

"It's not as simple as walking away. I'm... tied. Someone has me in their sights. And if I walk, I'm not the only one who pays."

A chill runs through me.

"Who?" I ask, my throat tight.

Suddenly he grips my chin, forcing me to meet his gaze. His voice is hoarse, dangerous—and broken.

"Don't ask, princesa. Not yet. Just understand this: if I try... I would lose you."

His confession leaves me breathless. I want to hold him, pull him out of that hell, save him. Instead, I sink deeper into him, into the secret that brackets his chest.

I am about to press again—the question burning in my throat—when he gives me no chance.

Adrián clamps my chin with uncompromising force and, before I can speak, his lips crash over mine. The kiss is brutal, desperate, as if he wants to erase the subject with the heat of his mouth. I try to answer, but he pins me to his chest, forcing my wrists to his torso, dominating me with his weight. His breath is a dark growl; his voice vibrates in my ear between bites and ragged gasps:

"No more questions, princesa. You already know what you need to know: you're mine."

The world tilts. My body yields to the fever of his control, and I understand this is his refuge—a way to silence me with pleasure and fury, with the force that always leaves me trembling. While he loses himself on my lips and his hands roam my skin with urgent need, I know he has slammed the door shut again. The small truth he gave me is buried beneath the only language that never lets me go: his absolute control.

"Come on," he says, voice low and dry, as if erasing what came before. "I'll take you home."

I look at him, stunned.

"Just... like that?"

A flash of fire ignites in his green eyes, then hardens into ice.

"Just that, princesa." His voice is firm, cutting—yet I know it's far from simple.

He offers his hand, and though my pride tells me to refuse, I take it. Night wraps around us, and the walk to his car feels like a forced return to a reality where questions multiply and answers stay hidden.

I get in silently; he starts the engine without glancing at me. Trapped between fury and desire, I promise myself I will uncover what he hides, even if it costs me my life.

The drive is quiet, broken only by the engine's roar and my ragged breaths. I watch the streets go by, trying to place each corner...

"Adrián..." my voice trembles; I make him turn his head for a moment. "I thought you were taking me to my place."

He clenches his jaw, knuckles white on the wheel. "I thought so too." His tone is low, heavy with something I can't read.

The car pulls up outside his house—dark and solitary. His green eyes search me—lit and dangerous, embers waiting to consume.

"But the truth is..." he growls, voice breaking. "I can't let you go. I don't want to."

A lump rises in my throat. Desire and fear braid together because I realize his confession isn't tenderness: it's obsession, a dark tether that binds him as tightly as it binds me.

His fingers brush mine on my lap, squeezing hard as if he fears I will vanish the moment I open the door. More than ever, I know Adrián is not a man who loves calmly—he devours me, even against his own will.

The engine has barely died when Adrián is already taking my hand. The door thuds shut, and he leads me into his house in long strides, never letting go, as if he truly fears I might run. The dim hall flickers to life as he flips on the lights, but I hardly see anything—I only feel him: his ragged breath, the tension in his grip. He presses me against the hallway wall; his body closes over mine, heat burning through fabric.

"Do you see what you do to me, princesa?" His voice is rough, almost a whisper. "It's not about letting you go… it's about how much I enjoy not doing it."

He gives me no time to answer. His mouth devours mine with contained fury, his tongue probing mine; the cold brush of his piercing forces an involuntary moan from me. His hands roam my body, hiking my dress up my thighs until I'm exposed under his hungry gaze.

He lifts me abruptly, gripping my hips; my legs lock around his waist. My back slams into the wall, his hands holding me tight, and I feel him hard and relentless against me—ready to claim me, to etch his obsession into every inch of my skin.

"Lucía…" His voice cracks, trembling against my skin. "You're destroying me… and still, even if it kills me, I'm not walking away."

His look darkens. There will be no calm this time. With a swift motion he tears the dress from me; the fabric falls to my feet as if it had never existed.

My body stands exposed before him, the air itself seeming to ignite as his eyes travel over every inch of me. He pins me to the wall; his hips collide with mine without mercy, and a raw cry rips from my throat. There is no preamble, no play—he plunges into me with a brutality that tears a scream from me, which merges with the ragged cadence of his breathing.

"Do you feel it?" he growls, voice hoarse, lips brushing my ear as he drives into me with a force that breaks me open. "This is what you do to me... you make me insane."

Every movement is punishment and reward at once. I try to resist the savage pounding that slams me against the wall; my body cannot decide whether to surrender or fight, but he gives me no choice. He drags me into his rhythm, into his absolute control.

His hands clamp to my hips with a grip I both fear and crave; his thrusts quicken, deepen, until it feels as if he tears me apart and stitches me back together in the same overwhelming wave. There is no room for air—only the brutal urgency of his obsession.

"You're mine, Lucía," he pants against my mouth, teeth grazing my lips before devouring them again. "Mine even if you hate me, mine even if you try to run."

He grants me no respite. He carries me to his bedroom while his lips never leave mine; each step thuds like the echo of a verdict—he will not let me go. He throws me onto the bed and mounts me immediately, green eyes glowing like coals in the dim. His hands map my skin with frantic desperation—marking, claiming—then plunge into me again with a thrust that rips a raw cry from my throat.

"Do you understand now, Lucía?" he growls, pinning my wrists to the pillow as he moves with possessive, relentless rhythm. "This isn't love… it's the curse of not being able to let you go."

The mattress creaks beneath each slam of his hips. My legs wrap his waist; my body arches, aching for more, unable to resist the delicious fury that devours me. His mouth drops to my neck, biting, leaving marks that burn like proof. My moans fill the room, braided with his, and for a furious, suspended instant there is no world beyond him—his brutality, my ruin.

Each thrust drags me nearer the abyss, and still he does not relent, he wants to break me, brand me, show me that however I crave it and however I fear it, I will never escape him.

"Don't look away, Lucía…" His voice vibrates— controlled, dangerous. "I want you to see what you do to me."

My hips grind against his; my body surrenders to the fury of his rhythm, unable to hold back. Pleasure swells until it is impossible to contain, detonating in a brutal surge that forces a ragged cry from me.

The orgasm devours me from the inside, so fierce I lose all sense of myself. I am not Lucía; I am nothing but his — a body trembling beneath his power, an echo of surrender that breaks me down and rebuilds me in the same heartbeat.

Adrián doesn't let go. He drives into the mattress, forcing me to ride that climax through its final shudders until his body tenses above mine.

"Lucía..." he roars, my name torn from him as a spasm runs through his whole frame.

Then I feel him come with me, plunging to the bottom with brutal force, unleashing fury and need in the same brutal instant. His moans braid with mine into a shared roar that fills the room. We move together, frantic, until the wave drags us under and leaves us trembling — panting, skin to skin, slick with the sweat that binds us like invisible chains.

I close my eyes, utterly spent, but the only thing I know is this: the shared climax doesn't free me; it ties me closer to him.

I'm still gasping beneath him, my body shaking as the aftershocks run through every fiber. I expect him to pull away, to raise his cold wall as always. He does not. Adrián stays on top of me, breathing hard, his chest pressed to mine.

Slowly his hand lifts to my face. With the back of his fingers, he strokes my cheek as if afraid to bruise me, as if I am too delicate for his hands. The lips that devoured me a moment ago rest on my forehead in a soft, warm kiss so unexpected it claws at my throat.

"You're the only thing I can't fight or avoid..." he murmurs, eyes closed, confessing a sin. "It terrifies me how much I need you."

My heart hammers — the contrast between the brutal man who ravaged me seconds ago and this one tenderly stroking me is unbearable. I look at him, lost in those green eyes where a dangerous tenderness cracks his steel mask, and I realize this moment says more than any confession ever could: I am the wound he keeps returning to.

The silence barely settles when a sharp buzz cuts through it. Adrián's phone vibrates in his pocket on the floor, insistent, as if the world he belongs to will not allow him a single unclaimed breath. He stiffens; his hand leaves my skin with a brusque motion that opens an empty place inside me. He sits on the edge of the bed, inhales, and answers.

"Yes." His voice flips to dry and sharp — the outward Adrián, the man he never shows me. I catch fragments: "tonight...," "I'm on my way."

When he hangs up he's already on his feet with a speed that tears me in two. His eyes burn from the shadows, filled with something between fury and resignation.

"I have to go." His voice is a blade.

I sit up, sheets tangled around my legs. "Where?"

He doesn't answer right away. He grabs his clothes, dressing with hard, efficient movements, each button sealed as if closing the distance between us for good.

"Don't ask, Lucía." He throws me a look that knocks the breath out of me.

But I already know. He doesn't have to say it. That call ripped him away, pulling him back into the dark world he refuses to name. The slam of the door behind him echoes in my chest like thunder. I lie frozen for a few seconds in the bed, wrapped in the heat he left in the sheets, wondering what demon could be strong enough to tear him away at this moment.

Half-dressed and still trembling, I step into the street. Dawn air slaps my face as I walk home, trying to sort the chaos in my head. Each step is a cruel reminder of how little I know about him...and how desperately I already need him.

At home the house is silent, but my mind is not. I lock my door, collapse onto the bed, and stare at the ceiling. What life does Adrián lead when he isn't with me? How deep does the world run that consumes him—the world that forces him to flee every time that damned phone rings?

I close my eyes, but sleep won't come. Only one strangling certainty settles over me: no matter how I try to escape, I am bound to him more tightly than ever—and his secret threatens to drag me under with a force as strong as his desire.

Chapter 16

✦ ✦ ✦ ✦ ✦ ✦

*D*awn is just beginning to tint the curtains gray when my bedroom door slams open. I sit up with a jolt, my heart still worn from a night that never let me sleep. "Where were you last night, Lucía?" My father's voice lashes the air like a whip.

His silhouette fills the doorway, framed in the hallway light—imposing, arms crossed, gaze sharp. I feel like a prisoner under interrogation. Every word from him falls like a sentence, and I know what's at stake isn't a harmless lie but the truth I'm desperate to hide.

"I went for a walk," I answer quickly, though even I don't believe the lie.

He steps forward, his eyes drilling into mine with a hardness that freezes me.

"Don't lie to me, Lucía. You came in at dawn."

I swallow, my mind screaming Adrián's name, though my lips stay sealed. My father exhales, but there's no relief in it—only restrained fury.

"Are you still seeing Adrián?" His tone allows no evasion.

Heat rushes through me; pride flares.

"I'm twenty-two. You don't need to watch my every move."

His expression darkens, chilling me to the bone.

"Lucía... you know perfectly well this isn't about you. It's about him."

"What do you have to do with Adrián?" The words burst from me before I can stop them, sharp with anger and fear.

Silence falls heavy. My father stares at me as if I've crossed a sacred line. His lips press tight, his jaw clenches. For a second I think he'll explode—but he doesn't.

"It's not your concern," he says at last, his voice low and grave, like a blow.

"Of course it is," I snap, breath ragged. "You talk as if you know him better than I do—like you're hiding something."

Something flickers in his eyes: anger, yes, but also guilt. He steps closer, his shadow swallowing me.

"Lucía, listen carefully. Stay away from him. For your own good."

"Why?" My heart pounds in my throat. "What are you hiding? What is it?"

His lips part, then clamp shut, as if the words themselves are too dangerous to live inside this house.

That silence tells me more than any answer—it confirms something enormous lies buried between them.

He looks at me as if I've spoken blasphemy, then spins on his heel.

"Don't ever look for him again," he spits, his voice like ice, refusing to meet my eyes.

The door slams behind him, reverberating through the room, as loud as the absence of his words.

I stand trembling, hands pressed to my chest. That reaction says everything: there's something binding them, something dark my father refuses to name.

And as silence closes in, I make myself a promise: I will not stop until I uncover the truth. Even if it costs me my soul, even if danger devours me, I need to know.

I can't stay another second in this house. The air is heavy, thick with his unspoken words and the echo of the door. I grab my bag and leave, abandoning his silence like an open wound.

Camila is the only person I can turn to, though I know she's drowning in her own doubts. When she opens her apartment door, her face lights with relief, as if she too has been waiting desperately for this conversation.

"Lu..." Camila says, taking my hand and pulling me into the living room. Half-finished cups of coffee sit on the table, as if she'd been waiting for company.

We sit, and for a long moment neither of us speaks. I fidget with my fingers; she bites her lip, and the silence presses until I can't bear it.

"Cami..." I sigh. "I need to ask you again—what exactly did you hear from Víctor?"

Her gaze clouds; her wide eyes fill with a worry that breaks my heart.

"It was late... he was on the balcony and thought I was asleep." She pauses, the memory costing her. "He was talking about fights, about money that was 'already secured,' about deals that couldn't be allowed to fail."

The coffee in my stomach turns to lead. I force a nod, pretend calm, but inside I freeze. Everything sounds too close to Adrián—too much like the shadows that cling to him.

Camila squeezes my hand. "Lu... do you think Víctor is involved in something dangerous?"

My heart climbs into my throat. I don't know if I should tell her what I suspect, if I can saddle her with the weight that eats at me. But I know this is only the beginning— that what ties our men together is darker than we imagine.

I squeeze her fingers back until she flinches. "Cami..." my voice trembles, but I press on. "What you heard... it might not be just about Víctor."

She blinks, confused. "What do you mean—not just him?"

I swallow, walking on embers. "Sometimes there are people closer to us than we think who carry the same things—things you don't see at first glance."

Camila studies me as if trying to decode my words. Questions crowd her eyes, but she won't voice them; I don't give her a chance.

"What I mean," I add, lowering my voice, "is that if Víctor is mixed up in this... he might not be alone." Her breath catches; she looks away, biting her lip hard.

"I don't know if I want to know more, Lu..." she murmurs, almost pleading.

I understand her. But I have no choice. What I hide is my own hell—the one that pulses under the name Adrián with every breath.

Camila stares into the bottom of her cup as if she could disappear there. I nod, though my mind is elsewhere, fixated on a name I won't say aloud.

The walk home feels endless, each step heavy with questions. Just as I reach for my bedroom door, my phone vibrates in my pocket. The screen lights with his name: Adrián.

"Princesa... I need to see you. Now."

I bite my lip, torn between desire and fear, knowing that if I go this time there may be no return.

I inhale, trying to think clearly—but clarity evaporates where he's concerned. My body ignites, my heart pounding with the certainty that, even if I wanted to,

I cannot refuse.

"Tell me where."

That's all I can type, fingers shaking. The reply comes as if he'd been waiting for me to surrender.

"Terrace."

A shiver runs down my spine. I glance at the window and lift my gaze: there he is—where everything began, leaning against the terrace railing, a cigarette glowing between his fingers, smoke curling around him and making him somehow more dangerous.

His silhouette is magnetic, as if time has paused for this exact moment. Adrián—back in the place of our beginning—waiting for me.

My heart threatens to betray me. I shove on my shoes and hurry downstairs. The air slaps my face; the terrace gleams in the bright light, and there he stands. His posture is arrogant and lethal as always: the cigarette ember still faint between his fingers, his green eyes fixed on me as though they'd been burning the whole time I was gone.

When he sees me, he exhales slowly, drops the butt, and crushes it under his boot. Then he smiles—the smile that undoes me: dark, dangerous, addictive.

"Princesa," he murmurs.

My legs tremble, but I step closer, knowing that though everything screams for me to stay away, there is no corner of the world I'd rather be in than in front of the shadow that consumes me. He straightens, a predator ready to pounce, and closes the distance. His hand finds mine across the railing—firm, hot, enclosing.

"Come," he says in that low tone that always breaks me. "I have a surprise for you."

Confusion and a racing heart. Whenever Adrián promises surprises, innocence is never on the menu. His crooked smile confirms my suspicion: this is no gift but another delicious sentence, a step deeper into his darkness. Still, I follow—because I can't do otherwise.

When the sun climbs high, we're still on the road, his grip unrelenting, questions forbidden. The journey is short and interminable; my anxiety stretches every mile. Then we arrive, and I'm left speechless. Before us unfolds an immense stable, green fields rolling away, and the distant chorus of neighs. The air smells of hay and freedom.

My eyes fill with tears despite myself.

"Horses?" I whisper, my voice trembling with a joy I didn't expect.

Adrián offers that faint, dangerous smile again—rare and lethal—and for a moment something like gentleness flickers in him.

"I know you love them. I thought you might want to ride again."

I stare at him, unsettled. This isn't the Adrián who pins me to walls or devours me in the dark. This is someone else—a man who seems to know every corner of my soul, and it confuses me until it hurts.

"And you?" I ask, teasing, as my hand strokes the back of a beautiful white horse. "Do you know how to ride?"

He steps closer, his shadow falling over me, those green eyes burning as always.

"Princesa... I know how to tame any beast."

He may be talking about the horse, but my body burns because I know he's also talking about me.

The stable hand brings us two mounts: for me, a gorgeous white mare with gentle eyes; for Adrián, a powerful chestnut seemingly built for him—strong, wild, and all his. I watch him swing into the saddle with a fluid ease that steals my breath. His body fits the animal like a second skin, his shirt clinging with every movement, hands steady on the reins. The sight is intoxicating.

I climb slowly and settle, the wind on my face and the gallop's rhythm reconnecting me to something pure. Even in the middle of that freedom my eyes find him. He rides beside me, that dangerous smile curving his lips as if he knows exactly what he provokes in me. Sometimes he urges his horse forward, forcing me to follow; other times he lingers, watching me with those green eyes that strip me bare even under the noon sun.

"You look stunning like this, princesa," he calls over the pounding hooves, his voice rolling through my chest.

I bite my lip, caught between a blush and desire. Though we're surrounded by sky and field, there is nothing innocent about this ride. Even here—among horses and laughter—Adrián marks his territory: master of my steps, my body, and every corner of my addiction.

The first drops touch my face and within moments the sky darkens. Rain pours down, heavy and sudden.

"Over there," Adrián says, steering toward a massive lone tree in the middle of the field. I follow, laughing nervously, soaked in seconds. He ties the horses calmly as if the storm were only a backdrop. Water traces the lines of his muscles; he walks toward me with steady steps on wet grass, and the world narrows to him.

He draws me close, his hand firm at my waist, his gaze locking mine as if escape were impossible. Rain slides along my neck and arms, and his fingers trace the same path, the water an excuse to touch. His green eyes flare brighter than the lightning overhead; his breath collides with mine as he leans in and the storm falls away.

All that exists is his heat against the chill of the rain, the delicious tension of knowing he will claim me even beneath the open sky.

"You're beautiful, princesa," he growls, voice low and rolling, his shirt clinging to his torso as the rain maps his skin. "All mine—even as the world crumbles around us."

The rain pounds around us, but he moves slowly, as if time itself bends to his will. His fingers trace my arm, from wrist to shoulder, following the silver trails of water across my skin.

The touch is so light it makes me shiver, unsure whether it's the cold—or him. His other hand finds my waist, guiding me closer until my back meets the wet bark. There's no haste, only that quiet, dangerous control that feels like a spell.

He leans close, lips a breath from mine, the warmth of his mouth setting me on fire before the kiss ever lands. He doesn't kiss me—he denies me, pulls away just enough to make the ache unbearable.

His fingers wander lower, tracing my ribs, my stomach, as though every raindrop whispers the way. I sink against him, undone by the exquisite torture of kisses that taste like sin and salvation.

I feel him toy with the ribbon of my blouse, untying it with practiced ease. The wet fabric parts, heavy and cold against my skin. His hands return to my waist. The faint metallic click of my belt unfastening mingles with the rumble of thunder, and with one sure tug he drags the drenched pants past my hips until they cling tangled around my ankles.

The contrast is savage: the icy rain, his firm touch roaming me with possessive calm.

My breath comes in ragged bursts. I want him bare too, vulnerable beneath the storm the way he has left me. With trembling hands I unbutton his shirt, let it drop, then tug at his pants, drawing them down slowly—as if the world itself could wait for this moment.

The sky roars, the water lashes, but nothing matters. There is only him and me—two bodies surrendered, defying the storm as if it were born of our desire.

Water slips between us like a second skin, cold and merciless. His hands, however, are fire. He doesn't rush to claim me—not yet. He prefers the game: stretching the wait, making me his ground before seizing it.

"Look at you, princesa..." he murmurs against my skin, his deep voice thrumming in my chest. "The storm can't conquer you, but I can."

A moan breaks from my throat as his mouth finds my nipple, trapping it in heat and hunger. His hands roam over my hips, my thighs, parting me with agonizing patience, like the rain itself were marking the tempo of his cruelty.

I close my eyes, surrendering, my body arching into his. He knows exactly how to drive me to the edge—with nothing but his hands and his tongue—teasing my need, breaking me down until I'm begging in silence. Then he lets go, only to guide me down, his body pressing mine into the wet grass. The chill bites, but I hardly feel it. He's there, covering me, his warmth a fever that claims me whole.

The rain lashes us, slick between our bodies as if trying to separate us, but Adrián holds me in place, his lips devouring mine, his fingers moving over me with a rhythm so slow it hurts.

The earth sticks to my skin, the thunder roars, and he explores me like a man worshipping what's already his. His hands slide down my ribs, over my stomach, stopping just long enough to make me beg for him—with only my eyes, with only the tremor of his name on my lips.

"Lucía..." —he bites my neck, his voice thick with possession— "even the storm feels small compared to you."

And I feel it. I feel that no cold could ever extinguish what he ignites inside me, that not even the fury of the sky could rival the obsession consuming me in his arms. He parts my legs with a force that leaves no room for resistance. The chill of the grass fuses with the scorching heat of his body, and before I can plead or stop him, he's already taking me—hard, deep, claiming me with every thrust.

The roar of thunder drowns my voice, but Adrián hears it. He feels it in every tremor of my body arching beneath him.

"You belong to me..." —he snarls against my lips, eyes dark and wild—." Mine, even if the whole damn world tried to pull you from me."

My nails rake his back—half attempt to halt him, half plea to hold him closer. Each strike rips me apart and mends me anew; my body becomes his in shards, each slam a challenge to the storm. Pleasure bolts through me like lightning braided with the sky's wrath. There is no refuge, no escape—only this brutal instant where nature screams with us and my body loses itself to his.

Thunder rumbles above, and Adrián's pounding grows more ferocious, the rain lashing our skin like a relentless whip.

I think I will break, drown in unbearable pleasure— then, just when I near collapse, he stops. He pins me to the wet grass, panting over my face, green eyes blazing with dark hunger.

"Not yet, princesa," he growls, tightening his hold on my hips. "Hold on a little longer."

A desperate cry tears out of me; my body trembles, begging in ways my tongue cannot. Adrián smiles— cruel—and moves again, slower this time, each thrust deep and wrenching, making me feel each inch until I teeter on the edge. Then he halts once more, his mouth seeking mine as he bites my lip until pain and pleasure spill together.

"You're so receptive... so addicted to me," he whispers in a broken voice. "I'll take you to the limit as many times as I want."

I've lost count of how many times he's dragged me to the brink, each scream swallowed by the storm. My body trembles, my throat burns, every fiber pleading for what he denies. I'm shattered, undone—and still his gaze keeps me chained.

Suddenly his hands dig harder into my hips, and his thrusts turn savage, relentless.

No more pauses, no more games—only a brutal rhythm that crashes through me like the storm above.

"Now, princesa..." he growls through his teeth, voice hoarse and dangerous.

Pleasure rips through me, unstoppable; a moan tears free and is swallowed by the storm's fury. My body tightens and surrenders at once, every muscle trembling beneath him as I come undone under his control. My nails rake his skin as my legs lock around him—both pleading and claiming—and the universe contracts to this searing instant where everything breaks and is reborn in his name.

Adrián follows, losing himself with me; his raw roar fills the tempest as his body tenses over mine. There is no gentleness now—only fierce punishment for pushing me *to the limit, and the cruel reward of dragging me with him into a shattering climax. Spent beneath his weight, gasping while the rain drums on our bodies, the only truth I know is that no heaven or hell could match what this man makes me feel.*

The storm begins to calm, thunder rolling off into the distance, leaving only the steady drum of raindrops on our skin. My fingers tremble as I slide them down his wet back, leaving marks from my nails. He does not move— he stays propped over me, chest heaving against mine, as if he needs the moment to remember how to breathe.

Chaos swirls around us—the bruised sky, the sodden earth, the restless horses—but here, in his arms, a strange refuge forms: intimate and disarming in a way his brutality never was. I close my eyes, tasting the contrast—the calm after the fury, the tenderness tucked beneath possession—and I understand that despite everything in ruins, there is no place safer or more dangerous than beneath Adrián, surrendered to the storm and to him.

"You're insane..." I whisper at last; my voice fractured between exhaustion and disbelief.

He only smirks, a dark curve on his wet lips, more lethal than any storm. He lowers his head and brushes my mouth with a slow kiss, as if sealing every unsaid thing.

"Maybe," he murmurs, voice low and raw with pleasure and restrained rage. "But you're already part of my madness, princesa."

My heart hammers so hard my reply sticks in my throat. He is right: what we lived under that broken sky is not love or mere desire—it is shared madness, an addiction that consumes me more with every second. I hold his gaze, waiting for that dangerous smile to turn into another claim. Instead, his hand rises slowly to my face, brushing damp strands from my forehead with a tenderness that disarms me. He tilts his head and kisses my cheek, then the corner of my mouth, as if tasting each fragment of my skin.

His warm breath contrasts with the cold rain still clinging to us, and for the first time I feel him touch me as if he fears I might dissolve in his hands.

"You're the only real thing in the middle of my chaos," he whispers, barely audible, as if even the storm should not overhear.

Tears sting my eyes, and I don't know if they come from the unexpected softness or from the fear the confession hides. My body still trembles from what just happened; it cannot reconcile how he can give me brutality, pleasure, and gentleness all at once.

And it's there, beneath the rain thinning into drizzle, that I realize what terrifies me most isn't his violence but his power to make me feel like his salvation.

His fingers linger on my face for a few heartbeats, and I swear there's a calm in his gaze I've never seen. Then, as if deciding we've had enough, he straightens and offers his hand to help me up.

He lifts me to my feet, picks my sodden pants from the grass, and hands them to me with a casualness that belies the madness we just lived beneath the storm. I obey in silence, my heart still racing. Without a word he loosens the horses' reins and strokes his mount's neck with an unsettling ease. I follow, trembling, still trapped in the echo of what he whispered: you're the only real thing in the middle of my chaos.

He helps me into the saddle with a calm, firm hand, as if this is merely another ride. As he mounts his horse and leads us down the lane toward home, I remain tangled in a whirlwind of feelings—desire, fear, tenderness—and a cruel doubt burning in my chest. How can a man who claims me with such brutality also touch me as if I were the single thing keeping him standing?

We ride in silence, accompanied only by the soft drum of hooves and the patter of fading rain. I think the tenderness will be buried under the routine with which he resumes command. But then, without turning his head, his hoarse voice slices the air.

"If you were smarter, princesa... you'd run far from me."

I freeze. I don't know whether it's a warning, a confession, or another cruel game. The taste of his words sears me more than the memory of his mouth. I long to ask why, to demand answers, but I don't dare—he will shut down if I press. So, I ride on at his side, mute and trapped by that sentence, more confused and addicted than ever.

The road home stretches in quiet, broken only by hooves on wet earth and the echo of his warning in my head. When we reach the stable, he dismounts first and helps me down with the same measured calm he used to lift me—acting as if the storm and our abandon were a dream. I remain trembling, not from cold but from the confusion that eats me. He hands the reins to the stableman without looking back; perhaps the deepest torment is this: we share skin and fire, yet his secrets remain a wall I cannot scale.

The engine rumbles beneath the humid night and the silence between us weighs heavier than the storm. I watch the road lights pool on the wet glass while he drives—one hand steady on the wheel, the other resting on his thigh so near me it burns.

"Thanks for today," I murmur at last, not daring to meet his eyes.

The curve of his lips appears for a breath, a dangerous shadow in the car's dimness.

"Don't thank me, princesa…" his hoarse voice strokes me like an invisible caress. "I never do anything out of kindness."

I swallow, unable to answer. The air in the car is so thick that every breath scorches my throat. As the city lights begin to appear in the distance, I understand the line for what it is—the most ambiguous and lethal of all: a reminder that what he gives me is never a gift... it is always a sentence.

The car stops a few meters from my house. The dark windows tell me my parents are asleep, but my heart pounds so loudly I fear they might hear it through the walls. I move to open the door when his hand clamps down on my wrist. I turn, and his green eyes catch me in the gloom—more intense than ever.

He says nothing at first; he just watches me, as if etching an invisible warning into my skin. Then he takes the back of my neck and kisses me. It isn't soft or slow— it's possessive and hungry, stealing my breath and reminding me of what I become under his control. He bites my lip, forces me to surrender into his mouth, and when he lets me go, I gasp as if surfacing from an abyss, still needing air.

"Never forget it, princesa," he murmurs against my skin, voice rough and dangerous. "You're mine. Always."

My hands tremble as I open the door and climb out, legs barely holding me. He drives off without looking back, his silhouette swallowed by the night. I stand there, the echo of his kiss burning on my lips, knowing that invisible mark will follow me even inside my own house.

Chapter 17

* * * * * *

The doorbell rings again and I rush to answer before my parents can. Camila stands there, drawn and wet-haired, as if she ran straight out without thinking. "Lu, we have to talk," she says, pushing past me before I can react. I lead her to my room and close the door; her face sets my pulse racing. Camila never loses composure—seeing her like this prickles my skin.

"What's wrong?" I whisper.

She breathes deep, eyes bright with fear and adrenaline. "I know where the fight will be tonight."

The world contracts. Something drops in my stomach. "What... what fight?" I force out, though the answer already smolders on my skin.

"Don't play dumb, Lu. You know there's something more. Last night I heard Víctor on the balcony. It wasn't work—he was talking time, place... and Adrián's name." Camila presses her lips together, shaking her head.

My breath snags. I stay quiet for a heartbeat, but inside the decision has formed. I turn to her, certainty surprising me. "Let's go."

Camila's eyes widen. "But... how will we get in?" she asks, naive panic threading her voice.

A crooked, dangerous smile crosses my face—suddenly I can speak Adrián's language. "By betting."

Silence yawns. Camila swallows, trying to process, and adrenaline floods me. I don't know what terrifies me more: moving closer to that forbidden world, or how irresistibly it draws me in.

The taxi slips through streets that grow darker with every block. Light drizzle taps the glass and the cab's silence weighs heavy. Camila can't sit still; her hands twist in her lap, eyes searching the window for answers that aren't there.

"Lu... what if they catch us?" she whispers. "What do we do if someone recognizes us?"

I glance at her and hide the storm in my chest. "You just follow me. Don't talk to anyone." She nods, though I can see she doesn't comprehend the full danger. She doesn't know that I'm walking straight into the fire because that is where he is—Adrián. His name drums in my blood louder and louder.

I picture him: sweat, bruises, a savage edge—the man who drags me into a world I don't belong to yet cannot leave. Camila squeezes my hand, searching for reassurance; I squeeze back—not for her, but to anchor myself against the hunger and fear threatening to undo me.

We stop at a red light and neon from a nearby cantina paints the cab in red. Camila's eyes go wide with real fear. "Lu... I don't know if I can do this," she whispers, fingers trembling over mine. I breathe, force a smile, and stroke her hand as if I own the calm I pretend to feel.

"Of course you can. It's just a place, Cami. You go in, look, and you leave with me. Nothing's going to happen."

She nods, swallowing hard, but I feel the tremor in her hand against mine. And that's when I realize I'm lying— not to protect her, but because even I don't know what will happen inside. My calm is only disguise. Underneath, anxiety tears me apart: my heart races at a frantic rhythm, my breath short, each passing mile burning me more. I'm not thinking of bets, or danger, or even Víctor. Only of him.

Adrián.
The name sears silently through me, and even though my mouth insists everything will be fine, I know the moment I see him I'll lose control.

The taxi stops at an abandoned warehouse on the city's edge. Graffiti and rust coat the façade, as if no one's stepped inside in years—yet the roar of voices and muffled music bleeding out betray the lie. Camila squeezes my hand so tight she nearly cuts off circulation.

"Lu... this looks awful," she whispers, eyes darting over the parked cars, their tinted windows hiding men smoking at the doors.

I feel it too. The air here is different: heavy with sweat, tobacco, alcohol—and danger. And still, adrenaline thrums in every vein. A massive bouncer blocks the entrance, arms crossed, gaze cold as steel. This isn't the kind of place you just walk into. Still, I hold my head high, pretending I belong.

"What if they don't let us in?" Camila trembles.

"They will," I reply without hesitation, though my heart hammers like it might break free.

The man at the door lifts an eyebrow as we approach. "What do you want?" he asks flatly.

I swallow. The answer comes on its own, carrying confidence I don't feel.

"To bet."

For an instant, silence presses like a weight. Then the guard smirks, crooked, and steps aside.

"Go ahead."

Inside is worse. The warehouse chokes with smoke and shouts. Men and women crowd an improvised ring in the center, the hanging lights barely piercing the stained walls. Bills pass between hands, liquor spills, and the air reeks of violence barely leashed. Camila grips my arm, terrified. I have only one burning question: Where is Adrián?

The noise is deafening—deep voices haggling over numbers, the scrape of chairs, the thud of footsteps. In one corner, under a yellow lamp, a long table sprawls with open ledgers. Behind it, men with sharp eyes scribble names and figures, counting stacks of cash like playing cards.

Camila clings to my arm, whispering, "Lu..."

I'm uneasy too, but I don't show it. My steps echo on damp concrete as I approach the table. One of the men looks me over, amusement flickering in his eyes.

"Betting?" he drawls, as though the idea is a joke.

I meet his gaze, steadying my voice even while my chest hammers.

"Yes. What's the minimum?"

His smirk deepens, not kind but mocking, a challenge.

"One hundred. And who are you betting on?"

I don't hesitate

"Adrián."

His lips curved a little more, as if tasting my answer.

"Good choice."

I slipped a bill from my purse and placed it on the table. His grubby fingers snatched it up.

"Name?"
"Lucía."
He jabbed it into a notebook stained with grease and sweat.

"Seats over there." He waved us toward the makeshift bleachers facing the ring.

Camila and I exchanged a look—me burning with anxiety, her hollow with doubt. Smoke and stale beer wrapped the room like a bad omen. She followed me like a ghost, pale and skittish; we sat on the hard planks among strangers shouting, laughing, and smoking without restraint. The ring lay empty beneath a single spotlight; the murmur swelled, and the air thickened with tension.

My heart hammered so loud it erased everything else. I couldn't take my eyes off the center of the ring; I knew he would appear at any second. Then the crowd erupted when he stepped inside. He wore no gold necklaces, no bluster—he didn't need them. His presence was its own gravity. Adrián radiated dark magnetism, a pull that brushed your skin like danger and desire entwined.

Women screamed his name, others reached toward him as if a touch might ignite them; some covered their mouths in reverence, staring at what seemed like a god in flesh. The announcer raised his arms, voice rasping with excitement:

"Ladies and gentlemen... Reaper!"

The nickname rolled through the room like thunder. He stood in the center of the ring—tall, unbending, no smile required. His gaze swept the crowd like a promise with teeth: Reaper had come to claim what was his. The roar swelled again as the announcer pointed to the other corner.

"And in this corner... El Toro Ramírez!"

El Toro climbed into the ring beating his chest, sweat slick, a massive body moving like a battering ram. He spat on the floor, raised his fists, and hurled obscenities to rile the crowd. Noise rose—whoops, whistles, jeers— but then the air shifted. The voices knifed higher, raw with hysteria and hunger.

El Toro slammed the ropes and roared; Adrián tilted his head, a panther appraising prey. In that stillness everyone understood: the fight wasn't fair. It was inevitable.

I stared at Adrián and forgot to breathe. He didn't seek applause—he radiated it. Under the yellow light his skin gleamed and his eyes felt like blades; even amid the press of bodies, they cut straight through me. Camila nudged my elbow; a nervous laugh tucked in her whisper:

"Lucía... he's looking at you."

His gaze lashed me like a whip. It wasn't desire. It wasn't pride. It wasn't the dark pull that had always poisoned me.

It was punishment.

That cold, cutting look stole my breath: What are you doing here, Lucía?

A silent reproach from a man who had never wanted me tangled in his world, in the darkness he himself couldn't escape.

I shrank beneath it. Shame burned across my skin, as though I had trespassed on forbidden ground, as if I had betrayed him simply by being there.

Camila tugged at my arm, her voice breaking in a whisper.

"Lucía, let's go—they'll find us..."

But I couldn't move. His eyes pinned me, that silent judgment hurting more than any blow he might take tonight.

Then a burly figure climbed into the ring, severing the invisible thread between us. His knuckles were misshapen; his brows split with old scars. He bellowed with a hoarse voice:

"To your corners!"

The crowd answered in a hungry roar. The referee raised a hand, his words cutting through the chaos:

"Fight until one can't go on."

The warehouse erupted—shouts, applause, cash flying through the air. Camila shuddered beside me, her nails digging into my arm. I still couldn't move. Adrián turned his back to me, as if I no longer existed.

The referee's hand dropped like a sentence.

"Fight!"

The first blow cracked like bone. I flinched, my breath caught. El Toro charged, all brute force and blind rage, fists smashing against ropes, flesh, anything in reach. The crowd howled, drunk on violence.

Adrián didn't move with the panic of a man trying to survive. He moved with the calm cruelty of a predator, dodging with lethal precision, letting El Toro's fury burn itself out against the air. His body glistened under the jaundiced light—every muscle taut, sculpted, vibrating with dark allure.

A brutal right hook came for him. I bit my lip until I tasted blood. Adrián pivoted—slight, elegant, lethal— and the punch carved only air. His counterstrike was surgical: a fist snapping across El Toro's face. The crack of splitting flesh froze my blood.

"My God..." Camila whispered, hiding behind her hands.

I should have looked away. I couldn't.

Because there was something hypnotic in the way he moved—in that terrible marriage of violence and beauty. It was like watching death dance.

Another blow—this time to El Toro's stomach— doubled the man over. Adrián held him there with an unblinking stare, merciless, immovable.

That wasn't the man I knew. He was something else entirely.

A dangerous shadow, cruel... yet magnetic enough to make my legs nearly give out beneath me.

The crowd screamed, delirious, demanding blood. I trembled too—but not only from fear. Something else burned inside me: that forbidden desire for him, for the darkness he now showed me without a mask.

He moved in that ring as if he had been born for nothing else. In his body, violence became elegance, destruction became beauty. Every strike was a whip cracking through the air, electrifying everyone... and me most of all.

I tried to look away, to flee the shadow clinging to him. But it was useless. I was chained—to him, to the dark attraction devouring me, to the side of Adrián he had never wanted me to see, now revealed mercilessly before my eyes.

And I understood, trembling head to toe, that I could no longer tell the difference.

Not between horror and desire.
Not between repulsion and attraction.
It was all one devastating sensation: I wanted him most at the very moment he terrified me most.

El Toro collapsed against the ropes with a guttural groan, but I barely heard it. The noise, the stench of sweat and blood—all of it vanished the instant my eyes found Adrián's.

The man pounding another into the ground before me wasn't the same one who had once held me in the shadows of my room.

I remembered it like a heartbeat: his breath steady against my neck, the gentleness of his hand threading through my hair. The way he had whispered, "You are my light, Lucía," as if it were a secret prayer meant only for us.

And now... that same hand that had caressed me with reverence was breaking bones. Those same lips that had kissed me with devotion twisted into a feral snarl.

A shiver ripped through me. Was it the same man? Or had there always been two Adriáns, and I had only ever known half?

The roar of the crowd dragged me back. Blood. Sweat. Screams. And there he was: Adrián—Reaper— unrelenting, brutal.

And me, caught between the memory of his tenderness and the horror of his violence.

El Toro spat blood on the floor, staggering, but lunged again like a wounded beast. The strike was clumsy, desperate. Adrián dodged with lethal calm and answered with a hook that cracked like a gunshot. El Toro crumpled to his knees.

The crowd erupted. Some celebrated, others demanded the kill. The referee hesitated, but Adrián didn't. He advanced like an unforgiving shadow.

"My God, Lucía!" Camila gasped, covering her mouth with both hands. "He's going to kill him!"

I heard her—but I couldn't look away. Camila trembled beside me, eyes darting to the exit, praying no one noticed us.

I, on the other hand, was nailed to my seat, paralyzed.

It was pure violence. Brutality. And yet every movement pulled me in with a force I couldn't resist. The contrast tore me apart: the tenderness of his memory still pulsing on my skin, while in front of me the man I desired sank deeper and deeper into darkness.

El Toro staggered, bleeding, barely upright. Adrián stared him down, merciless, and raised his fist again.

The roar of the crowd became unbearable. Camila tugged at my arm, on the verge of tears.

"Lucía, let's go. Now!"

But I couldn't. Not while his eyes—hard, unyielding, cruel—reminded me that this shadow was mine too, even if it tore me apart.

El Toro lifted his fists one last time, swaying, ready to die before surrendering. Adrián didn't rush. He studied him with lethal calm, then struck: one blow to the stomach that knocked the air from him, another to the face that spun him sideways, and then the last a devastating right hook that sent him crashing to the canvas.

For a heartbeat, silence. The echo of that impact reverberated through my bones. Then the crowd erupted in a savage roar.

El Toro twitched, tried to rise—collapsed. Tried again—fell flat. Finally, he lay on his side, gasping, defeated.

The referee crouched, checked him quickly, then grabbed Adrián's wrist and lifted it high.

"Winner... Reaper!"

The uproar was deafening. Bills flew into the air. Women shrieked his name as if a dark god had descended into the ring.

Camila clung to me, pale, her nails digging into my arm.

"Lucía, I can't take this anymore..."

Neither could I. And yet I couldn't tear my eyes from him. Adrián—triumphant, untouchable, cruel and beautiful. His chest heaving, another man's blood drying on his knuckles, that fire in his gaze still unbroken.

And when his eyes found mine again through the chaos, I shattered. Because that victory wasn't just his. It was mine too—a mark branded into me, reminding me I had no way out.

Around us, men hugged and shouted, celebrating their winnings. I seized the chaos, tugged hard on Camila's arm.

"Come on. Now." My voice shook more than I wanted.

She nodded, face crumbling, and we forced our way through the crowd, bodies slick with sweat pressing against us, shouts echoing in our ears. My heart hammered, desperate to escape before Adrián's gaze could bind me again.

But we didn't get far.

A rough hand clamped onto Camila's arm and yanked her back.

"And what the hell are you two doing here?"

Víctor's voice froze my blood.

Camila let out a choked scream, twisting to break free, but he held her tight, his eyes gleaming with a mix of fury and amusement.

"You're coming with me," he said, not even glancing at me, dragging her through the crowd that parted for him as if nothing were wrong.

"Camila!" I screamed, reaching out, but she vanished into the sea of bodies, swallowed by the darkness of that place.

Suddenly, I was alone. Surrounded by voices, by bets, by smoke... but alone.

And then I felt it.

The crowd shifted, parting just enough, as if they sensed it. Adrián was coming toward me.

There was no escape. His eyes were locked on mine, darker than ever, loaded with reproach and possession. My breath fractured into frantic gasps.

He said nothing. He didn't need to. His hand seized my arm, unyielding, leaving me no chance to resist. He dragged me with him, shoving aside anyone in the way, until the roar of the ring faded and we disappeared into the shadow of a narrow hallway.

The metallic tang of blood still clung to my senses when, with a slam of the door, I found myself in his locker room. Alone.

The echo made me flinch. The room was bare, oppressive—four walls, a wooden bench, air thick with sweat, blood, and the raw sting of leather.

Adrián released me abruptly, as if the mere touch of my skin burned him. He stepped back, fists still stained, his chest rising and falling violently.

His eyes cut through me—dark, sharp, merciless.

"What the hell are you doing here, Lucía?" he spat, each word a lash. "How did you find me?"

I froze, my back pressed against the wall, my heart pounding wildly. I had never seen him like this. Not even in his hardest moments had he worn that look—the look of a man torn between destroying me and protecting me from himself.

My voice came out in a whisper.

"Camila overheard Víctor."

His jaw clenched, his fists tightening until the veins bulged.

"No, Lucía. No." His gaze burned, full of fury and shame. "This isn't your world. You weren't supposed to see me like this."

Tears stung my eyes, but I didn't look away. Even though his anger cut me open, even though his voice lashed like punishment, something in me clung to him with a strength I couldn't break.

His breathing still crackled like lightning when he spoke again, lower now, but sharper.

"It's dangerous for you to be here." His eyes raked over me from head to toe—not with desire, but with the reproach of a guardian who had failed. "Where's Camila?"

I swallowed hard, my voice raw.

"Víctor... he grabbed her and took her away. I tried to stop him, but—" My throat knotted. "But I couldn't."

Adrián went rigid. His face hardened, another layer of darkness sealing over him. He struck the wall with his fist, the crack reverberating through the small room, making me jump.

"Damn it…" he muttered through clenched teeth, almost to himself.

I wanted to reach for him, to touch him, but his gaze snapped back to mine and froze me in place—fire and shadow at once.

"You don't understand, Lucía. You shouldn't be here." His voice trembled with contained fury.

My own voice shook, barely air.

"Do you think he could hurt Camila?"

Adrián held my stare. For an instant, the fury in his eyes twisted into something darker, heavier. His jaw tightened, and he gave the slightest shake of his head.

"I don't think so.". "He's a bastard… but he's in love with her."

A knot tightened in my stomach—relief braided with unease. Adrián stepped closer, so near I could feel the heat of his body, the scent of sweat and blood clinging to him. His voice dropped, as if speaking to himself.

"Just try to do what I try with you." He pierced me with his eyes and my skin ignited under that stare. "Keep you away from this world. But I can't."

His confession stole my breath. Part of me wanted to hold him; another part wanted to run. In his words there was something more dangerous than the blows in the ring: the certainty that he would never stop dragging me with him, even if he tried.

I was lost in the fire of his eyes. He held me in silence, as if my will meant nothing. It was strange how someone so violent could make me feel that, instead of destroying me, he gave me a place where only he and I existed.

Everything about Adrián was danger—bloodstained fists, a voice thick with fury, a shadow that wrapped him. And yet there was no room for fear inside me. Only that absurd, tearing need. I wanted him for myself.

I knew it with a shudder: a desire as dark as the world he dragged me into. And though it hurt to admit, there was no turning back. I stared at him, unable to look away—lost, broken, hungry.

Then he closed the distance. Adrián grabbed my face with a roughness that tore a strangled sigh from me. His fingers, still warm and stained, dug into my cheeks, forcing me to meet his gaze.

"Lucía... you don't know what you awaken in me when you look at me like that." —His lips ghosted over mine, a promise he refused to give. "I crave you with the same rage I use to resist you. And it's destroying me."

My heart exploded in my chest. There was no gentleness—only absolute domination, as if he wanted to tattoo on my skin the truth I kept denying. Yet in that brutality there pulsed a power that held me and made me feel alive. His breath hit mine; each word was a rough caress against my lips.

"I don't care if you run, I don't care if you hate me," his eyes burned, dark and voracious. "I will make you mine right here, whether you want it or not."

The world dissolved. There was no ring, no shouts, no blood—only that brutal promise chaining me to him, mixing fear with a desire so intense it made me tremble. His lips crashed on mine like a blow, punishment with furious urgency. His mouth devoured me—hard, hungry—and I tasted the metallic tang of blood under his breath. I tried to resist, to step back, but my body wouldn't obey. My fingers clung to his sweat-slick skin, desperate for more of what I refused to admit.

The kiss was fire: brutal, suffocating, full of what he wouldn't say aloud. It confirmed the threat—he was going to consume me, possess me, break me into pieces. And yet I wanted it.

"You disobeyed me," he murmured, his fingers squeezing my jaw so I couldn't look away. "I told you to stay out of this. Not to ask questions."

Each word seared my skin.

"What am I supposed to do with you, Lucía?" His lips brushed my cheek, slid to my neck, and his teeth grazed the skin like a delicious threat. "Because I don't know if I want to punish you... or never let you go."

What I felt was an intoxicating tangle: fear masked as desire; desire masked as fear. Though my mind begged to escape, my body had already chosen surrender. This man is made for me.

I don't care about his darkness. I don't care about the danger that breathes in every movement.

I am his. I have been long before I admitted it. Even if he hurts me, drags me to the lowest places, destroys me with every possessive gesture—I want him.

He is mine as much as I am his. There is no way out. No redemption. Only this abyss that calls me—and at its bottom, Adrián waiting.

I don't think. I don't reason. Everything I tried to hold together collapses the moment his hands grip me—force that is both punishment and refuge. I kiss him with the desperation of someone surrendering to a sentence. My fingers sink into the nape of his neck, into his back still damp with sweat and violence. I feel the heat of his body, the hardness of his muscles. I want him like that: raw, dark, real.

He lifts me easily and slams me against the wall. A moan rips out of me as his lips trail down my neck, marking me as if to carve on my skin that I belong to him.

"No one else gets to touch you like this" —he murmured, his tone rough, caught somewhere between hunger and threat.

My body arches to him, surrendering without reserve. I do not think of Camila, or Víctor, or the danger circling us—there are only the two of us in that locker room where violence still vibrates in his fists, and I give myself

He rips my soaked blouse from me, careless; the fabric yields, falling away as if nothing matters but my bare skin. His mouth trails down my neck with a violence that forces broken moans from me. His hands slide under my skirt; with one impatient motion he yanks it up and shoves my panties aside, as if no barrier remains but my surrender.

"Do you play with fire, princesa?" —he breathes against my neck, his voice a rasp of sin. "Then brace yourself... tonight, you'll become both the flame and the ash it leaves behind."

He does. He slams into me, hard and sudden, pulling a broken sound from my throat that collides with the metallic echo of the warehouse. Each thrust is ruthless, deep, a punishment and a need all at once. He drives me into the wall, over and over, until I can't tell where he ends and I begin.

My hands claw at his shoulders, desperate to anchor myself, but his pace is merciless, stealing every breath, every thought. He doesn't ease up. Doesn't give me a second to recover. His gaze locks on mine—wild, consuming—as if he wants to burn this moment into my memory.

And as pleasure and pain blur into one, I finally understand: this is his vengeance—taking me until the only thing left in me is him.

"Don't deny it, princesa..." he growls close to my ear, his voice raw with threat. "It's not just me. Risk calls to you; danger lights you up... and that's why you're here, surrendered under my control."

His words cut me, cruel, irresistible. The worst part was they were true. My body confirmed it, trembling under each brutal thrust, yielding to the very danger that should have driven me away.

Pressure built inside me, fierce and unstoppable. I clung to his shoulders as if that could let me survive the fire consuming me. When I could hold on no longer, my body detonated in a shattering orgasm; my torn voice ricocheted off iron and the broken silence of the room.

Adrián gave me no mercy. His hands gripped me tighter, as if branding me with possession, holding me to the wall while I fractured and reformed under his control. No escape, no respite—only him, his darkness, and the sweetest punishment I had ever surrendered to.

His rhythm never slackened; his thrusts robbed me of any control. I opened my eyes, trembling, and found him watching me with that contained fury that suffocated. His breathing was heavy, muscles tense—I knew he could come with me at any moment. He didn't. He held back. He mastered himself.

"That's the difference, princesa..." he bit into my neck, his words a burning poison. "I control my desire. You, on the other hand, have none that doesn't belong to me."

A muffled, broken sound escaped me—part frustration, part delirium—because I knew: it wouldn't end until he decided. That sentence consumed me more than his hands or his body ever could.

I thought I couldn't take any more. My legs trembled, my back burned against the wall, each thrust stealing my breath. I looked at him, hoping he'd give in and let me go with him. But his green gaze held something darker: absolute control.

He changed the pace. Movements grew deeper, more calculated—each drive designed to drag me over the edge without letting me fall free. He squeezed me harder, his hands white where they marked my skin, and I screamed, desperate, as another wave crashed over me— fiercer than the last.

"That's it, princesa..." his hoarse voice broke me— dangerous, lethal. "Surrender to me again."

And I did. The second orgasm ripped through me, shaking me whole, tearing a raw cry that filled the locker room. I felt myself break inside, overwhelmed, my body unable to bear so much pleasure turned into punishment.

When I finally collapsed against him—gasping, trembling—I knew it wasn't over. His breath was ragged, his erection throbbing against me, and yet he continued to hold back. That was the cruelest punishment: giving me more than I could resist while refusing himself.

"Adrián..." I whispered at first; then my voice hardened, full of fire. "I want you to come with me."

He tensed; his green eyes flared with a mix of fury and desire.

"Are you giving me orders, princesa?"

I grabbed his face, holding him, looking him straight in the eyes.

"Yes. I want to feel you. Inside me. Now."

A low, dangerous growl rose from his chest. In that instant I knew I'd broken him, pierced the shell of control that tormented him. His lips attacked mine with unleashed passion, and his rhythm went wilder, more urgent—my challenge had freed him from his own prison.

"With so many women out there screaming your name... you could have them all. Maybe you already do."

"But none of them make you feel what I do. None. And even if you deny it, you can't erase it."

His green eyes flare with dangerous fury, his jaw tight as if my words were gasoline on a fire he barely contains. I know I've hit his pride, his secret, his truth. And that makes him even more mine.

"*Lucía...*" *he roars my name, his voice broken, vulnerable and dangerous at once.*

Then we burst together. The climax hits me like liquid fire against the locker-room wall. My screams mingle with his, a shared roar that makes the air tremble, as if the universe itself opened to witness our destruction.

I collapse trembling beneath his body, his heavy gasps in my ear, my skin soaked with sweat and pleasure. And amid the chaos, the brutality and the fury, I feel that savage connection that consumes me: his addiction is mine.

He stares at me, so close I can feel the brush of his breath, and for a moment I think he's going to explode with anger. But no—only a crooked smile.

"*You're right, princesa,*" *he growls, his deep voice loaded with danger.* "*Out there I could have anyone... and yet, none of them break me the way you do. None drag me into this damn abyss where only you exist.*"

His words still burn on my skin when suddenly he pulls away. The heat of his body vanishes, and I'm left cold against the wall, my heart beating out of time, as if something vital has been ripped from me.

He runs a hand through his hair, jaw tight, breathing deeply as if to erase what he just confessed. There's no more sweetness in his eyes—only that cold shadow that always returns to cover everything.

"Get dressed," he orders in a hoarse, dry voice, not looking at me directly. "You shouldn't be here."

Tears threaten, not from physical pain but because in a second, he's rebuilt the wall between us. And yet the sickest part of me wants him more than ever.

"No!" The word bursts out stronger than I expected, echoing in the empty locker room.

He stops dead, his back to me, muscles tense, as if the very idea of hearing me is a punishment worse than any blow he might take in the ring.

"I want to know why you fight. Who's forcing you? What chain can't you break?"

He stays with his back to me, rigid, like a statue about to snap.

"And don't tell me it's just your choice," I press, taking a step toward him, my breath burning. "Because I heard Camila talk about Victor... and I know he has something to do with it. What the hell ties you together? What are you hiding?"

The words come out like a shot, loaded with the anguish that's been choking me since I saw him enter that damned ring. Though my heart races, all I want is to wrench the truth from him. He remains still, fists clenched at his sides, breathing as if every word weighs a ton.

Finally, he turns his head—just enough for his voice to reach me without looking at me.

"There are things you don't understand, Lucía..." he says, his tone low and rough, filled with a rage I don't know whether it's aimed at me or at himself. "I don't fight because I want to. There are debts, accounts that aren't erased so easily."

I swallow; my heart pounds in my chest.

"And Víctor?" I dare, my voice barely a thread. "What does he have to do with all this?"

A brutal silence falls. Adrián emits a dry, humorless laugh that chills my blood.

"Let's just say Víctor plays on the same board. Only you shouldn't be watching the game."

Then he turns, his green eyes locking on me with a dark, almost desperate gleam.

"The less you know, the better for you. Believe me, princesa..."

I look at him and feel that mix of anger and desire burning me. I can't keep quiet.

"Don't tell me to stay out," I spit, my voice trembling but steady. "I'm already in, Adrián—from the first day you looked at me like I was yours, from the first time you touched me."

He clenches his jaw, a muscle throbbing at the side of his face, as if my words are a provocation more dangerous than any blow in the ring.

"You can scream at me, push me away, try to bury me in your secrets... but I won't disappear. I won't step back even if you ask me— even if you order me." I step closer, my breath brushing his. "Because whether you like it or not, I'm already part of your sentence."

His green eyes devour me, furious, and for a moment I think he'll break me in two with a single look. But beneath that fire I see something else: fear. My voice trembles, but I don't back down. I meet his gaze, my heart beating like a drum.

"I'm going to find out everything, Adrián," I say, each word set like a promise. "And I'm going to help you get out of this world once and for all."

The silence that follows takes my breath away. He watches me, his green eyes shining with a contained fury that hides something deeper. His crooked smile isn't mockery—it's pain.

"You don't understand what you're saying, princesa," he murmurs, his voice hoarse like a broken roar. "I'm not a man you can save. And if you insist... the only thing you'll do is drag yourself with me into the same hell."

His words chill me, but something inside burns hotter. I know; that's the first crack in his armor—the admission that he needs me, even if he won't own it. I don't think. I don't care about his fury, his warnings, or the hell he promises.

I fling myself at him and kiss him—rage, desperation, addiction all rolled into one. His mouth tastes of danger and sin, and still I take it as if it were my only salvation. I grab his face with both hands, squeezing hard, refusing to let go.

"I don't care what you say," I whisper against his lips, gasping. "I won't leave you, Adrián. Even if you hate me, even if you drag me down, even if I burn with you... I'm not letting you go."

He holds my gaze, his green eyes burning with a dark fire that undoes me. Though he tries to stay cold, his hands clamp on my waist with desperation—answering my kiss with the same brutality he tries to deny. I know I'm breaking him. And that is my curse—that the more he resists, the more I cling to him.

Chapter 18

✦ ✦ ✦ ✦ ✦ ✦

I hadn't slept. Every time I closed my eyes the scene replayed: Camila at my side, the charged air, the warehouse vibrating with shouts—and then Víctor pushing through the crowd. His eyes were fixed not on me but on her; in an instant he grabbed her arm and walked her away, not giving me a chance to react.

I called Cami at first light, my heart knocking against my ribs. He answered quickly, as if he'd been waiting for the call.

"Cami..." I breathed. I took a steadying breath. "What happened last night? I barely had time to move— he just dragged you out."

She was silent a moment, then sighed.

"Don't put it like that, Lu. He didn't drag me. He got me out before things got worse."

"What did he say?" I asked, gripping the phone so hard my knuckles ached.

"That that world isn't for me—that I had no business being there. That he didn't want to see me in a place like that again."

I bit my lip. Her tone was soft, protective even, but something inside me burned.

"Cami, don't lie to me. I saw the way they looked at him. Víctor wasn't there by accident."

She hesitated, then answered in a whisper.

"He... he knows those people, Lu. He's part of the business. He doesn't fight; he doesn't show himself—but he moves the pieces. He recruits, takes bets, decides who wins."

A chill ran down my spine. My worst suspicions began to arrange themselves into a shape.

"And you... are you okay with that?" I asked.

"I don't fully understand it," she admitted, voice trembling. "But I love him, Lu. He swears it's for our future—that he's trying to secure something better for us."

Adrián's warning—not everything that glitters is gold—echoed in my head. Suddenly the pieces fit together too neatly. I listened to her in silence, fingers clenched so tight around the phone I could have broken it. Anger and dread boiled under my skin: Víctor, Adrián, my father—all orbiting the same dark core.

Still, Camila sounded vulnerable and determined, and I couldn't bring myself to say what I thought. I couldn't hurt her, not today.

"All right, Cami," I said at last, my voice softer than I meant. "If you're happy, I respect that."

I could feel her smile down the line; I forced one back though the silence I chose would cost me dearly. I hung up and let myself collapse onto the bed, staring at the ceiling. The room's quiet wrapped around me, but inside my chest a roar kept building.

Víctor: recruiter, manipulator—the man who treats people like pieces on a bloody board. And among those pieces was Adrián. The idea that his life depended on someone like that twisted my stomach. I couldn't bear to imagine him, blow after blow, a spectacle traded at another man's whim.

No. I wasn't going to sit idly by.

If Camila doesn't want to see, if she prefers to believe in her perfect love, let her. But I won't. This addiction is not just desire: it's the certainty that if I don't act, I will lose him.

I promise myself, in the suffocating silence of my room: I'm going to find out everything. I will discover the truth, even if it burns me in the attempt.

The echo of my promise still hums when my phone screen lights up. Adrián.

I catch my breath as I open the message.

"Princesa... I still feel your body trembling in my hands. And you've seen nothing yet. Tonight, I'm going to show you how far the danger you crave can take you."

A jolt runs down my spine, my skin prickling as if his fingers were touching me from afar. I press the phone to my chest and smile, the same dangerous mix of fear and desire that's held me captive from the start. My fingers tremble, but adrenaline steadies them. I type each letter slowly, a dare laid out with care:

"I'm not the one who seeks danger, Adrián... it's danger that can't resist me. Tonight, we'll see who makes whom tremble."

I hit send before regret can find me and stare at the lit screen with a crooked grin. For the first time I feel I can provoke him, make him lose control. The thought turns me on more than the fear. The phone buzzes almost immediately. His reply is short, direct—like a blade.

"I'll pick you up at our usual spot. Tonight, I've got a few small gifts just for you."

My stomach tightens. "Small gifts" from him are never innocent. It could be pleasure; it could be punishment. Both excite me the same. I bite my lip and answer, a challenge of my own:

"I hope you didn't get the wrong princesa, Adrián... I'm hard to surprise. You'd better make sure those 'small gifts' live up to your words, or maybe I'll be the one to give you one tonight."

I send it and sink back against the pillow, heart racing. I know my reply will light him up—maybe enrage him— and that mix is what I want: to provoke him, to nick his control.

His next message comes like a promise and a threat:

"I have only one princesa to tame... and that's you. Tonight, I'll remind you, until there's no doubt who's in charge."

I read it again and again until the words burn: only one princesa to tame... and that's you. Heat floods my limbs, my legs go weak, and I breathe fast, as if I'm already under his sway. I don't reply. Anything I write will sound small beside his magnitude. I close the phone, but I know I'm not disconnecting—on the contrary: I surrender to the waiting.

The clock crawls. Each minute is a slow-burning ember that eats at me. Deep down—though it pains me to admit it—I don't care about the danger, the chains, or the darkness that keeps him trapped. I care about him. I care enough to walk into the fire.

I open my closet and run my fingers over the fabrics until I find the dress that will drive him crazy: black, modest at the neckline, but designed to ignite the imagination and promise to lose it all under his gaze. The fabric slides over my skin like a whisper, tracing every curve, making me feel naked even when I'm dressed.

Below, I choose the boldest lingerie I own—fine lace I know he'll enjoy removing with his hands or his mouth. I study myself in the mirror; the reflection looking back is different: vulnerable, yes, but also powerful because I am the center of his obsession.

A few drops of the perfume he says drives him crazy at the base of my neck. Hair loose, rebellious, as if to announce that tonight I won't be submissive without a fight.

I take a deep breath and hold my gaze in the glass. I'm dressing for him, but also for myself—to remind myself I won't run. If his darkness wants me, I'll face it with everything I am.

When I close the door behind me, the beat in my chest no longer distinguishes between fear and desire. I know that the moment I meet his green eyes waiting for me, there will be no turning back.

I walk to the corner—the same one that has left me trembling so many times—certain each step brings me closer to my downfall. The night breeze brushes my skin but cannot cool the fire inside me. And then I see him.

The car appears, slow and imposing, like a predator stalking the dark. The headlights slice the empty street for a second and my breath catches. I don't need to see more to know it's him; I feel him in the air, in the tension prickling my skin.

The car pulls up a few meters away and the passenger window rolls down with that calculated calm that drives me mad. His green eyes meet mine, shining with dangerous intensity in the gloom.

It's a look that strips me bare without touching me, dragging me straight into that abyss where only he and my surrender exist. And still I smile, as if this game is as much mine as his. The night has just begun. The passenger door opens with a decisive gesture; I slide in without thinking, as if it's the only direction I can take.

No sooner is the door closed than his hand is on my thigh—firm, hot, possessive. He squeezes with just enough force to remind me there's no escape.

"Good evening, princesa," he murmurs, voice low, hoarse—so dangerous my stomach trembles.

The engine roars as he pulls away, but the only thing I feel is the heat of his palm slowly climbing my leg—a warning disguised as a caress that both paralyzes and ignites me. With every centimeter it rises, my breathing grows more uneven, more addicted to the sentence that waits for me.

His left hand stays tight on the wheel while his right slides between my legs. His fingers move without hurry, with a precision that pulls a stifled moan from me—and the most devastating thing is he never takes his eyes off the road. He drives, dominates, caresses—as if he could control everything at once.

Every turn, every brush of his fingers pushes me beyond reason. I grip the seat, fighting not to lose myself too quickly, knowing he won't allow it until he decides.

His fingers skim the soaked fabric of my panties, barely playing, as if testing my resistance. Then he tugs the lace hard, and I gasp.

His voice comes low and dark, an order I cannot disobey.

"Take them off."

The breath leaves me. His green eyes stay fixed on the road, as if he doesn't need to watch me to own me. But the yank of the fabric and the edge in his voice make clear there is no choice.

Trembling, I slide the garment down my thighs, breath ragged, feeling that with every inch that falls I surrender more. When the lace pools at my ankles and I pull it free, his crooked smile appears in the windshield's reflection.

I don't need him to say anything else. I know I'm completely his—even here, in the middle of nowhere, the world sliding by outside the glass. He holds out his hand; I take a shaky breath and hand him the fabric that still burns beneath my fingers. He accepts it without taking his eyes from the road, and for a moment I think he'll keep it—a token of my surrender.

He doesn't. With a cold, calculated motion he opens his fingers and lets the garment drop to the car floor, as if it means nothing.

I am naked under the dress, more vulnerable than ever, and the arousal scorches me like a delicious poison. He drives as though nothing has changed; his hand returns to my thigh, sliding higher. Trapped in this power game, I can do nothing but surrender to the truth: I've never been this lost, or this alive.

Each caress drags a stifled moan from me, and yet he never flinches or changes pace. He touches me with that cruel precision that keeps me taut, reminding me with every brush that I am his. The engine's roar, his fingers inside me, the world flashing past—everything blurs into a delicious vertigo that pulls me away.

His hand sinks deeper, relentless, his fingers setting a rhythm that drags me straight to the edge. The motor's growl mixes with my breath—more ragged, more desperate.

"Louder, Lucía. he commands; his gaze fixed on the road. — I want to hear you."

His voice shatters me. I can't fight it. My body arches off the seat, fingers clawing into the upholstery as a broken cry rips from my throat. —Yes...Fuck— The orgasm hits brutal and fast, wiping out everything—time, place, reason—until all that exists is him.

He never stops driving. Not once. One hand on the wheel, the other on me, owning me like he owns the night itself. I tremble, breathless, the fabric of my dress sticking to my skin. He smirks, that dark curve of his mouth a silent promise: this is only the beginning.

"That's how I like it," he murmurs, his voice hoarse, dangerous. *"Always under my control."*

"See how easily you fall, princesa?" he growls, never taking his eyes off the road. *"Just my hand and you're in pieces—trembling, begging."*

I swallow, my heart still racing; I don't know whether shame or desire burns me more.

"You're as addicted to me as I am to you. And the worst part—" his crooked smile flashes in the windshield *"—is that you know it. That you accept it."*

I close my eyes and squeeze my still-throbbing thighs, knowing he's right. Every word he speaks ties me tighter to this delicious sentence I cannot escape.

"Tonight, princesa..." he adds, his voice a dark vow, *"...there will be no limits."*

Just when I think he's already punished me enough, his hand returns to my thigh. This time he touches me not with violence but with a dangerous calm that makes me shiver.

"Lift the dress," he orders, voice low and steady, never looking away from the road.

I stare at him, incredulous, but his lips curve into a crooked smile that brooks no resistance.

"Obey. I want the world to know that under that fabric you're only mine."

My fingers tremble as I hook the hem and lift it slowly, exposing my bare thighs to the dim light spilling through the window. He never takes his eyes off the road, but I feel the power of his gaze anyway—heavy, green, relentless.

"Higher," he growls. "Until I say stop."

The air leaves me as I obey; the fabric slides up and my skin prickles with every inch revealed. I'm trembling. He barely nods, satisfied, then tightens his grip on the wheel.

"Perfect. Now stay like that. I want you to arrive remembering who's in charge."

My heart hammers. This waiting is delicious torture that consumes me more than any touch.

The car finally stops in front of an unassuming building—no flashy sign, just an atmosphere heavy with secrets: the kind of place people enter seeking forbidden pleasures and leave without looking back. A hotel of that sort where privacy is a spectacle—rooms designed for excess, mirrors on the ceiling, walls that reflect every move, every moan.

Adrián kills the engine without a word. At last, he looks at me, and the gleam in his green eyes burns me more than any caress.

"Tonight, I want you to look at yourself, princesa," he murmurs, voice deep and loaded with promise. "See with your own eyes how you belong to me."

The idea of seeing myself subdued, reflected from every angle, terrifies and excites me in equal measure. I know there will be no respite; every moment will be a brutal reminder.

The elevator opens silently; a carpeted hallway leads to a heavy door that Adrián opens with a confident movement.

The room is a temple of sex. The ceiling is entirely mirrored, reflecting every angle of the space—from the huge bed in the center to the glass-lined walls—multiplying details into infinite echoes. It's like being trapped in a maze of naked bodies that don't yet exist but that I know will soon fill every corner.

I walk slowly, heels sinking into the carpet, watching myself again and again in every direction. I can't escape my reflection, nor the image of him—powerful, upright behind me, dominating even the air I breathe.

I stop in front of the bed, trembling. I can see my face in the ceiling: my eyes shining with fear and desire. It's too much. The room screams there are no hiding places here, that every surrender will be exposed, that there will be no denying what he makes me feel.

I step back and collide with his chest. His firm hand at my waist pins me in place. He still doesn't touch me more, and yet I'm already lost. The wait is torture. Worst of all, he knows it.

My reflection returns the tremble of my lips, the feverish shine in my eyes, and I know he's watching that too.

"Look at yourself, princesa…" he murmurs in my ear, his deep voice brushing my skin like a blade. "Do you see what I see?"

I lift my gaze and find my smaller self in the ceiling mirror: me, trapped in his control, his powerful shadow holding me from behind. The air thins; there is nowhere left to hide.

His fingers travel slowly up my abdomen, stopping just beneath my breasts to press gently—only enough to make my back arch toward him.

"Look me in the eyes," he orders, nodding toward the mirror.

I obey. Suddenly everything shifts: it's no longer me watching myself, but me meeting his green eyes through the glass. A trap that lays me bare, exposed, even with the dress still clinging to my skin.

His crooked smile multiplies across every surface, reflecting my surrender before his hands have even finished claiming me. Then I understand: his game isn't only to touch me. It's to make me watch—to force me to witness my own addiction.

His hand stays fixed at my waist, but now he does not touch me more. Only his voice, low and dark, steals my breath.

"Take it off," he orders, and I don't need him to explain.

The mirror shows my flushed face, parted lips, fear and desire dancing in my eyes. I swallow, but the slight pressure of his fingers against my hip makes clear there is no choice.

I slip the straps of my dress down my shoulders, lowering them slowly. The mirror shows everything: fabric sliding from my skin, gooseflesh rising beneath his gaze. I feel his breath behind me—heavy, restrained—as if he savors every second of my torment.

"Slower," he growls. "I want you to see yourself— don't forget how you undress for me."

The dress pools at my feet. There I am, multiplied across a dozen mirrors, the last thread of lingerie barely covering me. My hands tremble as I unhook my bra, but I do it. Lace parts and my breasts are exposed to the air, to the reflections, to his eyes that possess me without touching.

I pant, naked before my own image, body multiplied in every direction. There is no escape, no modesty—only the certainty that I belong to myself less than ever.

His hand slides up to my throat, pressing firmly, forcing me to lift my chin and look at the ceiling mirror.

"That's it, princesa," he murmurs in a hoarse voice. "Watch yourself. You're mine... even in your own eyes."

He eases the pressure, and his mouth finds my shoulder, then my neck, moving with a slowness that breaks me. The warm, wet heat of his tongue contrasts with the cold glass that multiplies every moan, every shiver.
His free hand begins to explore—slow, torturing. It cups my breasts, squeezing with just the right strength while his tongue grazes my skin like electric fire. A moan escapes me, and he smiles against my neck, watching it all reflected above and around us.

"I adore you, princesa," he whispers, voice low and ragged with desire. "I can't resist you... and that drives me crazy."

My eyes stay fixed on the mirror. I watch my lips part, my nipples hard under his touch, my skin flushing where his mouth leaves invisible marks.

When his hand slides between my thighs I shiver. His fingers trace cruel, patient circles that pull me toward the edge.

"Don't close your eyes," he growls in my ear. "I want you to see."

And I do. I watch myself—thighs tensing, body arching, addiction mapping itself across every inch. In the glass I am only hers and his: a woman who belongs to no one but him.

Just when I think he can't surprise me, Adrián reaches for a black bag resting on a chair—discreet, invisible until now. He lifts it slowly; his green eyes shine with a dark fire that freezes and ignites me at once.

"Remember those 'small gifts,' princesa?" His crooked smile makes me tremble. "Well, here they are."

One by one he draws out the items: handcuffs, the thin riding crop I recognize with a jolt, and a small vibrator that hums in his palm. He places them on the bed like ritual pieces, each mirrored reflection multiplying the scene into infinity.

A current runs down my spine. My breath quickens. It's not only the fear of the unknown; it's the certainty that I'm about to give myself over to a pleasure I never dared imagine.

He strokes my chin, forcing me to look him in the eyes.

"You're going to try each one, princesa... and you're going to beg for more."

My body trembles. And yet, I nod.

He takes the handcuffs with a calm that makes my skin prickle. The sound of metal snapping open cuts the silence of the room, reverberating in the mirrors like a dark echo.

"Give me your hands, princesa," he orders, his voice so deep there's no room for doubt.

I obey, shaking, and he secures my wrists firmly—each click of the cuff like the seal of my sentence. He positions me standing in front of the bed so that my reflection in the ceiling, the walls, every corner, returns the same image: me, naked, bound, prisoner to his desire.

His hand travels up my back slowly and pushes me forward until I'm bent over the bed. I see my face reflected ahead: lips parted, eyes burning with fear and excitement. I can't look away because he's behind me, gripping my waist hard.

"Look at yourself in the mirror," he whispers in my ear, his fingers sliding cruelly over my skin. "I want you to see what you are when you're under my control."

Each of his words multiplies in the reflections, trapping me in a prison of images with no escape. I feel him step away, and when he comes back it isn't his hands that touch me first but something cold and firm that runs along my bare skin.

The riding crop.

I feel the leather glide slowly down my back, descending calmly, tracing my curves as if mapping my surrender. The contact doesn't hurt; it burns, it teases, it makes me arch as if each lit line were being branded onto my skin.

"How do you feel, princesa?" his rough voice surrounds me, dangerous. "This isn't punishment yet. It's a caress."

The riding crop pauses at the small of my back and slides down my thighs, grazing the inner parts until I'm forced to open myself wider for him. My reflection betrays me: my body shudders, my parted lips plead even though my voice won't dare to come out.

Then—one sharp, quick strike, barely on the meatiest part of my thigh. A stifled gasp escapes me, and his dark laugh cuts through me like lightning.

"That's how I like it... that you don't know when it's pleasure and when it's pain."

"The riding crop bites against me again, rising to the edge of my wet sex, brushing just enough to torture. In the mirror I see my body straining, my hips begging for him—and he knows."

The leather tip slides calmly between my thighs, grazing exactly where I need it most, provoking an unbearable tickle. Each brush pulls a muffled moan from me that multiplies in the mirrors, returning the image of my own desperation.

I'm wet, ready, burning for him, and he knows it. I feel it in the way he barely presses, in how he pulls the contact away at the exact second my body is about to break.

"So easy..." he whispers, his deep voice filling my ears. "With nothing, princesa, you're already trembling. But no. Not yet."

A gasp escapes me, my hips arching in search of more, but the rod jerks away, barely brushing me and making me let out a desperate whimper. The reflection shows me exactly as I am now: bound, vulnerable, begging with my eyes.

He brings it back close, slow, the tip vibrating against my damp skin, until again I'm on the edge. My nails dig into the palms locked by the cuffs, my legs shake... and again he pulls away.

A broken moan rips out of me, half anger, half pleasure. He laughs against my ear, that dark laugh that makes the hairs on my arms stand up more than any blow.

"That's your punishment, princesa. Feeling everything... and being left with nothing."

Desire consumes me, frustration burns me.

I breathe raggedly, trembling, convinced he'll give me a break. But the sound that follows freezes my blood and ignites desire at the same time: a low, electric hum that fills the room like a dark promise.

The vibrator.

He holds it in his hand like a weapon; the reflection multiplied in every mirror in the room. He approaches slowly, tracing from my chin to my neck with its tip, down to my breasts, making every nerve in my skin vibrate. My body arches, my lips plead without a sound.

"You want this, princesa?" his hoarse voice hits me straight in the gut. "It will be worse than the rod."

He lowers it slowly to my wet sex, barely touching the entrance, and my stifled moan fills the room, bouncing off every wall, every reflection. The vibration turns me on, lifting me in seconds to an unbearable brink.

But he gives me no mercy. Just as I'm about to break, he pulls it away with a jerk, pressing in circles around me, playing with my frustration as if it were part of the ritual.

"Be good, princesa... I'll let you come when I'm ready."

The constant buzz tortures me; the vibration drags me to the edge again and again, and every time I'm about to explode, he changes the angle, the pressure, leaving me balanced on the brink of the abyss without falling.

I look at myself in the mirror and what I see is devastating: my body arched, my eyes watering with desire, my mouth open, pleading without words. And behind me, him—absolute owner of everything.

The buzz sinks into my skin like a delicious poison. My hips arch searching for more, chasing a relief he denies me again and again. He pushes me to the edge.

"Look at yourself, princesa..." his hoarse voice resonates in my ear.

Sweat runs down my back, my wrists strain against the cuffs, my legs tremble uncontrollably. The vibrator presses again. My body tightens, shudders—and then he pulls it away once more. A tearing cry escapes me, a sound I can't tell if it's pleasure or despair.

"No... please..." I whisper, my voice broken, shaking.

He smiles against my neck, and that crooked smile is worse than any blow.

"Very good. Beg, princesa. I want to hear you say it for real."

My lips tremble: I resist one more second, but his hand presses the vibrator with a precision that rips a desperate gasp from me. I can't take it anymore.

"Adrián... please..."

The words come out in sobs and moans, multiplied by the mirrors, turned into an echo that strips me more naked than my own body. And he, satisfied, squeezes my waist harder, savoring my complete surrender.

A searing fire explodes from my belly and shakes me whole, as if every nerve in my body burned at once. My legs tremble uncontrollably, my back arches against the bed, and the cry that tears from me vibrates in the mirrors, returning again and again the raw vision of my body burning beneath him.

I feel the cuffs digging into my wrists, reminding me I'm trapped even in the fiercest climax. Pleasure devours me from the inside—deep, endless—dragging me into an abyss where there is nothing but him, his domination, and my absolute surrender.

"You're so beautiful, princesa... overflowing from my pleasure."

His fingers trace the line of the cuffs, making sure they remain tight, and a shiver runs through me. He's not going to let me go.

"You thought you were done, princesa?" His cruel smile haunts every mirror. "The night is just beginning."

He reaches back into the bag, and the sound makes a nervous gasp escape me. This time he pulls out a small steel clamp, gleaming under the dim light, designed for a single purpose. He holds it up, as if savoring my tremor while it's reflected dozens of times in the mirrors.

He leans over me, catching my nipple between his fingers, and brings the clamp slowly closer. The cold metal makes me gasp even before he closes it. When he does, a sharp flash of pleasure and pain shoots through me, ripping a stifled moan from my throat.

"Perfect mess," he murmurs, his low voice brushing my ear. "I want you to see what you provoke, how your body trembles with my toys."

The second nipple doesn't take long to receive the same punishment. I watch myself in the ceiling mirror: bound, naked, clamps shining on my skin like marks of his power. My body no longer obeys me; it answers only to him.

Then he picks up the vibrator again and turns it on.

"Get ready, princesa," he growls, bringing it calmly toward my wet sex. "I'm going to take you farther than you thought possible."

The vibrator's buzz fills the room again, more intense this time, as if the sound itself slips under my skin. Adrián brings it close with control, barely grazing me, and I'm already arching my back, trembling.

Suddenly, his fingers squeeze the clamps, and the vibration at my sex mixes with the sharp sting in my nipples. The clash of sensations forces a ripped scream from me—half pain, half pleasure—that rebounds off the mirrors and makes me hear myself in an endless echo.

"That's it, princesa..." his hoarse voice caresses my ear, dangerous and dark. "Your body doesn't know what to do. And that's why it belongs to me."

The vibrator intensifies and my hips jerk against it, unable to escape, seeking more even though every movement makes the clamps tug cruelly at my sensitive skin. I'm trapped between two fires, every nerve torn in opposite directions, and still the only thing I can do is beg for more.

I look at myself in the ceiling mirror: my naked body, bound, my breasts adorned with steel, my legs spread under his absolute control. And then I understand: I'm not only his. I'm the spectacle he forces me to watch.

The orgasm threatens to sweep me away again— fierce, uncontrollable—and just when I think he'll let me fall, his hand stops for a moment, holding my torture right at the edge.

"Almost, princesa..." he growls, tightening the clamps just a little more.

I'm on the edge, that I only need one more second. The vibrator keeps pulsing against me; each subtle tug of the clamps intensifies the current running through me, and yet I refuse. I look at him, my eyes blazing, chest rising and falling, clinging to that last flicker of control I have left.

He notices. He feels it. And his dark smile chills my blood.

"So, you want to resist me, princesa?" he growls, pressing the vibrator even harder against me. "Perfect."

His hand yanks the clamp, wrenching from me a gasp that tears out even as I try to swallow it. My reflection in the mirror gives me no mercy: I see my face contorted by pleasure and pain, my thighs spread, my back arched. This time I can't hold back the scream. It erupts from me, raw, savage, ripped out like an involuntary confession.

He leans in, his mouth at my ear, his voice deep and dark.

"That's what I wanted."

He gives me no respite. He increases the pressure, the pace, as if he wants to shred me with pleasure until every trace of defiance is erased.

A fierce burst detonates inside me, cutting through me from head to toe like a lightning bolt that never ends. My legs shake uncontrollably, my back arches against the bed, and the screams that escape me fill the room until they become unbearable.

I feel the cuffs digging into my wrists, the clamps pulling cruelly with each convulsion of my body, the vibrator tearing out a pleasure that consumes me and leaves me ashes. I am empty and, at the same time, overflowing with him.

Again, I collapse, gasping, soaked in sweat. It wasn't an orgasm of surrender so much as of submission. A delicious punishment... and yet I crave it again.

He grabs my throat, forces me to look at myself in the ceiling mirror.

"There's nothing more delicious than seeing you come like this... crazy for me." His hoarse voice vibrates against my skin, loaded with power and dark desire.

I'm still panting, trembling, unable to regain control of my legs when I see him take a step back. He doesn't touch me. He doesn't free me. He simply begins unbuttoning his shirt with calculated slowness, each button giving way like a silent threat that turns me on more than any hurry ever could.

My wrists remain trapped in the cuffs, tense above my head, and my body, spent, barely reacts. I'm motionless, reduced to watching the sight of him undressing before me.

He takes off his shirt slowly, revealing a torso marked by scars. Then he unfastens his belt and drops his pants with that same lethal precision, as if every movement is designed to remind me that he owns the show and I am only the spectator.

My throat burns as I swallow. In the mirrors I see him: powerful, virile, upright, with that savage certainty that steals my breath. Me, bound and shattered by pleasure; him, free, undressing with malice, like a predator savoring the moment before he lunges again.

When his green eyes lock on mine, I feel the whole room ignite.

—Every second of this belongs to you, princesa. And you'll remember it—even if you come back to life a thousand times.

He comes closer slowly, his shadow falling over me while my wrists remain trapped in the cuffs

His hand travels over my abdomen, tracing a slow path down to my hips. Then he leans in, removes the clamps, and his mouth takes my breasts, biting and sucking with that mix of tenderness and ferocity that drives me mad.

I arch, pleading, but he keeps me steady, his fingers exploring with calculated calm, grazing the most sensitive parts of me only to pull away at the exact moment when my body cries out for more.

"Wait..." he murmurs in that dark voice that cuts through my skin. "First I want to taste you again."

His tongue descends slowly, drawing wet circles over my belly until it disappears between my thighs. The piercing on his tongue draws a broken gasp from me the moment it touches my clitoris, and I feel my legs try to close, but he forces them apart with a firm, relentless gesture.

I see myself in the ceiling mirror: my body open, bound, completely surrendered to his mouth. The image makes me vibrate as much as his tongue, and I realize I no longer know where my pleasure begins, and his dominance ends.

Suddenly he sits on the bed, imposing, naked, with that dangerous look that devours me. Without giving me time to react, he grabs the cuffs and lifts me with a force that takes my breath away.

My bound arms fall forward, and in one motion he places me over his thighs—my body mounted on his, vulnerable and trapped. He forces my linked wrists around his neck, pinning me to him. The heat of his skin burns me. I feel him hard, ready, pressing against me, and a stifled moan escapes. In the mirrors I see myself on top of him, naked, my hands tied at his back.

He smiles, that cruel twist curving his lips.

"Just like this, princesa... bound to me, with no way out."

His gravelly voice cuts through me as his hands grip my hips, forcing me to rub against his erection.

"Here, you command nothing."

My body burns with every friction, desperation rising like liquid fire, and yet I can't move on my own: I depend on him, on his hands, on his rhythm.

A sudden movement changes everything. His hands force me down in one brutal motion, and my strangled cry breaks as I feel him invade me completely—wild, merciless—as if he wants to claim every corner of me.

My bound hands circle his neck, my wrists marking his skin as he manipulates me like a weightless toy, moving me at his will over his erection. Every thrust, tear, moans from me that bounce off the mirrors: me, exposed, surrendered, riding under Adrián's absolute control.

His mouth presses to my ear, his deep, dangerous voice caressing me more than his hands themselves.

"Like this... tied to me, surrendered in my body... you're the most beautiful thing I've ever had, princesa."

His fingers dig into my hips, guiding me hard against him. My back arches, my breasts rub against his burning chest, and I feel how he devours me with every movement—brutal, relentless.

His rhythm intensifies, but it's not savage—it's perfect, matching the pounding of my own heart. His hands on my hips guide me, bind me tighter to him than the cuffs themselves.

I feel him deep, filling me with every thrust, and the blend of force and tenderness completely undoes me.

Our bodies seek each other as if there's no other way to exist. My bound arms clutch him in desperation, and with every thrust I feel him closer, deeper, more mine.

"Lucía..." my name slips from his lips.

And then I'm gone. Pleasure tears through me from the center, deep and engulfing, like a current dragging me without mercy. I scream his name, trembling, as I see us in the mirrors: his strained face, his body burning with mine, his gaze locked on mine even as everything else blurs away.

He comes with me, a guttural growl ripping from his chest as he fills me the same moment my body clenches around him. In that instant there is no dominance or submission—only two souls burning together, chained to the same shattering climax.

I collapse on top of him, gasping, and his arms wrap around me for a few fleeting seconds—too warm, too tender for a man like Adrián.

Adrián doesn't move. His hands, once holding me with brutal force, now rest softly on my back, as if afraid to break me. His green eyes, still blazing, soften just slightly, revealing a glimmer I've never seen before.

"You have no idea what you do to me." —*he murmurs, his voice low, the words slipping out before he can stop them.*

I cling to his neck, trembling, and feel how he holds me tighter against him—strong, but different: not to dominate me, but as if he needs to hold on to me to keep from falling apart.

In the mirrors, the reflection feels almost unreal: we are not master and prisoner, not a dangerous man and the woman addicted to him. We are two bodies surrendered, unintentionally revealing the truth neither of us dares to say out loud.

I feel his breathing gradually steady against my neck, and then his hands move upward to my bound wrists. The metallic click echoes through the room as he releases the first clasp, the cuff loosening with a release that makes me shiver.

Then he frees the other, slowly, as if each second were a farewell. My arms drop, numb, and he catches them gently, massaging the marks on my wrists as if trying to erase the traces of his own dominance.

I remain still, stunned. This isn't the same brutal, savage Adrián who drags me to the edge; this is someone else — one who rarely lets himself surface. His green eyes, still burning, look at me as though he's made a mistake in letting me go… yet he doesn't regret it.

"Free," *he murmurs, his voice hoarse, almost a sigh.*

For a few seconds I don't know what to do. Instinct screams that I should pull away, reclaim my space, but I don't. Instead, I bring my hands to his face, brushing his jaw softly, feeling the tension that still hums beneath his skin.

He goes still—unmoving—as if my touch unsettles him more than any act of defiance. His green eyes search mine, lit not with fury this time but with something deeper, something he fights to keep hidden.

"You're a mystery that consumes me," I whisper, locking my gaze with his. "You say I'm yours, but it's you who keeps secrets... what is it you won't let me see?"

He closes his eyes for a moment, as if my words cut straight through him. His lips part, and for an instant I think he's about to speak.

I look at him, stroking his cheek, daring to reach for the man behind the danger—for the Adrián who, for a fleeting moment, showed me tenderness. But his eyes harden suddenly, even as my hands remain on his face. A heavy silence falls between us until his voice breaks the air—hoarse, laced with a pain he tries to mask with hardness.

"Fighting is all I know, Lucía..." he murmurs, looking away for a second, as if saying it weighs on him. "It's the only life they gave me."

My chest tightens, but before I can say anything, his green gaze locks back onto mine, more intense than ever.

"And even if I wanted something different with you, there's someone who would never allow it."

The echo of those words pierces me like an icy dagger. I want to ask who, to tear the truth from him, but he already squeezes my waist so hard that it seems he fears the question will leave my lips. His silence afterward is even more devastating than the confession.

He thinks that with ambiguity he can keep me in the dark, that his touches and his danger are enough to distract me. And yes, I lose myself in him, but I'm not naïve. Every word he withholds, every shadow in his eyes, only fans my obsession.

I hold him tightly, letting him believe I've given in, that I'm content. But something inside me breaks: I can't stay still any longer, waiting for Adrián to decide to tell me who that "someone" is—the one who will never let us be together. I will find out myself.

Suddenly his hand rises and pulls me toward him in a sharp, almost desperate motion. His lips press to mine, but it's not a wild, dominating kiss. It's different. It's a kiss that burns with need, as if he fears it might be the last.

I feel the tension of his body against mine, the hardness of his arms around me, gripping me tighter than necessary. Still, there is something broken in him—something I hadn't felt before.

His breath quavers against my mouth when he parts the kiss just enough to speak.

"You have no idea what I risk with you, Lucía..." he whispers, his voice hoarse with a truth that slips out of him against his will. "And I don't know if I'll ever be able to protect you from it all."

I fell silent, because any word might make him shut down again. I held him harder, as if my arms could erase all the shadows that chased him.

The night passed in his arms, the heat of his body wrapping me like a refuge I never imagined I'd belong to. We slept entwined, skin to skin, breathing in time, as if the outside world didn't exist, as if the shadows that followed him could not cross the walls of that room.

For the first time there were no chains, no power games, no unanswered questions. Just him and me—two bodies destiny might have meant to keep apart—clinging to each other as if the dawn could never separate us.

In the dim haze of my dreams, I thought maybe that was the real Adrián: the man who trembled when he let me go, the one who held me as if he was afraid to lose me. I fell asleep with a dangerous certainty burning in my chest: I was too far inside him... and he was too far inside me.

Dawn found me awake, the first rays of light slipping through the window. I opened my eyes slowly and saw him there, still asleep, his breathing deep, his brow softened in a way I'd never seen before. It was strange. The hardness that always surrounded him had vanished, and in its place was a young man—vulnerable, almost innocent. Not the fighter, not the brutal lover, not the dangerous shadow everyone feared. Just Adrián—my Adrián—lost in a dream that stripped him bare more than my own gaze ever could.

I stayed still, watching him in silence, afraid that if I blinked the image would disappear. With the tip of my finger, I traced the outline of his jaw without touching, as if I might break the spell. In that moment I understood: no matter how dark his world was, no matter how many secrets he tried to hide from me... he had cracks too. And it was those cracks that had me trapped.

His lips moved slightly, as if murmuring something in his sleep, and my heart pounded, wondering what ghosts haunted him even in dreams.

Suddenly his green eyes opened—clear as a storm—and caught me watching him. A shiver ran through me: I didn't know how long he'd been awake, but his steady gaze stripped me bare more than any touch ever could.

A dangerous, crooked smile formed on his lips as his hand rose slowly to grip my chin.

"Do you like watching me sleep, princesa?" he murmured, voice low, still rough with sleep. "Careful... you might end up dreaming of me even while you're awake."

His tone was soft, almost tender, but his eyes did not lie—behind those words was a darker reminder, a veiled warning. I bit my lip, unable to look away. In that instant

I wondered if I was really the one watching him... or if it had always been him watching me, even when I didn't realize it.

Adrián sat up first, his naked body outlined against the light of dawn. He stretched with the dangerous calm of a predator, then extended his hand to me—that strong hand that had so often subdued me, now inviting me to follow.

"Come," he murmured, and there was no room to refuse.

I followed him into the bathroom, the blush of sleep still warming my cheeks. Steam filled the air as soon as he turned on the shower, and when the hot water slid down his skin I couldn't help but watch him: every drop tracing over his scars, as if the rain itself longed to uncover his secrets.

He pulls me to him suddenly, pressing me against his wet chest. The contrast of the water and his heat makes me moan under my breath. His hands move slowly down my back, sliding to my hips, and I feel how the tenderness of the moment blends with the ever-present tension.

"Not even water can cool what you ignite in me, princesa... you're a beautiful fire only I know how to conquer."

I close my eyes, letting the water pour over me, and for a moment, the feel of his wet skin against mine speaks louder than any words.

His fingers trace the line of my spine, lower, gripping me hard—forcing me to feel every inch of him.

He meets my gaze, water dripping down his face like a crown of chaos, and that smile—dark, sinful—cuts straight through me.

"There's no escaping what we are, Lucía. My mark will live in you."

And I give in, because there's no place left untouched by him—no breath, no thought that isn't his.

He doesn't speak again, and neither do I. We just stay there, caught in the pause between destruction and desire, knowing it's temporary... and wishing it weren't.

Chapter 19

✦ ✦ ✦ ✦ ✦ ✦

*T*he car engine purrs along the road, and the silence between us feels strange—not uncomfortable, but heavy with the calm still lingering after the shower, as if we're both afraid to break it. I glance sideways at Adrián: one hand steady on the wheel, the other resting on my thigh, drawing idle circles that set my skin ablaze even though he says nothing.

Suddenly a phone vibrates insistently on the seat between us, the screen lighting up with a name I can't quite make out. Adrián glances at the device but makes no move to answer. His green eyes stay fixed on the road, as if the world on the other end of the line doesn't exist.

The phone buzzes again, longer this time, more insistent. My heart picks up speed, and I can't tell if it's from the tension of his ignoring it or the invisible weight of everything he never tells me.

"Aren't you going to answer?" I whisper at last, my voice low, bracing for his reply.

His jaw tightens, knuckles whitening on the wheel. "Not now." His tone is firm, cutting—an order that leaves no room for argument.

I bite my lip and turn to the window, but the quiet is no longer peaceful. It's swollen with secrets, so dense it chokes the air from my lungs. The phone rings again, this time more insistently, as if whoever is calling knows Adrián is deliberately ignoring them. The glow of the screen flickers, and I catch the name before he can move the device out of sight.

Víctor.

A shiver runs down my spine. I don't know if it's shock, rage, or the fear of seeing those two worlds collide—the ones I'd tried so hard to keep apart. Adrián notices my stare and, with a brusque movement, flips the phone face down. His lips harden into a thin line, his gaze locked on the road as if he could escape my question before I speak it.

But I can't hold it back.

"Why is Víctor calling you?" I whisper, my voice breaking between disbelief and restrained fury.

His answer is the slam of the accelerator. The car surges forward, the asphalt trembling beneath the tires as if speed itself wanted to drown out my words. The engine's roar swallows my voice. I search his eyes for any reaction, for a word—but Adrián doesn't yield. He releases the wheel with a chilling calm and grips my thigh with a force so tight it paralyzes me. He doesn't need to speak: in that pressure lies the warning—the message that everything we are rests on his absolute control.

His eyes remain on the road, but his voice—low, rough, razor-sharp—cuts through like a blade.

"Don't worry."

The weight of his hand burns into me, not only for the strength of his grip but for what it means: a line drawn, a veiled warning. I want to push back, to shout that he can't keep hiding everything from me, but the dominance in his gesture freezes me. My pulse hammers in my throat as I stare out the window.

Then Adrián breaks the hush with that low voice that always drags me to the edge.

"There are things you'll never understand, Lucía... and if you try, all you'll find is pain."

His eyes never leave the road, but his words fall on me like molten iron. I don't know whether it's a warning, a threat, or a confession disguised as both. My chest burns with unanswered questions, and yet, against all logic, the certainty settles over me: no matter what he hides, no matter how dangerous it is, I'm already too deep to turn back.

The car stops a few meters from my house. I expect him to say something curt, any word to put distance between us, but he doesn't.

Instead, he shuts off the engine and leans toward me. His hand, still damp from the shower, rises to my face and caresses my cheek with a tenderness that undoes me.

There's no rush, no anger—just that slow touch that contradicts everything he just warned me about.

Before I can process it, his lips brush mine in a short, almost sweet kiss so out of place it steals my breath. There is no possession in it, only something more dangerous: tenderness.

He pulls away immediately, returning to the rigid armor that shields him, and his voice—deep and resonant—strikes me even harder.

"Goodbye, princesa."

I stare at him, confused, the taste of that kiss lingering on my lips and the certainty that it wasn't an accident. When I step out of the car my whole skin burns. As I watch him drive away, I know I'll never escape the contradiction that consumes me.

I push the door open quietly, hoping silence will cover me, but a voice slices through my breath.

"You disobeyed me again, Lucía."

The light from the living room reveals my father's severe face. He's seated in the armchair, arms crossed, his gaze fixed on me with that mix of anger and exhaustion that cuts straight to my bones. My heart races—not just from fear of being found out, but because I know, deep down, his words hide more than a simple reproach. He knows something. He always has.

Standing there, the flush of danger still on my skin, I understand this won't be the last time he asks me to choose between obeying him or losing myself even more in Adrián. His gaze pins me like a sentence. He doesn't shout; he doesn't press. He only utters three words that chill my blood.

"I warned you."

He rises slowly from the armchair, his footsteps firm on the wooden floor, and without another word disappears down the hallway. The door to his room slams shut with a dull thud that leaves me frozen in the middle of the living room, my heart pounding.

I cling to the edge of my bag, trembling. I don't know which is worse: his silence or his words. I'm trapped—more confused than ever—between my father's fury, the secrets that surround us, and the man who has become my most dangerous addiction.

My father's phrase spins through my mind like a dagger turning inside me: I warned you. Warned me of what? Adrián, his dark world... or something even bigger that I can't yet imagine?

I pace my room several times, heart racing, trying to piece together the loose fragments: Adrián's silence, Víctor's calls, my father's hard look. Nothing fits, and the uncertainty eats at me more than any punishment.

The only thing I know is that my father knows something—something he's been hiding from me—and the way he said it, as if the outcome were already written, freezes me from the inside.

I looked at myself in the mirror at dawn. My eyes looked tired, but what scared me wasn't my reflection — it was the certainty burning in my chest: no matter what that warning meant, I wasn't ready to let Adrián go.

The phone rang early — Camila. Her voice was packed with an urgency that made me agree without thinking. We met at a café downtown, and when I arrived, she was already there, idly stirring sugar into her cup, wearing that nervous, confused expression I rarely saw on her.

"I had to see you, Lu," she says the moment I sit across from her. "Something weird is going on."

I leaned forward, my heart racing for no apparent reason.

"What is it?" I asked.

Camila lowered her voice, as if someone might overhear, and her words struck me like lightning.

"Víctor has been looking for Adrián for two days. He says he needs to warn him about something... something urgent. But he can't find him anywhere."

The coffee suddenly tasted bitter. My hands trembled on the table, and I tried to keep calm for her.

"Warn him about what?" I asked, my throat dry.

She shook her head. "I don't know. He won't tell me more, and when I press him, he changes the subject. But I can tell he's restless, like he's hiding something serious."

A strange chill settled in my chest. Víctor, Adrián, my father — all playing with half-truths. And me, caught in the middle, trying to piece together a puzzle that felt more dangerous by the minute. I forced a smile and stirred my coffee as if nothing had shaken me.

"He'll show up. You know Adrián — he always disappears for a while and then comes back like nothing happened."

Camila studied me in silence, brow furrowed, as if she suspected I wasn't telling her everything. I hurried to change the subject, asking about her family, anything to distract her, until her expression softened a little. But inside I was burning.

Every word she'd said pounded in my head. Víctor was looking for Adrián. Urgent. Something serious. And I knew that if I just sat and waited, I'd never find out what was really happening. So, I nodded and smiled, feigning calm. I let her talk, I listened, and finally we said goodbye.

I walked out into the street with a knot in my stomach, my heart pounding like a war drum. I moved quickly through downtown, ignoring the noise. My mind had only one goal: find him. If Víctor was after him, I couldn't sit idly by.

I started with the places I knew he haunted. The bar with its smoke-filled air and blaring music, where everyone seemed to know him, but no one dared to say much. I asked discreetly, but all I got were evasive looks and heavy silences.

From there I head to the gym on the outskirts, where I once heard his name whispered among the boys training. I recognize the smell of sweat and iron, the punching bags beaten nearly to shreds. But he's not there either—only an echo of his presence, an aura of respect and fear that follows him even in absence.

Every denial, every absence only fuels me more. Anxiety mixes with the certainty that something is moving in the shadows. As I step out of the last place, dusk begins to fall, and the city feels more dangerous than ever. And yet all I can feel is that I'm not getting any closer to him.

Adrián is nowhere to be found.

The days drag by—two, three… I lose count. No one knows where Adrián is. His phone is off, his house empty. His shadow seems to have vanished from the city, and I go a little insane with every hour that passes without a sign of him.

In the end I can't take it anymore. I go to Camila's house. The smell of fresh coffee still lingers in the air when she opens the door, surprised, her usual sweetness softening her face.

But I have no patience for pleasantries.

"I need to talk to Víctor," I blurt out, my voice harder than it should be.

Camila frowns, confused, but nods and calls him. A few seconds later Víctor appears in the hallway. His shirt is immaculate, his expression calm... too perfect, too calculated. He looks at me like he knows exactly why I'm here.

"Where is he?" I ask at once, my desperation shattering any pretense.

He sighs, runs a hand through his hair, and his gaze darkens with a mix of caution and something that almost looks like pity.

"I don't know, Lucía. Believe me, if I did, I'd already be with him."

"You were looking for him, Víctor. I know it. You called him. Why?" I press.

His eyes harden; his voice drops, and the atmosphere in the house shifts—heavy, charged.

"Because someone else is looking for him... and it's not good."

The silence steals my breath. A clock in the living room marks the seconds with an unbearable tick-tock.

"Who? What do you mean by that?"

Víctor shakes his head; the muscles in his jaw tighten.

"I can't, Lucía. I can't tell you more."

I step closer, my throat dry, almost pleading. "Then at least tell me how to help him."

He holds my gaze, and for an instant I swear I see fear in his eyes. His voice, deep and steady, sounds more like a warning than comfort.

"I can't tell you what I know... but I can help you look. Just promise me one thing: that Camila never finds out what's happening. And understand this—if you step into this, there's no turning back."

My skin burns, caught between fear and fury. I don't know if I can trust him, but he's all I have. I watch him in silence, searching for a crack in his expression— something that might reveal whether it's sincerity or just another disguise in this maze of shadows. His face remains firm, but in his eyes there's a flicker that makes me hesitate: protection... or manipulation?

I swallow hard, anger and anxiety colliding inside me until I give in—because I have no other choice.

"Fine. I'll believe you... but only because I need to find him."

A shadow of relief crosses his face, though it's fleeting, as if he too is hiding a secret. My skin prickles: something doesn't add up, but desperation forces me to cling to any thread that might lead me closer to Adrián.

"You won't regret this, Lucía," he says quietly, the weight in his voice sounding more like a warning than a promise. "Just promise me you won't tell Camila any of this."

Guilt rises like a knot in my throat. Still, I nod firmly.

"She won't know."

The words leave me steady, but inside I burn with the certainty that I'm allying myself with someone who's also playing his own game. Even if I accept his help, it doesn't mean I trust him.

When I say goodbye to Camila, I smile as if everything is fine, but the lie feels heavy. Night swallows us in silence as I climb into the car with Víctor. He drives without speaking, the city lights flashing across the glass, and with every passing mile I drift further from safety and sink deeper into the unknown.

At last, we reach the outskirts. A massive warehouse looms in the dark, its walls corroded with damp, a couple of yellow bulbs flickering at the entrance. The air reeks of metal and sweat, laced with a low murmur from inside: bets whispered, dull thuds, the rattle of chains. Everything about this place screams danger; everything tells me I'm about to cross a threshold from which there will be no return.

Víctor walks with confidence, greeting a few men who eye us with suspicion. I follow, my heart lodged in my throat, desperately searching for a trace of him. Every shadow feels like Adrián; every thud sparks hope—only to vanish instantly.

"He's not here either," Víctor mutters, frowning as his gaze sweeps across the room.

No trace of his shadow, his voice, or that green fire in his eyes. Only the crushing weight of his absence.

"And now what?" I ask, desperation cracking my voice.

Víctor clenches his jaw. "If he's not here… it's because he's hiding. Or because someone found him before we did."

A shiver races down my spine. The warehouse seems to close in around me. For the first time, I feel like I'm on the edge of uncovering the secret.

Víctor stands still for a moment, scanning every corner as if searching for something invisible. I want to scream at him to keep going, not to stop—to find him. But suddenly his expression hardens—cold, calculated. He comes closer, close enough that no one else can hear.

"We can't stay here."

"What? But we haven't even—!" I protest, anger and anguish choking me.

His firm hand on my arm cuts me off. It isn't rough, but it's final.

"Lucía, understand this. This place isn't safe for you anymore." His voice is low and sharp, carrying a nervousness he doesn't try to hide. "Adrián's not here."

I follow him reluctantly, trembling with helplessness as we cross the warehouse. The men watch us with suspicion, and for the first time I feel the true edge of that dark world: a place where a single glance is enough to brand you.

When we step outside, the night air hits my face—cold and biting. Víctor opens the car door for me without another word. His silence weighs as heavily as his words: if Adrián isn't here, he's somewhere even Víctor struggles to name.

I drop into the passenger seat without saying a thing. Víctor shuts the door, circles around, and takes the wheel. The engine growls, and we move forward in silence, the deserted road lit only by the headlights. I want to scream; to demand he tell me everything he knows. But I don't. I bite down on my lip until I taste the metallic tang of restrained rage, my eyes fixed on the window.

He thinks he's protecting me, that keeping me in the dark will save me. But all it does is let the anxiety burn hotter. Every mile we put between us and that warehouse is another promise I make to myself: I will find him, with or without help.

Víctor drives with a stern expression, his hands steady on the wheel, as if the quiet between us is explanation enough. Maybe he thinks he's convinced me. Maybe he thinks I won't push any further.

The car sinks into the darkness of night. So do I—this time with only one purpose burning in my chest: I won't stop until I have him in front of me again.

By dawn, sleep doesn't come. I'm in my bed, the glow of my phone illuminating the shadows of my room as I replay each place I searched, each silence from Víctor, each shadow from my father.

Then it vibrates.

My heart lurches. I glance at the screen and there it is: Adrián. The message is short, blunt, written in that same dark voice that dominates me even from a distance:

"Stop looking for me, Lucía."

A jolt shoots down my spine. My fingers tremble over the screen. I read it once, twice, three times; the shock hits first... but then I feel it. This isn't him. Adrián never writes to me like this.

A chill runs through me. The phone is in his hands— or at least it should be—but the voice behind these words isn't his. I know it with the same certainty with which I know I can't stop wanting him.

The realization hits like lightning: Adrián didn't send this. And if he didn't... someone else has his phone. That can only mean one thing: he's in danger.

I'm about to type, to challenge whoever hides behind that cold message, when the phone vibrates again in my hands. The buzz slices through the silence like a gunshot. This time it isn't Adrián's name on the screen. It's a private number. My heart pounds so hard it almost chokes me. My fingers hesitate before opening the message, as if touching the screen could seal my fate.

"He's in the hospital."

The air leaves my lungs. No explanation, no details. Just that blunt, brutal phrase that leaves me shaking. The phone nearly slips from my hands. Is it a warning? A trap? Or the one truth I can't ignore?

Panic propels me into motion before I can think. I rush out of the house, the lights behind me fading into darkness, and it feels like every shadow on the street is watching. The cold of dawn cuts into my skin as I sprint toward the avenue. I flag down a cab, the phone burning in my palm as if it were searing my skin.

Questions hammer at my skull, relentless. Who wrote to me? Víctor, playing a double game? One of the men who circle Adrián in those underground fights? Or someone else—someone who wants to use me as bait?

Fear bites at me, but my resolve is stronger: if Adrián is hurt, nothing will stop me from reaching him. Even if, by doing so, I'm walking straight into the wolf's jaws.

As the cab speeds through the empty streets, I stare out the window, my heart slamming in my chest. If someone knows where Adrián is, it means they're watching him. And if they told me, it's because they want me to see him like this—vulnerable, exposed. I don't know if I'm heading toward him... or straight into a dangerous game I won't be able to escape.

The hospital greets me with the sharp scent of bleach that tightens my chest. I walk straight to reception, certain my footsteps echo louder than my voice when I ask, "I'm looking for Adrián Suárez."

The woman behind the desk looks at me as if she's evaluating every detail of my face. She types slowly, too slowly, and when she finally looks up, her eyes are a wall. "There's no one by that name here."

Anger rises in my throat. I know she's lying. I feel it in the way she glances down the corridor, in the tension of her pressed mouth.

I try to push, but a nurse crosses in front of me, shoots me a sidelong look and whispers something to a colleague. They both turn too quickly when I catch them watching me. That gesture confirms it: Adrián is here. And they're hiding him.

I keep my mouth shut, swallowing my frustration, certain that if I want to find him, I'll have to do it alone, forcing my way through looks that mark me as an intruder. I move away from the desk pretending to give up, but the moment I turn my feet take me straight toward the corridor the receptionist glanced down. The sound of *my shoes echoes on the shiny floor, and I feel every pair of eyes following me from the corners.*

The hospital stretches on endlessly: closed doors, cold lights, a distant murmur of voices and machines. With every step my chest tightens. I turn left, trusting only instinct—how the nurses lower their voices when I pass, how someone steers their gaze toward the darker wing of the building.

I have no proof, but I know he's there. In that silent wing the air feels denser, more dangerous. And though everything in me screams to stop, I go on, because there's no turning back. The corridor narrows and grows quieter as if swallowing me into a tunnel with no exit. I walk slowly, holding my breath, until a number painted on the wall makes me stop: 312.

My heart skips a beat. The door is ajar, just a slit— enough for white light and a low murmur to slip out that chills my blood. I recognize that voice instantly, though I never expected to hear it here. I press myself against the wall, my body shaking, and listen.

"I warned you," my father growls from inside. "I told you to leave her alone."

My nails dig into my palm; blood buzzes in my ears.

"Your fate is in my hands, Adrián. I hope you learned your lesson."

The air leaves me. My father… threatening Adrián. Everything swirls in my head. And there I am, hidden behind the wall, not daring to move, certain that nothing will ever be the same.

My heart freezes when I hear the next sentence, sharp as a knife:

"Lucía is not for you," he says with a coldness I've never heard from him before. "Next time will be the last. Clear?"

I cover my mouth with my hand, stifling the scream that fights to get out. My skin prickles all over; my stomach churns. My father isn't just threatening him... he's warning him of an end.

Inside, the silence hangs for a few seconds, and I can picture Adrián's green eyes fixed on him, full of contained fury. I press myself to the wall and barely breathe. Every word sinks me deeper into a truth I don't know if I can bear.

For a moment I think the silence has defeated him. Then I hear Adrián's voice—hoarse, broken by pain, yet still charged with that darkness that makes him untamable.

"You can't control me forever."

My father's dry laugh chills my blood.

"Control you? Boy, it seems you still don't get it. I made you what you are. If it weren't for me, your father would've died owing me every penny and you'd be out on

the street like a dog. I put you in that ring since you were a kid... and you still belong to me."

The world spins. I barely dare to breathe. My father— owner of Adrián since childhood?

Inside the room Adrián growls with rage, though pain chokes his voice: "I'm not yours."

But my father's reply falls like a sentence:

"As long as I live, your fate will remain in my hands. And if you come near Lucía again... I swear there won't be another fight. It will be your end."

A brutal silence fills the room. Outside, I feel the ground open beneath my feet. I don't know what terrifies me more: my father's power, or the secret that has tied his life to Adrián's since before I could understand.

Every fiber of my body wants to burst into that room, to shout at my father, to hug Adrián. But I can't. Not now.

Air leaves me when I hear the chair scrape and my father's heavy footsteps approaching the door. I step back immediately, my heart hammering in my ribs. I tiptoe down the corridor, swallowing my fear, until I round the corner just as the door opens all the way. I hide behind a pillar, my back to the cold concrete, holding my breath. I hear his steps receding—steady, sure—as if he's just sealed a verdict. Only when the echo fades into the distance do I let out the air I'd been holding.

I go out into the street trembling, the night breeze clinging to my damp cheeks. I'm shaking, but it's not from cold. It's anger. It's fear. It's the certainty that my father has lied to me my whole life…and that Adrián has been a prisoner of his power from the start.

Even if I run away now, I know I'll come back sooner or later. I can't leave him like that; I need to know the whole truth. I get home with my legs still trembling, my heart pounding against my ribs as if it wants to escape. The echo of what I heard chases me like a poison I can't silence.

I can't take it anymore. If I don't let it out, I'll go mad. The only person I can turn to is Camila.

I call her with shaking hands. Half an hour later she's in my room, her silhouette outlined in the dim light, that worried look cutting straight to me.

"Lucía, what's wrong?" she asks in a low voice, as if she already knows what I'm about to say will split us in two.

The words spill out of me, jumbled, mixed with tears that burn my skin.

"My father… Cami, my father has something to do with Adrián. I heard it tonight at the hospital. Adrián was wounded, destroyed, and my father was there, threatening him. He said he put him in the ring as a child — that he owns him."

Camila's eyes fly open, and she brings a hand to her mouth, as if to stop a scream.

"Your father?" she whispers, incredulous.

I nod, my throat tight, feeling like each word tears a piece of my skin away.

"I don't know how far it goes, but I know it's true, Cami. My father controls him. And now I understand why Adrián always told me what we have was impossible..."

The silence that follows is so heavy it crushes my chest. I expect a cry, a warning — "You have to stay away now!" — but Camila does none of that. She stares at me, lips pressed together, and in her eyes there's something new: a dark, calm steadiness that chills me more than any reproach.

At last, she exhales. Her words fall slowly, like a knife sliding in without haste:

"If all of that is true... then it means your father has much more to lose than it seems."

I look at her, not understanding, but she doesn't look away. Her expression is different — calculating. For the first time, Camila doesn't seem just my friend; she seems like someone who keeps a secret too.

"What do you mean?" I ask.

She leans toward me, voice low, almost a whisper. "Maybe we can use this. People like your father always hide behind secrets. And now you know one that can break him."

A shiver runs through me. I've never seen Camila so cold, so sure. There's no fear in her eyes, only a dangerous spark. Suddenly I understand I'm not the only one willing to cross lines for the people I love. I take a deep breath, and when I speak, my voice surprises me by how steady it sounds.

"You're right. If I want to save him, if I want to free him... this is the only way."

Camila studies me, searching for any crack in my conviction. There isn't one. The fear burns inside me, yes, but it has turned into fire — and that fire gives me strength.

"That means the time has come," she says, voice low but cutting. "You're going to confront him, Lucía. And when you do... I'll be by your side."

I sink back against the headboard, heart pounding out of control. I don't know how or when, but I know I've just made the most important decision of my life. Even though Camila smiles at me with complicity, I can't help feeling that this decision has already dragged the two of us into an abyss from which there will be no return.

Chapter 20

✦ ✦ ✦ ✦ ✦ ✦

*T*he hospital greets me with the same coldness as
before: white lights, endless corridors, and the sharp
smell of bleach that seems to cling to my skin. I walk with
my heart racing, afraid that at any moment someone will
stop me.

*This time I don't go to reception. I don't want any more
excuses or evasive looks. I clutch my bag at my side and
head straight for the east wing, replaying from memory
every step I took last time — every turn, every closed
door, every shadow.*

*My legs shake, but I don't stop. The only thing I need
is to see him, even for a few seconds, even in secret. I
need to confirm with my own eyes that he's still here, that
he's still alive.*

*When I stop in front of room 312, my heart pounds so
hard it reverberates in my ears. The door is closed this
time — no crack, no voices inside. I swallow, lift my
trembling hand, and press my palm to the cold wood.*

*"Adrián..." I whisper, barely audible, as if he could
hear me on the other side.*

I push the door open carefully; my heart wants to leap out of my chest. The room is dim, lit only by the bluish glow of the machines.

And there he is.

Adrián lies in the bed, bandages covering his torso, one arm immobilized, bruises marking his face that make him look like a fallen warrior. Even so, his green eyes open when he senses my presence, shining with that wild intensity that even pain cannot extinguish.

"Lucía..." he murmurs, a barely audible thread of a voice.

I move closer slowly, swallowing the tears that threaten to betray me, and sit on the edge of the bed. I don't know whether to touch him or not — I'm afraid of hurting him more — but in the end my hand finds his: warm, trembling, alive.

I say nothing. I can't. I just look at him and let my fingers cling to his as if that contact were the only thing that can keep him here with me. His hand squeezes mine with the little strength he has left, and in his eyes a shadow appears that I've never seen before: fear.

"I thought..." His voice breaks, barely audible. "I thought I wouldn't see you again."

The air leaves me. I'm used to his growls, to his fierce dominance, to that darkness that always surrounds him.

But now, in that whisper, I hear something else: a naked confession, a truth that pierces my chest.

I squeeze his hand tighter, letting the tears I've been holding back finally spill. He looks at me as if I were the only thing keeping him alive, and for the first time I feel him vulnerable, human, devastatingly real.

I lean toward him, pressing my forehead to his, and the brush of his breath is a sweet poison that intoxicates me all over again. I could swear I'll protect him, that I won't let him fall... but deep down I know the truth: I'm the one who can no longer escape him.

"Don't say that" I whisper. "I'm here, Adrián. Whatever happens, I won't let go of your hand."

His breathing hitches, as if my promise is both relief and torment. His green eyes lock on mine, shining with an intensity that steals my breath. I caress his face gently, my fingers tracing the edge of the bandages with care. I don't care how his life has been until now or how dark the secret that ties him to my father may be. All I know is that I won't let him sink alone.

"I swear it," I repeat, pressing his fingers between mine. "I won't leave you."

For the first time I see his lips curve into the shadow of a smile—fragile, but real. We stay like that in a silence that says everything. The heart monitor registers a steady, almost hypnotic rhythm. His fingers still locked in mine, that faint smile on his lips. And yet I know it isn't peace I feel... it's the calm before a storm that's already too close. Adrián's eyes remain fixed on mine, as if trying to memorize every detail. I do the same: I lose myself in the intensity of his gaze, in the certainty that even like this—weakened and battered—he remains the man who consumes me, the one who drags me into his abyss though I don't want to resist.

I run my thumb along the back of his hand as if I could erase every scar, every mark violence has left on him. I lean closer and brush my lips to his, barely a sigh—a soft kiss that seeks not passion but a promise.

In that instant I understand that beyond the danger and the secret that surround us, here in this cold, silent room, Adrián belongs to me as much as I belong to him. Neither of us has an escape.

His fingers squeeze mine harder, and his voice cuts the calm with a whisper that takes my breath away.

"I don't know how you did it," he says with difficulty, his gaze fixed on me. "You've made me into someone I never thought I could be. You've made me need you. And that—" he closes his eyes for a second, as if it hurts to admit it— "that scares me more than any fight, Lucía."

The world stops. His confession hangs in the air, stronger than any touch, more intimate than any kiss. I look at him, unable to look away, my heart about to explode.

Adrián—the dark, dangerous man who drags me into his hell—has just bared his greatest secret: I am his weakness.

His words still echo in my ears when the door bursts open.

"We have to go," a firm voice says, urgent.

I turn and see him: Víctor, standing in the doorway, brow furrowed, eyes blazing. He looks out of place in this cold room, yet there's a determination on his face that chills me to the bone.

"What are you doing here?" I whisper, caught between anger and surprise.

Víctor doesn't look at me—his gaze is locked on Adrián.

"If you stay, you won't see another sunrise." His voice is low, sharp. "I'll help you get out."

My heart slams against my chest. I don't understand. My best friend's husband—the man who until now seemed woven into this shadowed world—stands before me offering a way out. Adrián struggles to sit up, the bandages pulling tight across his chest. His eyes narrow on Víctor, feral, mistrustful.

"And why the hell should I trust you?"

The silence that follows is heavier than any threat. I stand caught between them, feeling the ground crack open beneath my feet. Víctor steps into the room and shuts the door behind him with a snap. His eyes scan the hallway before returning to us.

"There's no time for questions," he says through clenched teeth. "If you want to get out alive, you'll have to trust me."

Adrián watches him from the bed, every muscle taut despite the bandages, like a wounded beast ready to fight to the end.

"I don't trust anyone."

"Then make an exception," Víctor replies, ice in his tone. "Because if you don't, everything ends here."

The silence steals my breath. My eyes dart between them as the tension thickens. The air feels heavier, more dangerous.

"What happens if we stay?" I ask, my voice more fragile than I want it to be.

Víctor meets my eyes, lips pressed into a hard line, as though words are a luxury he can't afford.

"Your father knows you're here."

A chill rips through me. I can't tell if it's fear, rage, or the certainty that the next decision will change everything. Adrián grinds his jaw, his green eyes sparking with restrained fury. Every part of him wants to refuse, to get up and smash his fist into Víctor's face. But he also understands something I can barely grasp, time is running out.

He lets out a low growl and slowly sits up in bed. The movement makes him groan in pain; he hisses through his teeth.

"All right…" he spits, the words torn from him. "But if this is a trap, Víctor… I swear there won't be a place in the world where you can hide from me."

Víctor holds his gaze—serious, unblinking. There's no fear in his eyes, only icy determination.

"Don't underestimate me, Adrián. If I wanted you dead, I wouldn't need a trap."

My stomach knots. The tension between them is so thick the air seems to crack, and I realize that in this dangerous game there are no true allies—only enemies who need each other. I move quickly to Adrián, sliding my arm around his back to help him stand. His weight presses into me, his heat envelops me, and even wounded he still radiates that power that obsesses me.

"I'll get you out of here," Víctor whispers, glancing at me as he opens the door. "No matter what happens, Lucía."

In that instant I understand that the escape isn't the end. It's only the beginning of something much darker.

The hallway seems longer than ever as we leave the room. Adrián leans on me, his weight making me stagger, but his steady steps remind me that even injured he refuses to appear weak. Víctor walks a few paces ahead, watching every corner. His dark jacket blends with the shadows, and his quick, precise movements give me goosebumps: he knows exactly what he's doing, as if he's used to moving through corridors where life is always on the line.

Voices in the distance. Hastened footsteps. A metal cart rolling over the polished floor. I hold my breath; my heart pounds so hard I'm afraid it will give me away. Victor stops abruptly and raises his hand. He presses us against the wall just in time for two men to pass—no scrubs, no hospital uniforms—dark suits, eyes that do not belong in this place.

Adrián tightens his bandaged hand around my waist, as if to make sure I don't move, that I stay glued to him. In that contact—more than in the danger—I feel the electricity of his control.

When the men disappear at the end of the corridor, Victor whispers without turning, "Now. Move."

Each step feels like an eternity, as if the walls could close in on us at any moment. I know, with a certainty that chills me, that if they catch us, it won't be to take us back to that room. It will be to finish what they started.

The hospital air is so thick I can barely breathe, but when the emergency door slams open and a gust of damp night hits my face, I feel reborn. The street is almost empty, save for a line of cars parked under the streetlights. The screech of the metal door still rings in my ears as Victor makes a brusque gesture.

"Hurry."

Adrián leans on me harder, and together we get him to a black car waiting a few meters away. His breathing is ragged, his steps clumsy, but he doesn't stop for a second. Every move is a battle against the pain, and still, he keeps going like a warrior.

Víctor opens the back door and practically shoves us in. "Crouch."

I fold over Adrián, his damp heat and the smell of blood soaking into my skin, while the engine roars and we pull away from the hospital. I don't dare look back. Inside I know that even though we left those walls behind, the danger didn't stay there. It's in the seat with us. It's in every secret they still haven't told us.

Inside the car, a silence so heavy presses on my chest. Adrián breathes with difficulty beside me, jaw clenched, and Víctor drives with his eyes fixed on the road, never taking them off the asphalt.

I can't hold it in any longer. "That's enough," I spit, my voice louder than I expected. "I want the truth. Both of you."

The car continues, the tension multiplying. Víctor doesn't answer. Adrián shoots me a quick, warning look, as if to shut me with a single gesture. But I won't be silenced.

"What exactly does my father have against you, Adrián? And you, Víctor—why the hell are you helping us if you've always been part of this?"

The silence that follows is unbearable. I can hear my breathing echo, the pound of my heartbeat in my temples. Víctor grips the wheel but doesn't turn his head.

"Lucía, you don't know what you're getting into."

"Yes, I do!" I retort, my voice breaking with anger. "My father almost killed him. And you, Víctor, you have no right to play savior when you've been in the same game for years."

"Don't lie to me, Adrián," I say, my voice trembling but sharp. "I was there. I heard everything through the door."

He goes cold. His lips part, but no words come out—only that thick silence that confirms what he won't admit.

"I heard my father say he put you in that ring since you were a child... that you belong to him," I whisper, each word tearing at me. My eyes burn, but I don't look away from him. "Is it true, Adrián?"

Adrián turns his face toward the window, as if the darkness of the night could hide him from me. His jaw tightens, and I see his fingers close into a weak fist on his thigh.

That silence breaks me more than any answer could.

"Tell me," I insist, my voice cracked but with a fury that cuts through me. "I need to hear it from you."

His breathing grows harsher, and when he finally speaks his voice sounds broken, as if each word tears at his throat.

"Your father..." he murmurs without looking at me. "He's not wrong. When I was a kid, my father was already up to his neck in debt. He drank more than he worked; he gambled what he didn't have. And when there was nothing left to sell... he sold me."

The words hit my chest like a blow.

"I was his payment," he continues, his gaze lost in the darkness beyond the glass. "The currency he used to settle his ruin. Since then, my life has never been mine."

I bring my hand to my mouth to stifle a sob. I had suspected it—I'd felt it—but hearing it from his lips tears me apart in a different way. Adrián is dangerous not only because he chose that life... he is dangerous because he was condemned to it.

He finally turns his face to me. His green eyes burn with rage and shame, but also with something that breaks my heart: resignation.

"That's why I always said this was impossible. Because I'm not free, Lucía. I never have been."

Adrián breathes deeply, as if summoning the strength to speak is another fight to endure. His hand trembles a little when it rests on mine, and then his low voice cuts through me like a sharp whisper:

"But I'm willing to change my fate... for you."

He looks straight into my eyes, and that intensity leaves me breathless. "I'll find a way."

Time stops. These are not empty words. Not a promise made in a moment of frenzy. It's the declaration of a man who was always a slave and who now, for the first time, is willing to defy his chains.

My heart feels like it will burst in my chest. I take his face with both hands, and my tears fall before I can stop them. He doesn't look away, as if he needs me to understand that he isn't speaking of mere hope but of war.

And in that instant, I know: if Adrián seeks that path, I will walk it with him. Even if it costs us everything. I need no more words. I draw him to me, careful not to hurt his wounds, and our lips meet in a kiss that is not just desire: it is an oath.

The taste of his mouth is bitter with blood, salty with tears, but in that moment, everything tastes like life. His breath mingles with mine, desperate, as if he wants to engrave me into his skin so he never loses me.

His fingers, trembling and bandaged, stroke the nape of my neck with a tenderness that undoes me more than any brutal possession ever did. I surrender, eyes closed to that kiss—not a furtive passion or a forbidden game, but the seal of a promise.

I feel everything in that contact: his pain, his rage, his sentence... but also the fierce spark of someone who, for the first time, believes he can break his fate.

The road becomes endless. I don't know how many hours we've been driving; the highway is empty and the night swallows everything around us. Only the hum of the engine and the uneven thud of Adrián's heart against my shoulder tell me we're still moving.

At last, the car stops. I look up and see a solitary house outlined against the horizon. It sits on the edge of the sea, so remote it seems ripped from the world, surrounded by silence and the distant roar of the waves. There are no lights nearby, no signs of life for miles.

I swallow, unable to hold back the question burning in my throat.

"Whose house is this?" I ask, looking at Víctor for a clue.

He turns off the engine, pauses for a second, and finally answers in a low voice, not looking directly at me. "Mine," he says calmly, as if that explains everything.

Inside, the house smells of damp wood and salt—a refuge frozen in time. The floor creaks under our steps and reminds me how far we are from everything, how isolated and vulnerable we are.

Víctor settles Adrián into a large armchair by the window that faces the sea. He hands him a clean blanket and a bottle of water without saying much, letting the gesture speak for him. I watch in silence, waiting for an explanation, some word that will reveal what's actually happening. But none comes.

"Rest," he finally says, his tone dry but sincere. "No one will bother you here."

He steps toward the kitchen, leaving us with the murmur of the waves crashing on the shore and Adrián's heavy breathing as his body sinks into the chair and his eyes close.

I sit beside him on the edge of the chair; knees pulled to my chest. The dim light barely lets me see him, but I know every line of his face by heart: the hardness of his jaw, the dangerous curve of his mouth, the shadows that follow him even in sleep. I reach out and, with my fingertips, gently trace the bandage on his arm. I don't want to wake him. I just need to convince myself that he's here, alive, that the darkness hasn't claimed him yet.

I think about everything he said—the confession that left me shaking: "I was the payment." A knot forms in my throat. I want to promise him I will pull him out of that world, uncover everything my father hides, and shatter the chains that bind him. But all I can do is stay here, watching over his sleep, as if my silence could protect him from the hell that surrounds him.

In the stillness of dawn, I find myself stroking his sweat-damp hair, and a thought embeds itself in me with force: Adrián is my addiction... but now he's also my war.

Sleep takes me without my noticing. I curl up beside him, my head resting on the arm of the chair, still holding his bandaged hand between mine.

When I wake, the gray morning light slips timidly through the window. I rub my eyes and then notice: Adrián is awake. He says nothing; he just watches me; his green eyes fixed on my face as if he's been studying every detail of my sleeping expression.

His hand, still weak, strokes my cheek slowly and moves down to my neck. The touch is so gentle it makes me shiver. There is no sign of brutality or possession, not even anger — only a tender, almost reverent gesture, as if he can't believe I'm here.

"You don't know how beautiful you are when you sleep," he murmurs, his voice hoarse, filled with a weariness that doesn't dull the intensity of his words.

My heart stumbles. The man who always dominates me, who dresses himself in danger and shadows, has just given me a gesture that utterly disarms me. The moment is broken by the sharp sound of the door opening. I straighten up at once, pulling slightly away from Adrián as Víctor comes into the room.

"I have to go back to the city," he announces without beating around the bush, his deep voice filling the space. "You two stay here."

"Here? Alone?" I ask, wide-eyed.

"It's the safest option," he replies. "No one knows about this house except me. If anyone suspects I'm helping you, we'll have half the world on us."

Adrián watches him from the chair, eyes sharp and distrustful. "And why should I trust that you'll come back?"

Víctor holds his gaze, unmoved. "Because if I don't, Camila will find out. And believe me, the last thing I want is to lose her."

The tension between them becomes unbearable. I press my lips together, trapped between two fires: the man I love and the man who, willingly or not, holds part of our fate.

Víctor walks to the door and, before leaving, stops and barely turns toward us. "Don't leave. Whatever happens, wait here. I'll come back."

The slam of the door echoes like a verdict, leaving us alone again in that isolated house by the sea. Adrián watches me from the armchair, eyes tired but burning, and that look grabs me as always. I approach slowly, letting the creak of the wood accompany my steps, and sit beside him.

"We're alone," I whisper, as if I need to remind myself.

Adrián raises an eyebrow, a dangerous half-smile forming. "And what will you do with that, princesa?"

Heat rises in my cheeks. I reach out and brush his jaw, feeling the roughness of his stubble against my skin. He's hurt, vulnerable, but in that moment all I see is the man who drags me to madness, to the most intense addiction I've known.

I lean in and kiss him. At first, it's soft, careful not to hurt him. He answers with that contained force that always breaks me, yanking me against his chest, as if even broken he refuses to release control.

In that house lost by the sea, between danger and secrecy, the only thing that exists is this moment: Adrián and I, devouring one another in silence.

His mouth takes mine with an urgency that disarms me, and although his body still bears the weight of his wounds, there is nothing fragile in his kiss. I feel him burning against me, his hands roaming my back with the strength that always leaves me trembling.

I settle onto his lap, feeling the heat of his erection hardening beneath the fabric, and a moan slips out before I can hold it back. Adrián tightens his grip on my hips, guiding me in a slow, almost torturous rocking that makes my breath break against his mouth.

"You don't know how much I need you right now, princesa," he murmurs, his voice rough and dangerous, his lips grazing my neck. "Wounded or not, I'm not letting you go."

My fingers tangle in his shirt, pulling at it until the buttons come undone one by one, eager, desperate to feel his skin against mine. Despite everything, he takes control: he grabs my wrist and forces me to look him in the eyes.

"I want you to see me," he growls, his gaze burning in the dim light. "I want you to understand that even broken, I'm still your addiction... and you're mine."

His lips seek mine with contained hunger, a deep kiss that steals my breath and makes me forget he's hurt. His tongue tangles with mine; the wet scrape of his piercing lights every nerve in my body.

His hands travel slowly, with the dangerous calm of someone who knows exactly where to touch. One strokes my neck down to my collarbone, while the other patiently slides up to lift the fabric of my dress. He removes it little by little, as if stripping me were a ritual, until my skin is exposed to the cool air of the room.

I run my hands over his chest, kiss him there, and he groans beneath me — that dark growl that melts me more than any word.

"Lucía..." he whispers, my name escaping his mouth like a secret he can't hold in.

His mouth moves down my neck, leaving a trail of burning kisses, and when he captures one of my nipples between his lips, playing with his piercing, a broken moan escapes me uncontrollably. I arch toward him, lost, while his fingers travel my thigh, slowly pushing my underwear aside.

He drives me crazy with unhurried pleasure — every kiss, every caress, every calculated brush bringing me to the edge and proving that his control over me doesn't need brutality, only time. Adrián pins me against him, forcing me to feel each movement with unbearable intensity. His breathing is heavy and rough, and yet he smiles with that dark arrogance that melts me from the inside.

"I don't need force to dominate you, princesa," he murmurs, his mouth brushing my ear, his tongue and piercing drawing circles that make my skin prickle. "It's enough to make you burn slowly."

He moves me with a deliberate cadence, sinking into me so slowly my body trembles with pure tension. I try to speed up, to take control, but his firm hands on my hips stop me, forcing me to follow his rhythm.

The pain from his wounds doesn't disappear — I feel it in the tension of his muscles — but even so his gaze burns with that indomitable fire. And it's that mixture — his vulnerability and his absolute dominance — that breaks me.

"I want you to feel everything," he growls, slipping a hand between my thighs, playing with my pleasure to the same torturing beat as his thrusts. "Every second, every moan, every drop of you... belongs to me."

Desperation sweeps me away. Every caress, every slow touch, pushes me closer to the edge, but he won't let me fall. And I know that although his body is wounded, his will is still my greatest sentence.

I don't understand how he does it. Each time I think I'm about to explode, that I can't take any more, Adrián barely changes the angle or the pressure of his hands or the touch of his mouth — and drags me to the edge again. When I fall, when the orgasm tears through me slow and deep, he doesn't stop.

My moans fill the room and blend with the roar of the sea beyond the windows, and I lose all sense of time. His torturous rhythm becomes a perfect cycle of unrelenting pleasure: he lets me tremble for a moment, barely catch my breath, and immediately lights me again until I lose control once more.

There comes a point when I stop counting. My body no longer belongs to me; it arches and opens only for him, convulsing beneath every slow, devastating wave that rips through me. I feel sweat sliding down my skin, my legs weakening, my voice dissolving into a sea of moans.

"That's it..." he murmurs in that deep voice that drives me crazy, holding me steady when I feel myself collapse. "Break for me, princesa. Again, and again."

And I do. I break, I melt, I lose myself in endless pleasure until I no longer know where my body ends and his begins. I only know that I am his — that in his hands, under his slow and cruel rhythm, nothing exists but the fire that consumes me.

His movements begin to lose the cruel calm with which he'd tormented me all night. I feel him tense beneath me; his breathing grows rougher, more urgent, and in his green eyes something I've never seen before: surrender.

I keep trembling, trapped in that endless chain of orgasms that breaks me again and again, when suddenly his hands squeeze me harder against his body and a low growl escape from deep within him.

"Lucía…" —my name in his mouth doesn't sound like dominance or threat. It sounds like a confession.

Then we break together. I feel his climax explode inside me — hot, fierce — at the same moment another wave hits me and tears a muffled cry from my throat against his neck. The world vanishes. There is only that devastating instant in which our bodies, our shadows, and our wounds fuse into one. I collapse on his chest, sweaty and exhausted, while his ragged breathing surrounds me. His hands, still firm, stroke my back as if he needs to make sure I'm still there.

For a moment, in that shared surrender, Adrián ceases to be the dark, dangerous man everyone feared. He is just him — broken and mine.

The silence after our climax hums on my skin. Adrián holds me to his chest, his fingers tangled in my hair, his warm breath against my ear. It feels as if the world could stop right there, in this house lost by the sea, where nothing and no one could reach us.

Then a sharp knock shatters the calm.

We both tense immediately. Another knock, harder this time, thunders at the front door. Adrián shoves me aside roughly, his green eyes alight again with that never-dying fire of danger.

The third knock leaves no doubt: someone knows we are here. Just before Adrián can move closer, a voice booms from outside, so familiar that my blood runs cold.

"Lucía!" —my father's voice, loaded with rage and threat—. "Open that door right now."

My heart stops. Adrián turns toward me, and in his eyes, I see the same fierce panic that consumes me. We both know that once again fate has come for us.

This time, there will be nowhere to hide.

And yet the only thing I feel is that I would choose him again.

Epilogue

The echo of his voice still reverberates in my chest, like thunder that heralds the inevitable storm.

My father.

Adrián.

And me, trapped between two worlds that should never have crossed.

I could run. I could give in. I could accept that destiny is already written.

But no.

Because I am no longer the same.

Because even if he drags me to hell, I would choose to fall again and again into Adrián's arms.

He is my addiction.

My sentence.

My forbidden truth.

And I know, with the burning certainty of someone who has tasted the abyss, that this is only the beginning.

www.ingramcontent.com/pod-product-compliance
Lightning Source LLC
Chambersburg PA
CBHW020648110726
47901CB00001B/100